Praise for *Born at Midnight*

"*Born at Midnight* is addicting. Kylie's journey of self-discovery and friendship is so full of honesty, it's impossible not to fall in love with her and Shadow Falls . . . and with two sexy males vying for her attention, the romance is scorching. *Born at Midnight* has me begging for more, and I love, love, love it!"
—*Verb Vixen*

"There are so many books in the young adult paranormal genre these days that it's hard to choose a good one. I was so very glad to discover *Born at Midnight*. If you like P. C. and Kristin Cast or Alyson Noël, I am sure you will enjoy *Born at Midnight*!"
—*Night Owl Reviews*

"I laughed and cried so much while reading this. . . . I *loved* this book. I read it every chance I could get because I didn't want to put it down. The characters were well developed and I felt like I knew them from the beginning. The story line and mystery that went along with it kept me glued to my couch not wanting to do anything else but find out what the heck was going on."
—*Urban Fantasy Investigations*

"This has everything a YA reader would want. . . . I read it over a week ago and I am still thinking about it. I can't get it out of my head. I can't wait to read more. This series is going to be a hit!"
—*AwesomeSauce Book Club*

"The newest in the super-popular teen paranormal genre, this book is one of the best. Kylie is funny and vulnerable, struggling to deal with her real-world life and her life in a fantastical world she's not sure she wants to be a part of. Peppered throughout with humor and teen angst, *Born at Midnight* is a laugh-out-loud page-turner. This one is going on the keeper shelf next to my Armstrong and Meyer collections!"
—*Fresh Fiction*

"Seriously loved this book! This is definitely a series you will want to watch out for. C. C. Hunter has created a world of hot paranormals that I didn't want to leave."
—*Looksie Lovitz: Books*

"The evolving, not-always-easy relationships among Kylie and her cabinmates Della and Miranda are rendered as engagingly as Kylie's angst over dangerous Lucas and appealing Derek. Just enough plot threads are tied up to make a satisfying stand-alone tale while whetting appetites for sequels to come." —*Publishers Weekly*

"Great for fans of Vampire Academy. This book has it all, and readers won't want to put it down. Hunter packs on the twists, and then leaves you hanging with an amazing hook ending, just waiting for more." —*RT Book Reviews*

"With intricate plotting and characters so vivid you'd swear they are real, *Born at Midnight* is an addictive treat. Funny, poignant, romantic, and downright scary in places, it hits all the right notes. Highly recommended." —*Houston Lifestyles & Homes* magazine

"*Born at Midnight* has a bit of everything . . . a strong unique voice from a feisty female lead, a myriad of supporting supernatural characters, a fiery romance with two intriguing guys—mixed all together with a bit of mystery—making *Born at Midnight* a surefire hit!" —*A Life Bound By Books*

"Very exciting, taking twists and turns I never expected. The main character grows very well throughout the story, overcoming obstacles and realizing things she never thought possible. And the author masterfully ended it just right." —*Flamingnet*

"I absolutely LOVED it. Wow, it blew me away." —Nina Bangs, author of *Eternal Prey*

"Fun and compulsively readable, with a winning heroine and an intriguing cast of secondary characters." —Jenna Black, author of *Glimmerglass*

ALSO BY C. C. HUNTER

Born at Midnight

Awake at Dawn

• a shadow falls novel •

c. c. hunter

ST. MARTIN'S GRIFFIN ❧ NEW YORK

This is a work of fiction. All of the characters, organizations, and events portrayed in this novel are either products of the author's imagination or are used fictitiously.

www.stmartins.com

Library of Congress Cataloging-in-Publication Data

Hunter, C. C.
   Awake at dawn / C. C. Hunter.—1st ed.
      p. cm.
   ISBN 978-0-312-62468-2
   [1. Supernatural—Fiction.   2. Camps—Fiction.   3. Love—Fiction.   4. Family problems—Fiction.]   I. Title.
   PZ7.H916565Aw 2011
   [Fic]—dc23   2011020378

10 9 8 7 6 5 4 3

*To my husband, Steve Craig—my partner, my best friend, and my hero.
Your love, support, and willingness to do laundry helped me take
my dreams and make them our reality. Thank you for
being a part of my dreams. I love you.*

Acknowledgments

To my fabulous critique partners, who laughed with me during lunches, gave me endless support when my characters were misbehaving, and drank chocolate martinis with me to celebrate every good moment of life. To the amazing and supportive booksellers at Katy Budget Books. You guys rock. To my daddy, Pete Hunt, and my mother, Ginger Curtis, who taught me the value of laughter and love. And to my daughter, Nina Makepeace, and my son, Steve Craig, Jr. By far, you two are the best things I've ever done in my life. And last but certainly not least, to my wonderful editor and agent, whose belief in me is the springboard of my inspiration.

Chapter One

"You have to stop it, Kylie. You have to. Or this will happen to some-
one you love."

The spirit's ominous words flowed from behind Kylie Galen
and mingled with the crackle and pop of the huge bonfire about
fifty feet to her right. The frigid pocket of air announced the spirit's
presence loud and clear, even if the words were only for Kylie's ears
and not for the thirty other Shadow Falls campers standing in the
ceremonial circle.

Miranda stood by Kylie in the people chain, completely un-
aware of the ghost, and gripped Kylie's hand tighter. "This is so
cool," Miranda muttered, and looked across the circle at Della.

Miranda and Della were not only Kylie's closest friends, but also
her cabin mates.

"We give thanks for this offering." Chris, or Christopher as
he referred to himself tonight, stood in the middle of the circle
and raised the sacred goblet up to the dark sky as he blessed its
contents.

"You have to stop it," the spirit whispered over Kylie's shoulder
again, hindering her concentration on the ritual.

Closing her eyes, Kylie envisioned the spirit the way she had appeared to her several times now—mid-thirties, long dark hair and wearing a white gown—a gown covered in blood.

Frustration bounced around Kylie's already tightened gut. How many times had she pleaded with this spirit to explain, to tell her who, what, when, where, and why? Only to have the dead woman repeat the same warning.

Long story short, ghosts just coming out of the closet sucked at communication. Probably as bad as beginner ghost whisperers sucked at getting them to communicate. Kylie's only option was to wait until the ghost could somehow explain her warning. Now, however, wasn't the optimal time.

I'm kind of busy right now. So unless you can explain in detail, can we chat later? The words formed in Kylie's mind, hoping the ghost could read her thoughts. Thankfully, the chill running down Kylie's spine evaporated and the night's heat returned—Texas heat, muggy, thick, and hot, even without the bonfire.

Thank you. Kylie tried to relax, but the tension in her shoulders remained knotted. And for a good reason. Tonight's ceremonial event, sort of a show-and-tell, was another first in her life.

A life that was so much simpler before she knew she wasn't all human. Of course, it would help if she could identify her non-human side. Unfortunately the only person who knew the answer was Daniel Brighten, her real dad. She hadn't known he existed until he'd paid a visit to her a little over a month ago. And he'd obviously decided to let Kylie deal with her identity crisis all on her own.

He seldom visited anymore, bringing a whole new meaning to the term *deadbeat dad.* Yup, Daniel was dead—died before she was born. Kylie wasn't sure if they offered parenting classes in the hereafter, but she was tempted to suggest he find out. Because now, when he did drop by, she would catch him watching her and just when she started to ask him a question, he'd fade away, leaving only a cold chill and her unanswered questions.

"Okay," Chris said. "Release your hands, clear your mind, but whatever you do, do not break the circle."

Kylie, along with the crowd, followed his directions. Yet as she released her hands, Kylie's mind refused to clear. A whisper of wind picked up a few strands of her long, blond hair and scattered it across her face. She brushed it behind her ear.

Was her deadbeat dad afraid she was going to ask for sex advice or something? That always had her mom disappearing from a room—running around in search of another give-this-to-your-teen pamphlet. Not that Kylie had actually asked her mom for sex advice. Honestly, she was the last person Kylie would go to for *that* kind of advice.

Why, the mere mention of her being interested in a boy sent her mom into a panic as the letters S-E-X practically flashed in her mom's eyes. Thankfully, since Kylie had been shipped off to Shadow Falls Camp, the supply of sex-related pamphlets had declined.

Who knew what she'd missed this last month? There might have been a few STDs discovered that she didn't know about. No doubt her mom was stockpiling them for when Kylie went home for a visit in three weeks. A visit she wasn't looking forward to, either. Sure, she and her mom had sort of mended their not-so-good relationship since her mom had confessed about Daniel being her real dad. But the new mother-daughter bond felt so fragile.

Kylie couldn't help but wonder if their relationship wasn't too delicate to actually spend more than a few hours together. What if she went home and found things really hadn't changed? What if the distance between her and her mom still existed? And what about things with Tom Galen, the man Kylie had perceived to be her real dad all her life, the man who had walked out on her mom and her for a girl only a few years older than Kylie? Kylie had been mortified at seeing him sucking face with his way-too-young assistant. So much so, she hadn't even told him.

A late-night breeze brought the smoke from the roaring bonfire into her face. She blinked the sting from her eyes, but didn't dare step out of the circle. As Della had explained, to do that would have shown a lack of respect to the vampire culture.

"Clear your mind," Chris repeated, and handed the goblet to a camper on the other side of the circle.

Closing her eyes, Kylie tried again to follow Chris's directions, but then heard the sound of falling water. Jerking her eyes open, she looked toward the woods. Was the waterfall that close? Ever since Kylie had learned about the legend of the death angels at the falls, she felt driven to go there. Not that she longed to come face-to-face with any death angels. She had her hands full dealing with ghosts. But she couldn't kick the feeling that the falls called her.

"Are you ready?" Miranda leaned in and whispered, "It's getting closer."

Ready for what? was Kylie's first thought. Then she remembered. Was Miranda freaking kidding?

Kylie stared at the communal goblet being passed around the circle. Her breath caught when she realized it was only ten people away from being placed in her hand. Drawing in a deep smoke-scented gulp of air, she tried not to look disgusted.

Tried. But the thought of taking a sip from a container after everyone had smacked their lips on the rim landed somewhere between gross and nauseating in her mind, but for sure the biggest yuck factor was the blood.

Watching Della consume her daily nutrition had gotten easier this last month. Heck, Kylie had even donated a pint to the cause—

supernaturals did that sort of thing for their vampire friends. But having to taste the life-sustaining substance was a different matter altogether.

"I know it's sickening. Just pretend it's tomato juice," Miranda whispered to their friend Helen standing on the other side of her. Not that whispering helped in this crowd.

Kylie looked across the circle of supernatural campers, their faces cast in firelit shadows from the bonfire. She spotted Della, frowning in their direction and her eyes glowing a pissed-off gold color. Her acute hearing was only one of her gifts. No doubt Della would call Miranda on her "sickening" remark later. Which basically meant Kylie would have to convince the two of them not to murder each other. How two people could be friends and fight so much was beyond her. Playing peacemaker between the two was a full-time job.

She watched another camper raise the goblet to her lips. Knowing how much this meant to Della, Kylie mentally prepared herself to accept the glass and take a sip of blood without barfing. Not that it stopped Kylie's stomach from wanting to rebel.

Gotta do this. Gotta do this. For Della's sake.

Maybe you'll even like how blood tastes, Della had said earlier. *Wouldn't it be cool if you turned out to be vampire?*

Not, Kylie had thought, but wouldn't dare say it. She supposed being vampire wouldn't be any worse than being werewolf or shapeshifter. Then again, she remembered Della practically crying when she talked about her ex-boyfriend's repulsion to her cold body temperature. Kylie preferred to stay at her own temperature, thank you very much. And the thought of existing on a diet that mainly consisted of blood . . . ? Well, Kylie seldom even ate red meat, and when she did . . . cook that cow, please.

While Holiday, the camp leader and Kylie's mentor, had said it was unlikely for Kylie to start exhibiting any huge metaphysical changes, Holiday had also said anything was possible. Truth was, Holiday—who was full fairy—couldn't tell Kylie what her future held, because Kylie was an anomaly.

And Kylie hated being an anomaly.

She'd never fit in the human world, and damn it if she wasn't a misfit here, as well. Not that the other campers didn't accept her. Nope, she felt closer to these supernaturals than she did human teens. Well, she did as soon as she learned that no one here was dying to have her for lunch. Why, Della and Miranda were now her two major best friends—there wasn't anything she couldn't or wouldn't share with them. The blood donation pretty much proved that fact.

Okay, there was one thing Kylie couldn't share with her two best friends. Ghosts. Most supernaturals had a thing about ghosts. Not that Kylie herself didn't have a thing about them. But it didn't stop the pesky phantoms from regularly popping in for visits.

Nevertheless, whatever type of supernatural she was, being a ghost magnet was her gift. Or . . . one of them. Holiday believed that ghost whispering was probably one of many of Kylie's gifts and that others would manifest over time. Kylie just hoped any future gifts were easier to deal with than the indecisive and communication-challenged dead people.

"It's coming," Miranda said.

Kylie watched someone pass the glass to Helen. Kylie's throat tightened again. Her gaze shifted to Derek, the brown-haired half fairy, standing three campers past Helen. Kylie had missed him drinking the blood. Not that she was sorry. The next time they kissed, she didn't want to think about him drinking blood.

He smiled tenderly and Kylie knew Derek could sense her emotional turmoil. As crazy as it seemed, his ability to read her emotions was both what attracted her to him and kept her from getting closer.

Well, it wasn't so much his ability to read her that kept her from allowing their relationship to deepen, it was his ability to control those emotions. Being half Fae, Derek not only could read her emotions, but with a simple touch, he could alter her emotions, turn fear into fascination, anger into calm. Was it at all surprising that she stayed in awe of the sexy-as-sin boy?

Call her paranoid, but after seeing how her dad—make that her stepdad—had cheated on her mom and then how Trey, her ex-boyfriend, had dropped her in the grease when she'd been hesitant to go all the way, trusting the male gender was difficult. Trusting one who had the power to manipulate her emotions was even harder.

Not that it stopped her from liking Derek or from wishing she could throw caution to the wind. Even now—her stomach clenched as she thought of drinking blood, surrounded by the entire camp—she felt herself being lured to him. Felt herself wanting to lean up against his chest, to get close enough to see the gold flecks in his pupils melt and mesh into the vivid green of his eyes. She wanted to feel his lips on hers again. To taste his kiss. She learned these last few weeks how good he could kiss.

A clearing of Miranda's throat brought Kylie back to the moment. When she saw Derek's caught-you smile, she knew he'd read her turned-on emotions, and her cheeks warmed and she shifted her gaze away from Derek to Miranda.

Oh crap. Miranda held out the glass for Kylie to take. It was showtime.

She took the goblet. It felt warm against her palm, almost as if the liquid inside had just been drained from its life source. Her stomach knotted and her throat followed course. She didn't know if the blood was animal or human.

Don't think about it.

She inhaled and the coppery smell, like old pennies, filled her nose, and before the glass touched her lips, her gag reflex prepared to bounce.

Just do it. Show Della that you respect her culture.

She swallowed hard, tilted the glass up a notch higher, and hoped like hell Della appreciated this. Telling herself she only had to taste, not drink, she waited for the moisture to dampen her mouth.

The second the warm liquid wet her lips, she went to pull the glass back, but somehow the thick red blood snuck through her tightened lips. Her gag reflex jumped but then the taste exploded on the tip of her tongue. Almost like black cherries but better, sort of like ripe strawberries but tangier and sweeter, the exotic flavor had her mouth opening and greedily swallowing. As the liquid slid down her throat, the smell of old pennies vanished, replaced with a spicy fruity scent.

She had almost downed the whole glass when she remembered what she was drinking. She yanked the glass from her lips, but couldn't stop her tongue from dipping out the corner of her mouth to catch a drop that tried to escape.

Immediately, the intensity of everyone's gaze on her pressed against her awareness and a deeper reality sank in. Murmurs filled her ears . . .

At least now we know what she is.

How come she's not cold?

Looks as if we're going to up our blood drive.

Della's victory yelp followed.

Kylie's hands started to shake. The smoke from the bonfire filled her nose and throat and made it hard to breathe.

Crap! Crap! Crap! What did this mean? Was she . . . a vampire?

She scanned the wide-eyed faces to find Holiday, wanting to see her reassuring smile that said it was okay, that said this . . . this meant nothing. But when she found the camp leader, her expression mirrored that of the others—shock.

Blinking, hoping to wash away the start of tears, she shoved the almost empty glass into the hands of the person beside her. No longer caring about showing respect, she took off at a dead run.

Five minutes later Kylie was still running. Running faster than she knew she could move. But was it vampire fast? The hot, muggy summer air filled her lungs and came out in gasps. Even with the night temperature clinging to the high eighties, a chill ran down her spine. Was she at this moment morphing into a vampire? Was she growing cold? Hadn't Della said it was painful? More like excruciatingly painful.

Was she in pain? Emotionally yes. But physically? Not yet.

She kept moving. The sound of her feet hitting the ground filled her ears, and the sound of the thorny vines snagging her jeans and then ripping away seemed too loud. Her consciousness throbbed right along with the beating of her heart. *Thump. Thump. Thump.*

How many times had she told Della she wasn't a monster? And yet the mere idea that Kylie might be a vampire seemed . . . too much.

The smell of the bonfire smoke clung to her clothes and filled her nose. Yet the taste of the sweet blood lingered on her tongue. She ran harder. Faster. Did her speed mean she was a vampire?

She didn't want to think about that.

Didn't want to accept it.

Her lungs finally gave out, declined the air she tried to force down. The muscles in her legs cramped and her knees shook. She stopped, her legs refusing to support her weight, and collapsed in the middle of a thorn-infested field. Pulling her legs to her chest, she hugged her shins and dropped her head on her knees.

She drew hot air into her lungs that now begged for oxygen. One breath, then two. Physically exhausted, she went still as the realization finally stuck. If she were a vampire, would she not have Della's stamina? Maybe that came with the change of body temperature. The dampness on her cheeks told her she'd been crying.

The air suddenly chilled. Turned cold.

Not vampire cold.

Dead cold.

She wasn't alone—another spirit had joined her. But who was it this time? Holiday had explained that in time, her abilities would increase and she would have to deal with more than one ghost at a time. But right now, there was only one ghost she wanted to see. Only one thing she wanted.

She wanted answers. "Daniel?" she called her father's name. And then louder. "Daniel Brighten. What am I?"

When he didn't appear, she screamed his name again and again. Her throat became sore, but she didn't stop. "You come here now. You give me answers or I swear to you, I'll never, *NEVER* acknowledge your presence again. I will shut you off, eradicate you from my mind, and refuse to see, talk, or even think of you again."

As the threat fell from her lips, she didn't even know if she had the ability to do it, but something inside her said she could. She dropped her head against her knees and tried to breathe.

Suddenly the cold grew nearer. She felt it surround her. Felt it wrap around her in a tight embrace. It wasn't just any cold, it was Daniel's cold.

She raised her face and saw his spirit kneel beside her. His blue eyes, the same light color as her own, met hers. His eyes, and most everything else about his facial features, from the oval-shaped face to the slightly turned-up nose, were so much like hers that it was a bit disturbing. When his arm curled around her shoulders, the knot in her throat doubled.

"Don't cry." He brushed a tear from her cheek. "My little girl should never cry." The icy touch shouldn't have been comforting, but it was.

"I drank blood and it was good." She spit out the words like a confession.

"And you see this as wrong?" he asked.

"I . . . It scares me."

"I know," he said. "I remember feeling much the same the way."

"Did you drink blood? Are we . . . vampires?" The word almost wouldn't come.

"I never tried blood." His expression filled with empathy. "But, Kylie, you didn't do anything wrong." His voice came out soft, his words soothing. The cold, his cold, lessened her fear of the unknown and she felt . . . loved.

Right then, she knew love had no boundaries, not even death. Love had no temperature. Maybe being cold wasn't altogether a bad thing. She leaned into him and drew comfort from his nearness.

Minutes passed. She blinked away her tears and sat up. He shifted from his kneeling position and sat beside her. Wiping her face, she stared at the father she'd never known in life. Yet, even separated by death, she felt the bond. "Tell me. Please tell me what I am."

The smile in his eyes faded. "I wish I could give you what you want, but I don't have the answers. I was older than you when I realized I was different from everyone else. But it wasn't until I was eighteen and away at college that things started happening."

"What kind of things?" she asked, and then somehow she knew. "You saw ghosts?"

He nodded and cupped his hands together. "I thought I had lost my mind. Then one day I met an old man fishing. He told me he was fairy."

"Did he tell you what you were?" she asked.

"No, just that I wasn't human and, of course, I thought *he* was crazy. It took me months before I believed him. When I went back to find him again, he was gone."

"But what about your parents?" Kylie asked. "Didn't they tell you?"

"No. And when my ability to recognize other supernaturals made sense to me, I realized they were both human. At that time, I didn't know that I couldn't have been their child. Since my death, I learned I was adopted. Not that it made them any less my parents. They loved me. And they would love you, too."

"They never told you that you were adopted? How could they lie to you like that?"

"Back then it was considered best to keep adoption a secret, even from the child. I have yet to find out who or what my real parents are. So you see, the answers you seek were the same answers I sought right before my death. Maybe you can discover them for us both."

"But . . ."

"But what?" he asked.

"I thought ghosts were all-seeing. They are in the movies, any-way. Isn't there someone on the other side who could tell you?"

He smiled. "You would think so. But no, even here, they want you to find your own answers."

"That freaking sucks," Kylie said. "Being dead should have some benefits."

He laughed. The sound echoed with familiarity. It was an-other thing she had gotten from him—the tenor of her laugh. Her thoughts went to her stepdad, the man whom she had loved so much and yet who had turned his back on her and her mom. She still didn't know if she could forgive him. If she wanted to forgive him. And then the strangest thought hit: she had loved the wrong father.

Her throat felt tight again. "I missed you all my life," Kylie said. "I didn't know I missed you, but I know it now. You were supposed to be there."

He placed a hand on her cheek. "I was there. I saw you take your first step. The day you fell off your bike and broke your arm I tried to catch you. You went right though my arms. And remember the day you flunked that algebra test and you got so upset that you ran off and smoked a cigarette?"

She frowned. "I hate algebra. But I hated the cigarette, too."

"Me, too," he chuckled. "I've been here, Kylie, but I can't stay here much longer."

His words bounced around her head and hit her heart with a thump. "That's not fair. I just got to know you."

"My time in this realm is limited. I've used much of it watching you grow to be the woman you are."

"Then ask for more time." Her throat tightened. She had lost one father already; she didn't want to lose another one. Not now. Not before she even got to know him.

"I'll try, but it may not happen. I don't regret spending my time with you then." The corners of his eyes crinkled into another smile. "I see in you the best of your mother and the best of me. And while I know you don't want to hear this right now, I see the best of Tom Galen. He is not all bad, Kylie."

She wanted to tell Daniel he was wrong, to insist she wasn't like Tom Galen, but her thoughts were interrupted by the whisk of wind. It came on so fast, as if something had shot past, something so fast that her human eye hadn't detected it. Something not human.

The dark silence that followed told Kylie she was right. "I'll bet that's Della." Kylie looked around. "Looking for me." But even as Kylie finished the sentence, she felt the cold of her father's presence fade. "No, please don't . . . go." Her last word rang out in the warm yet eerie and lonely silence.

Gone. He was gone.

Her chest tightened, then she came to the realization that even though he'd come to her, he didn't have the answers she wanted. Her surefire plan of solving her identity crisis had been squashed.

Biting her lip, she pushed away her thoughts of her father and prepared herself to face Della. Could she explain to her friend her reservations about being vampire without hurting her? Would Della be totally furious that she'd broken the circle and disrespected the vampire culture? Knowing Della, the answer would be a *hell yes*.

Della had a lot of unresolved anger and it didn't take much to infuriate her. Some of her angst could be blamed on being vampire—vampires weren't known for their loving dispositions, but most of Della's issues were from her family. Apparently, her super-strict father had noted the changes in his daughter since she'd been turned, and he didn't like them. Not being able to tell her dad about being vampire, Della had remained silent, which made her dad accuse Della of everything from drugs to just being lazy. The sad part was, Della loved her father so much that disappointing him was breaking her heart.

Kylie waited for Della to return, to come to a whizzing stop. She didn't. Had her ghost-fearing friend sensed her father's presence and kept going? The lack of sound suddenly seemed menacing.

"Della?" Kylie called out.

No answer came. Not unless you considered the dead silence

an answer. Kylie recalled Della's cousin, Chan, and the uninvited visit he'd paid to Della and her after she'd only been here a few days. His presence had brought on this kind of dead silence as well.

The memory of that night filled Kylie's head. Della had assured Kylie that he'd only been joking about her being a snack, but after Kylie's little run-in with the Blood Brothers gang of rogue vampires, when she'd nearly become a snack for real, trusting an unknown vampire took a little effort.

When the night's stillness continued, Kylie forced herself to speak. "I know someone is here." She stood up, hoping her false bravado would become real. The whisk of speeding wind passed again. "If that's you, Della, this isn't funny."

No one answered. Kylie stood there, trying to think of what to do next. Then she heard it. Very slight, but still the definite rustle of some bushes—someone was behind her. Breath held, she swung around to face the music.

Chapter Two

At first Kylie didn't see anything, then her gaze shifted lower to the ground and locked on to a pair of eyes—eyes that glowed golden in the night's obscurity. They weren't vampire eyes. Nope, they weren't Della's golden hue that expressed her anger. These weren't even human.

Canine?

No.

Wolf.

She nearly tripped taking a step back, as her heart screamed *run*. But the one word that whispered though her head next stopped her from attempting escape. *Lucas?*

Her chest clutched tighter but no longer from fear. Something akin to longing warmed her heart. Then the warm, gooey feeling slipped right into the feeling of betrayal. The hot-looking werewolf had kissed her senseless, made her want him, and then run off with Fredericka.

Kylie's gaze shot up to the cloud-covered moon. Even through the gray mist, she could tell it wasn't full. That didn't happen until next week, when the werewolves at the camp were planning their own ceremonial event.

Which meant the wolf staring at her couldn't be Lucas. Which meant it was a real wolf. A real wild-animal kind of wolf. Which meant she should be trying to get the hell away before it decided to attack.

Her gaze shot back to the wild animal, and while her mind created images of the creature snarling, ready to pounce, what she saw wasn't anywhere near as frightening. The gold eyes held hers. The cloud shrouding the moonlight must have shifted, and Kylie was able to make out the medium-size wolf in detail. Its coat looked thick and coarse, and it held a mix of colors from gray to red. She wouldn't call it beautiful, not exactly, but it sure as heck didn't appear threatening.

Lowering its snout, it slowly moved forward. Even though the thing still didn't look hostile, Kylie took a step back. As if sensing her fear, it crouched lower to the ground in a submissive position.

"What are you—someone's pet wolf?" Another thought hit. A real wolf couldn't have made the supersonic blast of air. But a real shape-shifter could.

She slammed both her hands on her hips and gave the beast a hard cold look. "Damn it, Perry, is that you?"

Perry, the powerful shape-shifter of the camp, loved to play jokes. But Kylie had had it up to her eyeballs with his tricks. Enough was enough.

"Game's over or I'm going for your ears." Kylie waited for the diamond-like sparkles to fill the air around the wolf as it changed back into human form. "Now!"

No sparkles.

The creature, down on all fours, inched forward.

"No," Kylie insisted, accepting that this was truly a wolf. "You stay there." She held out her hand and the animal seemed to listen. "Nothing personal, but I'm more of a cat person." Her voice rang loud and brought her awareness again to the lack of night noises.

No crickets. No birds. Not even the wind dared to blow. She looked up at the tops of the trees, which held so still they looked photographed. Even the Texas vegetation appeared frozen with fear.

She fought the sense of danger stirring in her chest and looked back at the wolf, more certain than ever that the danger didn't stem from the creature's presence. No, whatever was here was much more evil than a wild animal. Chills tap-danced up her spine, sending all her barely-there hair on the back of her neck standing at attention.

The wolf lunged up on all fours, sniffed the air, and snarled. It took a step away, then turned back around. Its golden eyes met hers almost as if to warn her of danger.

Not that she needed to be further warned. Her heart skipped a beat. The brush of cold wind passed again, only closer this time, and it left a foul odor that carried the stench of death. The wolf's snarl grew more intense.

"Kylie?" Her name echoed from the distance, the sound leaking from the thicket of trees. She brought her head around and the whisk of air shot past her again. Only this time, Kylie got the feeling that it kept going. Whoever, whatever it was, wanted her alone. She folded her arms over her middle and tried not to shiver from the thought.

The wolf made a soft whine and she turned her head and made eye contact again. It moved its head slightly, as though giving her a farewell greeting, then it turned and, causing only a slight rustle of vegetation, it disappeared.

"Kylie." Her name came again, carried with a slight whisk of wind. This time she recognized Derek's voice.

"I'm here," Kylie yelled, and, not wanting to be alone a second longer, she took off running.

• • •

She ran toward the sound of Derek's voice. Her heart pounded as she dodged trees and jumped over patches of thorns. She kept running. As if she could escape the fear she'd just felt, as if she could run away from her problems. Oh, yes, she so wanted to leave her problems behind. With each thump her foot made against the hard earth, she felt her fear slip farther away, but the problems not so much. They hung on, but exertion of energy still felt good. Good until she smacked right into something, or rather . . . someone.

Derek.

His muscled body let out a gush of air and he hit the ground with a thud. Kylie, thrown off balance, toppled down on top of him. His clean, spicy scent filled her nose at the same time his arms wrapped protectively around her.

"You sent the wolf," she muttered, still short of breath, as she just now recalled his ability to communicate with animals.

"What wolf?" His gaze shifted left then right. "Are you okay?" He rolled her over onto the ground. One of his legs still rested on top of hers and his left arm lay across her middle, while his palm fit right into the curve of her waist. Warmth and comfort pulsated from his touch. He pushed the curtain of hair from her face with his other hand. His gaze, filled with concern, met hers and she fought the lump of emotion crawling up her throat.

"Kylie, talk to me." His tone echoed the same caring she saw in his eyes, and that warm feeling she always got when he touched her spread inside her chest.

"Damn it, are you okay?"

She blinked up at him and she meant to say yes, but the truth came out. "No. I'm not okay."

"What happened?" His arm tightened around her waist.

All her problems came raining down on her like pitchforks and one made a direct hit to her heart. "I drank blood."

"We all drank blood. It was part of the ceremony," he said, and she got the feeling he was trying hard to say the right thing.

"But I enjoyed drinking it," she answered.

"I know," he admitted. "Your emotions were skipping all over the place when you drank it—passion, euphoria, joy."

She raised her head off the ground an inch. "What does that mean? Seriously, what does that mean?"

"Maybe you just like it," he answered with a cautious tone.

"Or maybe I'm vampire?" she countered, then she dropped her head on the ground and closed her eyes.

He didn't say anything for a minute, and then spoke up. "You saw a wolf? You said something about a wolf?"

"Yeah," she answered. "He was acting strange, almost friendly."

"He's not here anymore," Derek said as if his gift allowed him to check the nearby woods for animals. "It was probably just a stray dog."

"He looked like a wolf."

"Then he was probably a hybrid."

"Probably," she admitted, realizing she might be overreacting.

Neither spoke for a few minutes. Closing her eyes, she savored the feel of Derek's body next to hers and slowly relaxed. When she opened her eyes, the stars above sparkled with a fairy-tale radiance. The tall grass around them danced in the wind. Derek was doing it again, making the world around her appear utopian, too perfect. Even the air became fragranced with the spicy scent of plants, hinted with the floral aroma of wildflowers. She closed her eyes again, afraid to let herself be completely pulled into the world he created.

"Do you think you're a vampire?" he asked.

His question brought back some reality. She looked at him. "I don't know. I'm so friggin' confused."

He ran his hand over her cheek. "Does it really matter what you are, Kylie? It sure as hell doesn't matter to me."

"Of course it matters." She propped herself up on one elbow. "You don't understand because you know what you are. You've always known what you are. Everything about what I perceived about myself, who I am, what I am, who my father is, it's all been ripped away. All I'm left with is a bunch of questions. Nothing is like I thought."

Tears filled her eyes. "And—"

Derek's mouth met hers. Her eyes fluttered closed. The sweetness of the kiss sent all her emotional havoc out of her mental window. She let herself enjoy the moment. Let herself be pulled into the sensations of just feeling and not thinking. And, oh goodness, it felt good.

When he drew back she wasn't ready for it to end. She opened her eyes. No longer under the sweet sensations of his kiss, she wasn't sure how she felt about him shutting her up. She sat up. "Why did you do that?"

"Do what?" he asked.

"Kiss me when I was trying to talk."

A smile formed in his eyes. "You don't like me to use my gift to calm you down, so I thought I'd use my charm instead."

"If it is just your charm, and not your gift, how do you make everything so much like a fantasy world?"

He shook his head, and his brown hair brushed against his brow. "I told you, I'm not doing that."

She cocked her head to the side and sent him an accusing look.

"If I am doing it, I'm not doing it on purpose. I swear. Being with you makes me happy and maybe being happy ups my charm." His smile was contagious and any emotions taking up residence in her chest similar to anger or distrust vanished.

She thumped his shoulder with her palm. "You think you're that charming, huh?"

His smile widened. "I think you like my kisses." His gaze lowered to her mouth where she could still taste the moisture of his kiss.

"Really?" she teased. "You're that sure of yourself?"

"I'm sure that you're not feeling upset anymore. And that's what matters, isn't it?" He passed a finger over her lips. "Because I really hate seeing you upset."

Her heart squeezed and she wondered if that was a confession that he was indeed manipulating her emotions. Then again, was it wrong to want to make someone happy, to chase away their fears? Oh heck, what was she waiting for? What kept her from saying yes to everything Derek wanted? Yes to agreeing to go out with him. Yes to . . . to more kisses and to wherever those kisses led. She leaned in closer, wanting to taste his kiss again.

"See," he said playfully, and arched his eyebrows. "Admit it." He moved in. His mouth came so close to hers that she could practically feel it moving when he spoke.

"Admit what?" She put a little tease in her own voice, hoping she drove him as crazy as he drove her.

"Admit that you like my kisses. And then say yes to going out with me."

She cut her eyes up at him and grinned. "I'll admit I like your kisses, but do you like mine?"

"More than anything." He closed the tiniest bit of distance between them. "Go out with me." He kissed her again. Softly at first and then deeper. She felt his tongue slip inside her mouth. She felt herself gently being lowered back to the ground. Felt his hand slip up under her shirt and touch her bare skin at her waist. He'd touched her like that before but she got the feeling he wouldn't take that touch higher; he wouldn't push the intimacy any further until he had her approval.

And just knowing that made her want to approve. Knowing it was her choice and he would respect whatever she chose meant so much. But was it enough to take that leap?

She reached for his hand, seriously considering moving it higher, giving him permission to . . .

"You two need to go back to the camp." The deep voice penetrated Kylie's sensual haze.

Both Kylie and Derek jerked apart. Burnett, the temporary camp leader and a member of the Fallen Research Unit, a supernatural unit of the FBI, stood over them. Kylie's face grew hot with embarrassment at her and Derek being caught making out in the grass.

Derek didn't seem to be bothered. He shot to his feet and looked around. "What is it?"

Kylie stood up. Only then did Kylie recall Burnett's dark tone and notice that his eyes glowed red. A sign that he was on the defensive. Obviously danger lurked close by.

"What's happened?" Derek asked.

"Someone else was here earlier," Burnett said.

"Who?" Kylie managed to ask.

"I don't know. But they're vampire and not one of us. Now get back to the camp."

"Maybe I should come with you?" Derek offered.

"And leave her alone?" Burnett asked firmly, his frown deepening.

Derek cut his gaze back to Kylie and then back to Burnett. "You're right. I'll make sure she gets back safe. Do you want me to come back?"

"No," Burnett insisted. "I'll be fine. Just keep an eye on the camp. Let everyone know to be on the lookout. Stay together."

And leave her alone? Burnett's question kept playing in Kylie's head and with each repetition, she felt more annoyed. She wanted to insist she could take care of herself. God knew Della would be having conniption fits at being treated like she needed to be protected. Then Kylie recalled how frightened she'd felt before she'd started to run, before she'd found Derek. Obviously, Kylie wasn't Della.

Did that mean she wasn't vampire? Or did it mean she was just a vampire lacking anything that resembled courage? Did yellow-bellied vampires even exist?

Burnett continued, "Don't let Holiday leave either. Tie her down if you have to. Got it?"

"Got it." Derek reached for Kylie's elbow and started walking.

Kylie didn't budge. "I felt it earlier," she blurted out. "It moved past me several times. Almost as if teasing or testing me." She recalled how it kept flying past, making its presence known without letting her see it.

"That's odd. Vampires don't normally tease. Or test," Burnett said. "They see prey and attack to kill. Now go back to the camp."

Chills ran up and down her legs. Derek sensed her fear because he reached for her hand and offered her palm a warm emotion-quieting squeeze. Her fear lessened.

"Come on. Let's get back." Derek took her by the elbow. The sound of his voice helped her brain connect to her limbs, and she started moving.

They walked at a fast pace and without talking. The sounds of an occasional owl and crickets sang out into the darkness. Not that she minded their music. Music was good. Music meant intruders weren't near.

"Why didn't you tell me a vampire came at you?" Derek asked, frustration adding a new layer of intensity to his voice.

"I . . . at first I thought it was Della and then . . ." Then she had thought it was Chan, but she couldn't tell Derek about Chan. She'd promised Della. "Then I heard you calling. And I started running and I wasn't so afraid anymore." She looked at the frown etched on his face. "I told you about the wolf."

"I think the vampire was a bigger deal."

"Yeah and I would have . . . told you, but you started kissing me."

"So that makes it my fault?" His tone came out harsher than before.

"Sort of," she said, not liking it that he was annoyed with her when only a few minutes ago they'd been kissing. She started walking faster.

They continued moving in tense silence for another five minutes. With each step, she realized how silly their argument was. "I probably should have told you right away. I wasn't thinking." She stared away from him, afraid he wouldn't accept her offer for a truce.

She heard him inhale. "I'm sorry. I shouldn't have been grumpy." He reached for her hand again. His palm felt good against hers. "It just scares me thinking that . . . that you could have been hurt." He sounded older. His voice deepened and his need to protect gave his tone a new quality. In spite of still feeling a bit annoyed at his thinking that she couldn't protect herself, she liked the new quality. It made her feel safer.

Yes, with Derek she felt safe, but it didn't stop her from looking at the trees and praying the wind didn't stop blowing, that the night didn't go silent again.

Chapter Three

"What happened?" Miranda cornered her in the dining hall twenty minutes later.

As soon as Derek had told Holiday about the rogue vampire on the prowl, she called everyone and told them to gather here.

Deep down, Kylie still trembled. Be it from fear, or perhaps Della's icy mood, Kylie couldn't say for sure. Della's cold shoulder could be felt from clear across the room.

"Come on, spill it," Miranda said. "And then I've got something to tell you."

Kylie looked at Della again. "How mad is she at me?"

Miranda glanced across the room. "On a scale of one to ten, ten being totally vampire pissed off, I'd say she's about a fifteen . . . and climbing."

"Great," Kylie muttered.

Miranda shrugged. "She'll get over it. You know how she is. Now tell me what happened."

Kylie shook her head. "I ran off and . . ."

"But why did you run off? Why did you . . . drink the blood like it was a cold beer on a hot Friday night?"

Kylie looked down at her shoes. She didn't want to talk about this, not now. "I don't know."

"You liked how it tasted, didn't you?" Miranda sounded offended.

The most Kylie could do was nod.

"Okay, then what happened?" A frown marred Miranda's expression.

Kylie swallowed the tightness down her throat.

"Come on, give it up," Miranda snapped.

"I ran and then I felt someone there—a vampire someone. And then I heard Derek. I think he scared off whoever was there. I took off running and found Derek and then we just . . ."

"You what?" Miranda asked, hanging on to her every word.

Started making out. "Nothing. Burnett showed up."

A whisk of air blasted them as Della came to a sudden stop beside Kylie. "And you told him you thought it was Chan, didn't you?" Della obviously had been listening the whole time.

Kylie looked at Della. "No. I didn't."

"Who's Chan?" Miranda asked.

"Nobody," Della snapped at Miranda. "Mind your own business." Obviously, Della didn't want anyone to know her vampire and scoundrel cousin had broken one of the biggest Shadow Falls rules: no visitors without permission passes. That especially went for those who were against the FRU's attempts to govern the supernaturals.

Miranda, unhappy, glared right back at Della.

"Was it Chan?" Kylie asked, not caring if Miranda overheard. Kylie understood Della's loyalty to Chan. He'd been the one who'd helped Della get through the painful change. However, it made sense that if Chan had broken the rule once, he very well might break it again.

"I told you he wouldn't come back," Della snapped.

"But how can you be so sure?" Suddenly Kylie remembered how frightened she'd been in the woods when she'd met Della's smug cousin. She folded her arms over her middle and took on a defensive posture. Just because Della believed Chan wasn't a threat, didn't mean crap. He could be a part of the Blood Brothers gang as far as Kylie knew.

"Because I trust him, unlike other people. I thought you and Miranda were friends. All I asked was that you respect the fact that tonight was important to me. That—"

Kylie's frustration level peaked. "Damn it, Della. Why does everything always have to be about you?" The words hadn't fully left Kylie's mouth when she spotted the look in Della's eyes. The same look her friend got every time her parents came to visit. The look that told Kylie that Della felt like an outcast.

Kylie dropped her attitude. "I didn't mean to show disrespect. I just freaked out, okay?"

"Why?" Della's anger sounded in her voice, but it was hurt that colored her eyes.

"Why what?" Kylie asked, but deep down she knew what Della was asking her. She just needed a few seconds to figure out how to word it so it wouldn't sound so bad.

Della moved an inch closer. "You freaked out because you don't want to be a vampire, right? You think I'm a monster, don't you? You're scared to death that you might become like me. That's why you freaked out, wasn't it?"

Kylie opened her mouth to answer but no words came out. Probably because she couldn't lie to Della. The vampire would know the truth. Della turned to leave. Kylie reached out to stop her, but Della was gone.

"Where did she go?" Kylie searched the dining room twice and still couldn't find her. The room was filled with excited campers milling around.

"Just let her go cool off," Miranda said.

"I can't." Kylie knew how much this hurt Della.

Finally Kylie spotted Della's midnight-colored straight hair behind a group of shape-shifters. Kylie started walking over.

Miranda followed her. "Seriously, why don't you just give her some time?"

"Go away," Della growled before Kylie came to a complete stop.

"No." Kylie stood her ground.

Della's eyes glowed gold with anger. Then her top lip raised just enough to show her extended canines. There was a time when seeing Della like that would have scared the bejeebies out of Kylie, but not anymore. She wasn't afraid of Della.

"I don't think you're a monster," Kylie said. "But that doesn't mean I wasn't scared."

"Liar," Della growled.

"I'm not lying. Check my heartbeat if you want," Kylie said. "Listen to my heart, see if I'm lying."

Della turned to walk away, and Kylie caught her elbow this time. "Don't you dare walk away," Kylie insisted.

"Let me go," Della rumbled in a low voice. When Kylie didn't let go, the vampire swung around, her eyes brighter, her teeth fully exposed.

Kylie heard a few murmurs in the crowd. The argument had obviously drawn attention. Della heard it, too, because she looked around and hissed. The few people standing close by scattered like scared mice.

Kylie still wasn't afraid.

"Uh, we should leave, too." Miranda bumped Kylie with her elbow. "She's really pissed off now."

Kylie didn't look at Miranda. She continued to stare at Della, letting her know that she wasn't afraid. "I'm not leaving until she hears me out."

"I don't have to hear you out. I know what you think." Della's angry glare, filled with so much hurt, slapped against Kylie.

"That's unfair." Kylie glared right back at the pissed-off vampire.

"What's unfair is that I thought you were my friend." The hurt in Della's eyes shined brighter through the golden hue.

"I am your friend. I gave you my blood," Kylie said.

"Me, too," added Miranda, sounding nervous.

When Della's expression didn't change, Kylie continued. "And I also remember you telling me how scared you were when you found out you were turning. You said you were so afraid of what was happening. You said you didn't want to change."

Della turned to leave again. But Kylie kept talking and didn't let go of her elbow. "Are you the only one allowed to be afraid?" Kylie felt the emotion swell in her chest, and tears filled her eyes. "Are you so special that no one else can feel that?"

Kylie half expected Della to zip off. Maybe even pull her arm out of her socket when she did.

She didn't. But neither did her friend turn around. She just stood there for several long seconds. One. Two. Three. Kylie counted and waited, hoping this meant—

"Fine," Della bit out in frustration, and finally turned around. Her eyes were no longer gold. She looked down, then up again. "You're right." She looked away and then back at Kylie. "I'm sorry."

"Damn," Miranda said a little loud. "I didn't know vampires could or would *ever* apologize."

Della shot Miranda a cold look. "I didn't apologize to you. So why don't you go find your broomstick and fly to Timbuktu. That is if your dyslexic, screwed-up sense of direction will get you there. And don't bother coming back, either."

Miranda took an offensive step toward Della. "You are so mean—"

Della bared her teeth and growled. "I heard you when you told Helen that blood was disgusting. You promised you would respect—"

"Is it disrespectful to be honest?" Miranda asked.

Kylie moved between them. "You two can sling insults, call each other names, and even kill each other later. But right now . . ." She looked at Miranda. "I need a minute alone with Della. Please."

Miranda's chin notched up a few inches. She didn't like it, but she walked away. That was the thing about Miranda. She might get pissed in a flicker of a heartbeat, almost as fast as Della, but Miranda got unpissed just as quickly. Della on the other hand—that girl knew how to hold a grudge. And while she pretended nothing could hurt her, Kylie saw her vulnerable streak and it ran even wider than Miranda's.

Finally alone, Della and Kylie stood there staring at each other. Kylie spoke first. "I'm sorry, too. I didn't mean to disrespect your culture. I really just freaked out."

Della nodded. "I get it. Didn't get it at first but . . . I do now." Della sighed and a smile touched her lips. "You loved it, didn't you? The blood. It was good."

Kylie wasn't proud of it, but she admitted the truth. "It was awesome."

Della touched Kylie's arm. "But you're still warm."

Kylie nodded. "And if I am vampire, wouldn't I already be cold?"

"I don't know," Della said honestly. "Maybe you just haven't changed yet. But you're about to."

Kylie remembered Della telling her that turning had felt like boiling water running through her veins.

"I'll be here for you," Della said as if she'd read Kylie's mind. "To help you through it. If it happens. You won't have to be alone. I think I remember most of what Chan did to help me."

"I know you will." Kylie tried to smile. Right then, she spotted Miranda staring at them from across the room, looking like a lost puppy. Kylie felt bad asking her to leave. "So will Miranda. She will be there for me. And she'd be there for you, too. I really . . . really wish you two would stop fighting."

Della shrugged. "She's just so good at pissing me off."

"And you her," Kylie defended Miranda.

"Yeah, but she's not like you. You seem to know what I'm feeling, always manage to say the right thing." Della's brow crinkled as if in thought. "It's almost as if you're an empath. You know, like Derek and Holiday and you can read emotions?"

"No," Kylie said, but deep down she couldn't help wonder. Hadn't she always been good at reading people? Like with her mom, she'd always sensed the distance her mother kept between them, knew there was something keeping her mom from bonding with her completely.

"Is everything okay?" The familiar female voice came from behind Kylie.

Kylie and Della looked over at Holiday.

"Yeah," Kylie and Della said at the same time.

Holiday gave Kylie's arm a squeeze. "We need to talk about what happened tonight, and we will just as soon as things calm down."

Kylie nodded and while Holiday's touch offered a small amount of comfort, she couldn't help but wonder if Holiday hadn't touched her just to check her temperature—to find out if she'd changed into a vampire.

"Later, okay?" Holiday asked.

"Yeah." Kylie did want to talk to Holiday, yet she sensed the camp leader would tell Kylie the same thing she always did. *I don't have the answers. I think this is something you must find out for yourself.*

But how was Kylie supposed to find the answers? Her plan of getting information from Daniel had been flushed down the toilet. Where did that leave her?

The chirp of Holiday's cell phone brought Kylie back to the present.

Holiday yanked the phone to her ear. "Burnett?" Holiday's expression hardened. "No. You have the wrong number."

Kylie heard the frustration in Holiday's tone. No doubt the camp leader was worried about Burnett. A little of that worry wiggled into Kylie. She'd been the one to run off from the vampire event—if anything happened to Burnett it would be Kylie's fault. Looking off at the log walls of the dining room, she tried to deal with the guilt.

Then Kylie remembered that Burnett was probably the last person in the world who couldn't take care of himself. The man was six foot three of hard muscle and his vamp powers were some of the strongest. Or so Della had said. Since Burnett had stepped in as a temporary assistant, Della had become a bit of a Burnett fan.

"I'm sure he's fine," Kylie offered, and leaned into a dining chair.

"No one stands a chance against him," Della insisted.

But neither Kylie's nor Della's comments helped. Holiday's brow remained pinched with worry. And it was more than normal concern, too. Kylie sensed the attraction between the two of them the first time she saw them together. Just because Holiday didn't want to get involved, didn't mean she didn't care.

Holiday dialed a number and then snapped her phone closed.

"Why would he turn off his phone?" Holiday's eyes tightened. "He has to have known I would want to talk to him."

"I can answer that," Della said. "You see, when you're out in the woods looking for someone, hoping to find them before they find you, nothing takes away your advantage more than a ringing phone."

The truth of Della's words only brought a deep frown to Holiday lips. "He could have called before he left. He's just being . . . difficult. I swear, I can't wait until they hire someone else. I simply cannot work with that man."

Della grinned. "You can't work with him, you say you don't like him, but look how worried you are about him."

"I'm not worried . . . I mean, I am worried, but not . . . It's not like . . ."

"Like you really care about him," Della finished off Holiday's sentence, and then continued. "Like you have the hots for him? Or do you have the hots for him? You know one might assume—"

"You got the hots for me?" Burnett's deep voice rang out as he moved to stand behind Holiday.

Holiday's face blushed—from anger or embarrassment, Kylie wasn't sure. Then Holiday swung around and confronted the tall, dark vampire. Burnett's eyes briefly met Kylie's and he nodded.

Kylie recalled what she'd been doing the last time Burnett's presence had startled her, and was sure her face reddened right along with Holiday's.

"So you're alive," Holiday snapped. While her voice expressed anger, her expression told another story—genuine, heartfelt relief. Seeing the emotion, Kylie forgot about her own embarrassment. No doubt about it. Holiday cared a lot about Burnett. Probably more than she wanted to admit.

"You never answered," he said. "You got the hots for me, or not?" His dark eyes lit up with a smile.

Squaring her shoulders, Holiday started talking. "Della assumed I might have the hots for you. And you know what they say about assuming, right?"

"It makes an ass out of you and me," Della answered, and gave Kylie the elbow. "Get it. A. S. S. U. M. E."

Holiday cut her eyes to Della in visual reprimand, then started walking away. She got three steps and swung back around. "Are you coming?" she snapped at Burnett.

"You didn't ask me to," he answered.

"Well, I assumed you would know I needed to discuss what happened."

He arched one dark brow upward. "And what did you just say about assuming?"

Della grinned and appeared totally entertained by Holiday and Burnett, but Kylie's thoughts went in another direction. She cleared her throat. "Didn't you guys agree to be forthcoming with all of us from now on? So why do you have to leave? Why can't we all hear this?"

Holiday frowned.

"She's right." Burnett held out both his hands. "You did say that at the meeting. I believe it was the same one at which you called me a jerk," he added.

Holiday's eyes brightened with frustration. Obviously the man didn't know when to keep his mouth shut.

"Fine," Holiday said between her closed teeth. The two of them stared at each other, and neither of them blinked. When the silence became long, Holiday let go of a deep breath. "Why don't you address everyone then?" She waved at the front of the room. "The floor is all yours."

"I think I could do that," Burnett answered, but his expression said he didn't really like addressing the group. Kylie also got the feeling that Holiday knew it.

Holiday shot off, and Burnett watched her go. "I don't know which is worse, talking to everyone or talking to her alone." He looked up at Kylie and flinched as if he hadn't meant to say that aloud. Then before he moved to the front, he looked at Della. Kylie could swear she saw him mouth the words "Thank you."

When he left, Kylie studied Della. "How long did you know Burnett was in the room?"

"Pretty much from the time Holiday walked over here." Della grinned. "Hey, we vampires have got to stick together." She nudged Kylie with her elbow as if saying Kylie was one of them. Kylie wasn't so sure she was. Then again, she wasn't sure she wasn't, either.

The door to the dining room swished open. Kylie looked that way. Derek walked into the dining room, and his gaze went straight to her. The sweet smile he sent her reminded her of the kisses they'd shared earlier. A warmth brought on by the memory filled her abdomen at the same time an unnatural coldness brushed her skin.

Goose bumps popped up on her arms when she heard the words again. *"You have to stop it. You have to. Or this will happen to someone you love. Soon. Soon. It will happen soon."*

"Who? How soon?" Kylie muttered under her breath. The spirit materialized only a foot from Kylie's face. She still wore the blood-soaked gown, only this time the blood dripped from the hem of her gown and pooled around her feet. Kylie's breath caught, and while it was the last thing Kylie wanted to think, her mind took her there. To the sweet, addictive flavor of blood.

"Soon what?" Della asked. Kylie looked from the ever-growing puddle of blood to Della's slightly slanted eyes that hinted at her Asian heritage. Then she watched those eyes widen with fear. Della shivered and took a step back. "You've got company again, don't you?"

Della ran off. At the same time several other campers standing close by started backing away as if they had figured out what was happening as well. Feeling ostracized, Kylie's throat tightened and her sinuses stung.

She fought to keep the tears from filling her eyes. When she looked back to the spirit, it had faded and the air had lost its chill.

Kylie's lungs swelled with frustration. Frustration, no doubt, brought on by all her unanswered questions. Her whole freaking life was one big unanswered question.

"Excuse me." Burnett's deep authoritative voice filled the room. "Can everyone give me your attention? I know you're all curious as to what happened tonight. And since Kylie reminded Holiday and me that we said we'd be more forthcoming with situations, I figure I'd best explain."

Chapter Four

Hearing Burnett speak lessened the emotional lump in Kylie's throat. Everyone looked toward the front.

"We had an uninvited visitor to the camp this evening," Burnett explained. "A vampire."

"Was it from that gang? The ones who attacked you guys at the wildlife park?" Helen asked, and glanced over at Kylie.

Kylie moved a little closer to the front, not wanting to miss Burnett's answer.

"I don't know for sure." He looked around the room as if searching for someone. A second later, his gaze settled on Holiday and his expression softened.

"But," Burnett continued, "I don't think they were here to hunt. If he or she were here to kill, he had a chance at easy prey and didn't take it." His gaze shifted to Kylie, making it clear, at least to Kylie, that she was the "easy prey."

Easy prey. Prey maybe, but *easy*? That annoyed Kylie more than she wanted to admit. Okay, sure, she wasn't exactly Superwoman, but she'd held her own fighting the Blood Brothers that night at the wildlife park. Granted, she'd had some help from Daniel, but nevertheless, she'd kicked ass right alongside everyone else. Didn't she get any credit for that?

Burnett cleared his throat. "Chances are it was just someone curious about the camp."

Kylie recalled how threatened she'd felt those few minutes back in the woods when she'd felt the vampire's presence. It had felt like more than just curiosity. It felt menacing. If Derek hadn't shown up, Kylie didn't know what would have happened, but she suspected it wouldn't have been good.

"Or it could be the gang just wanting to let us know they haven't run scared. It could have also have been just a friend or relative looking for someone, and they didn't want to go through our visitor check. And if any of you have a vampire friend who might try this, please let it be known loud and clear that entering this camp without getting a visitor's pass is considered a serious offense. If I find them, I'll treat them like a hostile. And that goes for all species, even humans."

Kylie hoped Della was listening. Personally, Kylie didn't care too much for Chan, but she knew Della did, and for her sake, Kylie would hate for something to happen to him.

Burnett's gaze grew cold with his warning before he continued. "While I don't see this as an out-and-out threat, neither do I think we should totally let our guards down. The Blood Brothers gang was stupid enough to try something once. They might be stupid enough to try again."

"I still don't understand what it is they have against us," one of Miranda's witch buddies said.

"I'll take that question," Holiday said, and made her way up front. "If you'll notice, we have more vampires here than any other species. The reason is clear. The virus can be passed down so many generations and therefore parents of a newly turned vampire may not even be aware that supernaturals exist. This makes living at home extremely difficult, which leads many of them to joining the gangs. But since the camp opened, we've saved more than four hundred newly turned vampires from following that dark path. We've obviously cut into their membership immensely. They see Shadow Falls as standing between them and their gangs' growth potential."

She paused. "Any other questions?" When no one spoke up, Holiday added, "Now, it's almost two in the morning, so why don't you all go back to your cabins and try to get some rest? But remember what Burnett said. Don't let your guard down."

As the crowd started to leave, Kylie went to join Miranda, who stood by herself in a corner and played a video game on her phone. When she saw Kylie, she cocked her head to the side and smirked. Which reminded Kylie of a cute but pissed-off puppy.

"Oh, so when everyone else abandons you, now you want to be around me," Miranda said.

Kylie frowned. "I hurt Della's feelings and I just needed to apologize." *And I couldn't do it with you two verbally scratching each other's eyes out.*

"But you don't care if you hurt my feelings," Miranda said. "It's good to know where I rate."

"You don't believe that," Kylie said.

"I don't?" She shook her head, her multicolored hair—pink, black, and green—shimmering around her shoulders. "Is this the way it's going to be from here on out? Because you're both vampire, you don't want me around."

"No. It's not like that. And . . . we don't know if I'm vampire."

"You liked the taste of blood."

"That doesn't make me a vampire." Frustration built in Kylie's chest. But when she met Miranda's eyes and saw the insecurity lingering in her friend's eyes, Kylie stopped thinking about her own fears. "And for the record, I'm sorry I hurt your feelings. I didn't mean to do that."

"And for the record, neither did I," Della added, joining them in the corner.

"Wow," Miranda looked at Della. "That's almost an apology. And to a dyslexic witch."

"Don't push it," Della said.

"Fine." A smile lit up Miranda's eyes. "Let's make a pact that no matter what Kylie ends up being, no matter what happens, we'll always stick together."

Della snorted. "What planet have you been on? We already made that pact."

They started moving toward the door but stopped when Holiday called out Kylie's name.

"Can I see you a minute?" the camp leader asked.

Della and Miranda said they'd wait outside. Kylie walked over to Holiday.

"I know you want to talk about what happened tonight, but I'd like to get my talk with Burnett out of the way first. Is it okay if I stop by your cabin and we can chat in your room?"

Kylie remembered Holiday's comment about it being late. "If you'd like to wait and talk to me in the morning, we . . ."

"No." Holiday's brow wrinkled. "Don't you want to talk about this tonight?"

Kylie stopped trying to be polite. "Yeah, I would like to talk."

Holiday gave her a quick hug. "It's going to be okay."

While Kylie realized she wasn't as scared as she was earlier about the whole vampire possibility, there was still a whole heck of a lot of ambivalence bouncing around her insides. "I know." She smiled and hoped she sounded more confident than she felt.

When Kylie got back outside, everyone had disappeared except Miranda and Della, who sat in the big white rocking chairs on the office cabin's porch.

"What did she want?" Miranda asked.

"To tell me she's going to drop by the cabin in a few minutes to talk."

"To talk about what?" Della asked.

"Stuff." She didn't want to open up the whole vampire thing for another discussion with Della.

Miranda hopped up from her chair. "You guys ready?"

They walked down the trail to their cabin. Between the stars and moon, it wasn't too dark. The night sang out its song, of which Kylie was more than grateful. It was when the night music stopped that Kylie worried.

"I got kissed tonight," Miranda blurted out.

"Wow," Kylie said. "Perry finally made a move, huh?"

"About time that guy grew a pair of balls." Della giggled.

"It wasn't Perry." Miranda kicked at the dirt-worn path.

"Not Perry?" Kylie grabbed Miranda by the elbow. "Who was it?"

"Yeah, who was it?" Della studied Miranda really hard. "If you say it's Steve, I'm kicking your little witch's ass. You know I have a thing for him."

"It wasn't your shape-shifter Steve." Miranda frowned. "It was Kevin."

Kylie's mouth dropped open. "Not Kevin, Perry's roommate and good friend? Please tell me it wasn't *that* Kevin."

"Okay, I won't tell you." Miranda dropped her face in her hands. "What am I going to do?" She peered at them through her fingers.

"This is not good," Kylie said.

Miranda still stared at them through the mask of fingers. "I didn't mean for it to happen." She dropped her hands. "I . . . I was coming back to the cabin thinking you might be here and I ran into Kevin. I was worried about you. We started walking together and talking and then . . . then, he just kissed me and . . ."

"And what?" Della asked.

"And I didn't stop him."

"But was it yummy?" Della asked.

"Sort of. A little bit. I don't know. Why do I feel so guilty?"

Kylie stared at Miranda. "Because you've been acting like you like Perry."

"But Perry's not acting like he likes me. Sure, he sits with me sometimes at lunch and dinner, but don't you think if he liked me he'd have kissed me or something?"

"I think he's just nervous," Kylie said.

"I think he doesn't have a pair of balls," Della added.

"Stop it!" Miranda's face grew red.

"Stop what?" Della asked.

"Stop talking about Perry's genitalia. It's crude and I don't like it."

Della grinned. "Ooh-la-la, somebody likes Perry enough to defend his boys."

"So what if I like him. What's it to you?" Miranda placed her hands on her hips.

"It's nothing to me." Della's tone now sounded annoyed. "But it might be something to Kevin since you sucked face with him earlier tonight."

"Stop it," Kylie said. "I swear. Can you two not go fifteen minutes without getting pissy with each other?"

"She started it," both Della and Miranda said at the same time.

Kylie looked from one girl to the other. "Both of you started it. And both of you need to stop it. I'm up to here with it." Kylie put her hand on her forehead. "Seriously, I mean—"

"Shh." Della put a finger over Kylie's lips.

"What is it?" Miranda whispered.

"Do you not know what *shh* means?" Della asked.

Kylie pushed Della's finger from her lips and listened. A silence filled the night. Not the total kind of silence as it was back in the woods, because in the distance, sounding almost like background music, she could hear the insects and birds, but close by, everything had grown quiet.

Kylie leaned in and whispered, "Is it another vampire?"

Chapter Five

Della raised her nose in the air. "Not vampire. It's a wolf. It's been following us for a few minutes. I got a whiff of it a few minutes ago, and I thought it was just passing by. But it's not." She pointed toward the woods.

"What's a wolf doing this close to the camp?" Miranda asked.

Just like that, Kylie remembered the wolf from tonight. Derek hadn't made a big deal of it, so neither had Kylie.

"You wanna see me kick some wolf butt?" Della's eyes lit up as if the thought thrilled her.

Kylie remembered the wolf and its submissive posture. It hadn't been threatening. "No, I don't want to see you kick wolf butt." She grabbed Della's elbow.

"Why not?" Della asked. "It's not a werewolf. It's just an animal."

"Yeah, a real live animal. It's not hurting us," Kylie said. "So why would you hurt it?"

"It's following us. And that's creepy," Della answered.

Miranda leaned in. "I hate to say this but I agree with Della. It's creepy."

Kylie stared into the woods, and between the collage of trees she spotted the golden eyes staring back at her. A shiver ran up her spine. Creepy? Maybe, but it still hadn't hurt anyone. Then Kylie couldn't help but wonder if the wolf's presence wasn't some sort of message, or a piece of a puzzle. Or was it like Derek had said, just a hybrid animal wanting company?

"Oh man. Is that its eyes?" Miranda pointed into the woods.

"Yeah," Della snapped. "And I don't like it. I'm really in the mood to kick wolf butt."

Realizing Della was serious, Kylie snatched up a small rock and slung it in the direction of the wolf. "Go away," she yelled.

The rustle of underbrush filled the silence as the animal shot off. Then she looked up at Miranda and Della. "There, it's gone. Happy now?"

The sound of the insects started chiming again.

"Not really," Della said. "It would have been more fun if I'd done it my way. I could have used a snack."

"Tell me you wouldn't have killed it," Kylie insisted.

"Just a little bit." Della grinned.

Kylie rolled her eyes and hoped like heck Della was joking.

"Is it really gone?" Miranda looked down the line of the woods.

"Yeah," Della said, and they started walking again. But Kylie couldn't help but look back and question just exactly why the wolf was here. Then a thought hit and it felt as if Kylie's heart bounced around her ribs for a second. Could Lucas be trying to send her a message?

"Back to my problem," Miranda said as they approached their cabin. "What am I going to do about Kevin?"

"That's simple." Della jumped up onto the cabin porch. She turned around and looked back at Miranda. "You have to make up your mind." She held out her right palm. "Do you want Kevin?" She held out her left palm. "Or do you want Perry? It's not really that hard. Kevin?" She lifted her right hand. "Or Perry." She moved her left hand up higher.

"What if I choose Perry, but he never chooses me? Never makes a move. Never even kisses me. What if I end up being the oldest witch virgin alive?"

"Then you'll know you screwed up." Della shrugged.

"You're not a lot of help." Miranda looked at Kylie. "What do you think?"

"I think . . ." Kylie remembered kissing Derek tonight, wanting things to be different, but feeling as if something was always stopping her from taking that leap. Then she remembered feeling torn between Derek and Lucas.

"I think you shouldn't come to me for relationship advice. I suck at it." Kylie shot up the steps and went into the cabin.

Thirty minutes later, Kylie snuggled in her bed with her kitten, the kitten Lucas had given her. Outside her door, she heard Miranda and Della talking to Holiday. When the camp leader had knocked on the cabin door, Kylie pulled the blanket over her face and closed her eyes. She felt her kitten climb on top and paw at the blanket. It wasn't that she no longer wanted to talk to Holiday. It was more like she doubted this chat would help.

How many times did she have to hear Holiday say "I don't know, Kylie, this is something you'll have to figure out for yourself"? Why did Kylie think this talk would be any different? Wasn't that the definition of insanity? To do the same thing over and over again and expect different results?

"Kylie?" Holiday's voice penetrated the blanket as she tapped on the door.

Leaving the blanket over her head, Kylie called out, "Come in."

Kylie heard the door open into her tiny room, she heard it shut, and she heard Holiday come to a stop. "That wasn't a very enthusiastic welcome," the camp leader said.

"You want me to fake it?" Kylie moved the blanket off her head and sat up. Socks moved to snuggle in beside her.

Holiday smiled and sat down at the foot of Kylie's bed. "I know it's tough."

"You don't know the half of it." Kylie pulled her knees to her chest and watched Socks move over to the camp leader and rub his face against her arm. "I had a plan to figure it all out. All I needed to do was get Daniel to hang around long enough to tell me what he was, so I'd know what I am. He finally shows up tonight, but he doesn't have any answers." Kylie's throat tightened.

Holiday looked genuinely puzzled. "How could he not have the answers?"

"Because he was adopted. He didn't realize he wasn't human until he was eighteen. And I don't even know where to start to find the answers now."

"You'll figure it out," Holiday said, stroking Socks from his head to his tail. "I believe that with all my heart."

Kylie's eyes started to sting, which basically meant that the tears were on their way. "Does liking the taste of blood make me a vampire?"

Holiday hesitated.

"Wait. Let me guess. You don't know, do you? And then you're going to tell me that this is probably something I just need to find out for myself." Kylie wiped the first of the tears from her eyes.

Holiday let go of a deep sigh, then reached over and took Kylie's hand. "You're only partially right. Right in the fact that I don't know if you are vampire. But I think I can honestly say that liking the taste of blood doesn't make you one. I know of humans who enjoy drinking blood and that doesn't make them vampire. Even if some of them are freaks and they think it does."

"So this whole thing could be insignificant." Kylie pulled her hand away from Holiday.

"Yeah, it could be insignificant." Holiday's tone left a lot of doubt.

"But you don't believe that."

"I think it probably means something. I just don't know if it means you're vampire."

"But what else could it mean?"

Holiday gazed at Kylie with a ton of sympathy shimmering in her green eyes. "I don't know. But . . . I do believe that if you keep searching, all the answers you *really* need will be answered."

"*Really* need?" Kylie repeated Holiday's words. "As if I don't need *all* of the answers?"

Holiday raised her right eyebrow. "We never figure it all out, Kylie. Some things are meant to be a mystery."

"Maybe some things," Kylie said. "But not this. Not about what I am. I feel as if everything in my life is on hold until I have this answer."

"Then keep searching," Holiday said.

Kylie dropped her head on her knees and moaned. "See, I knew you would say that." Socks came running over as if to check on her.

Holiday put her hand on top of Kylie's head. "When one door closes, find another."

Kylie gazed back up. "And what if there isn't another door?"

"Then you try the window."

"And if there's not a window?" Kylie asked.

"Then you find a sledgehammer and make a window. Life isn't supposed to be easy. Generally speaking, the harder something is the more rewarding the results will be."

"But what if I fail?" Kylie asked. "What if someone is stabbed to death because I wasn't smart enough to find the right answers? I've done what you said and asked specific questions and all the ghost ever does is repeat the warning. She just keeps saying, 'This will happen to someone else,' if I don't stop it. She won't tell me who, when, or where. How the heck am I supposed to find those answers?"

"How do you know someone will be stabbed?" Holiday asked.

"Because she's bleeding profusely and it looks like her gown has been sliced and diced. Bullet holes are round."

"You've seen a bullet hole?" Holiday asked.

"On television."

Holiday bit back a grin. "Okay, I see where you might think it's about a stabbing, and she could be trying to tell you that, but remember when Daniel first came to you, you thought he'd been wrongly accused of a war crime."

Kylie slumped back on her pillow. "I suck at this."

"At what?" Holiday asked. "Communicating with ghosts? I told you, they're the ones who need a refresher course in getting their messages across."

"Not just the ghosts," Kylie said. "Everything. I suck at *not* being human."

"Not true." Holiday bumped Kylie with her shoulder. "You've done better than I ever thought you would."

Kylie cut her eyes up to the camp leader. "Is that supposed to be a compliment?"

Holiday chuckled. "Yeah, it is." She paused. "Hey, if it makes you feel any better, sometimes I'm pretty sure I suck at everything, too."

Kylie stared at Holiday and saw a touch of regret flickering in the depth of her eyes. "Do any of those things involve Burnett?"

"That is a subject I think I'll pass on right now." Holiday let go of a deep breath that hinted at frustration and Kylie felt certain it was all about Burnett.

Kylie remembered telling Miranda she shouldn't ask her about relationships, but for some reason Kylie couldn't stop herself from speaking up now. "Della was right tonight when she said you seemed to care about him."

Holiday twisted her ponytail in a tight knot. "I care about world peace. I care about the mangled moral compasses of today's politicians. I care about all the innocent creatures pancaked on that stretch of road two miles past our camp. Point is, I care about a lot of things, and my caring isn't going to change a thing—especially not a relationship between myself and that stubborn, egotistical, macho vampire."

"You're attracted to him," Kylie said. "And don't try to deny it. You've even admitted that much to me."

"Okay, I won't deny that. He's got that whole hard body, vampire magnetism going for him. But when I was young, I had a crush on Big Bird. That wouldn't have worked out either."

"Big Bird. Really?" Kylie asked. "It was the Cookie Monster for me." They both laughed, and then Kylie added in a serious tone, "It could work if you wanted it bad enough."

"I haven't got that much patience."

"Hmm," Kylie said. "Some very smart person just told me that the harder something is the more rewarding the results will be."

Holiday studied Kylie. "Do you really not have enough worries of your own to chew on that you want to take on my issues, too?"

"Everyone else's seems easier than mine." Kylie smiled.

"Ever heard that saying about the grass always looks greener on the other side? Well, it's the same way with problems. We all have our hurdles to overcome. So why don't you solve yours and let me take care of mine?" Holiday brushed a lock of Kylie's hair behind her ear. "But thank you for caring."

Holiday smiled and Kylie once again felt the bond between them inch closer. Kylie had long wondered what it would be like to have an older sister. She couldn't help but think this was as close as she'd ever get to that type of relationship.

Holiday studied Kylie and her eyebrows twitched. Kylie knew Holiday was testing to see if Kylie had opened up the doors of her mind. The first day at camp, Kylie had learned that supernaturals had the ability to read brain patterns. Supernaturals also allowed other supernaturals to read deeper, to get a glimpse of who and what they were.

Not Kylie, of course. The only brain pattern she'd been able to see had been that of the ghost of her real dad. And while other supernaturals could see Kylie's brain pattern, she had yet to learn to open up to let anyone get a deeper glimpse.

"Are you doing the mental exercises I told you to do?" Holiday asked.

"Yes," Kylie said, and watched the camp leader's brow crease. At least twenty minutes a day, Kylie was supposed to meditate. But so far it hadn't helped, or at least if it had, no one had told her.

"Anything?" Kylie asked, not wanting to be the odd duck anymore.

"No. You're still tight as a drum. Any luck reading anyone?"

"No. Maybe I'm a supernatural retard."

Holiday rolled her eyes. "If anything I think it's just the opposite. I think your brain is holding off giving you your powers until it thinks you're capable and mature enough to deal with them."

"Are you calling me immature?" Kylie made her point and stuck out her tongue.

"Not immature." Holiday chuckled. "I think you're wiser than a lot of girls your age." Her expression went serious again. "But that doesn't mean that you haven't got a lot to learn." Holiday stood up. "Do you think you can sleep now?"

"Maybe," Kylie said, but deep down, she doubted it.

Holiday got to the door, then turned back. "Oh, about the ghost problems. If she doesn't give you anything to work with the next time she shows up, tell her you're going to shut her out until she offers something more concrete. Then do it. If she doesn't give you something different, change channels on her. Nothing ticks off a ghost more than being ignored. That usually makes them figure out a better approach."

"How do I change channels?" Kylie asked.

"Concentrate on something else. It has to be something you want to think about." Holiday's brow rose as if she'd just remembered something. "Like making out with Derek."

Kylie saw something in the camp leader's eyes and she knew. "Burnett told you."

Holiday nodded. "And I'm not going to get involved with that, but just promise me you're not doing anything you'll regret."

"Nothing happened," Kylie said.

"This time." Holiday let go of another of her deep sighs.

Kylie sat up a little straighter. "Derek would never try to pressure me into . . . anything."

Holiday's chin lowered and her gaze zeroed in on Kylie with startling effect. "It's not Derek I'm worried about, Kylie."

Kylie looked down at her hands, feeling exposed. How did Holiday know how close Kylie was to giving in? Then Kylie remembered Holiday was just like Derek—she could read people's emotions. Obviously, just being around Derek had Kylie putting out turned-on vibrations. Good grief, she might as well just put a sign around her neck that said I'M HORNY. And wasn't that just lovely?

"Kylie . . . it's nothing to be embarrassed about. And I'm not asking you not to . . . What I'm asking is that when you do make that decision, it's a decision you make rationally and not one you just let happen. You understand the difference?"

Kylie nodded.

"Good." Holiday walked out.

Even after the door closed, Kylie's chest filled with even more emotion—embarrassment, uncertainty, and a touch of resentment. She didn't want Holiday or anyone knowing her deepest emotions or desires.

Then she recalled the sister-like bond she'd found with Holiday, the one Kylie totally valued. She supposed there was a downside to every good bond. She supposed a real older sister, even an all-human one, would have felt compelled to talk to her about sex.

As Kylie dropped her head back on the pillow, she remembered how it had felt to kiss Derek and wondered if she could ever make a rational decision where he was concerned. Especially when he had the ability to control her emotions.

Socks leapt up on the mattress, and Kylie was totally caught off guard when her thoughts went from kissing Derek to kissing Lucas.

Great. Just freaking great. She grabbed her pillow so tight that if it had a life, she'd killed it. Socks let out a pathetic meow and scurried back to the foot of the bed. Kylie moaned into the foam stuffing beneath the pillow case. She was already going to have a hard enough time sleeping and now she had the whole Derek versus Lucas thing to mull over.

Chapter Six

An hour later and she hadn't hit a lick of sleep yet. Well, not more than a few seconds. Every time she'd almost be there, she'd get this strange kind of sensation as if she was floating, or maybe flying, and the odd feeling would yank her from the light slumber. Once, right before she'd awoken, she'd spotted Lucas, as if she was about to dream of him.

He'd been surrounded with what looked like clouds, and a cool breeze stirred the foggy atmosphere. Just when she'd get a good look at him another cloud would float by, hiding him from her. He'd been wearing a button-down shirt, left unbuttoned, and that breeze would pick up the ends of the shirt, showing off his chest and flat stomach. That's when the cloudy atmosphere started moving faster and the sensation of flying grew stronger and yanked her awake.

Catching her breath, she sat up and pushed her hair from her face. Disappointment started to build, but she chased it away. She couldn't even think about the other "Lucas" dream—them in the water, only partially clothed—without blushing. She certainly didn't need to add a second dream to her couldn't-think-about list.

Rolling over, she punched her pillow as if the bag of foam

could be the blame. Then sitting all the way up, she turned on her light and without even knowing what she planned to do, she pulled out the letter. The letter from Lucas. The one Holiday had given her weeks ago but she hadn't read.

Hi Kylie,

I've started writing this letter a dozen times and crumpled it up and tossed it away. Maybe it's because I don't know what to say, when there is so little I can say at this point and time. Maybe it's because I just shouldn't write you, because . . . it's wrong. There are so many reasons why I shouldn't think about you all the time, reasons that have nothing to do with you and everything to do with me. I know I'm not making sense and if I could, I would explain it to you. Hell, maybe if things turn out the way I hope, I can explain it to you. Not sure that would change anything, but damn if I don't hope.

Do you see why I keep tearing this letter up? It doesn't make sense, does it?

What should make sense is this. You are so special, Kylie. And I'm sorry I didn't say this to your face. I'm sorry I didn't tell you right away that I remembered you. But I was so shocked to see you that first day at camp. Shocked and thrilled. You knew things about me that I'd tried to keep hidden—hidden from everyone including myself. My parents did some very bad things, and while I was young and didn't know better, I participated in much of it. You have no idea how hard I've tried to forget about that time of my life.

Actually, you were the only thing I didn't want to forget about. The little blond neighbor girl who looked like an angel, and who was a mystery. What were you? Who were you? You both scared and intrigued me even back then. I didn't understand how you made me feel inside. I wanted to kill the boys who threw those rocks at you,

I wanted to touch your hair to see if it was as soft as it looked. On full moons, I would watch you, hoping that you would turn. That you would end up being a were.

I think I just figured out why I have to write this letter. To tell you what you meant to me, just in case I never get to tell you that in person. Now if I can just put this in an envelope before I decide this is stupid and toss it in the trash.

Thinking of you.

Lucas

P.S. Dream of me.

His last line seemed to echo in her head. *Dream of me.* If only he knew . . .

Then all her other emotions were chased away by the residual anger. Just exactly what did he mean, dream of him? Dream of him doing what? Playing leap frog with Fredericka?

Kylie stuffed the letter back into its envelope and dropped it back in the drawer. Did he think his letter was supposed to make her feel better? If she was so special, why had he run off with Fredericka? Why hadn't he even tried to explain that to Kylie in the letter? Why was he being so secretive?

Did he think she wouldn't know that Fredericka was with him? Did he think it wouldn't matter? Duh, he'd admitted having had sex with the girl. He admitted that she thought they were a couple. And now he took off with her. How could he think Kylie wouldn't be upset about that? Were all men just dogs? No, wait . . . make that wolves?

No, she really needed to completely get over Lucas. Move on. And that was exactly what she intended to do. Cutting off her light, she dropped back on the pillow. Then she got a vision of

Lucas and the she-wolf making out and she gave the pillow one last punch.

The next morning Kylie had to drag herself out of bed to get dressed and comb her hair. She'd tried to go back to sleep after waking up at dawn with the icy chill of a spirit's visit. It hadn't worked. Now, with only an hour or two of sleep, she really would have loved to have buried her head under the pillow and ignored the daily grind. Who needed a thing like breakfast or nutrition? She dropped her butt back down on the bed.

She'd almost fallen back asleep when a thought jarred her fully awake again. Was she not hungry because she'd drunk the blood last night? Was she already losing her appetite for human food?

"You coming?" Miranda called out.

"Yeah, I'm coming." She fell back on her pillow, stared at the ceiling, and tried to decipher how she felt about all this in the morning light. So okay, the idea of becoming a vampire didn't feel like the end of the world anymore, but it still felt like a major calamity. Plus, she needed to know. Had a right to know what she was.

"You coming in the next century?" Della yelled out about three minutes later.

Calling Della a name under her breath, she started to sit up.

"Right back at you," Della yelled in return.

Yelled. Della yelled it back. Kylie tilted her head and tuned into the noises around her to see if her hearing had become super-charged overnight. But nope, she couldn't hear any better than she had last night. Which could mean Holiday was right. Her liking blood didn't mean Kylie was vampire.

Or at least not yet.

Forcing herself to get up, she ran a hand through her hair and went to face her roommates and the day.

"Good morning to you, too," Miranda said when Kylie stepped out of her room and didn't say a word.

Kylie shot her a mock smile. Then she did what she did every morning. She studied Miranda, twitched her eyebrows, and stared really hard at her campmate's forehead in hopes of seeing her pattern. But nothing. Just a tiny pimple near her hairline. Not that Kylie would inform Miranda of it. The girl would likely freak.

"You sure are perky this morning," Della said, joining them from her room.

"Didn't sleep well," Kylie said.

"Me, either," Miranda chimed in, and sighed pathetically. "What am I going to do if Perry finds out that Kevin kissed me?"

Della chuckled. "Run and hide before he turns into a fire-breathing dragon and scorches your ass."

"I'm serious," Miranda snapped back.

"And you think I'm not?"

Miranda glared at her.

Della shrugged as if conceding and started for the door. "First, you need to decide what you want to do."

"What do you mean?" Miranda asked as they walked out of the cabin. Then while waiting to hear Della answer, Miranda turned around and waved her hand up and then down at the door, putting a protective charm in place.

Miranda had started doing it last week, saying she felt an uninvited presence trying to come in. Part of Kylie wondered if it were the ghosts that Miranda wanted to keep out. Not that it was working. Every morning at the first sign of dawn, Kylie was awakened by the cold.

"I mean," Della answered, "are you going to start liking Kevin, or are you planning to hang in there with the shape-shifter in hopes that Perry will . . ."

"Don't say it. Leave his testicles out of your dialogue." Miranda pointed a finger at Della.

Della jumped the rest of the way off the steps then looked back up at Miranda with mock innocence. "I wasn't going to mention his testicles."

From the grin on Della's face, Kylie knew the vampire was lying. Nevertheless, she had a good point.

"She's right." Kylie put in her two cents' worth. "You need to make a decision."

Miranda frowned and pulled back her hair. They walked a few minutes without talking. Miranda seemed to be contemplating something.

"But I don't have to make it like . . . right now," Miranda said. "Do I? I mean, there's a chance that Kevin will just forget it happened. It wasn't really even that good of a kiss."

"Hey, Miranda." The voice came from about fifty feet behind them.

All three girls turned around and confronted the mediocre kisser moving down the walking path.

"Fat chance that he forgot," Della said and sniffed the air. "You don't even want to know about his hormones right now. The guy's got it bad for you."

"Really?" Miranda asked. "I thought you said you couldn't read the hormones and pheromones of a shape-shifter? When Perry was a bird, you said—"

"I said I didn't know what horny birds smelled like. But in their natural states, shape-shifters pollute the air with their lust just like everyone else does." She waved a hand in front of her face.

Miranda looked from Della to Kevin, who was closing in on them.

"Hi." He stopped right in front of the three of them. Kylie had never really noticed Kevin before, but she supposed he was kind of hot in his own way. Not anywhere near Derek's status, but he had some boy charm. And if you asked Kylie, he was even cuter than Perry, not that Kylie disliked Perry. The shape-shifter had sort of grown on Kylie these last few weeks.

"Did you sleep well?" Kevin asked Miranda, and dropped his hands inside the pocket of his khaki shorts. Kylie noted the navy T-shirt he wore hung a bit loose on his medium-size frame. His hair, a brownish blond, hung a little on the long side. He grinned, his blue-eyed gaze zeroing in on Miranda with obvious romantic interest.

"Yeah," Miranda answered, which was a lie, and Kylie noted Della rolling her eyes.

"I thought maybe we could walk together to breakfast," Kevin said.

"Okay. I guess."

Miranda looked to Kylie as if to ask if she thought her answer had been a mistake.

Kylie didn't know what to think, so she just smiled nonchalantly. No doubt, if Perry found out Miranda and Kevin were hooking up, he would be hurt. While Kylie wasn't afraid of Perry, a lot of other campers feared his powers. So hurting Perry could be a bad thing. But then Kylie saw the blush rise in Miranda cheeks and she also noticed how the girl stood a little straighter. Right or wrong, Kevin's interest in her was doing wonders for her friend's confidence.

When Miranda and Kevin took off ahead, Kylie and Della hung back. They stood there without talking until Miranda and Kevin took the turn in the trail that offered them some privacy.

"Whatcha think?" Kylie asked Della as they both started walking at a slow pace so as not to catch up with the two ahead of them.

Della rolled her eyes. "I think sooner or later some serious shit is going to hit the fan."

"Yeah, but did you see how her eyes lit up?" Kylie asked. "Everyone wants to think a guy likes her. Maybe Perry will see it and realize he needs to make a move."

"That's when the shit will hit the fan. You do not play with a shape-shifter's emotions, especially not one as powerful as he is. I'm telling you, the fact that Perry didn't turn himself into a wild boar and gore your ass the night you bobbed his ear is a miracle. It was the first thing Chan explained about the supernatural world to me. Beware of shape-shifters, they are one badass species."

Della tilted her head to the side as if listening. "Oh, shit. Make that sooner."

"What?" Kylie asked, not that Della answered.

Della had disappeared. Kylie didn't understand until she heard Miranda scream and some serious animal roaring punctuated the morning air.

Running with everything she had, which was amazingly fast compared to the speed she could run a month ago, Kylie got to the V in the trail just in time to see two huge black bears swinging claws at one another.

Della was holding Miranda, who fought to get away, as if she wanted to break up the fighting animals. It took Kylie about half a second to realize that these weren't your average giant bears. Nope. They had to be Perry and Kevin.

When the larger bear raked its claw across the other bear's shoulder and blood squirted onto the dirt path, Kylie screamed out, "Stop it!"

She would have gotten more attention from a brick wall. The

two angry animals continued to swing at each other. Suddenly, a few sparkles filled the air, and one bear transformed into a lion, a lion about the size of a minivan. Its roar rang so loud, it hurt Kylie's ears. Within a few more seconds, the other bear transformed into a lion—only larger. The sound of clashing teeth could be heard between the piercing roars, and more blood moistened the dry earth beneath their paws.

Kylie didn't know if the damage the two shape-shifters did to each other was permanent or if when they transformed they came back in one piece. When one lion grabbed the other by the throat, Kylie realized she couldn't just stand by and watch these two possibly kill each other. Not thinking about the consequences, she flung herself into the mix, grabbed the larger lion by its mane, and yanked as hard as she could.

"Don't do that," Della yelled out, and while Kylie couldn't see her, she suspected Della was talking to her. And just when Kylie actually considered listening to Della's advice, the huge cat stood up on his back paws, bringing Kylie up with him. With her two fists knotted in the orange hair of the lion's mane, Kylie's feet swung in the air. The beast opened its mouth, blood dripped from his teeth, and it roared with fury unlike anything Kylie had ever heard. The feline's angry eyes cut back at Kylie. She saw the eyes turn from a deep gold to purple. And somehow she knew this was Perry.

"Put me down and stop fighting!" she yelled.

Right then the other lion rammed Perry in the side. The hit jolted Perry back and Kylie almost lost her hold on the mane. She looked to the ground a good six feet below. The fall would no doubt hurt, might break a bone, but she would survive. However, the fall would also put her right in the path of Kevin's angry swipes and snapping jaws. Surviving that might be a little harder, so she tightened her hold on the mane and hung on for dear life.

Perry started shaking his head as if to rid himself of her presence. She swung from the right to the left like a not-so-loved stuffed animal in the hands of an angry child. Kylie's fingers started to slip. She glanced back down, trying to figure out an escape route, but her thoughts shifted when she saw Kevin's jaws sink into Perry's soft lion underbelly. Tightening her hold on the thick mane, she raised her foot and kicked the attacking lion right in the eye to stop him from killing Perry. Kevin let go, but when he retreated, Kylie saw blood dripping from his mouth.

Perry roared, from pain or fury Kylie wasn't sure. Maybe both.

Kylie heard Della yelling something. Next, Kylie felt her friend flying past as if in an attempt to rescue her, but each time she passed, Perry would shift direction, moving Kylie out of Della's reach.

"Enough!" Kylie screamed at the lions. "Both of you, stop it! Stop it or I'll get the death angels here."

The words no more than left her mouth when Kylie felt the temperature drop around her. The air in her throat felt icy. Her idle threat rang in her ears. But then she couldn't help but wonder . . . Did she have the power to call forth the death angels or was this just Daniel or another ghost making their presence known at an inopportune time?

Or maybe an appropriate time.

Hadn't Daniel helped her in the past? Suddenly it didn't matter, because she saw bright orange sparkles appearing around Kevin. Perry drew back his right paw as if to attack Kevin during his morphing stage.

"Don't do it, Perry," Kylie demanded.

Perry roared as if complaining, but he came back down on his four paws. Kylie let go of his mane and dropped. Still a couple feet off the ground, she landed off balance on her feet and then fell flat on her butt. When she looked up, there were sparkles appearing around Perry and she saw his human form take shape. With clothes, thank goodness.

He looked down at her, his eyes glowing bright yellow, and fury still filled his expression. But he wasn't bleeding. "That was stupid of you. Never, never ever get in the middle of a fight with shape-shifters. You could die."

"You're scolding me?" Kylie asked, flabbergasted that he had the nerve to reprimand her. "I wasn't the one trying to maul a fellow campmate. And I was trying to protect you." She leaned on one hip and rubbed her bruised backside.

"I didn't need protecting." His voice boomed and his gaze shot to Miranda.

Glancing back at Kevin, Kylie realized his changing process took longer than Perry's. As soon as Kevin appeared, he stepped away from Perry.

"This isn't over. We'll finish this later," Perry said to Kevin, his voice sounding more like a roar.

"Fine." Kevin stared Perry right in the eyes, and Kylie almost thought they were going to start again, but Kevin turned and walked off.

Kylie realized it took nerve to turn your back on Perry when you'd just taken a chunk out of his belly. But somehow the fact that Kevin was the one to walk away, that he never once looked at Miranda, left Kylie with little doubt which of the two held more power.

When Kevin disappeared into the woods, Kylie waited for Perry to say something to Miranda. But no one spoke. The birds in the distance started back on their song.

"Are you okay?" Miranda asked.

Kylie looked up to assure Miranda that she was fine, but then she realized that Miranda wasn't talking to her, but to Perry. Kylie shifted her gaze to him. He looked fine. Not a scratch on him. Which meant that when shape-shifters changed back into human form they healed from any injuries they'd received. And that meant Kylie had thrown herself in the middle of the fight and gotten a bruised ass for no good reason at all. She could have let them rip each other to shreds. She should have.

Just friggin' great. Still sitting on the ground, propped up on one side of her hip, she gave her backside another rub and watched as Miranda moved closer to Perry.

"Why did you do that?" Miranda sounded half honored he'd fought for her and half pissed because, well, he'd fought for her. "Tell me." She took another step toward the source of her anger.

"I felt like it," Perry growled back. Indeed, his anger became apparent in the way his body changed the moment she stepped closer. His posture hardened as if he was unable to bend. His blond hair hung scattered over his sweaty brow. His eyes were blue for a second, then changed to bright green.

He still personified the fierce appearance of an angry lion—gone was the jokester, the guy who always had something funny or sarcastic to say. And for the first time, Kylie understood why everyone was a little frightened of him.

"You didn't do it because of me?" Miranda asked, obviously not picking up on the fury he wore like an outer skin. "Because you were jealous?"

Perry didn't answer Miranda. He just stared at her and asked his own question. "So it's true?"

"What's true?" Miranda said.

"You kissed him," Perry said. "I didn't believe him when he

told me. I thought he was just trying to piss me off, but he wasn't making it up, was he? You really did it. You kissed him."

Miranda's eyes grew a tad larger. "Yes."

Silence hung in the hot morning air.

"No," she blurted out, and shook her head, sending the streaks of pink, black, and green in her hair intermingling with each movement. "I didn't kiss him. He kissed me."

"But you kissed him back," he accused.

Kylie held her breath. Della came to stand beside Kylie and extended her hand. Kylie accepted Della's help and, once upright, she reached back and gave her rear end another rub.

"Answer me," Perry demanded.

Kylie's gaze shot back to Miranda and Perry. The tension radiating from the couple seemed to suck all the oxygen from the air and made it hard to look away.

"This could get nasty," Della said.

Chapter Seven

Kylie crossed her fingers that this whole mess could somehow have a good ending to it—that the only thing nasty to come out of it would be her sore ass.

"Be honest," Perry demanded.

Miranda hesitated before answering. "I . . . I didn't kiss him back."

Della shifted her head closer to Kylie's ear and whispered, "She's lying."

Perry took a step closer to Miranda and studied her as if trying to figure out if he believed her. "Why don't I believe you?" He paused. "And even if you didn't kiss him back, you didn't stop him."

Miranda hesitated and then her shoulders dropped as if in defeat, and Kylie knew Miranda had decided to come clean.

"No. I didn't stop him. And yeah, maybe I did kiss him back just a little. But—"

"That's all I need to know." Raw and bitter pain filled Perry's color-changing eyes and for a second all Kylie could think about was feeling that same hurt when she'd seen Trey with his new girlfriend plastered at his side. Then there was the pain of seeing Mandy kiss Derek. And don't forget when she learned that Lucas had run off with Fredericka.

"That's not fair," Miranda said.

"Oh, it's not fair, but that's just too bad," Perry said. "It could have been good between us." He turned around and walked away.

He got about ten feet down the path when Miranda called out to him. "Aren't you curious about why I didn't stop him?"

Perry turned around and faced her. "I'm more curious as to why you think I should care."

Miranda's breath seemed to catch at Perry's words. She took several steps closer to him. "I didn't stop Kevin because . . . because I was tired of waiting for you to kiss me."

"Really?" Perry's feet ate up the few feet between him and Miranda. His right arm swept around her and pulled her against him. He didn't pause or even hesitate. He kissed her—not just a light peck, either. It looked to Kylie like the good kind of kiss, the kind Derek had given her last night. The kind of kiss a girl could feel all the way to her toes. And from the way Miranda leaned into Perry, Kylie could guess that Miranda's toes were feeling it all.

"Wow," Kylie muttered, and grinned.

"Yeah, wow." Della leaned in closer. "I think Perry just grew a pair."

Kylie bit down on her lip to keep from laughing. "If this was a movie, there would be some music playing in the background."

"I could sing," Della chuckled.

"And ruin it," Kylie teased back. "I've heard you singing in the shower." Both grinning, they looked back at the kissing couple.

Perry dropped his arms and stepped back. The abruptness with which the kiss ended seemed wrong. And it wasn't just Kylie who thought so. Miranda barely managed to catch herself.

Perry stared at Miranda, his expression not exactly one a person expected to see on a guy's face who'd just kissed a girl silly. The anger and hurt Kylie had noted earlier in Perry's eyes hadn't been wiped away with the kiss. If anything, he looked even angrier now.

"That," Perry said, his tone mirroring the emotion in his eyes. "That was just to show you that I would have been worth waiting for."

"Would have?" Miranda asked, her voice shaky.

"Yeah, would have." Perry turned and started walking away. But he stuck his right hand back and shot her the bird.

"What's that supposed to mean?"

"Figure it out," he said, but didn't look back.

Miranda swung back toward Kylie and Della. She put a hand to her lips and her eyes grew bright with moisture.

"Oh, crap." Kylie's heart clutched for her friend.

"Jerk," Della called out at Perry.

Holiday came running around the trail. She stopped and looked at the three of them and the departing Perry. "What just happened?" Holiday asked.

"Nothing," Della said.

Holiday glanced from Della to a teary-eyed Miranda who stood frozen watching Perry leave. Then the camp leader looked back at Della. "I heard it."

"Okay . . . almost nothing," Della said, and shrugged.

Holiday, as if reading Miranda's emotional havoc, walked over and wrapped an arm around Miranda. "Come on, let's go talk?"

"What are you doing?" Della asked, stumbling into the kitchen at two a.m.

Kylie looked up from the computer screen. "Using a sledge-hammer to make another window."

Della took a step back. "Are you having one of those funky dreams again?"

Kylie smiled. "No. I'm looking to see how many Brightens there are in the Dallas area."

"How many what?" Della dropped down at the kitchen table.

"Brightens. My dad's name was Brighten and Mom told me that his parents were in Dallas when they met. Since Daniel can't tell me what I am, I've got to find it out myself."

"But I thought . . . Didn't you tell me he was adopted?"

"Yeah." Kylie looked back at the screen and frowned. "Damn, there are over a hundred Brightens in the metropolitan Dallas area. Who knew that was such a popular name?"

"If he was adopted then how is this going to help you figure out what you are?" Della leaned over to peer at the screen.

"Maybe they will help me find his real parents."

"I'd love to be a fly on the wall for that conversation. 'Hey, Grandma and Grandpa, I'm your granddaughter you never knew you had, but not really since I know you adopted my dad who died before I was born and I really don't care about you guys, I just want to know my real grandparents.'"

Kylie frowned at Della. "You are not helping me any."

"I'm just calling it like I see it."

"Well, I wish you wouldn't." Kylie closed her eyes and tried to hold on to the tiniest bit of hope she had. But deep down she was afraid Della was right. The chances of actually finding the Bright-ens were near impossible. Getting them to tell her about his birth parents when she shouldn't even know he was adopted, well, it was probably going to take more than a sledgehammer to open that window.

"Hey," Della said, and nudged her shoulder. "Print up those numbers and Miranda and I can help you call them."

Kylie looked back at Della. "You would do that?"

"You gave me blood," Della said.

"Yeah, I did," Kylie said, and looked back at the computer screen. Then mentally she picked back up the sledgehammer and hit the print button.

"Let me go! Let me go!"

Two mornings later, something startled Kylie awake. Confused as to why she struggled in her own bed, she snapped open her eyes. The steam of her own breath floated above her face in snake-like patterns. The frigid air in the room told the time. Dawn.

She pulled the covers up to her neck and closed her eyes. And *bam*. The dream she'd just lived came crashing down on her.

Let me go! Let me go!

She heard her own scream like an echo, as if it was just now bouncing back from the dark corners of her bedroom. Her heart raced, pounded against her chest bone like a trapped animal. *Thump. Thump. Thump.*

She wadded fistfuls of blanket in her hands and mentally fought being pulled back into the nightmare. Her efforts were futile. The dream became her reality.

Cloth ties cut into her arms as someone attempted to tie her down. Blinking, she tried to focus, but her vision seemed impaired. Everything seemed impaired. Her head swam. She counted one, two, maybe three smeared and blurry figures standing over her. She kicked her legs, but an overwhelming sluggishness hampered her strength.

She pulled at the restraints, but the figures looming above multiplied. Their hands caught her limbs faster than she could move them. The ties around her wrists grew tighter. Unable to move, she watched in horror as another blurred figure came at her with a knife.

"No!" Her own scream jarred her from the nightmare. Snapping her eyes open, she clutched her fist and stared at the ceiling, afraid if she even blinked she'd be taken back.

"Just a dream. Just a dream." She repeated the words over and over. Rolling to her side, she tried to stand, but the dizziness from the dream now plagued her body for real. She fell back to the bed.

"Just a dream. Just a dream." She counted her breaths in and out, and only when the room's temperature dropped did she try to get up again. The wave of dizziness had passed, but the panic hung on. Her mind flashed through the frightening images, sending volts of fear coursing through her veins. Then she realized with horror that in the dream she had been the woman. She had been the ghost.

Grabbing her jeans, she slipped them on under her nightshirt. Not bothering to put on shoes or a bra, she scurried out of her room and out of her cabin. Her heart hadn't stopped racing when she came to the foot of the cabin steps. In spite of the hour, darkness hung like a cloak over the sky, only a glimmer of light clawing at the eastern horizon.

She started down the trail that led to Holiday's cabin, but remembered Holiday saying that she went to the office at first light.

Swinging around, Kylie ran down the path to the office. The ease and speed with which she moved should have been comforting, but it just served as a reminder that everything in her life was changing. And she didn't have a clue where those changes would lead her.

She'd gotten halfway to the office when her lungs finally demanded more oxygen. Drawing in deep breaths, she bent her knees slightly and rested her palms on her lower thighs. Staring down at her bare feet, she fought to keep images of the dreams from playing like a bad video in her head.

"Just a dream," she whispered into the dark silence.

And that's when she noticed it. The stillness. The dark dead silence.

The kind of silence that meant she wasn't alone. The lack of cold told her this wasn't a spirit. She remembered the vampire who'd dared to enter the camp. The one Burnett insisted could have fed on her if that had been its intent. Was it back to finish the job?

She stood erect. Her first instinct was to run.

Her second was to scream.

Her third instinct, not nearly as strong as the first two, was to pull up her big girl panties and face whoever—or whatever—it was.

Before she actually fully embraced option number three, the world around her came back to life. Finding comfort in the frogs, an occasional bird, and the chirp of insects, she pushed back the panic from her chest. No doubt the last few days had made her a bit suspicious. A second of silence in dawn's symphony didn't mean she was being followed.

Or at least not by a vampire. For some reason she remembered . . . She cut her eyes to the edge of the path, where the trees loomed as if guarding the woods. No golden wolf eyes peered out at her from the darkness. No creatures of the night either. Obviously, the only thing following her right now was her own paranoia. Brought on stronger by the nightmare.

Letting go of another deep gulp of held-in oxygen, she started back down the path. She got a few more feet when she heard it. Before she could react, the whish of early morning air blasted past her.

Prepared to fight for her life, thinking only of rogue vampires, determined to prove she was not easy prey, she raised her arms.

Then she saw it.

Not a vampire.

The huge bird—a cross between a large blue heron and something that might have existed in prehistoric ages—parked its feathered ass in front of her. It flapped wings that had a seven- or eight-foot span. Shocked, and still not quite believing her eyes, Kylie gasped. The thing towered over her by a good two feet. Unsure what to do, she took one step back. The sparkles started forming immediately.

Crossing her arms over her chest, she felt stupid for not guessing right away. "That wasn't funny," she hissed when Perry appeared.

"What wasn't funny?" he asked, in a serious tone that she'd seldom heard leave Perry's lips.

"You scared the crap out of me, that's what. I'm really sick and tired of—"

"Sorry. I didn't mean to scare you. I saw you running. I wanted to make sure everything was okay."

She didn't know if it was his tone or his expression, but she knew he'd told the truth. He hadn't been pulling a joke. He'd been concerned.

"Everything's fine." Yet when she got a better look into his eyes, she realized nothing was fine.

Perry, the practical jokester, was in a world of pain. Almost a mirror reflection of the pain she saw in Miranda's eyes. And it was so stupid. If they both cared so much why didn't they just move past the whole Kevin thing?

"She really likes you, Perry," Kylie said before she could stop herself.

"She likes Kevin, too."

"She doesn't like Kevin. He kissed her, that's all. And you two weren't even going out."

"She knew I liked her," he said. "I sat with her almost every day at lunch."

"Yeah, but a boyfriend is supposed to do more than just sit with you at lunch."

"I know that," he smarted back. "And I would have . . . I was just waiting for the right time."

"And why isn't now the right time?"

"It's too late," he said.

She shook her head. "You're really going to let a kiss come between you and someone you really care about? Are you that—"

"Stubborn?" he finished. "Yeah, it's part of being a shape-shifter. Which, obviously, you know nothing about because you almost got yourself killed."

"But if you care about her then—"

"Cared," he said. "I cared about her. Miranda's history." Little flickers of light started forming around him. "Oh," he said. "Thanks for trying to protect me the other morning. But seriously, don't ever do it again." The giant bird reappeared. The flap of its wings moving past sent Kylie's hair up in the air and at the same time a deep ache fluttered to the pit of her stomach.

The golden hue of light filling the office window met Kylie as she took that last turn. She stopped and let herself just stare at the window, remembering the somber look in Perry's eyes and wishing she could change that.

Moving up the steps, she opened the door and called out Holiday's name so she wouldn't be worried about who visited at this ungodly hour.

"In my office," Holiday called back, and Kylie moved into the room.

Holiday motioned for Kylie to sit down. Dropping into the chair, Kylie slumped back in the seat.

"Are you okay?" Holiday asked, sorting through a stack of mail.

Kylie sighed. "Miranda's still depressed. I just ran into Perry, and I tried to talk to him but he's not listening. Not that he doesn't look as miserable as Miranda. He's not even making any jokes. Della is PMSing and therefore is losing her patience with Miranda because all Miranda wants to do is eat ice cream and whimper over losing Perry."

Kylie stopped to breathe for one second, then continued. She was babbling, but she couldn't stop. "Not that it's really Miranda or the PMS making Della so difficult. It's the idea of going home for parents weekend and spending it with her family. But Miranda, even when she's not depressed, has never liked dealing with Della's mood swings. So now, Della and Miranda are threatening to rip each other's hearts out and feed them to my cat. Actually, I think Della wanted Miranda's liver, it was Miranda who's going for Della's heart. So to answer your question . . . No, nothing is okay."

Holiday looked up from the mail and offered one word. "Interesting."

"What's interesting?" Kylie had a vague flashback of being in Dr. Day's office and being psychoanalyzed.

Holiday's gaze shifted back to the mail. "Several things actually." She set a piece of mail apart from the others before looking up again. "But let's start with the fact that I didn't ask about Miranda, or Della, or Perry. I asked how *you* were doing."

"So I'm a freak because I care about my friends?" Kylie asked, suddenly feeling annoyed. And yeah, she was about to start her period, too, so it might be a bit of PMS. Or it could just be the hundred other problems sitting on her shoulders like an unhappy gorilla.

"I didn't mean to imply you were a freak." Holiday's soft, caring tone aggravated Kylie more than the psychoanalytical one. Probably because it made Kylie feel less like a freak and more like a bitch.

Holiday dropped her chin in her hands, a gesture so Holiday-like, that in Kylie's mind the camp leader's chin was permanently in her hand. "I was implying that I think you hide your own problems from yourself by concentrating on the problems of everyone else."

Kylie recalled that her reasons for her early morning jaunt to the office were not exactly about Perry or Miranda. So okay, maybe Holiday had a point. Not that Kylie really felt up to admitting it right now.

"Then again, maybe I'm just a nice person." Kylie sank deeper in the chair and regretted getting pissy. None of Kylie's problems could be blamed on Holiday, and if anything, Holiday and their growing relationship was one of the few things that felt right in Kylie's life right now. For that reason, she offered an apologetic smile at the end of the sentence.

"Nice? Oh, I don't doubt that." Holiday grinned. "So, let's try this one more time. How are *you* doing, Kylie?"

Kylie sat up and propped both her elbows on the desk. "How much time do you have?"

"However much time you need." Holiday let a few silent seconds pass and then asked, "What's going on with you and Derek?"

"Nothing. Why?" Kylie asked.

Holiday arched a suspicious brow. "I saw you skip out of the dining hall yesterday when he walked in, and the same thing happened at dinner."

"I just didn't want to talk to him." It was the truth. Part of it. Neither did she want anyone with the ability to read her emotions or smell her hormones to know how turned on she got by just looking at him. Until she could get her wayward thoughts in check, best not to be close to him in a crowd. Or alone, she admitted. And yeah, sooner or later she was going to have to explain that to Derek. Later being her first choice.

"So something is wrong?" Holiday asked.

Kylie crossed her arms over her chest. "Am I imagining things, or didn't you just tell me to be careful not to . . ." She didn't want to say it out loud. "You warned me to be careful around him? And now that I'm being careful, you act as if that's wrong. What is it you want me to do?"

Holiday pursed her lips to the side in thought. "Careful, yes. But I didn't mean for you to avoid him."

"You might not have meant that, but right now this is my way of being careful. My way of dealing with it."

Holiday held up her hand. "Fine. You deal with it your way." She paused, then let go of another deep sigh that told Kylie she didn't approve. "Have you spoken with your stepdad yet?"

Kylie rolled her eyes. "Did my mom call you again? I swear. I don't get why she thinks it's such a great idea that I forgive the man, when she doesn't have plans to forgive him anytime in the next century."

Holiday's mouth did another one of those twists to the right as if she was considering the words before she released them. "He's divorcing your mom, not you."

Yeah, Kylie's mom had sort of said the same thing, but Kylie didn't buy it. "It sure as heck doesn't feel that way." She could still remember begging him to let her go live with him. But no, he hadn't wanted her, and why? She looked up at Holiday again. "Did my mom also tell you he's screwing a girl who's only a couple years older than I am?"

"No," Holiday said. "But you told me. The day we went for ice cream." Sympathy filled her eyes. "Look, Kylie, I'm not saying he hasn't done something wrong. But this still isn't about you and him. If I let the relationship between my father and mother affect how I felt about them, I'd hate them both."

"I'm sorry, but I totally disagree. It might not be about him and me, but what he's done affected me," Kylie said. "It affected me in so many ways. For example, my mom called me yesterday and told me she's considering selling our house. The house I grew up in, the place I've called home all my life."

Holiday leaned back in her chair. "That's tough. I can still remember how upset I got when my mom sold our house. But . . ."

"No buts," Kylie said. "My mom shouldn't push me to do something that she can't even do. She can't forgive him. Maybe I can't forgive him, either. So just tell her *that* the next time she calls. Or maybe I'll tell her myself."

Holiday frowned. "It wasn't your mom who called. It was your stepdad. And he said he's—"

"Oh, crap. He called you?" Kylie remembered how embarrassing it had been when her dad had hit on Holiday, gawking at her as if she was candy and he had a sweet tooth. "Please don't tell me he asked you out or anything?"

"No. He sounded genuinely worried. He said he keeps e-mailing and calling you but you don't answer."

"If he was so worried he could just show up for parents day. But does he do that? No. And you know why? I'll bet it's because his girlfriend doesn't want him to come. Her parents probably won't give her permission to leave town."

"Or maybe he doesn't show up because he thinks you don't want to see him." Holiday shook her head. "I just think . . . maybe you should try talking to him." She bit down on her lip and then her mouth tightened to the right again. "Oh, hell. I've already tossed my two cents in. I might as well go for the quarter. I also think that you are using avoidance as a way of dealing with everything that's going wrong in your life right now. Your dad and now Derek. And frankly, I should add that avoidance is a poor excuse for a coping method. I know because I've tried it a time or two."

"Yeah," Kylie said, back to feeling pretty bitchy again, yet unable to stop. "But until another coping method magically appears in my bag of tricks, this one is going to have to do." She almost wanted to defend herself and tell Holiday that she wasn't avoiding everything. She'd spent the last day and a half calling Dallas area Brightens, trying to find her dad's adoptive parents, so she might find his real parents, so she might find out what she was.

Holiday frowned. "We all have to learn lessons the hard way, don't we?"

"I guess so," Kylie said, not sure it could get any harder. "I'm just not ready to deal with my dad . . . stepdad . . . or with what I'm feeling about Derek. Is it too much to ask to just be given a reprieve?"

"No, it isn't too much to ask. But generally speaking, the longer you put off dealing with something, the harder it is to solve. Sometimes, you just have to face things head-on. My dad used to say that you should look trouble right in the face and spit in its eye."

"I never mastered the art of spitting," Kylie said.

Holiday smiled then glanced at the mail again. Sighing, she raised her gaze. "Do you want to avoid this as well?" She pushed a letter across the desk.

"What?" Kylie stared at the envelope and saw her name scribbled in a familiar script.

Lucas's script. He had written her another letter.

Chapter Eight

A part of Kylie wanted to push the letter back across the desk. Hadn't she promised to get over him? She knew Holiday wouldn't force her to take it. Didn't Kylie have enough on her plate right now? Why willingly take on more crap?

Holiday pulled the letter back to her side of the desk.

Looking up at Holiday, Kylie expected to see some disapproval in the camp leader's eyes because, once again, Kylie wasn't so eager to confront her problems head-on. But all she saw in Holiday's expression was empathy.

"I'm not sure I want to read it," Kylie confessed.

"Why?" Holiday asked.

"He ran off with another girl."

"I don't think he thinks of Fredericka as—"

"But she thinks of him like that. And if she throws herself at him . . . well, he's a guy."

"I know," Holiday said. "However, not all guys—"

"But some are. And telling the difference is like math—it's hard. You think you understand it and then you get the answer wrong. And don't even try to disagree because it's the reason you won't give Burnett a shot."

Holiday dropped her chin back into her palm and didn't argue with Kylie's assessment. After several beats of silence, she said, "I could just stick it back in a drawer and if you decide you want to read it later, you can."

Yes, Holiday could do that, but could Kylie? Could she really walk out of here and not take that letter with her? Could she pretend that she didn't care about Lucas? That she hadn't worried about him since he'd left—worried about what it was that he couldn't tell her, and worried that some of what he couldn't tell her involved Fredericka?

Oh, and if she still cared about Lucas, what did she really feel about Derek? Or was her feeling about Derek even her own feeling, or was he messing with her emotions?

Oh, hell. Could her life get any more messed up?

Might as well take the letter and let the chips fall where they may.

Kylie reached out and pulled the letter out from under Holiday's palm. After staring at it for a few seconds, Kylie folded it and stuffed it in the pocket of her jeans. Later, alone, when she felt like spitting that problem in the eye, she'd deal with it.

When she looked up, Holiday nodded as if somehow telling Kylie she'd done the right thing. Not that Kylie was sure about that. Very little in life felt like a sure thing right now.

The room went back to the awkward kind of silence and Holiday shifted to another subject that was just as disturbing. "Has the ghost given you anything new?"

"New, yes. Helpful, no." Kylie frowned and wished she could avoid this problem like she did her stepdad and Derek. But the violence and the threat issued by the ghost didn't leave Kylie any option. "I think she was tortured by her abductors."

"Ouch," Holiday said. "And you really think this happened, or do you think it's just her trying to communicate something to you?"

"I think it happened." Kylie bit down on her lip, her thoughts going to the warning that this would happen to someone she loved if she couldn't stop it. "It felt too real, sort of like the dream I had where Daniel got shot. I was her in the dream. And they were coming at me with weird knives. I felt drugged and when I tried to fight back they tied me down." Remembering the terror, Kylie felt her heart rate quicken. Panic once again started building in her chest.

Holiday reached over and touched Kylie's hand. Her touch sent calming warmth up Kylie's arm. The fear collecting in Kylie's heart ran away like scared mice. And just like that, the panic faded into something less overwhelming.

Kylie looked up at the camp leader. "Thanks, but that's not going to fix anything. It's like a Band-Aid on a bullet wound."

"I know." Holiday frowned. "But when all you have to offer someone is a comforting touch, you want to offer it."

Kylie released a deep breath. "What's going to happen if I don't figure this out?"

Holiday's hand, resting on Kylie's wrist, grew warmer as if she sensed Kylie would need another shot of calm. "You accept that you did everything you could in your power to try to stop it and move on."

The enormity of exactly what Holiday was saying, coupled with the responsibility that rested on Kylie's shoulders, suddenly felt like too much. Kylie jerked her hand from under Holiday's palm. "No. I couldn't . . . I couldn't live with myself. I mean, if I understand this right, someone is going to die. Actually die and it's not going to be an easy death, either." All the problems in Kylie's life started bouncing around her head like ping-pong balls. Tears filled her eyes. It still hurt to think about her grandmother's funeral—she couldn't lose someone else. "Failure isn't an option."

Kylie's mind started racing, trying to figure out who she loved that could be in danger. Was it her mom? Was it someone from back home? Someone here at camp? It could even be Holiday. Oh lord, what if it was Lucas or Derek? She glanced at the door and fought the overwhelming desire to leave.

Holiday cleared her throat. "As much as we don't ever want to fail, our gift isn't a guarantee that we can help everyone. Sometimes we have to accept that we can't fix things."

Kylie shook her head. "You might be able to accept that, but I can't." She bit down on her lip until it hurt. "I should have refused this gift. I can't do it. I should have sent it back with a big note that said thanks, but hell no." The knot grew larger in her throat, crowding out her tonsils. "Is it too late to refuse it now?"

"I'm afraid so," Holiday answered. "You opened yourself up when—"

Kylie jumped up so fast that the wooden chair shot out from beneath her and hit the floor, filling the small office with a loud crack.

"Kylie, wait." Holiday's voice chased Kylie as she hurried out the door, but she didn't pay it any heed. Damn it. She had to figure out a way to decipher the ghost's message. Had to, because if not, someone she loved would die and Kylie couldn't live with herself if that happened.

With her throat still tight with emotion, Kylie moved up the steps of her cabin right about the time the sun finally crawled out of the corner of the eastern sky. The golden spray of light hit her back and cast her elongated shadow on the porch. As she took the next step, the sun must have risen higher because her shadow seemed to dance on the porch planks. Dancing shadows reminded her of . . . the falls.

Kylie's breath caught. She needed to go to the falls. As crazy as it seemed, it was as if something was telling her that she'd find the answers there. She let the idea sink into her tired brain. And like the sun against her back, the first glimmer of hope started to grow.

Taking in a big gulp of air through her nose, she suddenly felt refreshed, energized.

She could do this. She just didn't want to do it alone. Her gaze returned to the cabin's front door. Why should she have to do it alone? She had friends. Ghost or no ghosts, they would help her if she asked.

Okay, sure, she'd asked them to go before and they'd turned her down flat, but this time was different. This time, she'd beg. They would do it, wouldn't they? There was only one way to find out.

She hurried through the front door, zipped past the ankle-chasing Socks, and yanked open Della's door. "I need you. Wake up." She watched Della raise her head and study her through sleepy, nocturnal eyes. Morning just wasn't Della's best time.

Next, Kylie rushed over to Miranda's door and slung it open. "Miranda. Wake up. I need you guys."

Miranda rose up on her elbow. Her eyes were puffy—crying puffy, as if she'd stayed awake half the night sobbing into her pillow—which, knowing Miranda, she probably had. Kylie's heart squeezed for her friend and she almost said, *Never mind.* But then Kylie batted back the desire to give in because she really wanted both Miranda and Della with her. And maybe Della was right—it was time Miranda stopped moping and started moving past the pain.

"Please," Kylie said before Miranda had a chance to whine.

. . .

Kylie went to the kitchen table to wait, but she felt too anxious to sit. So she paced around the kitchen, waiting for her two best friends to get up so she could commence her begging.

"This better be important," Della said, and stumbled into the kitchen and dropped down in a chair. "Do you know what time it is? It's not even six yet. This is when I get my best sleep."

Miranda stepped out of her bedroom only seconds later, wearing a T-shirt, shorts, and bunny slippers. Kylie stared at Miranda's slippers; the ears bounced with each step as the sleepy girl shuffled over to an empty chair. Once she settled in, she looked up. "What is it?" she muttered.

"We're a team, right?" Kylie asked. "We're there for each other. Isn't that we've said?"

"Why is it that I think this is a setup?" Della dropped her head on the oak table, and her forehead thudded against the wood. If anyone else would have dropped her head that hard, it probably would have knocked her out, or at least left a goose egg of a knot. But not a vampire.

"Just tell us what it is." Miranda folded her arms on the table and rested her chin on top of her wrist. Her multicolored hair feathered out onto the table.

Kylie glanced from Miranda to Della, still facedown on the table, and her heart picked up a notch. If they said no, it was going to sting.

Della must have heard the thumping of Kylie's heart, because she raised her head and stared. "Spill it, ghost girl. How bad could it be?"

Swallowing, Kylie did it. Just spilled it. "I need you both to come with me to the falls. I just want—"

"Oh, hell no," Della said.

"Not happening," added Miranda at the same time, and sat up.

"But I have to go," Kylie said.

"Then go." Della waved her hand toward the door.

Kylie swallowed the knot down her throat. "I don't want to go alone."

"So you want us to sacrifice ourselves, too," Della bit back.

"Nothing is going to happen," Kylie insisted.

"Then why do we have to go?" Miranda asked, a frown marring her lips.

"Nothing bad is going to happen." Kylie dropped into a chair, losing hope due to their attitude.

"Says who?" Della asked.

"Says me," Kylie answered. "I just . . . I don't want to go alone."

"Because you're scared," Della insisted. "And for a damn good reason. Don't you know what death angels do?"

Kylie hesitated. "They are the ones who stand judgment of supernaturals." She repeated what she had heard, but truth was, she didn't completely understand death angels. How could she when no one really wanted to talk about them? Well, no one but Holiday, and most of what she would say was that she had never met one face-to-face.

"Yeah, they are the ones who stand judgment of us and sometimes they dish out the punishment, too," Miranda said. "I knew a girl, Becca. She was . . . toying around with spells on people who pissed her off. People who really didn't deserve it. So maybe she was being bad, but damn, her spells were more an annoyance than anything else. Then two days later, she walked outside and her clothes caught fire. Poof, just like that, she went up in smoke. She's disfigured now, scarred like crazy, and everyone says it was the death angels teaching her a lesson."

"Or maybe it was someone she'd cast a spell on getting even with her," Kylie said.

"They were all questioned by the witches council. Proven innocent."

Kylie shook her head. "We don't even know if death angels really exist. Chances are, they are just powerful ghosts," Kylie said, repeating another thing Holiday had said. If Della and Miranda had heard even half of what Daniel had done by pulling her into his dreams, and pulling her out of her own body and into his so she could relive his death, well, they'd probably think he was a death angel.

Della leaned her chair back on two legs. "If you don't believe they exist, then why do you even want to go?"

"Because if there's even the slightest chance that they exist, and are more powerful than regular ghosts, then they might be able to help me save someone I love." She'd never explained any of this to Della or Miranda. How could she when the moment either of them heard the word *ghost* they freaked?

"Save who?" Della, balancing the chair on two legs, started looking around the room as if they had company.

"I don't know. It could be you." Kylie stared right into Della's black eyes. "Or you." She pointed at Miranda. "There's a ghost who just keeps telling me someone I love is going to die. And it's up to me—"

"I hope it's not one of us," Miranda said.

Della snorted. "Maybe it *is* one of us and we die because you take us and offer us up as a sacrifice to the death angels."

"You know I wouldn't do that." Frustration buzzed around her gut even stronger than before. She tapped her left bare foot on the tile floor, trying to be patient, but her patience seemed to be in short supply lately.

Della shook her head. "I mean, it's bad enough that we have to accept that you have ghosts popping in all the time, but to actually go looking for the death angels . . ." She dropped the chair down with a whack. "I don't want to wind up with scars all over this face. Nope."

Kylie glared from one friend to the other. "Okay, even if they exist, what have either of you two done that is so bad that . . . that they would set you on fire?" She glanced at Miranda. "You aren't casting spells on anyone." She looked back to Della. "And you don't—"

"You don't know what I've done," Della snapped, her eyes glowed brighter. "Hell, *I* don't even know what I've done. There's a time when you turn vampire that you lose it completely, and I lost it. I don't know what happened for a whole two days. I don't want to know. Which is why I don't live in a glass house. Why I don't waste a heck of a lot of time judging others. And why I don't go to places where death angels are said to hang out. Maybe you haven't ever sinned, but I'm not perfect."

Kylie heard the undercurrent of guilt in Della's voice. "I don't think you would have done anything that bad."

"I wouldn't bet on it." Miranda made a face. "Look how mean she's to me," Miranda mouthed off.

Della glared at Miranda. "Oh, please, I haven't ever been mean to you."

"Bull crappie," Miranda said. "That's all you've been to me these last few days. I'm hurting and all you've done is poke fun at me."

"Yeah, but I do it out of love. Hoping to make you see what a dumbass you're being. Grieving over a guy who gets his shorts in a wad just because one of his friends kissed you. You should be out kissing all his other friends just to show him that you don't care. Not whining—"

"I'm not a dumbass." Miranda held out her pinky finger.

"I told you never to point that damn pinky at me." Della

jumped up and started screaming something about how all witches should be doomed to hell.

Kylie sat there, listening to them sling insults. Then frustrated and completely out of patience, she got up, collected her shoes by the door, and walked out. She stopped outside on the porch to put on her Reeboks.

Dropping her butt down on the porch, she slipped on her right shoe. Her toes felt cramped, just like her chest, and she loosened her laces before she tied them. Did Della or Miranda even realize she'd walked out? That's when she realized that frustration and impatience weren't the only emotions fighting for a spot in her chest. This hurt.

Didn't they realize how badly she needed them right now? Then taking her time to lace up her shoes, she hoped they'd have a change of heart.

That they'd decide their friendship meant enough to trust her on this.

Right shoe tied, Kylie slipped on the left and commenced the process. She could still hear them yelling at each other. They still hadn't realized she'd left. Or maybe they had and didn't care. That really hurt, too.

If either one of them had needed her, she'd have been there.

She stood, realized that she still wore her nightshirt over her jeans and was without a bra, but she didn't care. She jumped off the porch.

Taking off down the trail in a solid run, she wasn't even sure how to get to the falls. But something in her gut said she'd find it. She'd do this. And she'd do it alone.

Kylie came to quick stop at the edge of the woods, unsure which way to go. She recalled hearing the falls at the rock where she and

Derek had gone. She also recalled hearing it at the creek where the dinosaur tracks were. The falls had to be between the two, so she took off down the trail. She'd only moved a few feet beneath the thick umbrella of trees when the dusty dawn light faded to a foggy shade of purplish gray. She could feel the mist on her face.

The early morning heat chased away the night's coolness, forcing it to leave in the form of fog. But the cloudy haze clung to the trees and hung a few feet off the ground. Apprehension prickled the back of her neck. Believing she was slightly paranoid, she ignored the sensation and kept going. Going faster.

After about a quarter of a mile on the trail, she ventured off the cleared path, hoping the sound of the falls would call out to her as it had seemed to do before. She listened and she continued to sprint. No falls. Only the sound of the soles of her tennis shoes hitting the earth accompanied by the normal sounds of nature.

She kept moving between the trees, finding a path or making one as she went. The thorns in the thick brush snagged on to her jeans, as if trying to stop her from going any farther. She didn't slow down. Occasionally, a low-hanging branch would seemingly just appear in her way, but she either ducked in time or brushed it back with her arms.

She recalled trying to keep up with Della through a patch of woods very similar to this one on the night of the first campfire. She'd barely been able to walk it. That wasn't the case anymore. Her legs moved one after the other in succinct, effortless strides.

The thought hit again: change. Everything was changing. She felt it in how she moved, the speed with which she moved, she felt it in how her mouth pulled oxygen into her lungs. What else would change?

Not important, not right now, she told herself. The only thing that mattered was her understanding the ghost's message. Saving someone's life took priority. Then she could worry about herself.

She blinked, and then knocked a low-hanging cluster of leaves from her face. A loud crack sounded, and she could swear it was the limb breaking, but she didn't believe it. The deeper she moved into the woods, the thicker the brush was and the faster she ran. The faster her heart pumped with a mixture of fear and anticipation. Her whole body tingled with adrenaline.

Was she crazy for going to the falls? What if Miranda and Della were right? What if death angels looked at her sins and chose to punish her?

Her mind searched for the wrongs she'd accumulated though her life: lying to her mom, standing by and watching some girl bully another kid in school, hitting a squirrel during driver's education. The more she thought the longer her list of sins seemed to be.

Was she asking for trouble by going to the falls? Or saving someone she loved from something terrible?

Then she heard it. Or rather, she didn't hear it. The only noises bouncing off the trees were the sound of her shoes and the thread-ripping sound of the vines catching and being torn from her jeans as she ran. She stopped, folding her arms over her middle. Winded, she bent over at the waist. As she drew in shaky breaths, a stillness invaded the woods. The soundless air hung heavy, even heavier than the fog that had risen a few more feet and now snaked through the trees. And just like that she knew. She had company.

Chapter Nine

The sound of twigs being crushed underfoot told Kylie her company stood behind her. She froze, air caught in her lungs, fear sank into the pit of her stomach. Had the death angels found her?

She hadn't decided her next move when she heard, "Holy crappers, that was fun."

Kylie recognized the singsong voice. She fought back the panic and turned around. She couldn't believe what she saw. Miranda clung to Della's back and her legs wrapped around the vampire's waist. "Ride's over. Open your eyes. We found her." Della unlocked Miranda's ankles and nudged Miranda off her back, but her gaze never left Kylie.

"You okay?" Della asked Kylie. "Your heart's really racing. Is something wrong?"

Even with raw panic still running through her veins, Kylie couldn't help but smile. They'd come. Emotion filled her chest and shot upward and knotted in her throat. Unwanted tears filled her eyes.

"You let her ride on your back?" Kylie asked, hoping they wouldn't notice her watery weakness.

"It was that or wait on her. She's slower than a three-legged turtle using a broken walker."

"Am not," Miranda said.

"Are too," Della countered.

Kylie tried to swallow the lump in her throat.

"What is it?" Miranda and Della asked at the same time, dashing Kylie's hopes that her emotion would go unnoticed. Not that it really mattered. They'd seen her cry before.

"We're sorry we told you no," Miranda piped up again, elbowing Della. "Aren't we?"

"Yeah," Della said. "Are you really okay?" she asked. "Your heart's running super fast. Really fast. Not human fast."

Kylie blinked again. She did feel weird, but not completely a bad weird. "I'm fine. Actually, I'm better than fine now that you two are here. Thank you." The words came with sentiment and more tears formed in her eyes.

Della shrugged. "Yeah, well, if I die or something, I'm coming back and haunting your ass."

"Don't worry," Miranda said to Kylie and half smiled. "If she starts haunting you, I've got a spell that will lock her in purgatory for at least a dozen years."

Della shot Miranda a mock frown and then she reached out and latched on to Kylie's elbow. "Come on, let's go track us down some death angels."

"Can I climb on your back again?" Miranda asked, and rubbed her hands together.

"No. And if you tell anyone I gave you a ride, I'll break your kneecaps. I'm not going to become everyone's joyride."

"Unless it's a boy, right?" Miranda giggled.

"That's gross," Della said, and Miranda giggled harder.

Kylie looked at her friends and realized it was the first time in days she'd heard Miranda laugh. "I love you guys."

"Yeah, we know," Miranda said, and they all three started walking. The humorous mood slowly faded in the dark shade of the trees.

They walked without talking. A bird chirped above, the wind rustled the leaves. Kylie assumed she was going the right direction because Della never spoke up and she'd told Kylie earlier that she could find the falls just by listening to it.

As they moved, trampling over and sometimes through the thick brush, Kylie noticed her pace matched that of Della's. It was Miranda who seemed to be struggling to keep up.

They made about a hundred feet, and Kylie noticed Della eyeing her under her lashes. Had she noticed Kylie's newfound energy as well?

"What is it?" Kylie asked.

"Nothing," Della said. "It's just . . . your heart's still racing really fast and you look . . . different."

"Different?" Kylie asked, and looked from Della to Miranda and back. "How do I look different?"

Della continued walking but held her hands out in front of her boobs. "The girls."

Kylie looked down at her chest. "You've seen me without my bra before."

Della stopped. "It's not that your girls aren't supported. It's that they're bigger."

"They are not." Kylie stopped walking and protectively cupped her full size Bs in her palms. And the craziest thing happened. They didn't feel right. They felt . . . "Oh, damn." They felt bigger.

"She's right." Miranda cupped her own boobs as if checking them.

"Oh, God," muttered Kylie, staring down at herself.

"Hey, if you don't want them, pass me a cup or two over here." Della laughed.

Kylie recalled thinking that everything was changing. She just hadn't expected that to mean her boobs.

"That's not all," Miranda added. "You're taller, too. You must have had a growth spurt overnight."

"A growth spurt?" Kylie stood straight and visually measured herself against both Della and Miranda. She did appear to be a bit taller. Right then, her shoes felt tight, too. What was happening to her?

"My aunt Faye used to tell me every other week, 'You've just grown like a weed. Must have had a growth spurt.' "

Kylie wanted to believe that this was just a normal—human normal—growth spurt, but she didn't believe it. Her gaze shot to Della. "Did you . . . did you, like, get bigger right before you turned?"

Della looked down at her chest. "Do I look like I got bigger? I wish."

Kylie looked back down at her boobs. "What if it doesn't stop? What if I just keep getting bigger?"

"Then you'll have boys lining up for miles." Miranda snickered. "Hey, you know how they feel about boobs. The more, the merrier."

"You could always change your name to Barbie," Della said, grinning. "My mom wouldn't even let us play with Barbie because she said it was an unhealthy body image. I think it was because she knew that with us being part Asian, we would probably suffer from the no butt, no boobs syndrome. And she didn't want us to get our body image from a stacked piece of plastic."

"You've got a butt," Miranda said.

"Yeah, thank God. I at least got that from my mom. She's not short on bootie." She looked down at her chest. "Unfortunately, I took my dad's boobs."

Kylie tried to appreciate their lighthearted reactions to her situation, but it didn't dampen her concern. Okay, she'd admit that she'd occasionally wished she had a wee bit more up top. Especially when she compared herself to Sara, her best friend back home who no longer called, whose boobs were an eye magnet for guys. And sure, another few inches of height meant Kylie would look thinner.

None of that made her feel better. The idea that all this stemmed from some unknown, inhuman DNA she had coursing through her body made her nervous. Nervous because she didn't know how far it would go, or what would come next.

Would she end up having to have her size F bras custom-made like Sara's great-aunt did? Dear God, the woman nearly smothered Kylie when she hugged her at Sara's family's picnic.

Kylie still had her boobs in her hand when the chill ran down her back and up her arms, and her lips felt frosted from breathing in the icy air.

Company had arrived.

Standing right in front of her was the ghost. Only she looked even worse than before. She was emaciated, too thin. Even her cheekbones protruded from the sides of her face, giving her the appearance of a skeleton.

"You have to do something. Soon. You have to do something. They killed me. Killed me and they will kill her, too." Then the ghost folded over and barfed all over Kylie's too-tight tennis shoes and Della's pretty white running shoes.

"Gross." Kylie jumped back and slammed into Miranda.

"Gross what?" Della said, and looked down, and then Miranda moved in to see what was happening.

Kylie couldn't answer. She knew they wouldn't see the barf, she knew it wasn't really there, that as soon as the ghost left so would the vision, but Kylie was a bit of a sympathy puker, and real or not, right now it looked pretty damn real. Her gag reflex started to jump up and down in her throat. She looked away from her shoes.

"Do something," the ghost repeated.

"Oh, shit," blurted out Della. "They're here, aren't they?" Della started turning in circles, talking to things that weren't there. "I swear, I swear I'm sorry for everything I've ever done."

"Me, too," Miranda said, her eyes shifting from left to right.

Kylie stared at the ghost and, not wanting to freak out Della or Miranda any more than they were, she spoke to the spirit in her mind. *I'm trying to do something. But you have to tell me who it is. I need more information.*

"Killing me," said the ghost. Then she and her puke disappeared into the thin, icy air.

Kylie, realizing she still held her magically growing boobs in her hands, dropped her arms to her side. While she gave her chest one last look, her new boob size no longer seemed important. She had to get to the falls and see if the death angels could help her.

Glancing at Della and Miranda, Kylie said, "Let's go."

"I didn't catch on fire," Della said, sounding surprised. She elbowed Kylie. "Does that mean I didn't do anything that bad those days right after I turned?"

"Maybe." Kylie didn't have the heart to tell her that it hadn't been the death angels, so she just started walking. In a few seconds, she heard the almost hypnotic sound of the cascading water. She wasn't sure if it was real or from some mystical calling, but she kept walking.

They traveled another five minutes in silence. Then Miranda tucked a strand of her straight multicolored hair behind her ear and looked at Kylie. "Do you really think someone you love is going to die?"

"The ghost seems to think so," Kylie said, trying not to sound frustrated.

"And she won't tell you who?"

"According to Holiday, some ghosts have a hard time communicating."

"That sucks."

"Yeah." The overwhelming responsibility to save someone filled Kylie's chest with a heavy ache. If someone died because she couldn't figure this out, she wasn't sure she could forgive herself.

"Do you really think that the death angels might help you?"

Kylie considered Miranda's question. "I don't know for sure, but yeah, for some reason I believe they will."

"You really aren't afraid of them?" Della asked.

"Sure I am," Kylie said, but when she saw the fear appear in Della's eyes, she qualified it. "But I don't think they're evil."

Miranda piped up. "Do you think maybe you could ask them to . . . to make Perry forgive me?"

"Oh, please," Della said. "Perry just needs to pull his head out of his ass. You don't need forgiving."

"Not true," Miranda said. "I'd have been mad if he kissed someone else."

"Mad, yes. But to totally drop you because of it is ridiculous. I mean, it's not like you slept with Kevin or like you even gave the guy a blow job. He kissed you . . . big friggin' deal."

Kylie's mind shot to kisses. To both Derek's and Lucas's. They had felt like big deals to her. *Don't go there,* she told herself. But even as she tried to chase all thoughts of kissing from her mind, she remembered the letter she had in her pocket. Lucas's letter.

One thing at a time, first save someone's life, then worry about boys. And magically growing boobs. And the fact that she still didn't know what type of DNA she had coursing through her non-human veins.

"If you are going to be asking favors," Della said, "ask if they can get me out of going to see my parents for parents weekend. My parents are going to be watching my every move, trying to find the signs that I'm doing drugs. I'll probably be peeing in a cup every two hours so they can see if I'm using. I swear, if I make one wrong move, they'll yank me out of the camp and put me in a detox center with the washed-up child stars."

"I just want Perry to give me another chance. I . . ." Miranda continued talking, but Kylie tuned her out. Della grew quiet, as if lost in worry about spending time with her parents.

Kylie hated to let both her friends down, but right now she couldn't worry about their problems, not when it might even be one of their lives on the line. "I'm not going to be asking for favors. I just need to see if they can help the ghost communicate better with me. I've got to figure this out."

Miranda hurried her steps, still struggling to keep up. "Do you really believe it could be one of us that the ghost is trying to warn you about?"

"I don't know." The words the ghost had said replayed in Kylie's head. *You have to do something. Soon. You have to do something. They killed me. Killed me and they will kill her, too.* That's when Kylie realized that for the first time, the ghost had referred to the person with a pronoun. She said *her*. Hope that more answers would soon be revealed began to build in her chest as she continued toward the falls.

"Okay, this place is totally freaking me out," Della spouted the moment they stepped through the clearing and got their first glimpse of the falls.

"I agree." Miranda took a step back. "I don't think we should be here. I feel it."

Kylie kept moving, her gaze moving left and right, trying to soak it all in. It was . . . beautiful. No, more than beautiful. It looked picturesque. It looked photoshopped, as if someone had spent hours adding details. All those tiny details added up and created an ambience. The emotional essence of this place seemed as alive as the trees. As Kylie took in the fragrant air, it took her a minute to define what she felt. But she finally got it. The place breathed reverence—like an old temple or church.

Maybe it was the way the sun streamed through the trees as if spotlights from heaven. Maybe it was how the cascade of water tossed out tiny droplets of water that danced in the air and turned silver in the rays of light. Or how the verdant plant life glistened with all the pinpoints of dew. Or perhaps it was the noise. The rush of water filled her ears until she felt the same vibration in her blood. Or it could be the way the moist air tickled her throat and filled her chest with warm emotion. Not bad emotion. Acceptance.

"Okay, we said we'd come here with you. We did. Now let's go." Miranda took a step back.

"Not yet," Kylie said, unable to move her eyes from the rush of water falling from fifty feet above. Then, without thinking, as if she were being lured, she stepped into the creek bed. Just walked in, didn't even stop and think about removing her shoes, or rolling up her jeans.

"Whoa. I'm not following you," Della called out. "Really, we need to get back for breakfast. Let's leave, okay?"

"Just wait on me. A few minutes." Kylie didn't look back. Her shoes and jeans soaked up the shin-deep water like a sponge. She took another step and then another.

"Are you sure you should go in there?" Miranda's voice tightened with concern. "Come on, Kylie. Let's go, okay?"

"If you go in there, you might not be able to come out," Della warned.

Kylie didn't answer, not when she could swear she saw someone or something move behind the spray of glistening water. The figure shifted again. Someone was definitely there. She just hoped that it was someone with answers. And not someone ready to make her spontaneously catch fire for any past sins. But just to be sure, as she took her next step, she sent up a prayer for forgiveness for anything bad she'd done.

The tiny droplets of moisture sprayed on her face as she drew closer. She took the final step. The gush of water splattered on her head and shoulders.

Walking through the falls into the cavern-like darkness, she wiped a hand over her face, waiting for her eyes to adjust. Her skin pickled with goose bumps, not the kind of goose bumps that came from ghosts; no, they were the kind that came from fear. She stood completely still and hoped with the return of her vision came a bit more courage.

The sound of the falls echoed and closed off any noise from the outside world. When she blinked, the darkness suddenly didn't seem so blinding. She realized that the mouth of the falls was really a cave. Just when her eyes seemed to distinguish shapes, she saw someone dip behind a rock wall.

"Hello?" Her voice seemed lost in the rush of the water. When no one answered, Kylie continued, "I know someone is here."

"Then I guess I'll just come out," a voice boomed from behind the rock. It took Kylie a few minutes to recognize the voice, and she did recognize it, but she still couldn't believe it when she saw him step forward.

Chapter Ten

"What are you doing here?" Kylie asked.

His tall masculine figure kept moving toward her and Kylie actually took a step back. She wasn't so much frightened as she was surprised. And perhaps still awestruck at everything she felt. The whole reverent ambience felt even stronger in here.

"Probably the same thing you're doing here," Burnett answered. "Curiosity."

It wasn't her reason. She'd come for help, but she didn't correct him—and not because she didn't trust him. She met his gaze. If she were being completely honest with herself, she knew she hadn't gotten over being intimidated by him, but she'd grown to respect him as had most everyone else in the camp. She respected him enough that she wished Holiday would reconsider her no-vamp rule where men were concerned. The two of them would make a great couple. His dark side to her light. His seriousness to her teasing manner.

She felt him watching her and knew he was expecting an answer.

But she had her own questions. She took a deep breath. "Curious about what?" she asked.

"The whole ghosts thing. The legend." He tucked his hands into his jean pockets and looked around.

"That's strange," Kylie said.

"What's strange?" He turned and looked back at the cave as if checking his surroundings for safety. Oddly enough, Kylie wasn't worried about her own. The warm, good feeling filling her chest convinced her not to worry. She was safe here.

"Your being curious about ghosts. I thought . . . I mean . . . most supernaturals prefer to sort of stay in the dark about it all."

"Yeah, but Holiday's so fixated on them, I just thought . . ." His words faltered.

"That maybe understanding ghosts would help you understand her?" Kylie asked, somehow certain that she'd read him right. Again, she got a feeling that Burnett really cared about Holiday.

He nodded as if admitting it out loud might ding his macho ego. "Personally, I think she talks about it so much just to scare me."

"Probably hoping to scare you off." Kylie bit her lip when she realized she'd said that aloud.

He looked at her. "That, too." He paused a few seconds and then asked, "You wouldn't be willing to enlighten me on any of the reasons why she'd be doing that, would you?" Apparently he'd decided his macho ego could be damned.

Okay, now Kylie was up crap creek without a paddle and a huge leak in her canoe. Telling Burnett about Holiday's past felt almost like betrayal. "I . . . uh . . . I . . ."

He held up his hand. "Say no more. I get it." Shuffling his feet, he looked around again and then focused back at her. "So you're like Holiday, right? You feel spirits, and see them?"

She nodded.

"Do you feel the death angels?"

She started to deny that she sensed a strong presence of someone or someones, but considering the whole church-like ambience, she decided against lying. "I feel something. Don't know exactly how to describe it. It's like—"

"Really?" he asked.   .

"Really." She looked around and wondered if whatever she felt would give her the answers she needed. "You don't feel anything?"

"If I did, I wouldn't be here now." He chuckled, but Kylie could swear she heard a tad of nervousness in his tone.

"Doesn't the legend say that they come here at dusk?" He ran his hand through his dark hair that looked a shade darker than normal. Her gaze went back to the falls and she realized his hair was wet. She felt her own hair then, hanging damp on her shoulders and shifting back and forth on her back.

He took a few steps closer to one of the large boulders. His shoulders and arms shifted with corded muscle and appeared almost as hard as the rock walls. Once again, Kylie couldn't help but admire how attractive he was. Not that he made her body tingle the way Derek did, but she could appreciate the way he was put together. Holiday really should let herself fall for him.

"It says you can see them dancing on the walls at dusk. It doesn't mean they're not here at other times," Kylie answered honestly, hoping she was right. Hoping the presence she felt here was real and could give her answers.

He nodded and looked around again. "Why is it that the place wasn't so scary until you showed up?"

Kylie laughed. "It must be my magnetic personality."

He smiled. "Probably. You and Holiday." Just the way he said Holiday's name tugged at Kylie's heartstrings.

"It was another vampire," Kylie blurted out. "He hurt her a lot."

Burnett looked confused for a second, and then understanding filled his eyes. "So she's prejudiced against all vampires?" He sounded hurt.

"I would call it protective," she said. "And not all vampires. She doesn't seem to have a problem with any vampire but you."

He tilted his head to the side and looked at her. "You say that as if it's a good thing."

"It might be," Kylie said. "There has to be a reason you get on her bad side so quickly."

He seemed to consider her analogy. "I see what you mean." His gaze shifted to the wall of water again. "Why don't I walk back to the camp with you? Make sure—"

"Actually, I was hoping to stay here for a few minutes. Alone," she said before he offered to stay with her.

A frown pulled at his mouth. "I'm not sure you should be alone in the woods. Not after what happened the other night."

"I'm not alone," Kylie said. "Della and Miranda are right outside, waiting on me."

She thought he was going to say something completely macho, like tell her she should have brought a boy with her.

Instead he said, "Okay. Good."

Yeah, good, Kylie thought. Della would have had a conniption fit if she knew he considered her less capable than the opposite sex.

He tilted his head to the side as if to listen. "That's really strange. I can't hear them. Or smell them in here." His brow creased. "Then again, I didn't hear you until you spoke." His gaze cut around their surroundings. "Maybe this place is haunted." A grin pulled at his mouth. "And on that note, I think I'll head back to the camp." He took two steps and then turned back. "Don't be long. And make sure you guys stay together."

"Got it," she said.

He nodded and again tilted his head to the side and studied her. "Are you okay? Your heart . . . it's beating really fast."

She shuffled her wet tennis shoes on the rock. "Della said the same thing. I think I'm okay," Kylie said, not wanting to share her recent and unexpected all-natural but definitely not human boob job.

He studied her for a few minutes and Kylie got the craziest feeling he'd noticed more than her heartbeat, but he was careful not to make her feel uncomfortable. She appreciated that.

He started to walk out and then turned around. "Thank you for—"

"You're welcome," she said, not wanting to hear or think about how angry Holiday would be when she found out Kylie had told Burnett even the least bit about her past. And Holiday would find out, because Kylie had every intention of telling her. Keeping it a secret would make it feel like even more of a sin. And right now, right here, she especially didn't want to up her quotient of sins.

Five minutes after Burnett left, Kylie stood in the same spot. "Look, I got a ghost who is saying someone I love is going to die. I'm supposed to save this person, but the ghost isn't giving me a lot to work on. I'm getting scared. Really scared."

And she should feel sort of stupid talking to herself. Yet she didn't. While she couldn't see anyone here, she felt them.

"Can you . . . like, help me out here?" She waited. She listened with her ears. With her heart.

No answer echoed back, not in her mind, her ears, or her heart. Unless you considered the sensation of calm and rightness that made her chest feel lighter, her problem less urgent, and her ability to deal with everything almost manageable.

Was this the answer? That everything was going to be okay? Or was this like Holiday's and Derek's touch—just a quick fix to the emotional havoc living and breathing inside her? Doubt tried to sweep away the calm.

She dropped down on the uneven earth beneath her, a mix of rock and moist dirt, and rested her palms behind her for support. Tilting her head back, she felt her damp hair sway slightly and tickle her back through her nightshirt. Low on her back. Lower than ever before. Sitting up again, she reached back to touch the ends of her hair. Her hair, like her boobs, must have undergone a growth spurt. What did all this mean?

Trying to embrace the soothing emotion this place produced, she stared at the wall of water not five feet from her and felt the tiny droplets moisten her skin. *Don't worry, dear. Life is gonna be okay. One foot in front of the other.* She heard her grandmother's words echo in her mind.

"You really here, Nana? Or am I just remembering?" She posed the questions aloud.

The lack of cold told her she was alone. A tiny part of her wanted to rebel, to demand an answer, not just to her ghost's problem but to all her issues. Just as she was about to open her mouth, a bit of wisdom seemed to wiggle through the frustration. This, whatever "this" was making the falls feel special, wasn't open to demands or rebellion. In addition to the calm, Kylie sensed a power.

Not evil, but firm.

Not uncaring, but unyielding.

Unyielding enough to set a girl aflame and scar her for life? Kylie didn't know that answer, and for her own sanity she wasn't sure she wanted to know.

Then, realizing she was probably pushing Della's and Miranda's limit for waiting, she stood up. When she did, she felt the folded envelope in her pocket. Lucas's letter. Another thing she'd have to deal with soon. And while none of her issues had changed, she did somehow feel more confident about handling them. And maybe, Kylie thought, that was as much help as she was going to get.

The morning passed in a mind-numbing haze. Either due to her lack of sleep or the residuals from her growth spurt, Kylie wasn't sure. She dropped her lunch tray down beside Della and gave the dining hall a quick search for Derek.

His before-lunch group often got caught up in hiking and missed the meal. As her gaze swept the other side of the dining hall she realized how much she wanted to see him.

And how much she didn't want to see him.

God, she was so wishy-washy. If she was having a hard time dealing with her back-and-forth emotions, she could only wonder how Derek felt. He probably thought she was a few French fries short of a Happy Meal. And he'd be right, wouldn't he?

Without a doubt, the calm and confidence she'd gotten from this morning's trip to the falls was beginning to wane. When another visual sweep around the room didn't find Derek, she dropped in a chair and focused on Della, who sat there sipping her blood with very little interest. Then Kylie noted the empty seat next to Della.

"Where's Miranda?" Kylie asked.

"Don't know," Della muttered, and turned her glass in her hand.

Kylie tried not to stare at the blood in the glass for fear she'd recall how good it tasted. Instead, she picked up her ham sandwich and took a big bite. "You okay?" Kylie shifted the lump of bread in her mouth so she could speak.

"Yeah. Just mulling things over," Della said.

"About going home in three weeks?"

"Actually, I wasn't worrying about that, but now that you reminded me, I can add that to my worry agenda. Thanks." Sarcasm laced Della's voice.

"Sorry." Kylie stared at the sandwich with disinterest. "So what are you worrying about?"

"Just stuff," Della snapped.

"Ooookay," Kylie said, letting Della know her mood wasn't appreciated. Hey, Kylie got the whole vampire bad attitude, but at times—

"Sorry," Della said. "It's just that talk of death angels this morning got me worrying about . . . things."

"You mean about the time when you turned and can't remember the details."

"Yeah." Della sounded relieved that Kylie remembered, and she looked at Kylie as if seeking help. "What if I did something really terrible?"

How terrible? Kylie almost asked. Was Della actually worried that she might have hurt someone? Then she remembered who she was talking about. "First, I don't think you would do something really terrible. I mean, even the fact that you are worried you did something terrible means you're not a terrible person."

Della didn't look convinced. "But when you turn, it's so crazy."

"But you're not crazy," Kylie said. "And you're a good person."

Della nodded and looked as if she wanted to say something else, but then she looked away. Kylie had a sneaking suspicion that there was more to Della's concerns than met the eye. Did she remember more than she was saying? Whatever it was, Kylie wished she knew how to help.

"I wonder what's up with Miranda?" Della said in an obvious attempt to change the subject. "God, I hope she hasn't gone back into mourning over little boy wonder."

"She seemed okay earlier." Kylie looked to the table where most of the witches ate lunch to see if Miranda was there. She wasn't.

While the camp was supposed to encourage intermingling between the species, and it did, there seemed to be something about mealtime that encouraged the "birds of a feather flock together" mentality, the exception being a few interspecies couples and a few cabin friends. Helen and Jonathon took turns sitting with the vampires and the fairies. Until recently, it hadn't been unusual for Perry to join Miranda at their table. And a couple times a week, Derek would sit with Kylie during meals.

At least once a week, and never on the same days, even Della and Miranda would opt out of sitting with her and sit with their kind. Kylie told them they didn't have to sit with her. She understood if they wanted to sit with their same-feathered friends. They didn't listen.

Whether it was out of loyalty or because they felt bad for her, Kylie didn't know. But deep down, she appreciated it to no end. Who wanted to eat lunch alone? That would remind her too much of her old high school when Sara was sick or skipping school.

Thinking of Sara, Kylie pulled out her phone and checked to see if she had any messages from her best friend. It had been almost a week since Kylie had sent her several texts asking how things were going and telling her she would be home in three weeks for the weekend. It kind of hurt that Sara hadn't even gotten back in touch. Did that mean Sara didn't want to see her?

Sure, Kylie would be the first to admit that they no longer seemed to have a lot in common—Kylie not being human being at the top of the list—but what they had was a ten-year friendship, years of being each other's best friend. Didn't that merit her taking a few hours out of her weekend to at least pretend she still cared?

Kylie's phone rang. Thinking it would be eerie cool, almost psychic, if it was Sara, Kylie waited for the number to come across the screen. Not Sara. She cut off her phone and set it on the table.

"Don't tell me, either Trey or your stepdad," Della said.

"Two points for being right." Kylie grabbed her sandwich again.

"Which one?" Della asked.

"Dad. Stepdad." Even after meeting and learning to love Daniel, she sometimes forgot that Tom Galen wasn't her real father. Kylie sank her teeth into the soft bread, but didn't taste anything.

"Is he still banging his intern?"

Kylie swallowed. "Don't know. Don't care."

"Liar," Della said.

"Okay, how about . . . don't know, wish like hell I didn't care?"

"Now you're telling the truth." She studied Kylie and passed her glass of blood under Kylie's nose. "Do you want a sip?"

Kylie frowned and pushed the glass away. "No."

"You're lying again." Della arched a brow.

"Fine!" Kylie snapped, and even to her own ears, she sounded like Della had earlier. "I want it, but I don't want it. And don't go thinking it's because I think something's wrong with being vampire. I think it's fine. It's just that I . . . I'm a bit overwhelmed with trying to figure out what I am."

"Believe it or not, I understand." Della continued to study her. "You know, your heart is still beating faster than normal."

"I know." Kylie pulled her hair over her shoulder. "And look.

My hair grew, too." She sighed when she remembered how she'd only found one bra that allowed her to squeeze her size-bigger boobs into it.

"Damn." Della reached out and touched her hair. "Have you talked to Holiday about all this yet?" She glanced at Kylie's chest again. "I don't want to scare you or anything, but it's kind of weird."

Oh, great. Just when she'd almost convinced herself it was no big deal, Della was telling her differently. Kylie let out a deep breath. "No, I haven't told her yet. I have a meeting with her at two o'clock."

"You don't sound very happy about it," Della said.

"I'm not."

Della looked shocked. "What happened? You usually sing her praises. You pissed at her for something?"

"No. But she's gonna be pissed at me."

"For what? Going to the falls?"

"No. I don't think she'll be upset about me going to falls." At least Kylie didn't think she would. "It's what I did while I was there that's going to tick her off."

"What did you do?" Della looked confused as she sipped her blood.

"I kind of told Burnett about Holiday having had her heart broken by another vampire."

"Really? What happened?"

"He asked me about her and then—"

"Not that," Della said. "I mean with the other vampire?"

"I . . . don't know it all." Kylie realized she shouldn't have told Della, either.

"Okay, so what's wrong with telling Burnett that?" Della asked.

Kylie rolled her eyes. "It wasn't my place to tell him. Or you. So don't say anything."

"My mouth is sealed." Della reached over to Kylie's plate and stole a chip. "You know why you told him, don't you?" She studied the chip she held with the edge of her fingertips.

"Because I'm stupid," Kylie answered.

"No, because it's clear to you and everyone else that those two need to go bump uglies." She popped the chip into her mouth and made a face. "I used to love potato chips and now . . . ugg, they taste like toad ass."

Kylie completely ignored the potato chip/toad ass commentary while she tried to understand. "To do what? Bump what?"

"Bump uglies, bang each other, burn off some of those flaming hormones they put out when they're in the same room together."

"Uglies?" Kylie still couldn't wrap her head around it.

Della snickered. "I heard a comedian call it that. She was giving all the different names for doing the deed. Funny, isn't it?"

"Maybe," Kylie said, but couldn't be sure. Her sense of humor had taken a day off and so had her appetite. She stared at her sandwich, missing only a few bites. Was her loss of appetite a sign? Would she someday think potato chips tasted like toad ass?

"Speak of the horny little devils," Della said.

Kylie looked up. Holiday and Burnett walked into the dining hall. Holiday led the way, and Burnett studied her from behind. For a second, Kylie feared Burnett had told Holiday what Kylie had said. She envisioned an angry and hurt Holiday giving her a good talking-to, and Kylie's chest tightened. Oh, God, why had she said anything to Burnett? It had been wrong. So wrong.

Then Holiday met Kylie's gaze—no anger or hurt lingered in her green eyes, only a residual concern. Probably still worried about her and how she walked out of her office this morning. Holiday mouthed the words, "Two o'clock," and pointed to her watch.

Kylie nodded.

Holiday smiled and then walked up to the front of the dining hall and took a lunch plate. Burnett continued to follow her, his gaze taking in her every move, as if trying to memorize every inch of her body.

"Wait a minute," Kylie said. "If vampires can smell those hormones, how come Burnett doesn't seem to know Holiday feels that way about him? I mean, when I hinted that Holiday might be feeling something other than just annoyance, he seriously acted surprised."

"That's simple. We can't smell our own hormones and most of the time we can't smell the hormones of the people we're attracted to. I never smelled my boyfriend's." A sad smiled touched her lips as if some memory had tiptoed across her mind. "And I know Lee felt them."

Kylie sensed that Della still cared about Lee, but she also got the feeling that her friend wasn't about to admit it, nor did she want to talk about it. "That's weird how that works."

"Yeah. It's as if when we're attracted to someone, the emotion triggers the off button of our hormone sensor. Now, if you aren't attracted to someone and they've got the hots for you—oh yeah, we can smell that like a bad fart."

Kylie chewed on that information for a few seconds and then said, "But then how come Derek can tell when I'm thinking about . . ." Okay, Kylie wasn't sure she wanted to say that aloud, but curiosity provoked her to continue. "Are you saying he's not attracted to me?"

"No." Della grinned. "He's not vampire. He's not even smelling anything. He's reading emotion. That's a completely different thing."

"Oh." Kylie looked back down at her plate and forced herself to eat a chip but her mind continued to churn. Once she swallowed, she forced herself to ask the question, in a very low voice, of course.

"Do Derek and I . . . do we really spill hormones all over the place? I mean, is it so bad that it's embarrassing?"

Della's eyes widened, but she didn't answer. Which was so unlike Della. She never hesitated to tell you like it was.

"Oh, crap. Is it that bad?" Kylie asked.

Della cut her eyes upward. Kylie was just about to figure out what that eye shift meant when a warm breath whispered across her neck.

"Is what bad?" Derek asked.

Chapter Eleven

"Nothing is bad," Kylie answered Derek, and desperately tried not to emit any hormones or emotions that might have gone sailing in the air when her gaze locked on him. Problem was, she didn't have a clue how to stop them. Where the hell was her sensor button?

Off! Off! Off! She mentally jabbed at the off button in her mind.

Derek shifted and dropped down in the chair beside her. She didn't want to look at him, afraid that her doing so would increase the leakage of hormones, but not looking at a person was exceptionally rude. Or so said her mom.

"Everything okay?" Derek asked, probably aware she still hadn't looked at him.

"Don't be rude," she could almost hear her mom say. "It's fine." She looked at him. And because she'd been avoiding him for the last few days, she practically gobbled up his image. Her breath caught. Holy moly, did he look good.

Oh, yeah, she was so gonna blame this on her mom!

He was a tad sweaty, not yucky sweaty, but yummy sweaty. His skin glowed a bit, and he smelled a little like sunshine, as if he'd soaked up all the good scents from his hike. She figured his skin would taste a little like salty sunshine if she pressed her lips against it. His brown hair curled up on the tips and looked windblown. He wore a dark green T-shirt that hugged his torso. And the jeans he wore were his favorite. Or at least, it was the pair he wore more than others. She recognized them both because the knees were faded and they fit him snugger than most. And snug looked really, *really* good on him.

Della's snicker drew Kylie's attention away from Derek. The vampire grinned and waved a hand in front of her nose. Realizing what she meant, Kylie felt her face turn red.

When she stole another glace at Derek, his gaze had shifted and was now glued to her boobs. Which probably meant that he was at this second polluting the air with all kinds of pheromones as he tried to figure out how the girls had grown overnight.

"I . . . I gotta go find Miranda." Kylie popped up from her chair and shot out of the dining room like someone wearing white and in desperate need of a tampon.

"Miranda, you here?" Kylie called out as she entered the cabin five minutes later.

Her friend came scurrying out of Kylie's bedroom. She had panic plastered on her face and tears filled her eyes. Tears in Miranda's lovesick eyes had pretty much been the norm these last few days, but something appeared different. Kylie sensed it right away. And yeah, it had a little something to do with the fact that she'd stormed out of *Kylie's* bedroom immersed in a cloud of guilt.

"I'm so sorry," Miranda said, and hiccupped. "Really, really sorry."

"Really, really sorry about what?" Had Miranda found Lucas's letters and read them? Purposely invaded her privacy?

"I didn't mean to do it."

"Didn't mean to do what?" Kylie insisted, feeling her patience seep out like a balloon with a pinhole. Those letters were private. Heck, she hadn't even read the second one. When she'd returned from the falls, she'd stuffed it in her drawer with the other one. Told herself she'd read it tonight, or maybe tomorrow, or maybe even never. She wasn't sure her heart could handle dealing with whatever Lucas might say on top of everything else she had on her plate.

"I've done it dozens of times before, and I never had a problem undoing it until now. Please, please don't be mad at me."

Kylie suddenly got the feeling this wasn't about Lucas's letter. "What did you do?"

Miranda's gaze shot back to Kylie's bedroom, but when Kylie took a step, Miranda moved in front of her. "I'll fix it. I swear I will. I'll figure it out. I won't sleep or eat until I fix this."

"Fix what?"

"Please don't be mad."

Kylie physically moved Miranda. Then she walked into her bedroom to find out what Miranda didn't want her to see and swore she would fix.

Kylie's gaze shot first to the bedside table where she stored her most private things. The drawer was closed. No letters were strewn on the nightstand. A movement on her bed caught her eye. She shifted her gaze.

She blinked.

She screamed.

Then she hauled ass out of her bedroom in less than a flicker of a second.

She ran right into Miranda, who caught her by her forearms. "I'm sorry. So sorry."

Kylie caught her breath. "Why . . . ?" She inhaled. "Why is there a skunk in my bed?"

Kylie felt a familiar brush against her ankle. She looked down expecting to see Socks. But nope. No Socks.

Kylie screamed again and jumped clear across the room.

The skunk raised its pointed little head in the air, meowed, and came scurrying after her.

"I'm so sorry," Miranda cried.

Kylie looked up at Miranda and then down at the skunk quickly approaching her. Its paws pranced up in the air in a very familiar and very cute feline kind of way.

Socks?

"No," Kylie said. "Tell me that's not . . . Oh crap, you didn't!"

"I'll fix it. I will," Miranda said.

Kylie had just returned from art hour with Helen and Jonathon. Pacing, she stood in front of the office, waiting for her two o'clock appointment with Holiday. How was Kylie going to tell the camp leader that she'd ratted out her past romance with a vampire?

By the way, did you know that Burnett didn't know you used to date a vampire? Nope, that wouldn't do.

Hey, Burnett and I were talking and I happened to mention how you had your heart chewed up by one of his kind. That didn't sound like it would go over too well, either.

"Kylie?" Derek called out to her.

Oh, crappers!

She saw him walk though a crowd of campers waiting to sign up for kayak classes and she resigned herself to facing him. However, she did take several steps away from the crowd.

"Hey." He stopped in front of her and studied her carefully.

"Hey." She moved in backward steps, continued to motion him to follow her another ten feet away from the crowd.

His gaze stayed glued to her eyes as she continued to move in reverse. "Have I done something wrong?"

"No." She shook her head.

"Then have you been smoking something? Because you're acting really weird."

She completely understood why he thought she'd lost track of reality. However, in her defense, her reality for the last six weeks was completely different from the one she'd grown up believing in.

"It's not . . . it's . . ." She glanced around to make sure no one with super-hearing powers was in close range. "I'm embarrassed, okay?"

"Embarrassed about what?" His gaze lowered to her breasts. "That?"

She reached out, put her finger under his chin, and brought his face up. At least he had the decency to blush.

"Sorry. It's just they . . . you're . . ."

"Bigger. I know."

He reached out and caught a handful of her hair. "And your hair is longer."

"I'm taller, too," she said.

He took a visual measure of her and his eyes widened. "What happened?"

"I wish I knew." She attempted to keep the frustration from her voice. It wasn't his fault. "I woke up growing out of everything."

He grinned and his gaze lowered for a nanosecond before glancing up. "It looks nice."

"And why am I not surprised you feel that way?" She frowned.

His smile faded and he just stood there staring at her face. She wondered if it really took that much effort not to gawk at her breasts or if he had something else on his mind.

"Look, if I haven't done anything, then why have you been running away from me for the last two days?"

She shuffled her feet, painfully aware that her shoes were pinching her toes at this moment. "I told you. I'm embarrassed."

"Embarrassed . . . about getting bigger?"

"No. Well, yeah, that's embarrassing, too. But that's not why . . . why . . ."

"Why you've been avoiding me. Just say it. Because that's what you've been doing." He now sounded half mad, or at least half annoyed. But what she really heard in the tenor of his voice was insecurity. And honestly, she couldn't blame him. She'd feel all those things if he'd been dodging her the way she'd been doing him.

She bit down on her lip. "I'm sorry. It's not what you think."

"So what is it? Because I'm lost here. I mean, your emotions mostly seem okay when I'm around you, they actually seem really great at times, but then you run off."

"And . . . that's sort of why I'm running off," she said.

His brow creased. "And . . . I still don't understand."

Okay, she was going to spell it out for him. Her face flushed just thinking about it. "When I'm around you all I can think about is kissing and making out." *And going further than I've ever gone with anyone.*

His brow creased deeper, but at least some of the chip he seemed to carry appeared to fall off his shoulders with his new posture. "Okay." He tucked a hand into his jeans pocket. "Now can you explain to me why that's a bad thing?"

"It's not so much a bad thing, but it's . . . a private thing. I don't even want you to know what's going on inside my head. Much less all the vampires and other fairies wandering around the camp."

His shoulders tightened as if the chip had returned. "So you're embarrassed because other people know you like me."

"No. I mean . . . liking you is one thing. Wanting to . . . make out is another."

"You want to make out with me?" He almost grinned, and then ran a hand through his hair. "You know, I didn't think it was possible to feel complimented and insulted at the same time. But you've managed to make me feel both."

"I didn't insult you," she said.

"You did if you mean that you're embarrassed for people to know that you like me."

"I told you it's not about liking you."

"Okay, you just don't want people to know you're attracted to me."

She opened her mouth to speak, but wasn't sure what to say. "Yeah. Sort of. I mean, it's just private."

"Private?" He hesitated as if trying to figure out what she meant. "It's never all that private."

"It is for humans," she said. "And I may not be a hundred percent human, but . . . I mean, let's face it. I've had sixteen years of living as a human, and less than two months of trying to cope with being . . . Oh wait, I don't even know what I am yet." She shook her head, feeling her frustration level rise. "But yeah, I kind of like how humans do this."

"How they do what?" he asked, as if he wasn't following her.

Not that she could totally blame him, because she wasn't so certain she was following herself. "I like how humans keep their personal thoughts and feelings to themselves."

He stood there chewing on what she said. She could tell that her argument wasn't making sense to him.

"No," he said. "You're wrong."

"Wrong about what?" Now she was confused.

"It's not private for humans, either. They don't keep everything to themselves."

"Only if they chose to tell someone," Kylie said.

"Bullshit!" he said. "Look at Helen and Jonathon over there. Are you going to tell me that you, the human part of you, can't see that these two people are attracted to each other? And what about Burnett? You knew he was lovesick for Holiday before I did. You can see it."

Okay, he had a point. But she didn't like him jabbing her with it. "See it, yes. But I can't feel their emotions or smell the pheromones they put out because they want to . . ." *bump uglies* ". . . get it on. And knowing other people can . . . do that with me, well, it freaks me out a little, okay?"

He shook his head. "Are you sure it's other people knowing it that's freaking you out? Or is it you knowing what you feel for me that's freaking you out?"

She stared at him. "I don't know what you mean."

"I mean, that I'm not so sure you want this." He waved a hand between them.

"Want what?" Just like that, she got flashbacks. Flashbacks of having a similar argument with Trey. Oh, please. Not again.

"You and I. Us. You don't want us to become an 'us.' Every time I feel as if we get a little closer, you end up pushing me away. I've asked you to go out with me at least six times and you never answer me. What's up with this?"

Yup, she'd had almost this very conversation with Trey. "It's always about sex, isn't it?"

"What?" His mouth dropped open. "No. I wasn't talking about that."

"So you don't want sex?" she asked, getting angrier by the second.

He stood there staring at her as if she'd grown two heads and a tail. And God help her, considering everything that had happened to her lately, she almost wanted to check the mirror to make sure she hadn't sprouted a second head. Ditto for the tail.

"Where the hell is this coming from?" he asked.

Suddenly, she became aware that the crowd had gotten closer to them and several of the people in that crowd had the hearing of a gossip-hungry bat. She glanced at her watch and saw it was after two. "Sorry, I'm late."

Kylie stormed into Holiday's office. She dropped down in the seat across from the desk and looked her friend and camp leader right in the eyes. "I hate boys. I'm seriously considering going lesbian."

Holiday's expression was part grin, part groan. "If it was that easy, ninety percent of the women in the world would be gay." She made a funny little face and then asked, "So . . . boy problems?" She reached for a can of soda and took a sip.

"More like boys, skunk, and ghosts."

Holiday choked on the diet drink. "Skunk?"

Kylie sank into the chair, feeling defeated and frazzled from her argument with Derek.

"Miranda turned Socks into a skunk. And she can't figure out how to turn him back." No sooner had the words left her lips than Kylie realized it sounded as if she was tattling. "Not that I want you to say anything."

Holiday tried not to smile, but the edges of her mouth twisted up. "She was probably practicing for the show that her mom entered her into when she's back home."

"She explained why she did it. And I don't want her to get in any trouble . . . but what if she can't figure out how to change him back? I'm going to be stuck with a skunk for a pet."

Another smile threatened to appear on Holiday's lips. "I'm sure she'll figure it out."

Kylie shook her head and then dropped her hands into her lap. "You have no idea how much I wish my life could just go back to normal. Like human normal? Nobody trying to read my thoughts, change my feelings, or making it my job to save someone's life."

Holiday leaned back in her chair and stretched her arms up as if she'd sat too long in the same position. Hands still up in the air, she gave the papers scattered on her desk a frown. "Don't know about human, but normal does sound good sometimes, doesn't it?"

Something about Holiday's mood had Kylie's own concerns shifting. "Is everything okay?"

"Me? Oh, I'm fine." She dropped her hands and sat up a little straighter as if to put up a front. "It's you I'm worried about, Kylie. You seemed very upset this morning."

Kylie recalled how she'd stormed out of here. "I'm sorry. It sometimes . . . it just feels as if it's too much."

"I know it feels like that. But it will work out," Holiday said.

Kylie frowned. "You sound like my mom. She always says, 'God won't give you more than you can handle.'"

Holiday chuckled. "And we just wish He didn't trust us so much, right?"

"Yeah." Kylie saw the concern flare up in Holiday's eyes again. "What about your problems?" She motioned to the desk, sensing Holiday was upset.

"It'll be fine . . . just have a lot of financial crap to figure out with us going full-time here at the camp. There are teachers to be hired. Heating units to put into the cabins. And I don't have a clue how we're going to manage it."

"I thought the government, I mean the FRU, funded the camp."

"They do to some degree, but when they agreed to let me open the boarding school, they put us on a tight budget. These days even government programs are cutting back." She looked at the desk again. "It's probably not as bad as I think it is. It's just . . . Sky used to do all the financial work, and now I'm stuck with it."

"Burnett's not good with doing that kind of stuff?" Kylie asked, hoping to ease into a conversation about him.

"I don't know. But since he shouldn't be helping out here for more than another month, I don't see any reason for him to get involved with this side of the business."

Take the sugarcoating off what Holiday said and it basically meant she didn't trust Burnett. Was that because he was vampire, or could it be because she'd trusted Sky, her last co-camp leader, and Sky had let her down? Holiday never talked about Sky much, but Kylie sensed her friend's betrayal had hurt her more than she wanted to admit.

"Have they hired a new camp leader?" Kylie asked.

Now Holiday's expression turned into a full groan. "No. But they've promised by the end of summer I should have someone. And that can't come soon enough."

"Is he really that unpleasant to work with?" Kylie sensed Holiday's frustration came from Burnett, which only made Kylie worry about how Holiday would take Kylie's confession.

"We're just too different." Holiday's gaze lowered to Kylie's chest and stayed there for a fraction of a second too long. Which meant Holiday had noticed the growth spurt.

Kylie's thoughts shot away from her confession and turned on her own issues. "Can you explain this?"

"Explain what?" Holiday asked innocently enough, but it didn't convince Kylie.

Kylie held out her hands in front of her boobs.

Holiday's brows wrinkled. "I was hoping you'd just gotten a new Wonderbra."

"Afraid not. There's my hair, too." Kylie pulled it over her shoulder. "Plus, my shoes are almost too tight and I'm pretty sure I'm a whole inch taller."

"Mmm." Holiday almost appeared as if she worked at keeping her expression unreadable.

"Mmm, what?" Kylie leaned forward, pressing her hands on the desk.

"Mmm, it's odd." Holiday said, but something about the way the camp leader glanced back to her papers hinted that she wasn't being one hundred percent up front with Kylie.

"Please don't do this now," Kylie insisted.

Holiday looked up. "Do what?"

"Hide something. It's happening to me. I have the right to know what the hell is going on."

"I'm not hiding . . ." Holiday stopped talking and sighed. "I don't consider it hiding anything when I'm surmising, guessing. I'm not sure if it's fair to give you information when I'm not sure."

"What's not fair is to leave me completely in the dark. Because believe me, whatever you have to tell me isn't going to be half as bad as what I'm imagining."

Holiday nodded. "Okay, but just remember . . . it's speculation. Even Burnett said he didn't see it being a sure sign."

Kylie had suspected that Burnett had noted her boob increase. To his credit he'd dealt with it well, but to think he and the others were discussing it, well, it felt like overkill. Really dead stinky overkill. "You two discussed my boobs?"

"No. Well, yes, but not . . . Look, he said he noticed some changes in you when he ran into you at the falls. I insisted he tell me what they were."

The mere mention of Kylie seeing Burnett at the falls had Kylie remembering she needed to come clean, but first she had to know. "What's the speculation?"

"Some female werewolves—"

"Werewolf? Oh, damn! Not werewolf. Anything but werewolf."

Chapter Twelve

"Hey!" Holiday's hand came to rest on Kylie's arm. "You see, this is why I didn't want to tell you. I knew you'd jump to conclusions."

Kylie blinked. "What is it that some female werewolves do? Grow super boobs?"

"No. Well, sort of." Holiday bit back a smile. "When they reach a certain level in maturity, when they are close to mating age, they'll fill out rather quickly."

Kylie's heart pounded and all she could remember was what Miranda had said about seeing a werewolf change into wolf form, about how painful it appeared. "But that sounds just like what is happening to me. So how is this speculation or jumping to conclusions?"

Holiday shook her head. "Unless a werewolf had been turned, most start shifting into wolves when they are four or five. It would be very rare that it would happen to you at this age. And then there's the fact that werewolves undergo some rather strong mood swings a few days before and after a full moon. Dr. Day reported that she saw you during a full moon and saw none of these signs. And I watched you on the last full moon just to see if perhaps she missed something. I didn't note *any* changes in your behavior."

"Maybe I'm just a late bloomer," Kylie said, not that she was hoping it was true. "And I've never been one to let my emotions out too much. So maybe you just didn't see me being moody."

"There's also . . . your cat," Holiday continued. "All felines have an aversion toward weres. Not so with you."

Kylie recalled how, years ago, her cat had reacted to Lucas. She remembered how the kitten had reacted to Lucas the day he'd dropped it off. But then suddenly Kylie remembered something that might be important. "Oh crap. The wolf."

"What . . . wolf?"

"The other night . . . when I ran off after I tasted blood. I ran into a wolf. He hung around me. Even showed up again later that night, but—"

"It wasn't a full moon," Holiday said. "It couldn't have been a werewolf."

"I know that's why I didn't think . . . I mean, I just thought that it was someone's half-tame wolf. He knelt down in front of me and tried to crawl forward, like he wanted me to touch him or something." She had to remind herself to breathe. "Do you think that could mean something? Is it some kind of ritual that wolves hang out with werewolves before they turn for the first time?"

Holiday stared back at Kylie as if trying to think. "I've never heard of it. But I'm . . . Sky was always the one who took care of counseling the weres. So I don't have all the knowledge of it. But I'll ask around. Burnett will know."

"He's not a werewolf." Kylie wished Lucas were here. Here to advise her, to help her make sense of all this. But no, he'd run off with another she-wolf. And Kylie still hadn't read his letter because she was so pissed that he'd done it.

"Burnett's not were, but his job with FRU requires extensive research on all supernaturals. Believe it or not, he's as smart as he is arrogant. And I hope you don't think . . . I mean, when he spoke to me about your increase in size, there was nothing in his tone but concern about how you were dealing with these changes."

Even distraught about the idea of being werewolf, Kylie realized that Holiday was defending Burnett. Like it or not, Holiday had found some respect for the vampire. Not that this excused Kylie from the fact that she shared Holiday's private information. But couldn't Holiday see that she and Burnett should give the romance a shot? Just how mad was she going to be about Kylie telling him about her past relationship with another vampire?

"About the falls . . ."

"I understand," Holiday said.

"Understand what?" Kylie asked, hoping it could be that easy. That Burnett had told Holiday about his and Kylie's conversation and she wasn't upset.

"I understand why you went there," Holiday started, straightening some papers. "I go at least once a week myself. It's the best place to go to . . . think, to try to figure out things. Did you get any answers about the ghost this morning?"

Kylie shook her head. "Just a sense of rightness."

"Then you have to have faith that you're doing all you can," Holiday said.

Kylie suddenly remembered. "You told me you hadn't ever seen a death angel."

"I haven't," Holiday said.

"But you said you weren't even sure they were real."

"I don't think the version of the legends that everyone believes is real," Holiday said.

"Then what makes the falls so . . . special?"

Holiday hesitated as if trying to find the right words. "I think it's a holy place. I think the Big Cheese running everything up there in the heavens created it for those of us who have to deal with spirits. It's a place we can find some peace. And sometimes even answers."

"Like a church?" Kylie asked, recalling the reverence she'd felt there.

"Yeah, sort of like a church. There's a lot of spiritual power there. You felt it, right?" Holiday placed her hand over Kylie's.

Kylie pulled her hand back. "Yeah. But . . . why didn't you tell me? I asked you about the falls and you didn't say anything. I mean, I could have . . . I could have been going there all along. Maybe I would have figured out more what the ghost is trying to tell me by now."

Holiday dropped her hands on the desk, and empathy filled her green eyes. "You don't tell someone about the falls, Kylie. The falls has to call you to it. And I'm assuming it called you or you wouldn't have gone there."

Kylie couldn't deny she had felt the calling to go. Yet she still resented the fact that she had to figure everything out herself. What was wrong with a little direction, a little helping hand?

"I'm somewhat shocked that Burnett went there," Holiday said. "The only supernaturals who get called to the falls are those with ghost-whispering powers. The other supernaturals find it too emotionally stimulating . . . or I guess I could call it intimidating."

Kylie recalled how Della and Miranda had reacted. Yeah, intimidating was about right.

"Even Sky wouldn't go there." Holiday looked up at Kylie. "Did Burnett actually go behind the falls?"

"He was there when I went in." She hesitated. "He went there because of you," Kylie said, using this as her opening. If she didn't take it now, she might back out. Then her breach of confidence would be even worse.

"Me?"

"He wanted to understand you better. And I think he thought if he . . . could understand the whole ghost thing, then—"

"He said that?" Surprise widened Holiday's eyes.

"Yeah." Kylie hesitated and then just blurted it out. "I told him that you had your heart broken by another vampire. That it was why you . . . don't want to get involved with him."

Holiday's brow furrowed instantly and her eyes grew tight. It wasn't a look Kylie noted on Holiday's face very often. "You told him what?"

"I know I shouldn't have done it. But . . . he asked and at first I didn't tell him, but—"

"Why would he . . . No, why would you tell him anything?"

"He really likes you, Holiday."

"How he feels doesn't matter. I didn't share that with you to tell anyone else." She stopped talking, but the frustration flared in her eyes.

"I'm sorry. I am. And I know it was wrong, but I think . . . I mean, it's almost as if you're letting what your fiancé did to you stop you from seeing the possibilities with Burnett. You're punishing him for something that he didn't do."

Holiday's expression didn't soften. She swallowed a deep breath. "Kylie, what happens between Burnett and me isn't . . ." She closed her mouth and the muscles in her jaw clenched. "Why don't we stop this talk right now and we'll take this up later. I need some time."

Kylie felt a huge hole open up in her chest. "Please don't . . . don't be mad at me."

Holiday held up her hand. "I'm not exactly mad. I'm . . . disappointed."

"That's even worse," Kylie said, and her chest grew tighter. "Really, I'm sorry."

Holiday stood up and motioned for the door. "I'll see you to-morrow."

Tears prickled Kylie's eyes, and more than anything she wanted to argue, to beg Holiday to forgive her. To plead with her not to let her slip-up change the relationship they'd found. But something deep inside told Kylie it could be too late.

At almost nine that night Kylie lay in her bed staring at the ceiling with a dad-blasted skunk sharing her pillow. She'd opted out of going down to the dining hall and participating in pizza and basketball night. Burnett had put up a basketball court and all the guys had formed teams. With as little sleep as she'd gotten these last few days, you'd think she'd have been out like a blown bulb. Not.

She cut her eyes to the drawer where she'd placed Lucas's letter and for a flicker of a second her mind switched from her Holiday problems to her Lucas problems, and then it went to her Derek problems. Next her mind came against the idea of being werewolf. Oh, joy!

When her mind slapped against the whole issue of someone she loved being in danger, Kylie instantly recalled the feeling she'd gotten from the falls, that if she stayed on course, at least that problem would be okay.

Too bad all her other issues didn't seem so manageable.

The ring of her phone brought a moan to her lips—not that she couldn't use a mental break from juggling her problems. And maybe if she was lucky, it was Sara, finally calling her back. Sure they weren't as close as they once had been, but she still cared about Sara, and she'd been thinking about her a lot lately. But was she up to talking with her former best friend?

"Don't want to startle you," she told Socks, who may or may

not have the whole spraying thing down. "I need to reach for my phone." The animal opened one beady eye and looked at her and then let out a poor excuse for a meow.

Miranda had spent all day attempting to change Socks back to his ol' self. Kylie had finally told her to give it a rest. She even told her not to be so hard on herself, that this was just a hiccup. A huge, freaking hiccup, but Kylie didn't tell her that.

The phone stopped ringing and Kylie wasn't even compelled to check to see who'd called. She glanced at Socks again. "A really huge freaking hiccup," Kylie muttered. But considering she hoped that Holiday would forgive her, she decided it might be best to practice what she preached, or at least practice what she prayed for . . . forgiveness. And she had prayed. Remembering how Holiday had looked so betrayed brought a wave of pain to Kylie's heart.

How could telling Burnett about Holiday have felt almost right at the time? And now feel so wrong? And yes, telling Burnett the truth had felt right. She'd been compelled to do it, as if her gut had given her the push. So much for listening to her gut!

Her phone rang again. Pulling her cell over, not certain she wanted to talk to anyone, Kylie studied the number . . . and a sudden knot swelled in her chest.

Chapter Thirteen

Mom. The realization hit and hit hard, too. She never thought she'd feel this, but she missed her mom. Wished she were here to . . . to just be here. And it wasn't just because they'd sort of found new ground with their relationship. Kylie even appreciated the old ground they'd had.

As much as Kylie had sworn her mom had never loved her, the longer Kylie was away from her the more she began to see things differently. Sure her mom had been emotionally distant, and sure Kylie wasn't really *anything* like her. But for some reason now, Kylie saw all the other ways her mom had shown love. The pancakes every Saturday morning. The loaning her the credit card anytime Kylie mentioned she needing anything. Even the stinkin' sex pamphlets showed her mom cared—not that Kylie wouldn't be happy if the pamphlets stopped, but still . . .

Hitting the talk button, she fought back a wave of nostalgia. "Hi, Mom." Kylie swore she wasn't going to cry, and with effort she managed to keep her voice from shaking.

"Sweetheart?" The immediate concern in her mom's voice had the knot in Kylie's throat growing, and emotion stung her sinuses. "Are you okay?"

How could her mom know something was wrong when all Kylie had said was two words? Was her mom psychic? *No, she was only human.* It had to be maternal instinct. And her mom had never lacked that.

"I'm okay." Kylie bit the inside her cheek to keep from weeping.

"What happened, baby?"

Tears formed in Kylie's eyes. "It's nothing." She watched Socks reposition himself on the pillow and she prayed he wasn't about to spray her. Getting skunked by her skunk-cat would be the absolute last straw. "Just a hard day, is all."

"What kind of hard day? Do you want to come home? All you have to say is the word and I'll drive up there tonight and pick you up."

"No, Mom. I love it here." Kylie recalled her mom hadn't given her an absolute yes on signing her up for boarding school. Which meant Kylie shouldn't be talking about anything negative concerning Shadow Falls right now. She really had to get her mom to agree—especially if . . . if Kylie ended up being werewolf. How in the hell did one explain that to a human parent? "I just . . . I made a mistake today and someone I really care about is upset with me."

"We all make mistakes," Mom said. "You just need to apologize."

"I did."

"And they didn't forgive you? Are they still mad at you?" her mom asked.

"Not so much mad. Just disappointed in me." Kylie's chest swelled with regret as she recalled Holiday saying those words to her. Kylie knew what it felt like to be disappointed and hurt by someone you trusted. It was worse than being mad. Like her dad. Okay, with him she was both mad and hurt, but the "hurt" feelings had her heart breaking. While being mad and angry almost felt good, no good feelings came from feeling hurt. None.

"Do you want to tell me what happened?" her mom asked, sounding as if she didn't want to pry, but felt it was her maternal obligation to do so. Amazingly, Kylie wanted to answer. She couldn't and wouldn't tell her mother everything, but she could tell her some.

"Someone told me something in confidence. And I . . . told someone else. At the time, I really thought telling it might help . . . fix a problem. But . . ."

"But it didn't help?" her mom asked.

"No," Kylie said. "I mean, not that I can see yet."

"Kylie, it sounds as if you were trying to do the right thing. I wouldn't be so hard on yourself. This is just a little hiccup, girl." Kylie almost laughed at her mother's chosen words. Wasn't that exactly what she'd told Miranda? Maybe Kylie was more like her mom than she knew. Tightness gripped her chest.

"I love you, Mom," Kylie said without thinking.

"Oh, baby," her mom said, now sounding as if she was going to cry. "I love you, too. Is there anything I can do to help? I'll come there and kick ass if I have to."

A tear rolled down Kylie's check. "You'd kick ass for me?"

"In a New York minute."

Kylie chuckled and sniffled at the same time.

"Are you ready for a change of subject? Something fun?" her mom asked, sounding excited. "It's the reason I called."

"Yes." Kylie wiped her eyes. She really could use some good news.

"You'll never guess what I signed us up for that Friday night when you're back."

"What?" Kylie asked, and realized she didn't really dread going home anymore. It would be good to spend some time with Mom, to hopefully get away from the problems pressing down on her at the camp.

"You were the one who got me thinking about it."

"Thinking about what, Mom?" Kylie asked, sensing her mom's excitement.

"A ghost hunt. Remember, you mentioned the falls being haunted at the camp?"

"A ghost hunt?" Kylie couldn't believe her ears.

"It's a dinner at a reputedly haunted B&B and then they take us on a tour. Isn't that totally cool?"

Kylie dropped back on her pillow and now she really wanted to cry. "Yeah. Totally . . ." *not* ". . . cool."

Thirty minutes after Kylie had hung up, she started counting sheep, inviting sleep to come take her away. While sheep number one hundred took a flying leap across her bed, Kylie's mind started replaying her argument with Holiday.

"*How he feels doesn't matter. I didn't share that with you to tell anyone else,*" Holiday had said.

"*I'm sorry. I am,*" Kylie had said. "*And I know it was wrong, but I think . . . I mean, it's almost as if you're letting what your fiancé did to you stop you from seeing the possibilities with Burnett. You're punishing him for something that he didn't do.*"

You're punishing him for something that he didn't do.

You're punishing him for something that he didn't do.

Then her mind completely skipped to the argument she'd had with Derek.

"*It's always about sex, isn't it?*" she had said.

"*No. I wasn't talking about that,*" he had countered.

Kylie recalled all the anger welling up inside at that moment. Bottled-up anger, leftover anger. Anger she'd felt toward . . . Trey.

You're punishing him for something that he didn't do.

"Oh, shit!" She sat up. Had she done the same thing she'd accused Holiday of doing? The more she thought about it, the more she realized that Derek had never, not even once, pressured her about sex. His statement about her pulling away had everything to do with her dodging him. Not about her getting naked.

Then a bit of her mom's dialogue came into play. *We all make mistakes. You just need to apologize.*

Mom was right. Which Kylie realized was another thing she never thought she'd ever catch herself thinking where her mom was concerned. But damn it, her mom was right. Kylie needed to apologize. Standing up, she shucked off her nightshirt and slipped back into her too-short jeans, her too-tight bra, too-tight tennis shoes, and a T-shirt, then went to find Derek.

The moment Kylie stepped outside, the humid hot air surrounded her. She started to head toward the dining hall and then stopped. Derek generally left the nighttime events early to call his mom. Not that he told everyone what he was doing. But he'd confided in her.

Warmth filled her chest. She liked that he'd confided in her. Oh, heck, she really, really liked Derek, and with all her heart, she hoped he'd accept her apology. Because she didn't want to go into what she had to say around super-hearing individuals, she headed toward his cabin. She set her pace at a slow run, which only a couple of weeks ago would have been amazingly fast for her. As she moved, she felt the trees hovering above. She felt the wind stir her hair. She caught a glimpse of the bright stars, but she didn't care too much about the scenery. Instead she concentrated on what she would tell Derek when she saw him.

Halfway there, the feeling hit. The feeling as if someone was watching her. She slowed her pace and listened. The night was still chirping, there was no dead or unnatural silence, but she still felt it. Glancing from right to left to the edges of the woods, she checked to see if the wolf was back. There were no golden eyes peering back at her from the brush. She tried to convince herself it was nothing, but she picked up her pace, eager to find Derek—eager to have Derek's solid, bigger frame beside her.

His arms around her.

Her head on his shoulder.

Maybe his mouth melting against hers.

Oh yeah, thinking about Derek chased away her fears.

She made that last turn down the trail and saw there were lights on in his cabin. Someone was there. "Please let it be him."

She made it another hundred feet when she noticed that his cabin's front door was open. That was a little odd. When she got up the porch steps, she noted the smell. The ripe berry scent. She hadn't yet defined the aroma when her tennis shoe hit a slick spot and she went down.

Plopping down on her butt, she pressed her palm against the porch to lift up. But the sensation of something wet and thick beneath her palm gave her pause.

That's when she recognized the sweet berry scent.

Blood.

Her gaze shot to the porch.

A lot of blood.

The rectangle of light pouring from the doorway caught her attention and Kylie saw it. Dark red droplets led the way into the cabin like breadcrumbs in the forest.

Her heart stopped.

Oh, God. "Derek!" she screamed his name, but no answer bounced back.

She lunged to her feet and ran into the cabin, screaming his name over and over.

Chapter Fourteen

"Derek?" Her heart pounded. She followed the trail of blood, through the living room, down the hall. It led to a closed door. She grabbed the knob. Locked.

She heard a noise on the other side. "Derek?" she yelled. Again no answer.

Not thinking, driven by raw panic, she took a couple of steps back and rammed the door with her shoulder. Part of the door ripped off with the hinges; the other part splintered into two or three pieces and crashed on the bathroom floor. She crashed on top of it. Face-down.

That's when she realized the noise she'd heard behind the closed door had been the shower. That's when she saw a very naked and very wet Derek yank back the shower curtain.

His body was hard, corded with muscle. Defensiveness glinted in his eyes and his posture. He looked prepared to take on an intruder.

Which would be her, by the way.

He stared at her sprawled on top of the splintered piece of his bathroom door. She stared at him . . . naked with the shower curtain still clutched in his fist.

"Uh, I . . . I saw blood and thought . . ." *What had she thought?* Rogue vampire, ax murderer, serial killer on the loose. She hadn't put a villain in her fears. Her concern had just been for Derek's safety.

"You knocked the door down." Disbelief rang in his matter-of-fact tone.

"I know," she answered, unable to say anything else. Unable to look away from his body.

"But it's solid oak."

"I know." She felt the solid oak beneath her and was a little shocked that she'd done it, too. If it mattered at all, her shoulder felt a little bruised. And it was the slight pain that brought some reality back into the moment.

"You don't have any clothes on." Oh, God, did she really say that?

"I know. I usually shower that way."

Her face began to burn.

When he didn't seem to worry about his lack of clothes, Kylie decided that maybe it was her place to worry. After all, she had been the one to storm into his bathroom and break down his door while he'd been showering.

She turned her back on him. A totally useless, unproductive move. It didn't stop her from seeing him. The mirror hung over the low counter, which she now faced, offered her the same view.

A really awesome view, too. She'd seen naked men in the movies. Well, almost naked. And she'd seen naked statues. Beautifully posed, carved-in-stone statues that left nothing to the imagination. In person was definitely better. Oh, goodness, he looked good wet and without his clothes on.

Then she realized that while she'd been enjoying the view, he'd been watching her enjoying it. His gaze from the mirror locked with hers. That rush of blood returned to her face. She glanced away from his reflection in the mirror to her shoes just as he grabbed for a towel.

That's when she decided to explain again. "I . . . I saw blood and I panicked."

"Yeah," he answered. "Chris gave me a bloody nose when he elbowed me in the face playing basketball."

She looked up to the mirror to check out his face. "How bad was it?"

"Just a bloody nose." Holding the towel around his waist, he reached for his jeans on the floor, and then he met her gaze back in the mirror. "I'm gonna put on some pants. So you might want to look down again."

She did, and she blushed again, too. Only when she heard the zipper did she look up. He stood closer, right over her in fact, holding out his hand to help her up. She took it.

"Are you okay?" he asked as soon as she came to her feet.

She rubbed her shoulder. "Just a little bruised."

"I would imagine."

She saw him look back at the door. "I'll tell Holiday I did it," she said.

"It's okay." He picked up a piece of the wood and tried to bend it. When it didn't move, he looked back at her. Then he reached out and touched her arm and his touch shifted slowly up to her elbow.

His touch felt warm and moist, much like the air in the bathroom. Tingles climbed up her arm and filled her chest. Her gaze went to his broad shoulders and she wanted to kiss him there, in the place where she had rested her head so often.

"You're still warm," he said. "Normally, a vampire doesn't gain strength until after they've turned."

Disappointment shattered the mood. His reason for touching her had been to check her body temperature, not because . . . because he just felt compelled to do it, the way she felt compelled to touch him.

"I think that's the problem," she said. "I'm not normal." She bit down on her lip and then decided to just tell him. "Holiday said . . . she said some female werewolves have"—she glanced down at her breasts—"growth spurts around this age."

"So she thinks you're werewolf?" he asked.

"No, not really. She said that . . . nothing else seems to point to werewolf. So we're back at square one."

"Sorry," he said. "I know you want to figure it out." He ran a hand up her elbow again, and this time she knew it wasn't to check for temperature. The tingles and mood came back.

Letting go of a deep sigh, she met his beautiful green eyes. "That's why I came here."

"What's why you came here?" he asked. He moved out of the bathroom and to the first door on the right. She followed him and stopped when she realized it was his bedroom. She watched him grab a shirt from his closet. He held it to his flat stomach but didn't put it on. She had the craziest feeling that he'd left it off because he knew she enjoyed looking at him. He stepped closer to her. "Why did you come here?"

Focus. Focus. Quit thinking about his body. "To tell you I'm sorry. For being such a bitch this afternoon. I was . . . confused. I mean, Trey . . . He did me wrong and when you said what you did, I just jumped back to what Trey did. What he did really hurt me, and I think I just projected it all on to you."

He pulled her against him and pressed his lips to hers. The kiss was hot, passionate, and she didn't want it to end. And when it did, he was the one who pulled away, not her. She was happy, however, to see his breath was as uneven as hers.

"The answer is yes." Derek's lips were moist and still so close to hers that she felt the words whisper across her cheek.

"I'm . . . I'm not sure what the question is," Kylie said, thinking she'd missed something because she was drunk off his kisses.

"The last thing you asked me this afternoon was if I wanted sex. I want to make myself clear. I want you. I want you so badly that sometimes it's all I can think about. Some nights I wake up and I'm so . . ." He bit back his words and let go of another deep breath. "What I'm trying to say is while I want you really badly, the last thing I'd try to do is pressure you into doing something that doesn't feel right."

"It does feel right." She placed her hand on his chest. And oh my, did it feel right to touch his bare chest. The temptation to ask him to do it, to pull her over to the bed and teach her all about sex, was almost overpowering. However, there was still something that held her back.

"Or at least mostly right." She pulled her hand from his bare skin. "I think I just need to figure out who I am first." She stared at his chest, afraid if she looked him in the eyes, she'd turned candy apple red again. Unfortunately, he raised his hand and tilted her head back and forced her to look at him.

"I know who you are, Kylie. You're warm, funny, and beautiful. You are so good to everyone, everyone likes you. And you've got tons of spunk. I really like spunk."

"I mean *what* I am," she corrected, feeling his fingers brushing against her neck.

"*What* you are doesn't matter. Because what you are isn't going to change *who* you are." He dropped his hand from her chin. "And

I'm not saying this to rush you to have sex. I just want you . . . I wish you could see yourself through my eyes. I wish you could see how special you are. And I don't care what you turn out to be."

Tears prickled her eyes and she wrapped her arm around his naked torso and pressed her cheek against his warm wall of chest that smelled clean, soapy, and moist. "You're the one who's special," she whispered.

"Nope," he answered, and chuckled. "If I was special I wouldn't be thinking about how I could change your mind about having sex right now. So let's get out of this room before I decide to tackle you on my bed."

She laughed and looked up into his eyes.

He smiled and ran his hand up under her shirt and to her bare back where he cupped his hand in the curve of her naked waist. "That whole breaking the door down was really a turn-on."

"And not the fact that you were naked?" Had she said that? Instantly, she wished the floor would swallow her up.

"Nope, it was definitely the door thing. Now if you'd been naked . . ." He let go of a deep gulp of air. "Okay, we'd better quit talking about this." He pulled away from her, caught her hand, and tugged her out of his bedroom.

She let him lead her out into the living room. He eyed the couch and then looked back at her. His eyes looked heavy, sleepy, and hot. "Almost as bad as the bed."

She grinned and he pulled her out onto the front porch. He slipped on his shirt, then dropped down and leaned against the cabin on the blood-free end of the porch. Once settled, he looked up and patted the spot on the porch beside him. She lowered herself beside him, and scooted over so her arm was against his. Leaning her head on his shoulder, she said, "Thanks."

He shifted and lifted his hand around her shoulder and pulled her a tad closer. "You're welcome."

Neither of them said anything for several minutes. She just sat there, close and absorbing the feel of him beside her. Questions tumbled around her head like a pair of tennis shoes in the dryer. But embarrassment kept her from voicing them.

"Go ahead and ask it," he said, almost as though he was reading her thoughts.

She raised her head off his shoulder. "Ask what?"

"Whatever it is that's making you feel embarrassed and curious. I can read your emotions, remember?"

She frowned. "And I hate that, too. I don't want you reading me."

"But I can't help it. I don't know how to not read you." He chuckled and looked down at her. And just like all the other times they were together, the night had a fairy-tale feel about it. The stars twinkled like diamonds in the sky. The trees looked too full. The moon, less than a week from being full, gave off enough light that she could see his face. "I think you're going to have a bruise." She touched the side of his nose.

He caught her hand in his and kissed the inside of her hand. "So, what is it that's making you embarrassed and curious?"

"I'm just . . ." If she didn't tell him now, he'd probably envision the worst. Then again, what she was curious about might be the worst.

"Just ask me." He nudged her with his shoulder.

She hesitated and then just blurted it out. "I'm curious about how many girls you've been with. I know you're almost eighteen and . . ." Her words faltered. Kylie knew he wasn't a virgin, and not just because he'd said something that led her to believe it, but just how . . . he kissed.

His brow crinkled and she could tell he wished he hadn't pushed her to ask.

"Oh," he said.

"Oh?" she repeated. And now more than ever she wanted an answer. "You made me ask, now you have to answer."

He hesitated. "A few."

"That's vague." She pulled her fingers from his.

He breathed in and then out. "Okay, four."

"That's more than a few."

"Sorry." He didn't deny that he'd been lying. "It just feels awkward talking about it with you."

"Yeah, it does," she said, realizing she didn't like knowing. Didn't like thinking about him being with someone else. "Sorry I asked."

"Don't be." He leaned back against the cabin wall and went back to listening to the night. "Can I ask you something?"

"Sure." A nervous flutter tickled her stomach. But considering how personal her own question had been, she couldn't tell him no.

"If Lucas were still here, would you still be sitting next to me?"

Chapter Fifteen

His question ran across all sorts of nerves and not the good ones, either. "What kind of question is that?"

"Obviously a hard one." He pulled his knee up to his chest and stared down at his toes.

Something told her he was reading her right now—trying to understand her emotions. But how could he when she didn't understand them herself? "He's not here," Kylie said.

He looked over at her. "Rumor has it that he's coming back."

She felt her breath catch in her throat. "Doesn't matter," she forced herself to say. "He's with Fredericka."

"He'd drop her for you like this." Derek snapped his fingers. "He's not blind or stupid."

She shook her head. "Well, maybe I don't want anyone who'd run off with someone else."

He arched an eyebrow. "It's the 'maybe' in your answer that worries me more than the confusion you're feeling right now." He leaned his forehead down to hers. "Please don't break my heart, Kylie."

Her own heart almost broke right then. "It's the last thing I want to do."

He kissed her softly, then pulled back. "I should get you back to your cabin before everyone gets back here."

She nodded and accepted his hand to help pull her up. They started to walk off the porch when he stopped. "Oh, I forgot. I got something to give you." He ran back inside and returned after a few short seconds holding a piece of paper.

"What's this?" she asked when he put it in her hands.

"It's a telephone number of a private investigator."

When he didn't continue, she asked, "And I need it for . . . ?"

"You said you were trying to find your real grandparents. This guy is good at finding people. If anyone can find them, he can."

Kylie looked up from the paper. "Do you really think he could find them after all this time? I mean, I've been trying to just find Daniel's adoptive parents, but I can't even find them."

"He's that good," Derek said.

Her heart started to sink. "And probably that expensive. I can't afford him." She started to give him back the paper.

He caught her hand. "He's not charging you, Kylie. Call him."

"Why wouldn't he charge me? You said he was a PI."

"Because he's a friend of mine. And I used to do some work for him on the side."

"You worked for a PI?"

"Yeah. I went to him to see if . . . if he could help me locate my dad."

That piece of news also surprised her. She didn't think Derek wanted anything to do with his dad. "Did he find him?"

"Yeah," Derek said. "You missed a great pizza tonight," he added, making it clear he didn't really want to talk about his dad.

But Kylie couldn't stop herself from asking. "And did you see him?"

"No. I just wanted to know where the bastard was."

Kylie sensed Derek's pain. "So how did you end up working for the PI?"

"He found my skill of reading emotions very helpful."

Still wanting to soothe away the look of hurt from Derek's eyes, she reached up and planted another kiss on his lips. A good one. She pulled him close, so close that her one-cup-size-larger breasts were pressed against his chest. Derek's hands came down to hold her around her waist. One of his palms slid up under her shirt and slowly shifted upward. He caressed her upper back, stopping right below her bra strap as if not wanting to cross a line. A line she almost wanted him to cross.

When she pulled away, her breathing came faster. "Thank you, for this." She held up the paper.

"Wow," he said, smiling, and touched her lips. "If he actually finds them, what do I get?"

She elbowed him in the ribs. He laughed and then wrapped his arm around her shoulders as they started back to her cabin.

At eight a.m. sharp the next morning, Kylie had one roommate out of the cabin—Della had left for her vampire rituals—and Kylie was working on getting rid of the other. She told Miranda to go on to breakfast without her. Kylie would catch up later. Miranda had stepped out the door but she'd stayed there for five minutes or so performing some kind of ritual. Kylie finally poked her head out the door to ask, "What are you doing?"

"I told you earlier, I'm just trying to protect our cabin."

Kylie remembered her roommate claiming that an unwelcome presence lurked nearby, although Kylie hadn't really felt anything. Other than when she'd been alone in the woods or paths.

"Protect it from what . . . exactly?"

Miranda tossed up some kind of herbs in the air. They crackled and popped on their downward descent, telling Kylie they weren't just regular herbs. "I don't know . . . exactly."

"Didn't you already do something to get rid of it?"

"Yup, but the bad boy is still here. Just won't go away."

Kylie didn't want to ask, but she figured she had to. "Could it be a ghost?" Because if it was, Kylie wasn't so sure Miranda should attempt to keep it away. Like it or not, dealing with ghosts was sort of Kylie's job. Not that so far Miranda's rituals had prevented the ghosts from visiting. However, if Miranda's herbs were in any way keeping Daniel away, well, Kylie couldn't have that. She really needed to talk to Daniel.

"No, it's not like one of your spirits," Miranda said.

"Then what is it like?" Kylie felt a tad apprehensive and remembering the unwelcomed vampire visitor from the other night. "I mean, wouldn't Della know if it was like something rogue?"

"Yeah, but this isn't . . . normal. It's involving magic. I can't put my finger on it yet, but I'm working on it," she said.

Working on it like she was working on changing Socks back to feline form? Kylie didn't say it, because that would have hurt Miranda, but Kylie couldn't help thinking it.

"Have you mentioned it to Holiday?" Kylie asked.

"Not yet. Let me try to deal with it first."

Kylie nodded, but she wasn't too sure.

"You ready to go yet?" Miranda asked after tossing up one more sprinkling of herbs.

"No." Kylie brushed a few of the tiny crackling herbs from her hair. "I . . . got a few phone calls to make."

"Okay, but don't be too late. After Campmate Hour, we've got cooking together, and today we're supposed to bake brownies, and you're supposed to decorate them. And they won't let us eat them until after you've done your thing. And I love, love brownies. And don't want to have to wait."

"I won't be that late." Kylie was actually enjoying the food art lessons she'd signed up for last week. Who knew she'd get off on decorating cupcakes and such? Drawing with pen and paper had never been her thing, but working with icing was kind of cool. Then again, she'd always kind of enjoyed watching those cake-decorating shows on cable.

Miranda started to walk away and then turned back. "Who are you calling?"

Holding the phone number of the private detective in her hand, she almost told Miranda the truth, but decided she wasn't ready to share. "I'll explain later."

"Trey?" Miranda asked.

"No way," Kylie answered.

"Sara?" Miranda asked.

"I'll explain later." Kylie frowned, remembering Sara still hadn't tried to call her back.

"A secret admirer," Miranda continued as if were a game. "A hot stud muffin who kisses like no tomorrow that you haven't told us about? Oh, I want to meet him."

Kylie groaned. "I don't have a stud muffin."

"Really? The way you blushed when you talked about Derek naked, I thought he was your stud muffin."

"Go to breakfast." Kylie waved her off.

"Oookay," Miranda said, and started off.

Kylie shut the door and looked at the scrap of paper she held in her hand. She finally felt as if she might be closer to finding answers. She hadn't had any luck finding Daniel's adoptive parents, or even knew if they were still alive, and she didn't have a clue how to go about looking for his real ones. But if Derek was right . . . if this guy was that good, then maybe he could find them. And because they were supernaturals, or at least one of them had to be, and considering they had a longer life expectancy, then there was a good chance they could be alive.

And if she found them, she would find her answers. She would finally know what she was. God, she really, really hoped this guy was as good as Derek believed.

Just thinking Derek's name, or maybe it was Miranda's whole stud muffin talk, either way, Kylie got flashbacks to last night. To the whole shower scene and to the hot kisses they'd shared.

"Wow. If he actually finds them, what do I get?"

Derek's question played in her head. She knew he was joking, he didn't expect payment of any kind for helping her. And perhaps that was part of the reason she wanted to reward him. Or not exactly reward him. She just wanted . . .

Don't go there, she told herself. It was way too early to start thinking about those kinds of things. Think about decorating cupcakes. Or think about making the call.

Grabbing her phone off the kitchen counter, she sat down at the computer desk. Taking a deep breath, she dialed the PI's number.

"Brit Smith Agency," he answered.

"Hi." She didn't exactly know where to start. "Uh, my name is Kylie Galen."

"Derek's girl?" the man said.

Kylie felt her stomach wiggle at being called "Derek's girl." It sounded really nice, even though Kylie wasn't officially his girl. Then again, seeing him naked . . . *Don't go there.*

"Derek said that you might be able to help me find someone."

"Yeah, something about your dad being adopted. Let me get to my computer and I'll take notes."

"Sure." While Kylie waited, she looked up at her computer and decided to check her e-mail. She moved the mouse to wake up the computer.

Seconds later, a *Springville Times* newspaper article appeared on the screen. When Kylie started reading, she realized it wasn't just any article. It was the *Springville Times* obituaries. Springville? Wasn't Della from Springville, Texas? But why was she . . .

"Ready," Mr. Smith said. "What's your father's name?"

Kylie looked away from the computer. "Daniel Brighten."

"Parents' names?"

"I don't have their first names," Kylie said.

"Okay," he said. "What county was he born in?"

"I . . . don't know."

"But it was Texas, right?"

Kylie started feeling less and less hopeful that this would lead her anywhere. "I'm not really sure."

"Okay," he said, and this time his okay sounded less enthusiastic. "Maybe we should start by you telling me what you do know."

Her mind started gathering information. "His parents lived in Dallas when my mom met him. I've been . . . calling all the Brightens in the Dallas area. So far I haven't found anyone who claims they knew my father." She went on and told him about how Daniel had died in the Gulf War. And even told him a little about how her mom and Daniel had first met. It wasn't a lot to go on and she knew it.

"That's not a lot to go on," Mr. Smith said, just proving her point and making her even less enthusiastic. "But I'll see what I can dig up. I'm working a big case right now, and it might take a while before I start on this, but when I have something I'll let you know. Meanwhile you keep on asking questions."

"Questions to who?" Kylie asked.

"Your mom, of course."

"I think she's told me everything she knows," Kylie said.

"Maybe," Mr. Smith said. "But parents are funny about divulging info about relationships and things like this."

Kylie bit down on her lip and wondered if he could be right. For certain her mom wasn't the most open-book type of person. "I guess you could be right."

"Yeah, and even if she's not keeping something from you on purpose, she might not see something as important. She does know you're looking into finding his family, doesn't she?"

"Uhh. Not really."

There was a silence. And she supposed Mr. Smith was wondering if he could get in trouble doing work for an underage kid.

"I plan to tell her," Kylie said. "I just haven't really had the chance." *Or decided how to do it.*

"Good. Believe me when I say that these kinds of things work out best if you're up front about them."

"Yeah," Kylie said, and tried to figure out how that conversation would go with her mom. How could she explain that she wanted to meet Daniel's real parents, not just his adoptive parents, because she needed to know what species of supernatural she was?

Hanging up from the PI, Kylie sat there feeling let down. The PI thing didn't sound like the answer anymore. And if that didn't work, what would? If only she could get some more information from Daniel.

She looked up at the ceiling. "You wouldn't be able to come for a visit, would you?"

No spiritual cold filled the room. Kylie was about to get up when her gaze went back to the computer screen and the obituaries. She noticed that the dates on the deaths were back eight months ago.

A terrible thought hit. Was Della looking at obituaries because . . .

she thought she might have killed someone during those blackout days when she turned?

Kylie's gaze went back to the screen to faces of the people who had died. Only a few obituaries listed cause of death, and none said, "drained of blood." While her heart knew that she should feel bad for the deceased, she couldn't help but think of Della. How hard would it be to even think you might have killed someone?

The next few days passed in an uneventful blur. Kylie had tried to talk to Della about what she found on the computer, but Della refused to talk about it. She'd tried to ease into a conversation about Daniel with her mom, but her mom had brushed her off.

While every morning she woke up right at dawn to a blast of icy temperature, the spirit left without any visual or verbal contact. Nothing from Daniel either. So it appeared even everyone in the spirit world was giving Kylie the brush-off.

Kylie wasn't sure what that meant. She got Daniel's absence. He had said his time on earth was now very limited, but what about the female spirit who insisted that someone Kylie loved was about to die?

Holiday told Kylie not to worry, that when the spirit needed to talk, she would speak up. Holiday even tried assuring her that, more likely than not, the ghost's lack of presence was more good news than bad. Either she'd realized things weren't as imminent as she had first thought, or the situation had been handled. Kylie hoped it was the latter. But her gut told her not to get her hopes up.

While Holiday and Kylie had met twice since she'd confessed her mistake of passing info on to Burnett, Holiday had remained almost distant, very matter-of-fact. Kylie had tried apologizing again, but Holiday had stopped her and said it was forgotten.

Forgotten maybe, forgiven not so much. Kylie sensed it when she looked into the camp leader's eyes. And the pain of knowing that her mistake had altered their relationship left an empty spot in Kylie's chest. To make matters worse, there seemed to be even more tension between Holiday and Burnett. Obviously, Kylie's interference not only hadn't helped, but it had made the rift between them even wider.

"You ready?" Kylie heard Miranda call out from the living room. Socks raised his little skunk face off the mattress and hissed. No doubt the kitten/skunk was tired of Miranda following him around and trying to undo her screw-up. Kylie wouldn't be surprised if Socks didn't end up spraying her. If he could spray, that is.

"No. I haven't even touched my hair," Kylie called back, and looked around for her hairbrush. "Why don't you go down to breakfast and meet up with Della and I'll meet you as soon as I can?"

"Got it!" Miranda called. "But hurry, I can't wait to head off. It feels like years since I've gotten to go shopping. And hey, when you leave, make sure you shut the door and don't just break it down."

Kylie frowned and wished she hadn't told Miranda and Della about the whole shower scene at Derek's. But not sharing didn't feel right, even if they teased her about it.

"Did Holiday say we had to be back at a certain time?" Miranda called out again.

"No," Kylie said.

Holiday, in spite of her emotional distance, had agreed to let Kylie, Della, and Miranda take one of the school vehicles into town and do some clothes shopping. It was either that or Kylie was going to have to borrow someone's shoes and bras. Thankfully, the growth spurt appeared to have come to an end. Not that it stopped Kylie from worrying. What did it all mean? And when would she know for sure what to expect next? The full moon would be here on Monday. The weres of the group had planned their show-and-tell event for that night, planning on allowing the group to actually watch one of them turn.

Every now and then, whenever Kylie let her mind go there, she worried she might be doing some show-and-telling that night, too. If her body's change was because she was werewolf, didn't that mean she might do a little morphing herself? Her heart raced at the thought. Would she know what to do? Would she remember who she was?

Kylie heard the cabin door shut and she reached for her phone to make sure she hadn't missed a call from Mr. Smith the PI. Looking at the phone, she realized she did have some messages. Her hope rose that it was him with good news.

But nope. No call from the PI. Two more messages from her stepdad and one from Trey. Great. Just friggin' great! She deleted all three messages without listening to them.

When she reached inside her drawer to find her brush, her eyes landed on Lucas's letter. Curiosity ate at her to open it, but another emotion—one Kylie could best describe as guilt—kept the letter sealed and unread.

Please don't break my heart, Kylie.

Derek's words played across her mind. She had no intention of breaking Derek's heart. She had no intention of getting involved with Lucas. So would someone please explain why she felt guilty about reading his letter?

Maybe because she kept dreaming about him. Almost dreamed about him. Oddly enough, the dreams always stopped before they really got started. However, Kylie had a feeling that was best. She somehow sensed that they would be all too similar to the dream she'd had about him before. Dreams that involved kissing and touching where clothes were considered optional.

Why did she keep almost dreaming of him?

Because you have unresolved feelings for him, a voice from within answered.

A voice Kylie really wished would keep her mouth shut. Kylie didn't want to have any feelings for Lucas. He was off with Fredericka. And Kylie was now with . . . well, almost with Derek. They hadn't even kissed since the night she'd seen him naked. A memory that never ventured too far from her mind. However, since that night, he'd sort of kept his distance from her. Kylie didn't know if it was because he sensed she still felt embarrassed about everyone picking up on her uncontrollable desires for him, or if it was something else.

It could be his way of trying to show how it felt to be avoided. Though Derek didn't seem the type to play head games.

Maybe it was simply because she still hadn't made any verbal commitment to being a couple, to going out with him. Not that this had anything to do with Lucas or his letter. Nope. Not at all. Lucas was history. Even if he came back. He'd made his choice when he took off with Fredericka.

Not that she would be rude to Lucas if he did come back. They could even be . . . friends. If his little she-wolf allowed it.

Thinking of Fredericka shot Kylie back to the night she'd been trapped in the bedroom with the lion. The Blood Brothers, a rogue vampire gang, had started terrorizing and killing the wildlife at the animal preserve next door hoping the FRU would blame the camp and then close it down. They had sent the lion into the camp as part of the setup. However, Kylie couldn't help but think that someone had made sure that lion had gotten in her bedroom. That someone would be Fredericka. Was she wrong to suspect her? Kylie didn't think so.

Oh, heck, this trip down memory lane was stupid. So was the fact that she hadn't opened Lucas's letter. She snatched up the envelope, opened the seal, and was just about to pull the letter out when her phone rang.

Dropping the letter on the bed and checking the number, she took the call. "Hi, Mom."

"Hi, sweetheart." Her mom sighed. "I'm afraid I have some bad news."

"What is it?" Right then, the room's temperature dropped. Kylie felt her stomach twist into a tight knot. Had someone she loved been hurt, like the ghost had warned? "Are you okay, Mom?" Kylie asked as panic began to pull at her heartstrings.

"No. I'm not okay."

Oh, God! The temperature in the room dropped another ten degrees. "What is it? What's wrong?"

"I just received an e-mail and my company is insisting I fly out today to a meeting in New York. It's with a big client and . . . I'm going to miss seeing you on parents day. I checked to see if there was a red-eye flight back and it's already booked."

The chill hung on, even as Kylie's panic lessened. "It's okay." Kylie looked around to see if the ghost had materialized. She hadn't. Kylie reached over and petted Socks, who looked around with nervous, beady skunk eyes. Socks always knew when a spirit was here.

"I wanted to see you. I feel as if I haven't seen you in months."

"It hasn't been months," Kylie said. "Just two weeks." Yet deep down, Kylie realized she was going to miss seeing her mom, too. "I'll be coming home in a couple of weeks for the weekend, anyway. We'll have plenty of time to catch up then."

"And we have the haunted B&B dinner and tour," her mom added, sounding so thrilled.

"Yeah. That, too." Kylie tried not to let her dread leak out in her tone.

They talked a few minutes about her mom's schedule and about her mom's cousin who wanted to come down for a visit. Kylie almost brought up Daniel again, but couldn't figure out how to turn the conversation that way.

As they talked, Kylie pulled the blanket up closer. The cold from the spirit lingered and even grew colder, but she still didn't materialize.

"Oh, guess who I saw at the grocery store?" her mom asked.

"Who?" God, it was getting even colder.

"Sara."

Kylie's heartstrings gave her emotions another tug. "How's she doing?"

"Actually, she didn't look good at all."

"What did she do, dye her hair or get a nose ring?" Kylie asked, knowing how Mom felt about such things. She might have suddenly found common ground with her mom, but that didn't make the woman perfect or change the fact that she was judgmental.

"Not that," her mom said. "Sara's not that kind of girl."

Her mom would be surprised at some of the things Sara had done with drinking and boys—not that it made Sara a bad person. She was just . . . going through something.

"She just didn't look . . . good," her mom continued. "She's thinner than she should be. I hate it that you girls feel as if you have to be size zero to look good. I hope you aren't losing weight."

"Nope, if anything, I think I'm growing." Frowning, Kylie looked down at her boobs, a tad worried what her mom would say when she saw her.

"Which reminds me, have you gone shopping yet?" her mom asked. "Your camp leader called and confirmed it was okay if you drove to town. I told her I'd already given you permission."

"Actually, we're going today." Kylie shivered again from the ghostly cold.

"Well, have fun. And keep it reasonable." The maternal tone filled her voice.

"I will," Kylie promised. "Under a hundred dollars. I remember what you said."

"Okay, go up to a hundred and fifty. But no higher."

"Mom, I didn't ask—"

"I know." Her mom chuckled. "But I'm offering." She grew quiet a second. "Ahh, my baby is growing up." Her mom let go of a deep, heartfelt sigh. "Oh, I forgot to mention it, I told Sara you were coming down. She said you'd texted her and told her and that she owed you a text. And she'd probably be in touch in the next few days."

Sara owed her about four text messages, not including the phone calls and e-mails, Kylie thought.

She and her mom chatted a few more minutes. Mostly about her selling the house—another subject Kylie had to bite her tongue on. "I'll still do my best to come see you on Saturday. Maybe I can get a flight out first thing in the morning. If I get in by ten, I might be able to make it. Even if I'm a little late."

"Mom, it's okay. Don't worry. And they're pretty strict about visiting hours here." *As in if you come in without a pass, you might be taken down by a vampire.* "So really, don't worry, okay?"

"I just miss you," her mom whimpered.

"I miss you, too."

When Kylie hung up, the spirit's chill still lingered in the air. Kylie got the crazy sensation she'd been listening in on the conversation. But why?

"Do you have something to say?" Kylie asked. "Something to show me?" she muttered with less enthusiasm. Kylie really didn't like the freaky visions or dreams, but if that was what it took to solve this and protect someone she loved, she'd do that and more.

No answer filled the cold air and a few seconds later, the chill faded. She looked at her clock on the bedside table and moaned. She was late, which meant Della and Miranda were probably already pissed.

She grabbed her brush, phone, and purse and headed out. Right before she shut the door, she looked back at Lucas's letter on her bed.

"No time now," she muttered, and shut the door and left, but as she took off in a run down the trail she could almost hear Holiday: *"Avoidance isn't a very good coping method."*

Yeah, yeah, yeah, Kylie thought. One thing at a time.

"Hey," Miranda called from the dressing room three hours later. "You two still out there?"

Kylie and Della, both checking out some tops on a nearby rack, walked back to the dressing room area. "Yeah, we're here," Kylie answered.

They were two hours into their shopping spree, and were having a great day so far. The only negative blemish had been seeing the sidewalk where she'd watched her dad and his slutty intern getting it on.

Miranda stepped out of the dressing room modeling a pair of jeans. "Okay, tell the truth. Do these make my butt look good?"

"Turn around," Kylie said.

"Did you say good or big?" Della asked, and grinned.

Kylie would admit the few downtown Fallen stores didn't offer the same experience that shopping at her mall back home did, but it hadn't stopped them from having a blast. Kylie would even admit the town had a certain quaint charm about it. Obviously, she had really needed some time away from the camp.

"Is that a slam because I don't have much of an ass?" Miranda looked over her shoulder as if to see her butt.

"They look great," Kylie interjected.

"Hey," Della said. "Considering I'm lacking in one department," she glanced down at her chest, "I don't pick on body parts. Unless they're really bloody and then—"

"Shh," Kylie said, realizing a couple of other teens were lurking nearby.

Della, not appreciating being hushed, frowned. The frown added to the overall intimidating don't-screw-with-me air she carried on her shoulders all day. Not that the air was intended for her and Miranda. Nope. Rumor had it that the homegrown teens, as well as some of the campers in the area, had it out for all the Shadow Falls teens. Kylie hadn't experienced it the few times she'd come into town, but Holiday had mentioned it at their last camp meeting, so Kylie knew the stories had merit.

"Shh, why?" Della asked.

Kylie cut her eyes to the two girls. Della's frown deepened to a full-blown scowl.

Kylie wondered if Della hadn't picked her all-black outfit on purpose, as if dressing like trouble would keep trouble away. In truth, Kylie wasn't sure the outfit didn't do more harm than good, but arguing with Della was useless, so Kylie hadn't said a thing.

One of the girls started moving closer, and Kylie sent up a quick prayer that this wasn't going to spoil their day.

"Hi, my name's Amber Logan," the cute redhead said, looking at Kylie. "Are you new in town or here with one of the . . . camps?"

The way she said *camps* led Kylie to believe this wasn't going to end well.

"A camp." Kylie put a bit of extra nice into her voice, hoping to ward off any trouble.

"Which one?" the tall blonde standing behind Amber asked, and she cut Della a cold look.

Nope, this wasn't going to end well.

"Shadow Falls," Della answered with attitude, and her dark eyes grew a little golden. Kylie just hoped the girls didn't notice

"Boners," the blonde whispered to Amber.

"What did you say?" asked Della, her shoulders coming back as she took a defensive step forward.

Blondie grinned. "The camp used to be named Bone Creek Camp. So they call you guys . . . boners. It's not personal."

"It feels personal," Della growled.

Both Amber and Blondie took a step back.

Kylie saw Miranda stick out her little pinky as if ready to cast a spell. Kylie shot her a warning glance, but it wasn't Miranda who Kylie worried about.

"Nice to meet you," Kylie told the girls, and latched a hand on Della's elbow, hoping the touch would help her see reason. She couldn't go vampire badass on these girls. She couldn't even threaten to kill them without stirring up a whole big pot of trouble.

" 'Bye," Kylie added, and motioned for them to leave with her free hand.

Amber shot Della another calculating look. From the spark of fear in her eyes, Kylie figured the girl wasn't all that stupid. She turned around, nudged her blond friend, and the two went their own way.

"You better tuck your tails and run," Della muttered, pulling away from Kylie.

"I could have given them the worse case of pimples you've ever seen," Miranda snapped.

"Oh, I could have done much worse," Della snarled.

"But you didn't." Kylie latched a hand around each girl's arm, just in case they changed their minds. "You both showed an amazing amount of restraint. I'm very proud of you."

Della shot Kylie a huge frown. "Don't you ever just lose it? I mean, don't you ever just wanna rip somebody's heart out and beat them over the head with it?"

"I get mad, yes," Kylie said, and grinned. "Don't know if I've ever wanted to bludgeon someone to death with their own heart, but I have my moments."

"Yeah, what do you do when you're really pissed? Frown at someone?" Della chuckled.

"Yeah," Miranda piped in. "But have you seen her frown? It's very effective."

They all laughed.

An hour later, after shoe shopping and trying on a few more pairs of jeans, they moved to the lingerie section. Because she'd already spent close to a hundred dollars, Kylie headed to the clearance rack. They all dropped their packages and browsed through the array of underwear.

"Do either of you wear thongs?" Miranda held up a red stringy pair of panties.

"Not me," Kylie said. "I like regular bikini."

"Personally for me, wearing a thong is like flossing your ass," Della said, and all three of them burst out laughing.

After the giggles subsided, they went back to checking out bras.

A store attendant walked up. "Would you like me to measure you to make sure what size you are?" she asked Kylie.

Kylie looked up at the store clerk and back at the four bras she held in her hands. "Uhh, no . . . thank you. I think I can figure it out."

"Okay, but it's very important you get the right size."

Kylie nodded. "I will."

"It will only take a minute," the attendant said, a tad more insistent that time.

"I know . . . but I'm fine. Thank you," Kylie added.

The woman's expression said Kylie was making a mistake, but she walked off.

"Ugg, no way would I let a stranger handle my girls," Miranda whispered. "These are virgin girls." She giggled.

"I think the ol' biddy just wanted to see your boobs." Della growled at the clerk's back.

Kylie elbowed Della and tried not to snicker. "She was just doing her job."

"Duh, she was like eyeing your boobs like they were candy, and I'm standing here holding a bra and she didn't even ask to measure me!"

"I think there might be a reason for that." Miranda snickered again.

"Bitch!" Della said it with a smile.

Relief swept through Kylie when she saw Della's smile. The last thing Kylie wanted now was for Miranda and Della to start smacking each other around verbally.

Della cupped her A-cup boobs. "At least these puppies aren't virgin. And believe me, Lee didn't complain."

Miranda laughed. "I'm surprised you didn't tell me that I didn't have an ass."

"I'm saving that insult for next time," Della said.

"I'm going to try on these." Kylie studied the bras she held.

"Can you hold these?" Kylie handed Miranda her bags containing two pairs of jeans and two pairs of shoes.

"Here, try this one on, too." Della held a bra out.

"I don't like black bras," Kylie said.

"Yeah, but I'll bet Derek does." She grinned and wiggled her brows.

Kylie rolled her eyes. But she snatched the bra from Della and headed off to the dressing room. Behind her, she heard Della and Miranda laughing.

Trying on bras reminded Kylie of the Goldilocks fairy tale. One felt a bit too big. One was a bit too lacy, and one, the black one, was a bit too . . . sexy.

Now to decide which ones to take home. Kylie glanced down at the pile of bras and had just slipped the strap of her old bra up onto her shoulder, when she heard:

"I like the black one best."

The deep male voice that came from behind her had her heart leaping into her throat. Her eyes shot to the mirror.

Before she saw his face, she saw the blood.

He stood right behind her. Big splotches of red color stained his shirt. Even his auburn-colored hair was soaked in it.

His eyes flashed a vivid red color. He shot her an evil smile and his elongated canines showed at the edges of his mouth. Recognition hit—Blood Brothers.

Chapter Sixteen

Kylie opened her mouth to scream, but neither air nor words came out. Panic gripped her throat and blocked off all oxygen and verbal communication. She swung around, not certain if it was to fight or to run.

He wasn't there. Her gaze shot back to the mirror as if only his reflection had been real. He wasn't there, either.

Her gaze shot to the open door to the dressing room. It had been closed. He'd really been here.

She slammed the door. Sucked a bit of oxygen into her lungs. Tried to scream again, but stopped when the dressing room door swung open and whacked against the wall.

Every muscle in her body clenched. *Fight.* The one-word command echoed inside her. Then Della appeared behind the door that now hung half off the hinges.

"Was someone here?" Della asked. Her eyes shined bright amber. Her canines appeared sharp and threatening under her raised upper lip.

Still unable to speak, Kylie nodded.

Della careened forward when Miranda rammed into her back.

"What happened?" Miranda peered over Della's shoulder. "Why did you take off like that?"

Tears stung Kylie's eyes. She sometimes cried when she was scared, and she had been scared—mortified, actually—but these weren't frightened tears. These were tears of anger. No, make that fury. Fury from feeling violated. *I like the black one best.*

His words rang in her ears. How long had that slimeball been watching her try on bras?

"Is someone here?" Miranda asked. "Ghost? Non-ghost?"

"Vampire," Della snapped at Miranda, and looked back at Kylie. "You okay?"

Kylie nodded again. "Is he gone?"

"For now." Della snatched up Kylie's purse and bras and handed them to Miranda. "Go pay for these while she gets dressed."

Miranda took off. Della looked back at Kylie. "You really okay?"

"I think I'm mad enough to rip out someone's heart and beat him with it." She bit down on her lip to keep from crying. "How long was he here playing Peeping Tom?"

"Just seconds." Della's color grew paler. "It wasn't Chan, was it? I mean, it didn't smell like him, but . . . all I could mostly smell was blood."

"No." Kylie grabbed her shirt and yanked it over her head. Her mind flashed the image of the blood dripping from the guy's hair.

"So you did see him?" Della asked.

Kylie poked her head through her T-shirt and met Della's eyes. "It was . . . it was that creep that we fought at the wildlife park. The one who grabbed me."

Della lifted her nose in the air. "Oh, shit!"

"Is he coming back?"

"Somebody is." She grabbed Kylie by the arm and hurried her out.

When they walked out of the dressing room, Miranda was taking the package from the woman at the checkout counter. Della motioned her to follow and she did without questioning. Obviously, Miranda could see panic in both of their eyes.

"What's going on?" Miranda asked.

"We have to get back to camp," Della said.

"Is he here again?"

"Let's just go," Della snapped.

The moment they stepped out of the door, a black SUV came to a screeching stop in front of the store. Della growled and then pushed Kylie and Miranda behind her.

The window lowered and Burnett stared out. His own eyes were a fierce golden color. "Get in."

"What about the car we drove?" Kylie asked, though she didn't know how she could even think, let alone drive responsibly with the panic still bouncing around her gut.

"Get in!" Burnett's tone demanded obedience.

And they complied.

"What's going on?" Della asked Burnett once they'd all piled into the backseat.

Burnett didn't answer. He focused on driving. The SUV took off before Kylie realized someone was sitting in the front seat with him. It was a dark-haired woman around Burnett's age. She looked familiar and Kylie realized she'd been among the crowd of FRU the night of the fight at the wildlife park.

"Toss them the scrubs," Burnett told the woman.

Three plastic bags with what looked like a pair of hospital scrubs tucked inside each were thrown in the backseat. "What are these for?" Kylie asked.

"Take your clothes off," Burnett ordered. "Put all your clothes back in the bag. Shoes, socks, underwear. Everything. Then put the scrubs on."

"Do . . . what?" Kylie asked.

"You heard me," he snapped.

"Why?" Kylie and Della asked the same question.

"Do it," the woman ordered.

Della and Miranda started to undress, but Kylie grabbed their hands and stopped them.

"No. We're not taking our clothes off until you explain why. And it better be a damn good reason because I don't take my clothes off just because someone tells me to. Just ask my ex-boyfriend!"

The woman turned in her seat and glared. Her eyebrows twitched as if trying to get a reading on Kylie. Too bad it wouldn't work.

Not that the woman gave up immediately. She continued to stare. Her amber-colored eyes grew a bit brighter, and somehow Kylie suspected that she was werewolf. Pissed-off werewolf. "Do it," the woman insisted.

"No." Amazingly, Kylie didn't feel intimidated. She glared right back. She even did her own twitching and tried to see the woman's brain pattern. It didn't work, but the were didn't know that.

"Do as he said! Or I'll do it for you," she ordered.

Burnett caught the woman by the shoulder. "Selynn, let me handle this." His gaze shot to the mirror and Kylie met his golden reflection. "Kylie, please . . ."

"No!" Kylie honestly didn't know where her newfound gumption stemmed from, but it felt good. It gave her some small sense of control. She really needed to feel in control to help combat the feeling of being victimized.

"Do you realize what you're asking?" Kylie continued to hold both Della's and Miranda's hands. "For us to take our clothes off in a car with a man sitting in the front seat with a rearview mirror. And you aren't going to explain why?"

Burnett reached up and ripped the mirror from the car's window.

"Damn!" Miranda said.

"Two girls were killed in town," Burnett said.

"Shit," Della said.

"Oh, hell," Miranda said.

The only thing that came out of Kylie's mouth was a gasp.

Burnett continued, "I need your clothes to prove that you three weren't involved with their murders. The FBI and FRU will demand it. So, please, do as I say."

Kylie let go of their hands and started undressing. In a few minutes, all three of them sat in green scrubs, looking like surgical doctors. No one said a word during the process.

Miranda collected the three bags and handed them to Selynn. "Here."

"Do you really think anyone will think we had anything to do with this?" Kylie asked, remembering the blood all over the rogue vampire's head and shirt.

"No," Della said. "But they'll believe I did." She sounded hurt. "It was a vampire kill, wasn't it?"

"Yes," Burnett said. "But I don't believe you did this. I'm just taking precautions until we know who did."

"We already know who did it," Della said. "Kylie saw him."

"Saw who?" Both Selynn and Burnett swung around.

"It was the rogue vampire," Kylie said. "The one who attacked me at the wildlife park."

"Damn it!" After almost running off the road, Burnett pulled over and rammed the car into park. He twisted in his seat again and met Kylie's eyes. "You aren't hurt, are you?" His eyes shot to her neck as if . . .

"No. I'm not hurt." A big wave of I-wanna-cry, I-wanna-cry-right-now filled her chest.

"Did he say anything?" Burnett asked.

I like the black one best. "No," she said.

Burnett's stare deepened. "Now isn't the time to be lying."

Kylie swallowed. "He didn't say anything that would be helpful."

"Let us be the judge of that?" Ms. Badass Werewolf sitting in the front seat said.

Kylie frowned. "He said he liked the black bra best. I was in the dressing room." The feeling of being violated hit strong again and the anger accompanying it welled up in her chest.

Burnett's expression changed from demanding to empathetic in a split second. "Are you sure you're okay? He didn't . . ."

"I'm fine," she managed to say, but she felt the tears fill her eyes and looked away from Burnett's concerned expression.

"He came and left so fast that by the time I sensed he was there he was gone," Della said.

The memory of his reflection in the mirror filled Kylie's head. "He had blood . . . all over him. His shirt. His hair."

Miranda slipped her hand into Kylie's and gave it a squeeze as if offering moral support.

Burnett's frown deepened and he turned back around and started the car. He looked over at Selynn sitting in the seat beside him. "Make the call. Tell them it's a Code Red."

"You sure you want to attempt that?" Selynn asked.

"What's a Code Red?" Della asked right before Kylie posed the question.

Burnett answered hesitantly. "Right now, the only ones who

know about this are the FRU. Code Red means we'll fix it so it looks like a car accident."

"You're going to let him get away with it?" Kylie asked.

"No," Burnett said. "But neither can we let something like this leak out. Any rumors start floating around, making higher-ups nervous, and they'll close down the school."

Selynn held up her hand as if to silence everyone. Then she spoke into the phone. "It's a Code Red." She paused. "I know." She cut her eyes to Burnett. "He gave the order, I'm just the messenger."

Burnett frowned and Kylie got the impression that whatever Burnett was doing, he was doing it for the school and maybe even Holiday. But she couldn't help but wonder about the good of the townspeople—the human people who would never know that a murderer had come and taken two of their own.

When they walked into Holiday's office thirty minutes later, Holiday practically leapt out of her chair and ran over to them. "Thank you, God," she yelped, and wrapped her arms around all of them in a group hug. Della was the first to pull away.

"We're fine," Della said.

Speak for yourself, Kylie thought. She could have used a few more seconds of a hug. It was the closest she'd felt to Holiday since the whole Burnett issue.

"Look." Della pointed to the television screen mounted on the wall.

Kylie glanced up and her breath caught. The screen showed a wrecked car and then two pictures of girls. *It couldn't be.* She felt suddenly nauseous.

Holiday grabbed the remote and turned up the volume.

"Two girls were killed today in an automobile accident. It appeared . . ." the reporter continued.

"We met them in town," Kylie blurted out, her chest filled with heaviness. "We talked to them." For some crazy reason, that short encounter made their deaths even more personal. "The redhead is named Amber. I don't know the blonde's name."

"They weren't very nice." Della voice sounded tight. "But they didn't deserve to die."

"No, they didn't." Miranda put her hand over her lips and just stared at the screen.

Kylie would have verbally agreed, but she couldn't. She recalled with clarity the blood on the rogue vampire's shirt and emotion closed her voice box. It had been their blood she'd seen. When the tears prickled Kylie eyes, she felt like a crybaby, but then she noticed both Della and Miranda had a wet sheen to their eyes, too.

"I feel . . ." Kylie forced the words out. "I feel as if it's somehow my fault."

Holiday stabbed at the remote and turned it off. "It's a terrible thing. But the only person responsible for this is the rogue who did it." Then she just stared at each of them as if needing to visually memorize them. "When I heard two girls were found . . . I thought . . ." Holiday's eyes pooled with tears. And that pretty much made it a cry fest. Even Della joined in the tear party.

Right then, Burnett walked into the office. His gaze went from one female to the other. Kylie could almost hear him groaning inwardly.

"I . . . I'll be . . . right out here." Obviously even a hard-bodied vampire trained by the FRU wasn't capable of dealing with four crying women.

Fifteen minutes later, Burnett poked his head back in the room, and when he saw they were no longer in tears, he walked in. On his heels came Selynn, the werewolf who'd been with him in the car. She stood so close to Burnett's side that her shoulders brushed up against his forearm. Burnett stepped to the side and started explaining that he needed to interview them separately. He opened the door and told Kylie and Miranda to wait outside of Holiday's office.

As the two of them started out, Selynn looked over at Holiday. "You should leave as well." Selynn's voice held such a condescending tone that Kylie decided right there and then that she really didn't like her. Not even a little bit.

Holiday shot the woman a look that Kylie could only describe as fiercely protective. "Sorry, but I don't take orders from anyone when it involves my campers. Or has Burnett not informed you of this?"

"She can stay," Burnett interjected.

Selynn placed a palm on Burnett's forearm. "I really don't think that's wise."

"The girls will feel more comfortable with her here." He stepped away from her touch. But Kylie noticed Holiday's gaze take in the familiar way the woman treated Burnett.

Jealousy flashed in Holiday's eyes. Not that it lingered more than a second. One blink and the emotion vanished. And probably for a reason, too. Selynn glanced at Holiday as if looking for a reaction. Which led Kylie to assume that Selynn had feelings for Burnett. Not that Kylie sensed that Burnett returned any of the feelings.

Then again, he might just be good at hiding his emotions. Could this be part of the reason Holiday refused to get too close to Burnett, because she knew he was already involved with someone? Instant distrust for Burnett stirred inside Kylie.

Burnett motioned for Kylie and Miranda to leave. Kylie, suspi-

cious of Burnett for Holiday's sake, didn't move until Holiday
confirmed the order.

"Who do they think is in charge?" Selynn asked, annoyed at
Kylie's show of authority for Holiday.

"Can we please just get started?" Burnett said.

Kylie and Miranda walked out into the front room of the office.

"He's checking to see if we're lying. That's why he wants to talk
to us separately," Miranda whispered.

"I don't think he thinks we're guilty." Kylie defended him, though
she wasn't so sure she could say the same about Selynn. Then Kylie
wondered again about the relationship between Burnett and the rude
were.

"God, it sucks." Emotion gave Miranda's voice a raspy tone. "I
can't believe we actually met the girls who were killed."

"I know," Kylie said but, honestly, she didn't want to think
about it. She still had this overwhelming feeling that it was her
fault. She dropped down onto one of the two desk chairs filling the
small entry room and stared at her hands. Was this the bad thing
that the ghosts had been talking about? No, the ghost had insisted
it was someone Kylie loved. That thought sent another wave of sorrow sloshing in her gut. She hadn't loved those girls, but someone
had. They had mothers, friends . . . Closing her eyes, Kylie tried to
reconnect to the calm she'd found at the falls. How long could she
hang on to that feeling when bad shit just kept happening?

"It could have been us." Miranda pulled at a thread attached to
her light green scrubs.

"I know." Kylie gripped her hands together.

It was only a few minutes before Selynn and Della walked
out. Kylie stood up. Selynn motioned at Miranda to follow her. Then
she turned to Kylie and Della. "We prefer if you don't speak. And

Burnett can hear you if you do." She practically smirked before following Miranda into the office.

Della snarled at the werewolf's back. "Bitch," she mouthed the word. And when the werewolf was in the other room, Della said it out loud. "Bitch." She glanced at the office door. "I don't care if you can hear me, Burnett. She's a bitch. You know it. I know it. And Holiday knows it."

Footsteps sounded on the office's front porch. Kylie glanced toward the door just as it opened and Derek rushed in. "Thank God." He stopped and just stared at her as if noting the hospital scrubs. Right behind him followed Perry, looking just as worried.

Perry's gaze shot around the room. "Where's Miranda?" Fear and some other deep emotion filled his now copper-colored eyes.

Kylie didn't have a chance to answer because Derek swooped her into a big hug. She let him hold her, even rested her head on his chest and sighed at how good it felt to be this close to him.

"Why do you want to know?" Della mouthed off. "You don't like her, remember?"

"Is she okay?" Perry demanded, his voice a deep rumble of emotions. Kylie didn't bother to pull away to see, but she imagined his eyes were changing colors as he spoke. She'd noticed his eyes shifted with his emotions.

"Don't go all T. rex on me." Della lost her smartass tone. Whether out of fear of Perry or if she heard the emotion in his voice, Kylie didn't know.

"You okay?" Derek whispered in her ear.

"Yeah." *Hell, no.* Kylie pulled back to look in his eyes and she saw the same concern flashing there that she noted in Perry's. A rush of calm flowed from Derek into her. She didn't argue this time. She really needed it.

The door to Holiday's office opened. Miranda walked out. Perry met her eyes, then he turned and left the building. Miranda watched him go. "What did he want?" she asked.

"To make sure you were okay," Derek answered, and slipped a hand around Kylie's waist. "I saw him right after I heard what happened and I told him. He was worried about you."

"But not worried enough to even speak to me, huh?" The look on Miranda's face was half sad and half angry. She met Kylie's gaze again. "Your turn." She pointed to the office door. "Watch out, the she-wolf bites."

Kylie gave Derek's hand a tight squeeze and then walked into the room to face Burnett and the she-wolf. Kylie was no longer as intimidated by Burnett as she was the first time she'd been interrogated by him, but a nervous tickle still fluttered in her chest.

Chapter Seventeen

Burnett made Kylie go over what happened several times. Then he asked specific questions. "You said the rogue vampire was bloody. Did it look like fresh blood? How much time passed from when you saw the girls to when he appeared?"

Then Burnett asked the same questions in a slightly different way. At one time she'd have thought he was trying to catch her in a lie, but now she suspected his intent was to make sure she wasn't forgetting something and hoping a slightly different question might lead her to remember some minor detail that could be useful. Problem was, Kylie didn't want to remember. She longed to forget, to wipe it from her memory forever. And seriously, what else could she tell him that might be helpful?

"Could you describe the blood to me?" Burnett straddled a straight-backed chair in front of Kylie, reminding her of their first interrogation. Only this time she sat on the sofa with Holiday beside her.

"I already did." She felt her patience being pulled like a tight rubber band.

"One more time." His tone demanded obedience.

It was the tone that finally made Kylie snap. "You know who

did this. You know who his victims were. So is any of this *really* necessary?" She gritted her teeth and tried not to start crying again.

"We decide what's necessary," Selynn answered in her haughty tone, moving in behind Burnett.

Kylie glared up at the werewolf, not trying to hide her contempt. Selynn's tone annoyed Kylie even more than Burnett's harsh tenor. At least with Burnett, she heard real concern. With Selynn, it seemed to be all about power. She liked having it and enjoyed using it.

"You think we did this, don't you?" Kylie asked Selynn.

"I think—"

"Stop." Burnett frowned at Selynn, then glanced back at Kylie. "Kylie, I know you didn't do this. And I know this isn't easy. However, blood patterns might tell us if he was killing for sport or for food."

His statement made her stomach churn. "And why does that make a difference? Those girls are dead no matter what his reasons were for killing them."

"I think she's had enough questions." Holiday placed her hand on Kylie's wrist, offering moral support and a strong surge of calm. The rush of peaceful energy slowed Kylie's heartbeat and lessened the tightness in her chest. Not that it could make it all go away. Kylie didn't think that power existed.

Burnett looked at Holiday, then at Kylie. "It won't change what happened. But right now, we need all the information we can get on this creep to be able to catch him. To stop him before he does this again."

Burnett's words shifted around inside her head and pulled at her conscience. Two girls had died. Violently died. Was it too much to ask for Kylie to suffer through a few more minutes of questions? No, it wasn't. Taking in a breath, she sat up straighter.

Holiday stiffened. "For a vampire, your hearing is really bad. I said she's had enough."

"It's okay." Kylie turned her palm over and gave the camp leader's hand a squeeze. "If it helps stop this guy, I can do it." But she didn't let go of Holiday's hand.

Ten minutes later, apparently when Burnett felt he'd drawn every detail about the incident he could out of her, he stood up and looked down at her. "Thank you, Kylie. I know this wasn't easy."

She nodded and after she let herself breathe in and out a couple of times, she decided it was her turn to ask the questions. "Do you think he wanted it to look as if we'd killed these girls? Like they tried to frame someone at the camp for killing the animals?"

Burnett shook his head. "No. There's nothing to lead us to conclude that."

"Do you think . . . do you think he followed us into town?"

He considered her question for a second. "No, I don't. I think it was a coincidence that he ran across you."

Holiday squeezed Kylie's hand. "I told you, this isn't your fault."

"No, it isn't," Burnett said. "This has nothing to do with you, Kylie."

"Then how come it feels so . . . personal?" Kylie asked. "I mean, he keeps showing back up. At the park and then last Friday. I didn't actually see him then, but I'm assuming it was him. And even after that I . . . I've felt as if someone was following me."

"When did you feel this?" Burnett asked.

"Yesterday morning when I came to the office before breakfast. At first, I thought it was the wolf but—"

"Wolf?" both Burnett and Selynn said at the same time. While Burnett looked concerned, Selynn immediately started twitching, trying to read Kylie again. It took everything Kylie had not to reach up and cover her forehead. Maybe even give the woman the finger.

"When was this?" Burnett asked.

"A couple of days ago," Holiday answered. "It wasn't a were-wolf. Kylie said it appeared to be semi-tame. Nonthreatening."

"Was it a shifter?" Burnett asked.

"I'm . . . not sure. But I know it wasn't Perry." Kylie hesitated and then recalled what this conversation was really about. "But the wolf isn't important. Two girls are dead and I . . . I feel as if it's somehow my fault. I think he was after me, not them."

Burnett dropped back down in the chair facing her. "I can understand how you might feel that way. But if he was out to hurt you, he could have done so the other night in the woods. I don't think this is personal. Not toward you. To the camp as a whole . . . maybe."

"Then why does he keep coming to see me? It doesn't sound like a coincidence."

Burnett frowned. "It's not a coincidence. You put yourself in situations that offered him the best opportunity with the least of amount of risk. And the first time, he didn't come to you. You had gone to the wildlife park where the Blood Brothers were. And if he was here the other night, and we're not sure it was him, then he probably spotted you when you ran off in the woods and saw it as an opportunity. And today, he was probably . . . hunting when he sensed other supernaturals in town. Again, you were the one alone in the dressing room. He took advantage of it."

And got himself an eyeful, Kylie thought. "But you even said that if he'd wanted to kill me the other night, he could have but he didn't even try. So what did he want with me then?"

Burnett hesitated. "I think he wanted to send a message to the camp. To let us know that the gang hasn't moved on. I'm sure the arrest of several of their gang members has dented their egos. If they pulled out right away, it would appear as if they lacked courage. If they stay around, they at least save face. I'm sure he realized that killing you would have brought too much trouble down on the gang."

Kylie tried to grasp exactly what Burnett was saying. "But he killed those girls. Are you saying that didn't cause trouble? That doesn't make sense."

Burnett looked at Holiday as if asking for her help.

Holiday squeezed Kylie's hand. "When a supernatural kills another supernatural, it's easier to deal with the offense. We have our own justice system."

"And when they kill a human? What happens?" Don't let them say "nothing," Kylie thought. Please God, don't let them say "nothing." She might be part supernatural, but she was still part human.

"That's part of the FRU's job," Burnett said. "But as you might guess, it can make getting justice tricky."

Kylie felt her shoulders getting tighter. "Are you telling me that he's actually going to get away with this?"

"No." Burnett said in a deeper tone. "You have my word, Kylie, I will do everything I can to make sure this guy pays for this."

Exactly how Burnett intended to make him pay wasn't clear. Nor was Kylie sure she even wanted to know. But something about the way he said those words told her this wasn't a promise he made lightly. And for that, she was grateful.

That night, the camp leaders held a meeting of all the campers at the dining hall and served up both pizza and sage advice. Burnett spoke about being extra careful. "Stay on the main paths and trails and don't go through the woods without having someone with you," he explained. "Depending on how dense the trees are or how the wind is blowing, an intruder's scent could go undetected."

Della shot a grin at Kylie and then turned back to Burnett. "Maybe you should cancel parents weekend," she suggested.

Burnett looked at Della. "That's over two weeks away. I hope to have this problem resolved by then."

"Hey, can't blame a girl for trying," Della muttered.

"I have a meeting with the High Council next week," Burnett said. "I'm hoping I'll get some assistance to deal with what happened here."

Kylie leaned in closer to Della. "Who are the High Council?"

"Sort of like the Senate, made up of a bunch of elders from the different species." Della smiled. "I just learned about it this afternoon. Chris did a talk about it in our vamp meeting."

"A Senate? I didn't think all the species got along," Kylie said.

"They don't. But neither do the Democrats and Republicans and they still meet."

"I guess so," Kylie said, and then another question popped up. "What kind of assistance will they offer us?"

"Depends. Chris said the council has to vote to even look into the case."

"Vote? Two girls murdered, how can they say no?"

Della shrugged. "You have to remember that not all the elders are in line with the government's way of thinking. "

"You mean some of them are rogue?"

Della nodded. "According to Chris, most of the elders respect the government, but don't want to be controlled by it. So they follow some of the rules, but not all of them." One of Della's eyebrows rose upward.

Kylie shook her head. She had enough trouble trying to understand human politics—did she really have it in her to grasp this, too? "If they take the case, then what?"

"They either allow the council of the accused species to do the punishing and deal with things or they turn the guy over to the FRU. And I don't want to think about what happens to them then."

"Me, either," Kylie admitted.

Della glanced over to the door and her mood seemed to have changed. "I'm going to head on back to the cabin. I've got some stuff I want to do."

"What kind of stuff?" Kylie remembered the obituaries she'd found on the computer screen.

"Just stuff," Della snapped.

Kylie leaned in. "You could never do anything like this."

Della glared at her. "I'll see you later."

"Do you want me to walk with you?" Kylie asked, remembering Burnett's caution to stay together whenever possible.

"Are you kidding me?" Della asked. "If something attacked, I'd just end up having to protect both of us."

"Hey . . . I'm not so helpless anymore." After thinking about what those girls might have gone through, Kylie wasn't so upset about her new found strength, either.

"Just because you broke one door in, and don't lag behind when hiking through the woods, doesn't mean crap." She grinned, letting Kylie know she was mostly teasing. "I'm fine. I'll see you later."

Della took off, and Kylie watched her go. Her heart ached for Della. Then she saw her vampire friend turn and give a couple of boys the finger. No doubt they'd probably said something rude and crude.

"Hey." Holiday stopped beside Kylie. "Is Della okay?"

"I hope so." Kylie realized that ever since they'd returned from town, the distance that had seemed to come between her and Holiday because of the whole Burnett issue had vanished. Had they bridged a gap, and could Kylie keep it from reappearing?

"Are you doing okay?" Holiday asked.

"I've been better," Kylie said honestly. "I just keep thinking about those girls."

"Maybe Sunday we can take a walk to the falls," Holiday said.

"That sounds good." The thought of going there with someone who could feel the same thing Kylie did seemed nice.

Right then, Burnett looked over at them and Kylie saw Holiday notice it, too. Kylie cringed, worrying that Holiday would remember she was mad at her.

"I should apologize," Holiday said, obviously reading Kylie's emotions again. "I . . . I overreacted about the whole thing with Burnett."

Shocked, Kylie looked at her. "No you didn't. I was wrong to say anything to him."

"Maybe, but your heart was in the right place. When we care about people, we sometimes overstep our grounds. I of all people should know that. I'm a famous overstepper." Holiday's voice tightened. "Today when Burnett first came to me and said they had two teens down and I thought . . . Well, let's just say our issue really felt stupid." Holiday put her arm around Kylie and gave her a sweet, sisterly hug.

"Thank you." Kylie fought the swell of emotion in her throat. "But you are going to make me cry."

Holiday looked up toward Burnett. "Hey, if you cry, maybe it will send him running again. If I knew all it took were a few tears to get him to leave, I'd have been crying for the last seven weeks. "

Kylie grinned and when she looked up at Burnett, she saw Selynn walk up to him and say something. "What's she still doing here?"

"Don't know for sure," Holiday said in a whisper. "I'm sure she wants something. And I bet it starts with a B and is tall, dark, and good-looking."

Burnett listened to something Selynn said and then walked out the door with her. "And she may have just got it," Holiday said, her voice revealing rejection.

Kylie hesitated to ask, but then it just popped out. "Are those two . . . you know?"

"Dirtying up the sheets?" Holiday said.

"Yeah." Kylie mentally added that to Della's list of ways to say getting it on.

"This afternoon he came into my office and made the announcement, 'I know how things looked between Selynn and me. And it's not that way. Or at least not anymore.'"

"So they were together and they broke up?" Kylie asked.

"He said they ended it two months ago. That they were never serious."

Kylie raised her eyebrows. "And how long ago was it that you met him?"

"Two months," she said.

"Hmm," Kylie said.

"Hmm, what?" Holiday asked.

"Just a meaningless hmm," Kylie lied. "So what did you tell him?"

"I told him that I didn't have a clue why he felt as if he needed to tell me about Selynn."

"Could he tell you were lying?" Kylie asked.

"Yup," Holiday chuckled. They just stood there for a minute looking out at the crowd. "Any more info from the ghost lately?"

"Nothing," Kylie said. "It scares me that . . . I've messed up somehow."

"I don't think that's it at all. She's probably trying to figure out how to tell you what she needs you to know."

"I hope so," Kylie said.

Angry sounds exploded from across the room. "What did you call me?" a loud voice boomed. Kylie and Holiday looked up. Two werewolves stood nose-to-nose, about to go fist-to-fist.

"My work is never done," Holiday said, and took off to break up the fight.

Kylie watched her go—watched her calm the tempers of two very high-spirited boys. After a few minutes of feeling a bit like a lone ranger, she spotted Miranda hanging with her witch sisters. She knew Miranda wouldn't mind if she joined them, but Kylie decided against it. Helen and Jonathon sat at a table playing chess. She could go watch Helen embarrass Jonathon again with her natural talent for chess, but for some the reason, the two seemed to be enjoying being alone.

Another sweep of the room and Kylie found Derek. He leaned against a wall, arms crossed, watching her. A slow smile widened his lips. Something in his smile told her he could really use some company.

She gave the room a quick check to see how many individuals could either smell her hormones or read her emotions. They were everywhere. What to do? What to do?

She glanced back at Derek, remembered how good it had felt when he'd held her those few minutes in the office, and she thought . . . *what the hell*. She started walking toward him.

"Wanna go eat pizza in the moonlight?" Derek whispered in her ear when she stopped in front of him.

Standing this close, she could smell his freshly showered skin. A vision of what he'd looked like standing in the buff wearing only a few water droplets filled her mind. She blinked the vision away.

"Is that like dancing in the moonlight? It's supposed to be

seductive." She smiled and then bit her tongue. Why was it when she got within three feet of him, all she could think about was . . . him?

He grinned. "It could be. With the right person. And the right pizza." He laughed. "Hey, I'm hungry."

They got themselves two slices each of pizza and a couple of drinks and walked out of the dining hall.

"I know the perfect place," he said as they left the chatter of voices and the air-conditioning behind in the dining hall. The night air was warm and smooth. He pointed to the two large, white rocking chairs at the front of the office. She followed him. She was just about to sit down when the phone in her pocket chimed.

Sitting her drink down, she balanced her plate in one hand and pulled out her phone to check the number. She frowned when she saw her dad's number and she hit the off button.

"Who was it?" Derek moved the second rocker over so they faced each other.

"My dad . . . I mean, my stepdad," she corrected herself.

"You still aren't talking to him?" Derek sat down and picked up a piece of pepperoni pizza and took a big bite.

"Nooooo." She stuffed her phone back in her pocket and dropped down in her rocker. Their knees touched and it felt nice.

"Why not?" Derek asked between bites of pizza.

Kylie stared at him. "Why would I want to talk to him?" She positioned the plate in her lap.

He finished chewing and swallowed. "Because you care about him. Because up until the shit hit the fan with your parents' marriage, he was a pretty good dad." He held up his finger. "You're the one that told me that."

"Yeah, but I didn't tell you to use it against me." She picked up the slice of pizza and stared down at the oozing cheese. Her mouth watered and her stomach grumbled. Thankfully, she was finally hungry. For a while there, she thought the blood had ruined her for eating regular food.

"I'm not using it against you." He took a sip of his drink. "I'm just . . . trying to help. Because when you saw it was his number, your emotions went all lonely and sad. I felt them all the way to my gut. Maybe if you talked to him, you wouldn't have to feel that anymore."

"He cheated on my mom." She fought back the slight annoyance she felt toward Derek and took a small bite of pizza. The spicy sauce along with the gooey cheese made her taste buds jump up and down.

"That's just it," Derek said, taking another bite of his slice. "He cheated on your mom. Not you."

Kylie swallowed the pizza and frowned. "Why does everyone keep saying that as if his infidelity didn't affect me? It broke their marriage up. Nothing is the same for me anymore."

Derek studied her over the rim of his drink and started his rocker moving. "Maybe if you spoke with him, some of it would be the same. The relationship between you and him could be the same."

She dropped her pizza back on her plate, frustration chasing away her first sign of hunger in days. "You know, for a guy who won't even think about talking to his dad, you're a fine one to talk. I mean, you had a detective find your dad, and you still won't even contact him."

His jaw tightened. "And your point?"

She narrowed her own eyes and steadied her stare at him. "My point is, back off, okay?"

Derek scraped his feet on the porch, brought his rocker to a fast halt, and stared at her. "How far back do you want me to go? I'm already scared to even talk to you in public. Isn't that far enough?"

Frustration filled his voice, but it was the hurt in his eyes that made her see reason.

Why was she being such a B with an itch?

"I'm sorry." Kylie said. "I shouldn't have snapped at you. And I don't mean that you can't ever talk to me in public. I just . . . I'm just . . . I'm so moody." Kylie remembered what Holiday had said about the mood swings in werewolves before the full moon. Was that why she was acting this way? She looked up at the dark navy sky and focused on what almost appeared to be a full moon. Come Monday she'd know, wouldn't she?

When she glanced back at Derek, he'd continued eating. Not that he looked all that happy. He wouldn't even look at her. Her thoughts shifted from what might happen on Monday to the anger that had just passed between them.

"Hey," she said to get his attention.

When he looked up, his discontent showed more on his face.

"I'm really sorry," she said again.

He dropped what was left of his pizza back on his plate. "You shouldn't be," he muttered, and used the back of his hand to wipe his mouth. He closed his eyes for a second. "You're right. I wouldn't want you trying to tell me I needed to call my father. It's just . . ."

"Just what?" she asked.

"I feel everything you feel and it can be a tad overwhelming."

"Bad overwhelming?" she asked.

"Not really," he said, and glanced away.

"So we're okay? I'm forgiven for being a bitch?" she said in a soft, pleading voice.

"I don't think you've hit the bitch mark yet." He smiled. "But yeah, you're forgiven for being grumpy." He set his plate on the porch and stood up. Bracketing his palms on the arms of the rocking chair, he leaned down and kissed her. The kiss wasn't overly sexy, but the soft way his lips brushed against hers had her heart swelling with emotion. Emotion that was as gooey as the cheese pizza she'd abandoned.

"Mm." He pulled back, smiling. "I don't know if it's you, or the pizza, but something tastes good."

She touched his cheek. "Will you still like me if I'm werewolf?"

"What do you think?" His lips met hers again. This kiss came with a touch of his tongue and had her pulse racing even faster than its abnormally fast pace.

But when he pulled back this time, he wasn't smiling. He didn't look happy.

"What is it?" she asked.

"Nothing." He sat back down in his rocking chair.

She looked at his expression through the moonlight. "I hate it when people do that."

"Do what?" he asked.

"Say nothing, when it's sooo obvious that it's something."

He let go of a sigh. "Okay, if you must know. It just occurred to me that maybe I wouldn't be so thrilled if you turn out to be werewolf."

"Because I'll get all hairy?" Kylie asked.

"No." His expression darkened. "Because . . . because Lucas is werewolf."

Chapter Eighteen

Later, after Derek walked her back to her cabin in an uncomfortable silence, Kylie decided to go to bed early. She'd only been in bed a few hours when she felt herself having a dream. She knew it had to be a dream from the moment she became aware of the floating sensation. She rolled over and tried to force herself awake, but then she saw . . .

Him.

Again.

Lucas.

He looked at her and smiled. His bright blue eyes looked heavy, sleepy. She realized that she was no longer above him, but stood beside him. He wore jeans and a light blue button-down shirt that wasn't buttoned. Her gaze went to his chest and then up again. All the way up, away from his open shirt. His black hair looked mussed, as if he'd just gotten out of bed himself, and the dark strands appeared to be a tad longer. It even had a bit of waviness to it.

"You came," he said.

"Came where?" she asked, feeling out of her comfort zone.

He didn't answer her, instead he said, "Come on, let's go for walk." He held out his hand as if wanting her to take it.

She hesitated. The idea of touching him tempted her, but she remembered she was angry at him, although she couldn't quite recall why.

"I don't bite." He smiled again.

It was just a dream, she told herself, and slipped her hand into his, forgetting about the hint of anger she felt inside. His palm felt so warm against hers that it made her giddy.

"I missed you," he said.

She didn't know what to say, so she didn't say anything. Or at least not about missing him. But she had, she knew she had.

"Where are we going?" she asked when he started walking.

He stopped. "Where would you like to go?"

All of a sudden, Kylie realized they were standing in a patch of woods; large trees with sweet-smelling flowers hung overhead.

"Paris? The mall?" He looked around as if just noticing the scenery. "Or would you like to go back to the lake, like in the last dream?" His voice grew deeper, huskier. "Is that where we're going?"

Blood rushed to her face. *How did he know about that dream?* Then she remembered this was just a dream. Nothing had to make sense. Right? Yet this dream seemed even stranger. Different.

He laced his fingers through hers. "We could go anywhere, as long as I'm with you." His irises appeared to darken and his eyelids looked heavier.

She recognized the emotion. Desire. Hunger. Passion. She'd seen it in his eyes the day they'd kissed at the creek by the dinosaur footprints. But that wasn't the first time she'd seen that look. She'd seen it first in her dream. The dream of them swimming—of him touching her.

"We can even do anything . . . because . . ."—he moved in closer—"because this is just a dream. It's not real. Just like the first one. But it's your choice. You're the one in the driver's seat."

His head dipped down an inch, and his face felt lightly scratchy against hers. Then his lips brushed across her cheeks until he found her lips. She let him kiss her. At first, she didn't respond. At least not until his tongue slipped between her lips.

Unable to think of anything else, she gave in and started kissing him back. It was hot. It was wonderful. It was just a dream. His hands were on her back, and then shifted to her front. Her breasts felt swollen when he brushed his palm across them.

Then . . . she remembered Derek. Strong, kind, beautiful Derek. And then she remembered Fredericka. Yeah, that was why she was mad at Lucas.

She jerked back. She was breathing hard. He was breathing hard, too.

She started floating away.

"Don't go, Kylie," he said. "Come back. Please."

Kylie suddenly became fully awake. She jackknifed into a sitting position. Her heart raced as if she'd run a marathon. Her palms felt sweaty. Her body tingled in front. It tingled darn near everywhere.

Socks, still in skunk form, meowed from the foot of the bed.

"Weird dream," she said aloud, and it felt good to hear her own voice. "A very weird dream."

Then she remembered Lucas's letter. His first letter.

Dream of me, he'd signed it.

Was it a coincidence?

Crazy possibilities started forming in her head. What if . . . ? What if werewolves had the power to get inside one's dreams? What if these weren't just dreams, but something more? Did that kind of power even exist?

The more she thought about it, the more she started to believe it, and the angrier she got. How dare he just come into her dreams and . . . kiss her. Touch her. Wasn't Fredericka enough for him? Did the she-wolf know Lucas was skipping out on her to come visit Kylie in her dreams?

So many questions and no answers. She realized one place she could look for answers.

Turning on the light, she yanked open the drawer and pulled out his letter. She'd already unsealed it and it slipped from the envelope easily enough. She blinked to adjust her eyes.

Hi Kylie,

Another letter from me. For all I know I'm the last person in the world you want to hear from. But it doesn't stop me from writing you. Or from thinking about you. But damn, I think about you all the time—wonder if you have discovered what you are and the many talents that you have. I've spoken to Burnett and when I asked about you, he only said you were fine. I think he knew I wanted details but for some reason, he wasn't willing to give them. It makes me wonder what you're doing that Burnett won't share. I don't want to think about it too much, because I'll start worrying.

You could say that I feel very possessive of you. I'm not saying it's right, but I did meet you first.

Do you remember when we met? You were in your front yard, lying on the ground, staring up at the sky. When I came over, you didn't even say hello. You looked at me with your big, curious eyes and asked if I saw the elephant. At first I thought you were crazy, but then you pointed to the clouds.

Kylie stopped reading as the tiny piece of memory started floating around her head. She did . . . remember. Taking a deep breath, she went back to reading.

I remember I told you I didn't see the elephant in the clouds. But I did. I don't know why I lied, probably because you made me nervous. I could see you weren't human, but I couldn't tell what you were and it seemed strange. Not really a bad strange. You were just like a puzzle I wanted to figure out. Ha! It's been ten years, and here I'm still trying to figure you out. Part of me wonders if it's because you are a female, girls are always a mystery, or if you are really that big of a puzzle.

Anyway, I hope you'll think this is good news, but I may be able to come back to the camp. I've spoken with Burnett about it and he said he has to get clearance from a couple other people and if they say it's okay, I'll be back. Hopefully, I'll be able to explain more then.

Okay, I hope to see you soon, but until then . . . dream of me.

Your admirer and friend forever,

Lucas

Kylie dropped the letter and just stared at those three words. *Dream of me.*

Exactly what did he mean by "dream of me"?

Did it mean anything? It had to, didn't it? Kylie folded the letter and stuffed it back in her drawer. Her emotions ran all over the place. Then she realized a second place she could look for answers. The place she always went for answers. Holiday.

Kylie looked at the red glowing numbers on her clock. Still too early. It wasn't quite . . . five.

But what happened to the regular cold that always came at dawn?

She looked at the window and saw the vaguest sign of sunrise. For some reason, her mind moved away from ghosts and to the two girls who'd died yesterday. They would never see another sunrise.

Never experience another day. Or have another dream. She clutched two handfuls of blanket and fought back the emotion.

She'd just gotten her breathing back to normal when the cold crept into her bedroom like a bad omen.

"Okay," Kylie said, searching for patience that she seemed in short supply of lately. "How about let's have a talk? What can you tell me that I don't know? Give me something. You gotta give me something so I can help whoever it is that needs help."

"You can save her." The ghost's words filled the frigid air and her spirit appeared. Her long dark hair flowed over her shoulders. She didn't appear as thin or sick this time. And there was something about her, something that looked vaguely familiar. Kylie wondered if that meant anything.

"You can save her. You don't know you can, but you have the ability," the ghost said.

"How am I going to save her?" Kylie asked, hoping this might lead her to understand the identity of the person. She needed something, damn it—something to help her figure this out. "Who do I need to save?"

"She's scared. She needs you."

"Who?" Kylie gritted her teeth. "Just tell me who, and I promise I'll do everything I can to save her. Can you understand that I can't save anyone until I know . . ." The ghost vanished.

"Damn it!" Kylie dropped back on the bed. She breathed in and out and tried not to think about her frustration with the ghost. Tried not to think about the frustration with Lucas and the so-called dream. Tried not to think about the girls who'd lost their lives yesterday.

With so many limitations on what she could think about, she found one she could. Today was parents day.

That sent a whole new wave of frustration over her. Her mother wouldn't be here. Her dad . . . her stepdad . . . was off bumping uglies with a girl practically Kylie's own age, and Kylie would probably be the only one whose parents didn't show up.

Didn't that make her feel special?

"Daniel?" she said her father's name aloud. "Could you maybe drop in a minute?" *For moral support. Maybe answer a few questions about your parents?* "Please." No answer came. She counted to ten. Said a prayer. And waited another minute before she lost her patience.

She pounded her fists on the mattress. It felt like a juvenile and stupid thing to do, but in her mood, it also felt good. So good, she continued to do it for a few more minutes.

Socks let out a frightened cry and Kylie felt him take a flying leap off the bed. She might have felt sorry for him if she wasn't in such a piss-poor mood. And that's when she remembered what the whole mood swings problem could possibly mean. She, Kylie Galen, might be morphing into a wolf in two days. Could life get any more friggin', fraggin' messed up?

Chapter Nineteen

After Kylie had given her mattress a good beating, she got dressed, apologized to Socks for acting silly, and left her cabin in search of Holiday.

The mornings were getting hotter and muggier. Welcome to July in Texas, Kylie thought as she made her way to the office to ask questions. The frustration buzzing in Kylie's gut encouraged her to run, but as eager as she was to find answers about the dreams, she was equally uneager to ask the questions. Holiday, with her emotion meter, would probably read what kind of dreams Kylie was talking about.

However, her need for answers obviously weighed in more than her need to avoid embarrassment, because she kept walking.

The moment Kylie stepped onto the office cabin porch, she heard angry voices coming from inside. She stopped by the white rockers where she and Derek had eaten pizza last night and listened. Not to eavesdrop, but to make sure Holiday was okay.

"What the hell is wrong with my money?" a male voice boomed, and Kylie immediately recognized it as Burnett.

"Nothing is wrong with it," Holiday answered. *"I didn't say I wasn't going to accept it. I said give me a few weeks to decide."*

"A few weeks to try to find another investor, you mean. Tell me that isn't what you're doing."

"Fine," Holiday answered back. *"That's what I'm doing, but—"*

"Do you hate me and vampires so much that you'd risk having Shadows Falls shut down?"

Kylie flinched when she realized she had shifted from concern for Holiday to . . . eavesdropping. Not wanting to infringe on Holiday's privacy any more than she already had, Kylie stepped off the porch and moved a good fifteen feet out of hearing range.

"I'm not going to let Shadow Falls close down!" Holiday's voice still reached Kylie's ears. Wincing, Kylie turned and moved another twenty feet back.

"But you won't deny hating me, will you?" Burnett snapped.

"Hate is pretty powerful word," Holiday said.

Kylie looked at the office in the distance, frowned, and moved another ten feet back.

"Damn it," Burnett said, his voice, loud and clear, still reaching Kylie's ears. It was as if . . . as if he stood right next to her.

"Not good," Kylie muttered, realizing she shouldn't still be able to hear Burnett and Holiday. They were inside. She was outside. And a good—she measured her distance—a good fifty feet from the office.

Oh crappers! Things must be changing . . . again. Kylie grabbed her boobs to make sure they hadn't grown another cup size. Thankfully, they felt the same.

"I just want to help," Burnett continued, and so did Kylie. She continued to move back. Back. Back. Back far enough so the conversation wouldn't reach her ears.

"Then help me by trying to understand," Holiday countered.

"What the hell am I'm supposed to understand? That you'll do anything to get rid of me? That's why you're doing it, isn't it?"

"I don't . . ." Holiday's voice wavered.

"Because you're afraid if you take my money you'll have to put up with me. Are you so attracted to me that it's that difficult to be around me? Hell, let's just have sex and get it out of your system. Maybe then you can stand being with me!"

"You are so arrogant," Holiday snapped. *"Having sex with you is the last thing I want."*

"Ahh, finally. Now, I know you're lying," he said. *"You are attracted to me."*

"La, la, la, la." Kylie started singing and covered her ears. She didn't want to hear this. Nope. Not even a little bit. She turned away and started back to the trail that led to her cabin.

Seconds later, she heard a door slam shut. Felt a whish of air. She blinked and when her eyes opened Burnett stood there raking a hand through his hair. "That woman is the most difficult, the most stubborn redhead I've ever had the displeasure of meeting."

He shot off, leaving only a blurry streak in his wake.

"And you're falling in love with her," Kylie whispered. She didn't know how she knew it, but she did. And somehow she realized she'd sensed it back at the falls, too. The genuine emotion she'd heard in Burnett's voice and seen in his eyes had been what encouraged Kylie to tell him the truth about Holiday's past. Not that it nullified the fact that it wasn't her place to tell. Still . . .

Kylie looked back at the office and remembered her questions about her dream, remembered her newly discovered hearing abilities, too. Was this a werewolf talent? She recalled asking Lucas if he could hear her heart beating and he'd told her that weres' hearing wasn't really set to do that, but to hear enemies approaching. What kind of hearing ability had Kylie just experienced? Was it werewolf or vampire?

Turning her head to the side, she listened to see what else she could hear. Nothing. Sure, she heard the normal noises, but nothing seemed too loud or out of the ordinary. Della had said she could hear the animals at the wildlife park. Kylie couldn't hear that. So why had she been able to hear Holiday and Burnett's fight? What did this mean?

Staring up at the sky soaked with pale early morning colors, she tried to accept all the things about herself that were changing. Problem was, to completely understand, she needed to know what the hell she was! With a chest full of emotion, she started walking back to the office, praying Holiday might have the answers.

"Holiday, it's me." Kylie called out when she stepped inside the main office ten seconds later.

"In my office," Holiday answered.

When Kylie stopped at the door, Holiday swept her palms over her cheeks. She was crying. Or she had been.

Her eyes were still washed with wet sadness, and her face looked red. Angst and sorrow filled Kylie's chest. "Are you okay?"

"It's nothing." Holiday waved a hand in the air. "Burnett and I just had . . . words."

"I know," Kylie said, deciding the best approach was to come clean. "I heard."

A frown appeared on Holiday's lips and Kylie wasn't sure if it was because she thought Kylie had been intruding or if the expression stemmed from her lingering frustration with Burnett.

"I didn't mean to eavesdrop," Kylie said quickly. "When I stepped up on the porch and heard arguing, I wanted to see if you were okay, but then I moved off the porch, but I could still . . . hear. So I moved farther. And I could still hear." A little of her panic crept in Kylie's voice.

Holiday's frown deepened. "Were we that loud?"

"No. And that's what's so freaky. I shouldn't have been able to hear you. I kept getting farther back and I . . ."

Holiday's eyes widened. "And you could still hear us? Are you sure we weren't just loud?"

"Positive," Kylie said. "I was at the beginning of the trail."

"Wow," Holiday said.

"Yeah, wow!" Kylie dropped down into a chair. Her gaze shifted to the bills strewn out over the desk. Holiday's emotion and frustration still filled the room. Kylie looked at Holiday. "Are we really in financial trouble?"

Holiday eyed the stacks of bills. "A little bit. But it'll work out in the wash."

"Are you going to take Burnett's money?"

Holiday's eyes tightened in worry. "I will before I let Shadow Falls suffer. But this issue isn't important right now. You're important. Are you okay with . . . this?" She studied Kylie. "I mean your sensitive hearing."

"Do I have a choice?" Kylie batted back a bad mood. "If I say I'm not okay with it, will it just stop?"

Holiday shot her a sympathetic smile. "I can only guess how hard this must be on you. I mean, I grew up knowing certain things would happen and expecting there to be some surprises, but I'm sure for you, it's really a shock. These last few weeks have been a real eye-opener for you, haven't they?"

"Just a little bit," Kylie said sarcastically, and pushed her palms into her eye sockets. When she looked up, Holiday studied her. "I just want to know what I am. If I knew that, then . . . I think I could deal with it. I'm so tired of thinking I'm this, and thinking I'm that." She gripped her hands together. "I've been . . . so moody lately. A real bitch. I grew a cup size, half a shoe size, and added an inch to my height overnight, and now I'm hearing things I shouldn't be hearing. Do you think this means I'm werewolf?"

Holiday chewed on her bottom lip as if considering. "Sensitive hearing is one of the gifts of being werewolf, but it's also part of being vampire—though I'm told they each have different types of hearing."

Kylie hung on Holiday's every word, hoping she would tell her something Kylie didn't know. But some of it she already knew.

"Like I told you," Holiday continued, "when you mix human with supernaturals, or different species mix, sometimes the offspring are born with different abilities, but they always inherit the DNA and the main gifts from the dominant parent. And they fit into one pattern of a species. I'm sure your pattern will emerge soon. With all the changes happening to you so quickly, it's bound to become apparent any time."

Kylie struggled to understand. "But you also said if I was werewolf or vampire you thought I'd already have experienced some of the basic transitions."

"I did say that," Holiday admitted. "But I also said I've never seen a case like yours."

"I'm just a freak."

"No. You are unique."

"I don't want to be unique." Kylie sighed. "Do fairies ever have sensitive hearing?" She looked at Holiday.

A smile whispered across Holiday's lips. "Not commonly." She continued to study Kylie as if reading her disappointment. "You want to be fairy?"

"Yeah. I mean, if I have a choice, I'd go with that or a witch. Something that doesn't . . . you know . . . change me or my body temperature." Kylie thought of Della and how she'd feel if she knew Kylie felt this way.

"Am I terrible for wanting that?" Kylie asked. "I love Della and I don't want to hurt her feelings, but I just . . . I'd rather be witch or fairy. I mean, most of the gifts they get are not so complicated, not so hard to live with."

Holiday chuckled. "Are you forgetting about the ghosts? That's mainly seen in fairies or elves. And believe me, most supernaturals would die before wanting to deal with spirits."

"True." Kylie blinked. "I did sort of forget about that. And yeah, it's a royal pain in the ass. At first, it terrified me, but now that I've had some time to deal with it . . ." She paused and remembered the ghost's little visit this morning and the nightmare from the other morning. "Okay, it sometimes still terrifies me and frustrates me. But at least now I'm almost used to it."

Holiday leaned her elbows on her desk. "Whatever you are, whatever gifts you end up getting, you'll find that time will make those changes less scary as well. Whatever happens on Monday, I know—"

"Monday? Because it's a full moon. You think I'm werewolf now?"

Holiday held up her hand. "I don't know. I do know that you are an amazing young lady and no matter how things end up, you're going to be okay."

Kylie leaned her head back in the chair, stared at Holiday, and moaned. "I hate this. I really, really hate this." Then she remembered the reason she'd come here this morning. She sat up again and took a deep breath.

Then she nipped at her bottom lip, trying to remember how she'd planned to ask about it. Hadn't she come up with a less embarrassing way to approach the dreams? "One more thing . . ."

Holiday sat there, patiently waiting.

"Dreams . . . ?" Kylie only got out the one word.

"What about them?" Her expression grew concerned. "Has the ghost been giving you more dreams?"

"No."

"Night terrors?" Holiday asked.

"No." Oddly enough, Kylie hadn't had one of those in a long time. That is, if you didn't call the vision dreams with the ghost night terrors.

"Are you sleepwalking again?" Holiday asked.

Okay, it was going to get weirder if she didn't start talking. "I've been having strange dreams. I know I'm dreaming in the dream. And in the dream the people I'm dreaming about know it's a dream, too. I almost feel as if . . . as if he's breaking into my dreams."

"He?" Holiday asked.

"Lucas." Kylie felt her face flush. "Is it possible for someone, for Lucas, to actually come into my dreams? To actually . . . visit me? It feels so real. And I . . . if it is real, I want him to stop doing it. I mean, in both letters he mentioned dreams. And if it's real, he needs to stop it."

Holiday's eyes widened, but she didn't say anything.

"What is it?" Kylie asked.

"I . . ." Holiday stumbled as if trying to decide what to say.

"Don't lie to me, or keep something from me, even if you're just guessing. Just tell me what you think is the truth." She reached across the desk and placed her hand on top of Holiday's. "Please."

Holiday's brow creased in concern. "Okay, but you probably aren't going to like this."

Oh, great. That was not what she wanted to hear.

Chapter Twenty

"He's really doing it, isn't he? He's breaking into my dreams." Kylie's heart filled with resentment.

Holiday slowly shook her head. "I don't think . . . I mean. I'm only guessing, but it's probably not him."

"Oh, it's him. I saw him." She put her hand in front of her face about an inch away from her nose. "He was this close to me." *And closer.* She recalled how he'd kissed her.

"No, I didn't mean it wasn't him in the dream. I mean, it's not him coming into your dreams."

Kylie tried to wrap her head around what Holiday was saying to her.

Holiday continued. "What you're talking about is what we call dreamscaping, and I've never heard of a werewolf with this gift."

"Well, you've heard of one now." Kylie felt herself getting angrier, remembering the dream with them swimming. "And the thing he's doing . . . he shouldn't be doing."

Holiday held up her hand. "However, it is a very common gift with those of us who share the gift of ghost whispering."

Kylie sat there, staring at Holiday, not wanting to believe the camp leader. "Are you saying that . . . I'm . . . I'm doing this?"

Okay, Kylie had put her foot in her mouth before, but she'd never had it in there so deep she felt her toes wiggling against her tonsils.

Holiday leaned in, her expression almost one of apology. "Yeah, that's exactly what I'm saying, Kylie."

Kylie nearly choked on a big breath of air. "So the person I'm dreaming about, do they . . . I mean, can they remember the dreams?" Her heart stopped as she recalled the first dream, the one of them swimming, the one where she'd practically flashed the girls at him.

Okay, so she'd totally flashed the girls at him.

"Some do," Holiday said. "Some don't."

Thank you, Jeeessus! She was definitely going with the "some don't."

Holiday continued, "However, supernaturals would remember."

Okay, I take back that thank-you.

Kylie really wanted to die now. Then she recalled Lucas saying, *You're the one in the driver's seat.*

"So . . . whatever happens in these dreams . . . Am I, like, in charge of it? Am I responsible for what happens in the dream?"

From Holiday's expression, she must have just realized what kinds of things Kylie was eluding to. "Our emotions often guide our dreamscapes just as they do our dreams."

"Our?" Kylie asked. "Do you . . . do this, too?" Hey, misery loved company.

Holiday held out her right hand, her thumb and index finger pinched close together. "I'm slightly gifted in this area, but yes, I've experienced it some." She waited a few seconds before continuing. "Ultimately, you are the one in control—if you are in control of your emotions."

Well, that pretty much left Kylie in the dark. How many times had she admitted feeling no control when it came to boys and kissing, let alone . . .

Holiday continued, "The dreamscaper sort of sets the stage for the dream. You offer a script to the person you are dreaming about and, depending on the strength of your abilities, and the person you are dreaming about, he or she can either refuse the script or attempt to alter it."

Kylie's head started to throb. No doubt from stress. "But it feels so real."

"It is real, but it's not." Holiday reached over and took her hand. A lot of Kylie's stress began to fade. "Think of it as going to see a movie. If you go see a movie with someone, you both share the experience. You live through the emotions, but it didn't actually happen."

Holiday released Kylie's hand, and then leaned back in her chair. "I'm impressed by this new ability of yours, Kylie. Really. If someone is highly skilled in dreamscaping, it's considered a very powerful gift. You can learn a lot from it and even teach others through the use of dreamscapes. And very few of us are lucky to have it."

"Lucky me," Kylie said with zero enthusiasm. "I don't suppose it's one of those returnable gifts?" she asked, feeling overwhelmed.

"Not returnable. I'm afraid the time has already passed to refuse your gifts. When you accepted your role as a ghost whisperer, you pretty much accepted it all." Holiday smiled. "But believe me, in time you will probably feel more in control of it. Seriously, Kylie, this is a very special gift."

Kylie crossed her arms over her special extra-size breasts and tried to take it all in. Holiday's words replayed in her head. *I've never heard of a werewolf with this gift.* "So . . . if I am gifted with this, does it mean I'm not going to be morphing into a werewolf this Monday?"

Holiday didn't say anything, but Kylie saw that look on the camp leader's face again. The one that said she was either trying to figure out if she should say something, and if she did, how to say it in a way to soften the blow.

"Just spill it," Kylie told her. At this point, she might as well hear everything.

Holiday wrinkled her brows. "You are good at reading me," she said. "Really, too good," she said as if that could mean something, too.

But Kylie was too focused on the werewolf issue to care what other things Holiday was thinking. "What are you telling me now?"

Holiday shook her head. "I was going to talk to you about this later. But first, I want to say up-front that it's still surmising." She paused.

"Okay . . ." Kylie waved her hand to hurry Holiday along.

"After our talk yesterday where you mentioned the wolf . . . Well, Selynn and Burnett told me that . . . there's an old legend about real wolves being drawn to weres who are supposed to be in the hierarchy of the pack."

"So, I'm like an important werewolf?" Damn, she didn't even want to be a regular werewolf—she for sure didn't want to be an important one.

"I said it was just surmising on our part. Because frankly, Kylie, all the other stuff, the fact that you've never turned, that your other gifts aren't those common with weres, it doesn't line up. Especially when you realize that most all hierarchies in a were group are full-blooded. No human blood. So, you see, I don't want you to start thinking this really means anything. Because frankly, I'm not sure it does."

"Or it could mean a really big something," Kylie said, and wondered if she'd ever figure it all out. Or if she was destined to go through her life not knowing who or what she really was.

Before Kylie left Holiday's office, the camp leader asked Kylie to help her greet the visitors, deliver cold water and hot coffee, and keep peace in the dining hall during parents day. She got the feeling Holiday didn't need her help as much as she worried Kylie would go back to her cabin, fall into bed, and crawl into a deep state of insurmountable depression. Since Holiday could actually read Kylie's emotions, that was a big possibility.

Now, prepared to play the part of a greeter, the door to the dining hall opened and several parents came rushing in and looking around for their kids.

Kylie realized a problem with Holiday's no-depression plan. Seeing eager parents walk in and embrace their kids wasn't exactly cheering her up. Remembering the call with her mom and how upset her mom was about having to miss the visitation helped chase away some of her melancholy. But then her mind shot to her stepdad and the reasons he wasn't going to show up. Too busy bumping uglies with his skanky girlfriend!

Kylie turned around and went to the table to start pouring glasses of iced water.

Ten minutes later, the noise in the dining hall rose as more parents arrived. Kylie looked around and her thoughts went to her mom again. Not that her mind lingered on Mom too long. Nope. She had better things to knock around in the batting cage of her mind. Like the realization that Kylie had been barging into Lucas's dreams and handing him a dream script that read: let's get naked, go for a swim, and make out.

Not that he'd exactly been complaining about it.

Oh, and the best part, according to Holiday, was that Lucas would remember these dreams, too. So when he came back to the camp—if he came back—she'd have to face him.

Nope. She definitely didn't want to think about that.

She grabbed another tray and started lining up glasses to fill with water.

"It's Kylie, right?" A soft voice spoke beside her.

Kylie glanced up from the tray. The woman appeared to be in her early fifties. She wore her dark hair short in a classic older lady cut, and her soft green eyes studied Kylie with a smile.

"Yes, it's Kylie." She forced herself to smile back and she was glad she did. It took her only another second after noticing the eye color to recognize the woman. "Hi, Mrs. Lakes."

Kylie looked around to see if she could find Derek, thinking his mom was obviously looking for him. "I haven't seen him, but I'm sure—"

"Oh, he's right over there." She pointed in the opposite direction from where Kylie looked. Kylie was tempted to turn around and find him, but something kept her from it. She recognized the emotion right off the bat. Guilt. Guilt about her dreams.

Please don't break my heart. Derek's words echoed in her head and she realized it would break her heart if she knew Derek was skinny-dipping in his dreams with some other girl.

Staring back down at the plastic glasses lined up like dominos on the tray, she hoped Derek wasn't close enough to read her emotions.

The woman put a hand on Kylie's arm and leaned in. "I told him I wanted to snag a glass of water."

"Oh, here," Kylie reached down and picked up a glass.

"Thank you, dear," Mrs. Lakes said, but she winked. "Actually,

I just wanted to say hello and tell you . . ." She leaned in again. "You are practically all he ever talks about."

The guilt in Kylie's chest doubled, but this time she couldn't stop herself from looking over the woman's shoulder at Derek. He made a face at her as if he was worried about what his mom might be saying.

"I think my son is sweet on you," Mrs. Lakes said.

Kylie shifted her focus back to Mrs. Lakes but she didn't know how to answer. "I . . ."

The woman smiled. "I'm so glad he found nice friends here." She looked down at her glass. "Now, I'll leave and stop embarrassing you. Thank you for the water."

As Kylie watched the woman walk away, she muttered, "I'm sweet on him, too." And she was. What wasn't to like about Derek? She liked him for his easygoing ways, she liked the way he was nice to everyone and didn't think he was better than anyone else. She liked him in other ways, too.

The vision of him standing naked in the shower filled her mind. She was really, really sweet on Derek.

So, why hadn't she barged into *his* dreams? Why wasn't Derek the one whom her subconscious went to for fulfilling some kind of naughty fantasy? Feeling her face heat up just thinking about this in public, she looked back down at the glasses of ice water.

"Hi, Pumpkin."

Thoughts of fantasies immediately took flight. *Hi, Pumpkin. Hi, Pumpkin.* Realizing who stood right behind her, she froze. Even if she hadn't recognized the voice, only one person called her pumpkin.

She turned and lifted her eyes to her dad . . . stepdad. "What are you doing here?" she blurted out, and damn it if she didn't want to drop to the floor, curl up in a ball, and start to cry.

"What do you think I'm doing? I came to see my girl." He

smiled and looked at her the way he used to when she did something cute, or when she showed him a good report card.

Yup, she wanted to cry all right. The tightness in her throat made that crystal clear. "You didn't tell me you were coming." Was that enough of a reason to walk away? "You should have told me."

The loving father look on his face quickly changed to an unhappy father look. "I would have told you if you'd taken my calls," he said in a disgruntled voice. It was a voice he didn't use a lot, because her mom had always been the heavy.

"I've been busy," she answered.

His eyes tightened. "We both know I left you about seven voice-mails, two texts, and a couple of e-mails. And I don't think you've been so busy that you couldn't have returned just one of them. I even called your camp leader."

The tears she didn't want to come started filling her eyes just as anger started filling her chest. But she welcomed the anger, because it crowded out the hurt. She looked into his eyes. He had no right getting angry at her. No right to tell her what she'd done wrong when his wrongs had totally ruined her life. Ruined her mother's life, too.

"Do you really want to talk about right and wrong?" she asked.

To his credit, his expression went from annoyed to ashamed in zero flat. "I guess your mom's been talking to you. Damn it! She really shouldn't have told you about our problems."

"What? Are you kidding me? Are you seriously going to stand here and blame this on Mom?"

He blinked. "I just . . . I don't think she should have said any—"

"Stop." Kylie gripped her hands to keep them from trembling . . . or from punching him in the nose. Right then, she wasn't sure which was more likely to happen. "Mom didn't tell me anything." Tears spilled down her face. "Mom didn't have to tell me anything.

You told me. No, wait. I misspoke. You didn't *tell* me anything. You showed me."

"What are talking about, Kylie?" He leaned in and lowered his voice as if hinting she should do the same.

But she was too mad, too hurt to care who heard their argument. He'd left her. He'd left her and her mom for some bimbo. The vision of him and his slutty little intern making out in front of the downtown B&B filled her head.

"Well, first you hit on Holiday when you came to visit me," she said. "That was embarrassing enough, but then I saw you in town later that day. You hadn't come alone. And I saw you and your intern standing in the middle of downtown Fallen. You want to know why I remember it so well, Dad?"

He opened his mouth as if to say something, but nothing came out.

So she continued, "Because you had your *tongue* shoved down her throat while she had her *hand* jammed down your pants." Kylie blinked and felt more tears spilling over onto her cheeks. "Lovely," she seethed. "It was such a lovely sight, seeing your dad practically get a hand job in public."

Instantly, she realized that the entire room had gone deadly silent. *Damn!* Had she really screamed that out in the middle of the entire camp and their parents?

She glanced out at the crowd. Staring at her and her father. And from the look on everyone's face, yeah, she had.

Okay, now she really, *really* wished she'd taken her dad's hint about lowering her voice. Turning around, not looking at her dad, not looking at the crowd, she walked out of the dining room, hoping she could get outside before she started crying in earnest.

She would have run, but exhibiting her superfast supernatural running skills would have caused even more of a scene.

So she walked slowly toward the exit and pretended she didn't feel the tears gliding down her cheeks.

She pretended her heart wasn't breaking.

She pretended that she didn't know that about one hundred pairs of eyes were watching her go.

But pretending could only take her so far.

This . . . this was too damn real, and it hurt her too much.

Chapter Twenty-one

The knock sounded on her bedroom door not three minutes after she crawled into her bed and pulled the covers over her face and continued to cry. "Go away," Kylie called out.

The door opened. She yanked the cover from her face, expecting to see Holiday. But nope, Derek stood there with a heck of a lot concern for her shimmering in his eyes.

Seeing it only made her start crying harder. She cried because of her dad, and she cried because she felt bad about the dreams she'd had about Lucas. Derek rushed over to the bed and pulled her against him. If he read any of her emotions about guilt, he didn't say it. He just held her. And she loved him for doing that, too.

She buried her head on his shoulder and continued to sob in his arms. She didn't care that she was getting tears and snot all over his shirt. His arms felt so good wrapped around her and while he didn't say it, the way he held her said he didn't care about his shirt, either. Good thing, because when she got through crying, it was really going to be a mess.

"Hey?" Another voice came from the open door.

Kylie pulled away and saw Della and Miranda standing there.

"I could turn him into a toad if you want," Miranda said, waving her pinky. "Or maybe a skunk. I could use the practice."

Socks, who'd been sleeping at the foot of the bed, raised his head, meowed loudly as if in agreement, and then shot off to hide under the bed.

Della snarled. "I could pick him up and drag him up a tree and then drop him on his head a few times until he comes to his senses."

Kylie cried harder and then for some reason she started laughing. She wiped her eyes and looked at three of the most beautiful people in her world right now. "Did I really say that in front of all your parents?"

"Yup. I think my dad had a stroke," Della said, grinning from ear to ear. "It came just at the right time, too. He'd been grilling me about drugs again."

"My mom passed out cold," Derek teased.

Then they all started laughing. Kylie collapsed against Derek again. When she pulled back, she wiped her face and looked up.

And that's when it happened. That's when Kylie's whole world opened up in a way it never had opened up before.

She blinked. At first, she thought there was just something wrong with her eyes. But nope. There was no mistaking it. She could see inside their foreheads. She could see into them the way she'd seen into Daniel's head in the vision. She, Kylie Galen, could finally see supernatural patterns.

"I'm doing it, guys! I'm finally doing it!" She started bouncing up and down on the bed. "Holy crap, I'm really doing it."

"Doing what?" a familiar voice asked from the doorway.

He didn't call her pumpkin this time, but she recognized her dad's voice. He stood beside Holiday, who glanced at Kylie with a huge apology in her eyes. Obviously, her father had demanded she bring him here.

"Can I have a word with my daughter alone?" He stepped inside her bedroom.

"Only if that's what she wants," Derek said, sounding defensive and older.

Kylie rested her hand on Derek's arm. "It's okay."

Derek stood from the bed, but he didn't stop glaring at her dad for one minute. To her dad's credit, he just stood there and took Derek's angry stare as if he knew he deserved it. Della actually growled, and Miranda twitched her little finger at him.

Kylie hoped she remembered to give each of them a big hug later.

"Come on, guys," Holiday said, and motioned for them to leave. They all stepped out of the room. Then Holiday reached in, her concerned gaze meeting Kylie's eyes right before she closed the door.

Kylie pulled her knees up to her chest and wrapped her arms around her shins. Her heart must have dropped to her stomach because she could feel it pound in the pit of her gut. She stared at the top of her jeans-covered knees and not at him, because looking at him hurt too much.

Besides, if she looked at him, she might start crying again, and she didn't want to do that.

He sat down beside her on the twin bed. From the corner of her eye, she saw him fold his hands together in his lap. She heard him breathe. She heard herself breathe, too.

She closed her eyes.

Sooner or later, one of them had to talk. But for once Kylie decided not to be the bigger person here. Let him do all the work.

"I screwed up," he finally said. "I never dreamed I could screw up so badly."

Opening her eyes, she forced herself to look at him. The first thing she noticed was that he looked like her dad again. He wasn't wearing those tight jeans. His hair was combed like it should be and not spiked. He still had the highlights in his hair, but alone, they weren't so bad.

"I don't blame you for being furious at me, but I do love you, Pumpkin." He rested his hand on her knee and his touch sent tiny pinpricks of pain rushing to her heart. Tears filled her eyes.

She blinked, but didn't trust her voice to say anything just yet. And even if she did trust it, she wasn't sure what to say.

"I never wanted to hurt you," he continued. "I never dreamed that you'd be in town that day." He shook his head, closed his eyes, and when he opened them back up, she saw something she'd never seen before. Her dad was crying. Real live tears, too. The ache in her chest doubled.

"I don't know what got into me, Kylie. I lost my head. I turned forty and then your grandmother got sick and she died." He inhaled. "All I could think about was getting old. Then Amy—the girl at the office—she started flirting and it made me forget everything for a little while." His breath caught. "It made me forget that the most important people in the world to me are you and your mom."

Kylie knew it was her turn to talk, but she still didn't know what to say. She couldn't say she forgave him, because she didn't. Then a thought struck.

"Did your girlfriend break up with you?" Was that the only reason he was here now?

"Yeah." He looked embarrassed. Kylie was surprised he hadn't tried to deny it. "But that's not why . . . I'd already realized how badly I'd screwed up before we broke up."

She remembered her mom telling her how her dad had deserved someone to love him as much he had loved her all those years. That's when Kylie felt a small part of herself give in. She couldn't stay mad at him forever. She just couldn't. Maybe she *was* ready to forgive.

He reached over and ran his hand over her head, the way he'd done all her life. "I love you, Kylie. You're my daughter."

No, I'm not. She remembered that he'd made her mother promise not to tell her about her real father and her anger returned.

She batted at her cheeks to remove her tears. Then she offered him the only thing she could. "I'm hurt and I'm really mad at you right now. As soon as it stops hurting so much, I might be able to forgive you. But not now."

He nodded. She watched a tear slip from his lashes. He wiped it away. Then he leaned in and pressed a soft kiss on her forehead. "I love you, Pumpkin. Just remember that."

As Kylie watched him get up to leave, she realized that just because you couldn't forgive someone didn't mean you stopped loving them. She bounced off her bed and wrapped her arms around her daddy. He hugged her back. He hugged her so tight. And it felt so good, she wept on his shoulder. Big tears. Dinosaur tears he'd called them when she was young.

She knew that in just a second she was going to have to let go, and that she still wouldn't tell him he was forgiven, because he wasn't. But for just a few seconds she wanted to feel that her daddy loved her. And while she wasn't up to saying it yet, she hoped he understood she still loved him, too.

A few minutes after her dad left, Kylie was still stretched out on her bed when Holiday knocked on her door.

"You okay?" Holiday poked her head in the door.

"I'm working on it." Kylie had stopped crying. Something about her daddy's hug had eased some of the ache.

"You mind company, or would you like to be alone?"

"Company would be nice." She tried to see around Holiday. "Is everyone still out there?"

Holiday stepped into the room. "Just me. I made them go back and visit with their parents for a while."

"Good," Kylie said, and then recalled the scene she'd caused in the dining room. "I'm sorry about everything. I just lost it."

"Please." Holiday dropped onto the bed beside Kylie. "We needed a little excitement. I mean, if something crazy doesn't happen every fifteen minutes, it just doesn't feel right." She giggled.

Kylie grinned and then she remembered, excitement buzzing in her chest. "I did it. I . . ." She twitched her eyebrows and looked at Holiday. "I'm doing it now. I can see your pattern. You've got some horizontal lines and then . . . and then triangle shapes on the left."

"That's great!" Holiday hugged her. "I knew it would happen for you. Congratulations."

"But does this mean I'm opening up, too? That people can read me now and I won't come across like a snooty bitch anymore? And can . . . oh, man!" Hope started to build. "Can you see what I am? Look and tell me."

Holiday stared at Kylie's forehead. Her expression told Kylie the answer before Holiday spoke.

"Sorry. You're still a snooty bitch." Holiday grinned. "But it will happen any time now. Opening up takes more practice. Are you still doing your visualization exercises?"

"Not as often as I should," Kylie admitted. "But I'll start being better, I promise."

"Have you experienced any more of the sensitive hearing?"

"No. Why? Does that mean anything?" Did Holiday know

something she wasn't saying? Did she think Kylie was back to being a werewolf now?

"No. I was just curious." Holiday reached up and tucked a
strand of Kylie's hair behind her ear. "Are you really okay? You've
had a rough few days."

"Tell me about it." Kylie's thoughts went back to the girls
who were killed. She looked at Holiday. "What if . . . What do I do
if those girls from town—their ghosts, I mean—come to me to help
them?"

Holiday gripped Kylie's hand. "That won't happen."

"How can you be so sure? If their spirits are still here and—"

"It won't happen," Holiday said with more certainty this time.
And that's when Kylie understood. "They came to you?"

She nodded. "I'm helping them cross over." Then Holiday gave
Kylie a feel-better hug. Its soothing effects did wonders.

"Now, let's go back to you," Holiday said. "Are you okay?"

"Not completely okay," Kylie said, and then admitted a piece of
truth that Holiday deserved to hear. "You were right. I feel a little
better after seeing my dad. I didn't let him off the hook, either. I'm
still furious at him, but . . . I know he loves me. And I love him
and sooner or later, I'm sure we'll be back to something that is almost normal."

Holiday leaned back on Kylie's pillow. "Normal is overrated,
anyway."

"I'm beginning to wonder if I'd even recognize normal now."
Kylie raised her thumb to her mouth and nipped at the corner of her
nail.

"Well, if you did recognize it, you probably wouldn't like it anymore," Holiday teased.

"I just want to figure out this whole mystery with the ghost, if someone really needs me or doesn't need me. Do these ghosts have a clue what they put us through?"

"I don't think so." Holiday touched Kylie's arm again. "But I really believe everything is going to be okay."

For the next few minutes, only silence filled the room. Kylie looked down at Holiday resting on the bed. "Can I ask you something?"

Holiday cocked an eyebrow at her. "It doesn't involve Burnett, does it?"

"No," Kylie said. "But it's about boys."

"Okay, shoot." Holiday sat up.

"Is it . . . normal if you really like one guy to still be infatuated with another?"

"The whole Derek and Lucas issue, huh?"

"Yeah." Kylie frowned. "But I liked it better when I didn't name them."

"Okay, no names. Two guys." She held out one finger. "First, we can't always control our attractions to other people. Take my aunt Stella, for example. She's been married to my uncle for fifty years, but the woman is goo-goo over Tom Selleck. Owns every movie and TV show he ever made, she spends hours every week watching him strut across her fifty-two-inch flat screen." Holiday gave Kylie a soft look as if she realized the whole Tom Selleck talk wasn't working. "I think I've said this to you before. You are too young to worry about things like this."

"You're wrong," Kylie said. "Why wouldn't I worry? Just because a person is young doesn't mean that being loyal to someone isn't important. And it still hurts if someone isn't loyal to you. It hurt like hell when Trey hooked up with another girl. It hurt Perry when Miranda kissed another guy, and they weren't even going out yet. Okay, I admit that at this age, it might not bring about the

same disastrous outcome as . . . as my dad cheating on my mom,
but it still hurts. So I have to worry, because I don't want to hurt
anyone."

"Wow." Holiday frowned and sat back up. "When you put it like
that, you are so right, and I am so wrong. I'm sorry."

Kylie stared at the camp leader for a moment. "I appreciate your
admitting you were wrong," Kylie said. *Adults don't always do that.*

"Is it okay if I try again to offer some advice?" Holiday asked.
Kylie nodded.

Holiday paused in thought for a second. "Can I guess that this
is all about the dream you had with Lucas?"

"You could guess," Kylie said. "But I won't confirm or deny it."

Holiday smiled. "Kylie, you didn't intentionally seek out the
dream. You didn't even know you could do it. So you really aren't to
blame. And the fact that you find yourself attracted to more than
one guy is completely normal. I've got three guys right now that all I
have to do is think about and I start tingling all over."

Kylie gave Holiday's words serious thought. "But did you feel
that when you thought you really cared about someone else?"

"Yeah. Even when I was engaged, I still could appreciate a good-
looking guy." She paused. "Being committed or loyal to someone
doesn't mean you won't ever be attracted to someone else. It means
you won't physically act upon the attraction." She grinned. "My aunt
Stella, she used to tell my uncle he'd better pray Tom Selleck didn't
show up on her doorstep asking her to run away with him. But
the truth is, I know she'd turn Tom down flat. She loves my uncle
Harry."

Holiday made a face. "Don't ask me why, though—he's bald,
has a gut, and snores." She chuckled. "That said, I'll bet that woman
has had some really hot fantasies about Tom."

Kylie laughed and then they both reclined back on the bed.

The twin-size mattress offered just enough room for them both to stretch out with their shoulders pressed against each other. For a second they didn't talk. Kylie stared at the ceiling and finally posed another question. "Is Burnett one of the guys who makes you tingle all over?"

"No Burnett questions, remember?"

"Okay," Kylie said. "But if I was older, he'd make me tingle."

Holiday laughed. "You and half the world. Including Selynn." The humor in her voice faded.

Silence reigned again. Maybe it was thinking about Selynn and Burnett that brought on Kylie's next question. "Lucas told me in his letters that he was trying to get permission to come back to the camp. Do you know if he's coming back?"

Holiday hesitated. "He'll be here either tomorrow or Tuesday."

"Is Fredericka coming with him?"

"Yeah," Holiday said.

"Great," Kylie muttered. So if she did morph into a werewolf, Fredericka, who would also be in wolf form, would probably chase her down and rip her wolf ass to shreds.

Her day was just getting better and better.

Chapter Twenty-two

That afternoon, Kylie decided to skip the picnic dinner at the swimming hole. First, she didn't have a bathing suit that would fit; second, she really wanted to make a few calls to see if she could locate any Brightens who might know something about her real dad. And third, well, she hoped the ghost would drop by again. Something about the way she'd shown up when Kylie had been talking to her mom felt odd.

Kylie knew she couldn't start fixating on trying to guess who the ghost was talking about being in danger. But deep down, the fixating had bit. Could the ghost be talking about her mom? Could her mom be in danger?

Worried that it might be true, Kylie had called her mom. Twice. But her phone was turned off. Probably because she was in mid-flight. Kylie sat down at the computer desk, telling herself everything was fine, and pulled out the printed list of phone numbers. Her cell rang. Hoping it was her mom, she took the call without checking the caller ID.

"Mom?" Kylie asked.

"Not Mom. It's Sara."

"Oh, hi," Kylie said, trying to figure out which one of the

multitude of emotions about Sara she should let control the conversation. There was the hurt she felt that Sara—whom she'd considered her best friend for years—hadn't returned any of her calls in almost a month. There was the concern she felt knowing that Sara was . . . going through something. And then there was the melancholy she felt because she knew her friendship with Sara would never be the same again.

When the silence seemed awkward, Kylie jumped in. "My mom said she saw you in the grocery store the other day."

"Yeah, she did. She's looking good, too. I like her new look and hairstyle. She said you talked her into getting a makeover."

"Did she do it?" Kylie asked. "She hasn't told me she did it."

"Oh, I hope I didn't ruin her surprise."

"Nah, I appreciate the warning. Does she look good? Or dumb?"

"Good. She looks . . . younger, I guess. You know, kind of like she might be about to start dating."

"Dating?" Kylie knew this was a possibility, she'd even suggested it, but for some reason now the idea hit her stomach like a bad piece of chicken. "Did she *say* that or are you just guessing?"

"No, she didn't say it. She just looked, you know, like a woman who wanted to be noticed by a man. Tighter jeans and a fitted top that showed off her girls. I almost didn't recognize her."

Was Sara saying her mom was dressing like a ho? That wasn't the makeover Kylie had suggested. Realizing the conversation had gone quiet again, Kylie started talking to fill the silence. "Mom said you looked . . ." Kylie had almost lied and said good, but at the last minute decided not to do it. ". . . thinner. Are you on some new diet again?"

Sara was the first to try every new diet endorsed by Hollywood: low carbs, no carbs, all fruit on Tuesday, all brown rice on Wednesday, the crazier the better.

Not that she ever stayed on any of them.

"Not really," Sara said. "I think it's the birth control pills. I heard they'd cause me to gain weight, but they seem to be doing the opposite with me."

Sara was on the pill? It struck Kylie again how much things had changed between them. The old Sara would have certainly told Kylie something as big as getting on the pill.

But then, Kylie hadn't exactly been in a sharing mood with Sara lately, either. Of course, trying to explain to a normal about being a still unidentified supernatural was a little—well, a lot—more difficult than discussing birth control pills.

"Did your mom agree to you taking them?" Kylie asked, knowing Sara's mom was a bit of a religious fanatic and constantly preached against premarital sex.

"Are you kidding? She'd die if she found out. I went to the clinic and I faked her signature."

Kylie had heard about some other girls doing the same thing to get around the Texas law that required a parent's signature before dispensing the pills.

Another long pause followed.

"So, who are you dating?" Kylie asked.

"A couple of different guys." Sara sounded purposely vague. Kylie couldn't help but wonder if Sara was having sex with the couple of different guys, too. Once upon a time, she might have asked.

"So," Sara said. "You're still coming home in a couple of weeks, aren't you? Camp from hell is almost over? No more being a boner, huh?"

Annoyance chomped down on Kylie's stomach. Obviously, Trey had told Sara about the whole boner reference, because Kylie couldn't remember mentioning it.

"Actually, I'm only coming home for the weekend. And I really like it here." Kylie didn't tell her about the whole boarding school possibility just because she didn't want to go into it. But she sent up a silent prayer that her mom agreed to it. The thought of going back to her old school and not having the old Sara at her side was just too much.

"Really, you like it? You hated it at first. Camp Freaky, isn't that what you called it?" Sara sounded shocked.

That was before I actually realized I was a freak, too. Well, not a freak, but not all human, either. "I guess things change." Kylie meant her relationship with her one-time best friend, as well as her feeling about the camp.

"Yeah, I guess so." Another pause. "Well, text me when you get in town and hopefully we can meet up."

She wasn't even going to get a definite "Yes, I'll see you" from Sara. That hurt like a paper cut to the lip. Pushing away the feeling, she answered, "Yeah, I'll do that." But she wasn't so sure she would. Seeing Sara might just be too weird to deal with right now.

"Okay, my mom is calling me to help with the dishes," Sara said.

Kylie couldn't hear anyone calling in the background. Not that she wasn't eager to end the call as well. This had been hard. Really hard.

"Okay, bye," Kylie said. *Have a good life. Nice knowing you.*

As soon as Kylie hung up, the phone rang again. This time, she looked at the caller's phone number.

Derek?

He didn't normally call her. "What's up?" she asked with a touch of worry.

A ghostly cold invaded the room as she waited for Derek to speak. A wave of dizziness had Kylie grabbing the computer desk.

She had experienced this enough to know that it meant a vision was about to occur.

Or was occurring, she corrected when she saw the casket sitting where the kitchen table had been seconds earlier. The woman in the casket was the ghost. A few people moved around the casket with tears in their eyes.

"Kylie?" Derek's voice came on the line.

"Yeah." She stared at the casket and the people and wondered what she was supposed to learn from this vision. That was why they happened, right? The ghost was trying to tell Kylie something. But what?

"I'm scared, Mama." From the back, Kylie saw the little girl reach up and take her mom's hand.

"It's just Grandma." The couple walked up to the casket.

"Kylie, are you there?" Derek's voice sounded upset . . . or something.

She recalled her concern about Derek calling her. It was so out of character for him.

"Yeah. I'm here. Is everything okay?" Kylie asked, and her concentration on Derek made the vision fade like an old photograph. It lost its color and went into black and white mode as if dating the scene as something that happened a long time ago. Then the vision grew weaker, almost transparent. "Don't go," she said.

"Go where?" Derek asked.

"Not you," she said, but it was too late, only a vague outline remained of the scene. The woman holding the little girl's hand turned around. Kylie got only glimpse of her face, but something about her looked familiar.

Shaking her head, and remembering Derek was still on the phone, she asked, "Is everything okay?"

"No," he said. "It's not okay."

"What's wrong?" she asked.

"You're not here."

She rolled her eyes. "I thought you were serious."

"I am. I've been looking forward to this afternoon all day, thinking you'd be here."

"But I wanted—"

"Please," he said. "I . . ." His voice lowered. "I haven't ever seen you in a bathing suit."

"And you still wouldn't. I've grown out of my bikini top, remember?"

"Don't remind me," he said with a tease in his voice.

"You're terrible," she reprimanded, but she wasn't all serious. She liked the fact that he was attracted to her.

"Just put on a pair of shorts and a T-shirt and come down."

Kylie bit down on her lip. She looked at the computer screen, which displayed the list of the Dallas Brightens she hadn't called yet. Della and Miranda had been helping, but so far nothing.

"Please," Derek said.

His plea echoed in his voice and she felt herself giving in. On top of just wanting to make Derek happy, she remembered that she could read everyone's brain patterns and realized seeing everyone all together would be fun. She could compare one brain pattern to another.

"You had a rough day," Derek said. "You deserve some fun in the sun."

I've had a rough few months. "I'll be there in a few minutes."

"Really?" he asked, almost shocked that she'd given in. Didn't he know how much he meant to her?

"Really," she said, and smiled. The smile warmed Kylie inside and out. The memory of how he'd stood up for her even to her dad

played in her mind. And that's when she knew that the next time
Derek asked her to go out with him, she'd say yes.

It took her fifteen minutes to decide which pair of shorts and
T-shirt to wear. She wanted to look good. Extra good. Maybe she
and Derek could sneak off together and . . . and hopefully he would
ask her to go out with him. Heck, maybe she might even ask him.

When she realized how much time had passed, she tore out the
door. The shortest route to the swimming hole was through the
woods, so she took it. The speed with which she moved shocked
even her. Her foot-eye coordination of where to step and how to
miss the trees flabbergasted her.

While speed and agility had never been something she longed
for, she found herself feeling a sense of pride at her new talents. If
only she knew from what species these new talents stemmed.

She was over halfway to the swimming hole when she felt it.
Felt that sensation of being followed. The hair on the back of her
neck stood up. And wouldn't you know that's when she recalled
Burnett's warning about staying on the paths and out of the woods.

Listening, hoping to hear something other than the sound of
feet pounding against the earth, she felt better when the normal
sounds of the woods filled her ears. Whatever presence loomed close
by wasn't so ominous that birds and insects stopped their songs.

Not that she should stake her life on the wisdom of the birds
and insects. The feeling hit stronger . . . someone was here. What
should she do?

Logic said for her to keep going; turning back would only put
her farther away from the help of the others if trouble struck. Her
mind went to the girls who'd been killed in town and amazingly,
she found herself running even faster.

The clearing in the woods appeared in less than a minute. The bright sun hit her eyes and she could hear the other campers laughing and splashing in the water. When nothing attacked her, when no evil presence appeared wearing a bloody shirt and tried to yank her back into the woods, she wondered if this feeling of being watched wasn't all in her head. Could she be that paranoid?

She stopped in the clearing beside a tree and tried to catch her breath, feeling completely winded from her run. She almost had her breathing back to normal when she saw Derek coming toward her. He wore only a pair of swim trunks. His chest was bare and wet like the other night in the shower. The trunks were regular boy trunks, a little loose on him, even hung a little low on the waist, but they were wet so they molded against his form. Since she knew what he looked like without them, she found herself feeling breathless again.

"Hey," he said, and when his gaze fell to her mouth, she could tell he wanted to kiss her. He looked around and saw that they had an audience. So instead of kissing, he reached out and took her hand. "Come on, the water feels great."

It did feel great. And for the next hour, Kylie played water volleyball, splashed around, studied everyone's brain pattern, and completely forgot about the problems pressing on her shoulders. The only downside was watching Perry watch Miranda. She looked really good in her bathing suit and Kylie wasn't the only one who noticed, either. The guys were all stealing glances, even Derek, and then Perry would cut them glances, and not the friendly kind of glances either. His eyes would turn jet black, reminding Kylie of some kind of serpent.

Nevertheless, between the water and the laughter, Kylie hadn't had so much fun in . . . well, forever.

Then all the fun came to a jarring halt when she spotted Holiday running out of the woods in a panic and heading straight for the lake.

Her expression grew tighter with each hurried step. What was wrong? Holiday's gaze found Kylie's and suddenly she knew that whatever was wrong involved her.

Kylie started moving out of the water, but her toes sank into the mud at the lake's bottom the closer she got to shore. All the stresses in her life lined up like dominos in her mind, and she wondered which one this new problem involved.

Selynn appeared behind Holiday and her gaze shot to Kylie, as well. This wasn't going to be good.

Kylie met Holiday at the edge of the water and purposely ignored Selynn. "What's wrong?"

"We have a problem." Holiday's gaze shot back to the water and she waved someone else in. Kylie turned and saw Derek swimming in to join them.

"What is it?" Kylie asked again, still ignoring Selynn, who had moved in.

"You're coming with us," the werewolf spouted out. Her hand clamped down on Kylie's wrist. "Now."

Chapter Twenty-three

Kylie frowned and shook Selynn loose.

"I'm not going anywhere until you tell me what's going on." Kylie's gaze went back to Holiday who watched Derek step up on-shore. "Will somebody please tell me what is wrong?"

Holiday glanced back. The line of stress furrowing the camp leader's brow told Kylie this was serious. "It's your mom."

"My mom?" Kylie took a deep breath. Bits and pieces of her mom's conversation filled Kylie's mind. Then the ghost's warning echoed like a bad song in her head. *"You have to stop it. You have to stop it or someone you love will die."*

Oh, God, no.

"What's wrong with my mom?" The words barely spilled from her lips. She remembered her mom was flying home sometime today. Kylie's heart clutched as she envisioned a plane crash. Oh God, was her mom . . . ?

"She must have come to see you." Holiday said. "Late. For some reason, the new security alarm on the gate didn't work. And she got in without anyone knowing."

"She's here?" More than Kylie wanted air, she wanted to know her mom was alive and well. That her plane hadn't crashed. That some freak hadn't kidnapped her and was torturing her the way the dreams seemed to imply.

"Yes. She's here," Selynn said in her haughty tone. "Against school policy. Visiting hours were over hours ago."

Kylie's gaze went to Selynn. What was the she-wolf saying? Was her mom okay or not? Kylie looked back at Holiday.

"What happened?" Kylie repeated her question. "Is she okay?"

"She's . . . upset." Holiday's frown deepened. "She was trying to find your cabin and got turned around. She . . . she saw some things she shouldn't have."

"What?" Kylie remembered how stunned she'd been when she first saw Perry change into a unicorn. "What did she see?"

"She needs to be erased," Selynn snapped. "And quickly."

Erased? "What . . . is that supposed to mean?"

The she-wolf grabbed Kylie by the arm and started pulling her toward the woods.

Kylie put on the brakes.

"What does erase mean?" she asked again, not anywhere close to understanding, but miles from liking how it all sounded. She yanked her arm away from Selynn and then took a step closer, so close Kylie could count the woman's eyelashes.

"You better not lay a finger on my mother!" Kylie growled, and the sound of her voice seemed unnatural to her own ears. It was deeper. Coarser.

"Kylie, listen to me." Holiday's hand came down on Kylie's back, sending a surge of calm into her tense shoulders. Kylie might have listened, might have even accepted the calm emotion from Holiday if Selynn hadn't been there.

"We don't have time for this," Selynn snapped. She grabbed

Kylie by both arms, her fingers digging into Kylie's biceps hard enough to bruise. When Kylie tried to pull away again, Selynn tightened her hold.

"She's human," Selynn said. "She has to be dealt with. Now."

"Dealt with?" Fury, anger, and fear for her mother's safety threatened to overwhelm Kylie. "Damn you, where's my mother?" Kylie's voice sounded deeper than before.

"Stop it, Selynn!" Holiday said. "You're upsetting her. She doesn't understand what is going on."

"Yeah, stop it!" Derek's voice rang out.

Kylie felt Holiday's touch come against her shoulder again. The fairy attempted to fill Kylie with a peace-inducing emotion, to curb her fury, but Kylie somehow rejected the flow from moving inside her.

"Your mom is going to be okay," Holiday said, her voice seeming to echo from some other place. "She's at Helen's cabin right now. She—"

Once Kylie heard her mom's location, she again tried to pull away from Selynn's grip. But the she-wolf tightened her hold, her fingernails cutting into Kylie arms. Kylie recognized the pain, but it felt as if it was happening to someone else.

"Let go!" Kylie hissed in Selynn's face.

When the woman didn't release her. Kylie, acting on some instinct she didn't even recognize, grabbed the woman by her shirt and slung her out of the way.

Several gasps echoed around her. One might have even been from Kylie when she saw Selynn flying like a rag doll through the air before she landed in the water with a loud splash. The werewolf came up covered in mud and spitting mad. She roared and started swimming back to shore, and once on dry land, she locked gazes with Kylie, slung her head back, growled, and charged.

Holiday jumped in front of Kylie and held out her hand. "One step closer and I will summon the wrath of the death angels. And if you think I'm joking about that, you don't know me very well."

But Selynn didn't stop. She kept coming.

Then Derek and Della tackled her, sending the she-wolf tumbling to the ground with a grunt.

Kylie didn't stick around to hear or see what happened next. She took off through the woods, her blood pumping through her veins as she ran with everything she had to reach her mother.

As she moved with inhuman speed, she felt a blast of air pass by her and she spotted a blur of movement. The sudden silence of the woods told her it was vampire. Not that she cared.

She only wanted to reach her mother before anyone touched her. If anyone hurt one hair on her head . . .

Kylie heard her mother's screams right before she exited the woods near the path that led to Helen's cabin. Panic clawed at Kylie's chest like a wild animal seeking escape. She cut through the last of the trees, flew over the path, and arrived at Helen's porch.

Burnett, with a windblown Holiday at his side, stood there blocking the door. And Kylie knew Burnett had brought Holiday here.

"Let me out of here!" Her mom's scream reached Kylie's ears.

The rich berry scent that she now knew as blood filled her nose. She stared at Burnett. "Move!"

"Kylie." Holiday jumped in front of Burnett. "Listen to me, okay? Your mom is fine. She's very upset and we're going to have to calm her down."

"She's hurt." Kylie struggled to breathe and fought the desire to break through Burnett and the door to get to her mom.

"She's not hurt," Burnett insisted.

"I smell blood," Kylie seethed.

"That's not her blood," Burnett answered, his eyes turning a burnt orange color.

"I swear," Holiday said, and attempted to touch Kylie, but Kylie jumped back. Holiday lowered her hand. "Your mom isn't hurt, Kylie. I promise you. Please calm down. We're going to fix this. But we need your help."

"Trust them, Kylie," a voice said at the same time a familiar coldness invaded her breathing room.

Kylie turned to see Daniel standing next to her. "Trust them," he repeated.

Tears filled Kylie's eyes as Daniel wrapped her in his cold embrace. "It's okay." His icy breath came at her ear, as comforting warmth filled her chest.

An awesome sense of peacefulness flowed though her body. The same kind of peacefulness she'd felt at the falls. The kind that said things weren't as bad as she thought. The kind that said she should have faith.

She raised her head to look at Daniel, but he was gone. Feeling overwhelmed, her legs wobbled and she dropped to her knees on the porch.

Holiday crouched beside her. "She's going to be fine, Kylie. I promise."

Kylie looked at Holiday. "What . . . what did my mom see? Perry . . . ?"

"No." Holiday brushed Kylie's hair from her face. "I had given permission for Helen to donate a pint of blood to Jonathon. He was bleeding her, and against my rule he was . . ." Holiday paused and then firmly added, "He was drinking from the tube when your mom stepped in. I'm sure it looked really bad to her. She panicked."

Kylie dropped her face into her hands. "Oh, God." How the hell was she going to explain this to her mom?

"Jonathon was startled," Holiday continued. "He grabbed her and pushed her into Helen's bathroom, shoved the dresser against the door, and sent Helen after me. I got Burnett here as quickly as I could."

"I didn't hurt her," Jonathon said, stepping up on the porch. "I probably should have handled it differently, but I swear, I didn't hurt her. I'm sorry this happened."

Kylie looked at Jonathon. His shirt had stains of blood, Helen's blood, she told herself, not her mom's blood. Following him up the steps was Derek.

"Here's what we have to do," Burnett said. "It's called erasing."

"No," Kylie said, instantly being reminded of her emotions and her fight with Selynn.

"It's not a bad thing," Holiday said. "Erasing means that the memory is removed from her mind. It won't hurt her. But the calmer she is, the easier it is and the more successful it will be. And right now she's not calm. I think if you talk to her, you can calm her down."

"Talk to her? She saw someone drinking blood from an IV tube. What am I supposed to tell her that will calm her down?" Kylie asked. "Oh, don't worry, Mom, they're just vampires?"

Holiday looked Kylie right in the eyes. "She's worried about you now more than she's scared," Holiday assured her. "Just let her know you're fine and then Derek will come in—"

"Derek?" Kylie swung back to look at Derek. "Why Derek?" Something that looked like guilt clouded his eyes.

"We've recently discovered that Derek has the gift of erasing," Holiday said.

Derek nodded and for a fraction of second, Kylie wondered why Derek hadn't told her about his new gift. She thought they shared everything. Then her thoughts went back to her mom. "But if he's new at this, then . . . what if he messes up?"

"He won't mess up," Burnett said. "He's practiced on me numerous times."

Kylie looked back at Derek. She didn't know what all went into erasing someone's memory, but the idea scared her. "Don't you have someone with more experience?" Much to Derek's credit, he didn't appear offended by her request.

"He's on another case right now," Burnett said. "And the sooner we take care of this, the better it is. If we wait too long, he might have to remove more data from her mind. It could require he remove hours before what happened. Obviously, the less memory time that we have to remove the better."

"Is it at all dangerous?" Kylie looked at Holiday for the answer.

Holiday shook her head. "When it's done soon enough, the biggest side effect is a headache and confusion at the loss of time."

Kylie looked back at Derek. "Promise me you won't mess this up."

"I won't," he said. But was that doubt in his voice?

"What do you have to do?" Kylie asked.

"Just touch her," he answered.

Kylie nodded. She remembered Daniel's assurance that she should trust them, and she stood up. "Okay. I guess." Then she heard her mom start screaming again. She looked at Burnett. "Nothing better go wrong."

"Mom," Kylie called to her mom five minutes later from behind the large dresser that Jonathon had moved in front of the door.

"Kylie?" her mom screamed. "Oh, baby, are you okay? Tell me you're not hurt. Tell me these crazy people—"

"I'm fine. I'm going to get you out, okay?"

"Hurry, baby," her mom said. The rawness in her mother's voice told Kylie her mom had been screaming and crying for way too long. "We've got to get out of here. There are some very bad people here."

"It's okay, Mom," Kylie said.

"Hurry, baby. Hurry before they come back."

Burnett motioned that he planned to move the dresser and then leave. Derek nodded. Then Burnett, with one hand, pushed the heavy piece of furniture out the way and, in a flash, was gone.

Her mom yanked open the door and flew out, wrapping her arms protectively around Kylie. "We gotta get out of here!" She spotted Derek and pushed Kylie behind her. "Stay away," her mom yelled.

Derek looked at Kylie as if he was unsure how to proceed.

"It's okay, Mom." Kylie's heart broke when she saw her mom's tear-streaked face. "This is Derek. He's a nice guy."

"I don't trust him," her mom said. "We can't trust anyone here. I just want us to leave. Now." Clutching Kylie's arm, she started moving toward the door, keeping herself between Derek and Kylie as if in protection.

Unsure what to do, Kylie stopped moving. She couldn't let her mom walk outside. If her mom was freaking out with just Derek, she would surely lose it if she saw Jonathon and Burnett.

"Mom, Derek is a good guy. He's going to help us leave," she lied. "Aren't you, Derek?" Kylie looked at him.

"Yes . . . Mrs. Galen. I'm going to help you and Kylie get away."

Her mom looked at Derek and back at Kylie. Panic shone in her eyes, but she didn't jump back when Derek took a step closer.

"Let me get the door," Derek said. He moved in and when he did, he reached out and touched her mom's arm.

Kylie hadn't known what to expect when a person's memory was erased, but when her mom's eyes rolled back in her head and she collapsed in a dead heap on the floor, Kylie screamed.

Shaking, and still in mid-scream, she dropped down beside her mom to make sure she was still breathing.

"It's okay." Derek dropped beside Kylie and touched Kylie's elbow. "She's just unconscious. I promise, Kylie," he said, as if reading her fear.

Burnett appeared and scooped her mom up in his arms. "I'm putting her in her car. You come with me," he said to Kylie. "We'll need you there when she wakes up."

His gaze held Kylie's for a second. "It's all going to be okay," he told her. "Follow me. It's almost over now."

Burnett disappeared. Kylie took off, too. She wasn't anywhere near as fast as he was, but with luck, and considering he had her mother in his arms, he could bet she wouldn't be far behind him.

"Mom, you okay?" Kylie tapped on her mom's car window only five minutes later.

When her mother didn't instantly wake up, it took everything Kylie had not to yank open the door to see if she needed CPR. But Burnett's list of don'ts still echoed in her head.

- Don't show panic, because she might pick up on it and it will make her even more nervous.
- Don't try to explain too much; let her come up with her own conclusions of what happened.
- Don't start crying for no reason.

And as he'd said that one, he'd pointed to Kylie's tears.

It was the "crying for no reason" part of number three that Kylie would have argued about if she hadn't been so damn worried about her mom.

Kylie tapped again on the window. "Mom?" She fought to keep her voice calm.

The way Kylie saw it, she deserved to go on a crying jag that lasted for a good two weeks. The emotional trauma she'd endured this last half hour would go down as one of the top worst half hours of her life. Even the fight at the wildlife preserve hadn't kicked her in the gut so hard.

She glanced down at her arms, expecting to see bruises and nail marks from where Selynn had grabbed her. Oddly enough, her skin was smooth and unmarked. Weird. Had she just acquired a new quick healing gift, too?

Her mom's eyes fluttered open and Kylie refocused on the situation before her. Her mom sat up and looked around, obviously startled. Kylie's first thought was that the erasure hadn't worked.

Then her mom turned her head and her confused eyes met Kylie's.

Kylie plastered a smile on her lips, hoping to appear as if everything in the world was just peachy. "When did you get here, Mom?"

Her mom's brow creased and she raised her wrist to see her watch and then opened the door. She turned and put her feet on the pavement, but didn't climb out of the car. "I . . ." She blinked. "I rushed over here from the airport." She ran a hand through her dark hair, which now had highlights of red running through it.

"You must have fallen asleep after you got here." Kylie bit her lip, realizing she'd broken one of Burnett's rules.

"Yeah." Her mom pressed a hand to her temple, a sure sign of the headache Holiday had said might come. "I was up all night at the airport hoping to get a flight on standby."

"You must be really tired," Kylie offered.

"Yeah. Gosh." She looked back at her watch and then stood from the car seat. "I hardly even remember arriving here. I must have parked and zonked out. Which is a good lesson for both of us. Don't drive while under the influence of exhaustion." Her mom reached over and gave Kylie a hug. "It feels so good to see you."

Damn it, if Kylie didn't feel herself breaking another rule. Tears filled her eyes and she hugged her mom really hard. Ahh, but her tears weren't just because of the last thirty minutes. No, they were because of Kylie's last sixteen years and the rarity of hugs from her mom. And because it brought to mind the hug she'd given her dad . . . stepdad, before he'd left a few hours ago.

When her mom pulled back, she looked at Kylie. "Are you okay?"

"Yeah." Kylie batted at her tears. "It's just . . . you don't hug me a whole lot."

"Something I guess we need to work on, huh?" her mom said, and touched her temple again.

"Yeah, we need to work on that," Kylie said. "But we're off to a good start." And they were. Kylie could feel it.

Her mom looked at her watch again. "I must have slept for an hour."

"You probably needed it," Kylie said, and started walking back through the gates.

"Yeah. I was going to call and let your camp leader know I was going to be here a little late. I remember what a big deal they made over visiting hours, but wouldn't you know it that my battery died in my phone. It's completely dead."

"Yeah. Luckily I walked by and saw your car and told Holiday you were here. But they are very strict about visiting hours." *Please God, don't let me have to go through this again.*

"Which I think is silly," her mom said. "It's like they are trying to hide something."

"Nope." Kylie lied through her teeth and almost felt bad doing it. "Not trying to hide anything." Except things like: people drinking blood, changing into any kind of creature imaginable like super-size bears or unicorns or wolves. Or girls who accidentally turn kittens into skunks. In other words, the usual stuff that happened at Shadow Falls.

"But they're still strict," Kylie said. "They say it's for our safety. Besides, you know, like you used to tell me. Rules are rules."

"I know and I'll try to follow the rules from now on."

Thank you, Jeezus! "Would you like to go sit in the dining hall?" Kylie asked.

"Or your cabin," her mom said.

"Sure." And then Kylie remembered Socks—her little skunk. "Uhh, I forgot that . . . Della and Miranda invited a few girls over. The dining hall might work better."

"That's fine," her mom said. "Maybe I could grab something to drink so I could swallow a couple of aspirins. My head is pounding like I'm going to have an aneurysm."

An icy coldness suddenly settled around Kylie again. For a moment, she thought the ghost was back.

She looked at her mom. "Don't say that."

"Don't say what?" she asked.

"The aneurysm crap." It had been one of the many unsaid possibilities Kylie had considered happening with someone messing with your mind, and erasing your memories, and it still freaked her out.

Her mom smiled. "I'm just being a drama queen. I'm fine."

"Good," Kylie said. And when she looked at her mom, she recalled how frightened she'd been that she might never see her again. Another wash of emotion filled her chest. Kylie almost reached out to steal another hug. She didn't. Not just because it might make her mom suspicious, but because where her mom was concerned, she'd probably handed out her quota of hugs for the month.

Amazingly, thirty minutes later, they hadn't run out of things to talk about. Of course, they'd talked a good fifteen minutes about her mom's new makeover. All of which Kylie admitted liking. Sure, Kylie was still a little hesitant about the thought of her mom dating, but Kylie decided to cross that bridge when she came to it.

Then her mom noticed Kylie's "growth spurt."

"Tell me that's one of those Wonderbras making you look so big."

" 'Fraid not," Kylie said. "I'm a growing girl."

That conversation led to her mom asking about Kylie's shopping trip. But Kylie didn't want to talk about shopping, or anything that occurred during her recent trip downtown. So she told her mom that her dad had come to visit. They talked a good five minutes about him. Kylie hadn't given any details about the embarrassing scene she'd caused. She'd never even told her mom that she'd seen her dad in town.

She also opted out of telling her mom that her dad had broken up with his little girlfriend. For some reason, she didn't want to remind her mom about that.

"I'm glad you two talked," her mom said. "No matter what mistakes he's made recently, he is a good father."

"Yeah," Kylie agreed.

Then Kylie spent another five minutes telling her how much

she loved camp and her interest in the cake decorating class, all prep work for getting a commitment from her mom about signing her up for the boarding school in the fall. Not that she planned to ask about it today. Face it, whether her mom remembered it or not, she'd had a pretty lousy day.

"Seriously, you really enjoy decorating cakes?" her mom asked. "I do, too. Do you remember that I took that class when you were younger and made you the Cinderella cake?"

"Yeah," Kylie said. "I loved it." Another big freaking lie. She'd been fourteen and embarrassed out of her mind when her mom had served a fairy-tale cake at her soccer meet, but hey, what did one more little white lie count compared to the others she'd told today?

Lies aside, this whole new direction in their relationship was really going well. So well, Kylie decided to chance asking for more info about her real dad.

Picking up her soda, Kylie twirled the can in her hand. "Mom, can you tell me a bit more about Daniel?"

Her mom's eyes widened. "Sure. I guess. But I think I pretty much covered everything the last time you asked."

"You hardly told me anything. Like . . . where were his parents from?"

She smiled. "I remember him telling me that they were originally from Ireland."

"They're Irish?" Kylie asked, not sure it would help, but not sure it wouldn't. "When did they come to America?"

"I don't know."

"Was Daniel born in the States?"

"I'm guessing he was. He didn't have an accent."

"But you don't know for sure, right?" Her hope started to wane. If he was adopted in Ireland, wouldn't that make it almost impossible to trace him?

"I think he would have told me if he was born somewhere else."

Kylie nodded. "You said his parents were in Dallas, right?"

"Close to Dallas. You know, somewhere up there."

"Where?" Kylie couldn't believe she'd spent this last two weeks calling Dallas numbers only to learn they didn't even live there.

"I can't remember." Her mom studied Kylie. "You're not thinking of trying to find them, are you?"

Okay, decision time. Kylie had told the PI that she would eventually tell her mom about her quest. Maybe this was showtime. "Would it upset you if I was?" Kylie asked, not wanting to add any more stress to her mom's day.

Her mom frowned. "I . . . I just . . . We don't even know if they're still alive."

"They could be," Kylie said, and couldn't tell her mom that her real interest was in finding them so they might be able to lead her to Daniel's real parents. Soon, her mom might find that out, but one thing at a time. Besides, she didn't have a clue as to how she could explain that she knew Daniel was adopted. Well, not a clue without going through the whole ghost thing, and that was totally a conversation she didn't want to have with her mom.

"Seriously, would you mind if I tried to find them?"

Her mom let go of a deep breath. "I don't mind, Kylie. I guess I'm just worried they will be very angry at me if you did. There have been so many times that I felt guilty for not letting them know about you." There was something in her mom's voice that drew Kylie's attention.

She suddenly realized if her mom felt guilty about not telling them, then she had to know where they were.

"Do you know where they are, Mom? Do you know how I could find them?"

Chapter Twenty-four

Her mom looked down. "I . . ."

"Please, Mom," Kylie said. "Please. If you know anything, tell me."

Her mom seemed preoccupied with her soda as if fascinated by the condensation running down the can. "I couldn't bring myself to throw away his obituary," she said finally. "I put it in the back of the frame of your baby picture hanging on the wall. It has their names and the town they lived in."

Hope flared anew in Kylie's chest. "When you get home, can you scan and e-mail it to me? Please."

Her mom nodded. "If they are still alive, they are going to hate me."

"I don't think so, Mom. They'll probably just be happy to meet me now."

Her mom touched Kylie's cheek. "I'm sorry, baby. I did what I thought was best at the time, but now . . . it looks as if I didn't make the best decisions."

"You did fine," Kylie said. And without thinking, she gave her non-hugging mom another hug.

• • •

An hour later, Kylie watched her mom's car move down the road until it was a tiny blue dot that finally faded from view. Both Burnett and Holiday were waiting on her at the gated entrance when she returned.

"I think my mom is going to be fine," she told them, assuming that's why they were there.

Then she realized Burnett had probably been listening to their conversation the whole time. That's when she got a feeling they weren't here just about her mom.

"Am I in trouble for fighting with Selynn?" she asked. The thought had crossed her mind during her conversation with her mom. Like it or not, Selynn was FRU.

Holiday shook her head. "No. Selynn deserved what she got. She handled the situation all wrong. Terribly wrong."

Holiday glanced up at Burnett as if she was saying this to him as much as to Kylie. "If anyone says one thing about what went down out at the swimming hole, I'll be the first to tell them how the cow ate the cabbage."

When Kylie was about to ask Holiday what she meant about the cows and the cabbage, Burnett shrugged. "I don't think anyone will be saying anything," he said, humor dancing in his eyes. "I never have understood that saying. How does a cow eating cabbage translate into giving someone hell for something?"

"I have no idea." Holiday looked back at Kylie. Burnett's gaze followed Holiday's, and they both returned to that weird kind of staring. And Kylie went back to wondering what the heck was going on.

"If it's not Selynn, then what is it?" Kylie asked.

Burnett stuck his hands into his jeans pockets. "I think we just wanted to make sure you're okay."

She started to answer him, but realized they both were staring at her again. "If that's all, why are you two gawking at me as if I'm about to grow a tail?"

"Do you think you might grow a tail?" Concern filled his voice.

Oh, shit! He was serious.

Kylie swiped her hand over her butt to make sure nothing had suddenly appeared. When nothing was there, she frowned at them. "What is it that you're not telling me?"

"You showcased some new talents today," Burnett said.

"You mean running fast?" Kylie asked.

"And taking on Selynn," Holiday said. "A were this close to a full moon is . . . pretty hard to take on."

"So you're back to thinking I'm a werewolf now?"

Holiday glanced at Burnett and then they both looked back at Kylie.

"We're still not sure." He started studying Kylie anew.

"What is it?" she demanded.

"It's your brain pattern," Holiday said, her tone making it sound like a confession.

"What about it?" She touched her forehead. "Have I opened up? Can you tell what I am?"

"No," Holiday said. "It's just . . . your pattern is shifting."

"Shifting? You mean, it's changing?"

Burnett and Holiday both nodded.

"What does that mean?" Kylie asked.

Holiday's expression went from curiosity to sympathy in a flash. "It's just . . ."

"Surmising, I know. Just tell me." She motioned with her hands for the camp leader to hurry up.

"The only brain pattern that shifts and changes is a shape-shifter," Holiday said.

"So, you now think I'm a shape-shifter?" Kylie tried to wrap her head around being a shape-shifter. Turning into giant lions and . . .

"It's not changing like a shape-shifter," Burnett corrected. "A shape-shifter only changes when they change forms."

Kylie looked down at her chest and lower, almost to make sure she hadn't morphed into anything, and to make sure her boobs hadn't taken on another cup size. Then she gave her butt another swipe, praying again that she hadn't grown a tail. "I'm not changing."

"We know," Burnett said.

Then, as if sensing Kylie had about had her quota of crap for the day, Holiday came over and dropped an arm around her. "Come on, why don't we take a walk to the falls?"

Kylie nodded. She'd been thinking about going back to the cabin and having a good long cry, but a trip to the falls sounded even better.

"I'll come with you," Burnett said.

"I think we'll go alone," Holiday replied.

"I don't think you two should be that deep in the woods alone," he countered. "We still don't know why the security gate wasn't working."

"I don't think we're exactly vulnerable." Holiday nodded her head to Kylie.

"I would feel better if I went with you." He frowned. "You won't even know I'm there. I'll stay at a distance."

Holiday rolled her eyes, as if to say "whatever," then she guided Kylie to turn around and they started walking toward the trail that led near the falls. "I might be happy with a fifty-mile distance."

"When are you going to remember I can hear you?" Burnett said from about fifteen feet back.

"When did you ever think I forgot?" she countered in a low voice.

• • •

Monday morning Kylie woke up to the chill of the ghost. She opened her eyes, but the spirit hadn't materialized yet. "You do know just coming here and waking me up isn't going to help me, don't you? You need to give me something, find a way to show me who it is I need to help."

No answer came back and Kylie pulled the covers over her chin and just stared at her breath making little clouds of mist rising above her nose. The visit to the falls with Holiday had been both amazing and amazingly disheartening. She and Holiday hadn't even talked; they just sat beside each other, staring at the wall of water cascading down in front of them. The same ambience Kylie had found existed there last time seemed even stronger this visit. That was the amazing part.

And the amazingly disheartening part? The message she took away from the visit wasn't so much everything was going to be fine. Nope. It was more like: stay focused and keep the faith.

And if Kylie had thought she could argue with the presence at the falls, she would have looked up at the rock ceiling and roared, "Really? That's all you're going to give me?"

Honestly, how was she supposed to stay focused when she didn't know what to focus on? Sort of hard to focus on ghosts when they wouldn't even appear, wasn't it?

The temperature dropped another few degrees.

"Yeah, I'm talking about you," Kylie said aloud to the spirit.

Keeping the faith was almost equally impossible. Having faith meant believing nothing bad was going to happen. Didn't two girls being killed by a rogue vampire qualify as bad? Who could consider having your mom's memory erased to be a good thing? Add her changing brain pattern that had everyone staring at her as if she were a freak—and let's not forget her uncontrollable desire to barge into people's dreams—and, well, her faith could use a pack of steroids to build it back up again.

Kylie let go of a big gasp of frustration when the cold of the spirit started to fade. Great! Just another day of being shocked awake at dawn with nothing to show for it. Rolling over, she punched her pillow and felt her mood grow darker by the second.

Oh, it wasn't just a general Monday blues kind of mood, either. Nope, this was more. Tonight was the full moon. Who knew what was going to happen? But the fact she'd awoken in such a piss-poor mood was even more of a sign that she might be werewolf.

Not that morphing into a wolf was the only bad-mood trigger. After finally making up her mind to say yes to going out with Derek, she hadn't had a chance to get him alone and give him her answer. There was also the particular werewolf coming back to the camp today or tomorrow. Make that two weres coming back. She wasn't exactly looking forward to getting reacquainted with Fredericka. And facing Lucas after the whole dream fiasco? Oh yeah, that was going to be so much fun. Not!

Kylie let out a groan, punched her pillow, and pulled the covers over her head.

Five minutes after Kylie was up, and two minutes after checking and realizing her mom still hadn't sent her the scan of Daniel's obituary, Kylie managed to piss off both Della and Miranda. After they both managed to piss her off. So Kylie made up her mind—she was taking a day off. A complete day off from people. And that included all the supernatural varieties, too.

Today, it was just her and her skunk.

Snatching a bottle of soda from the fridge, she scooped up Socks, told her roommates to tell Holiday she was taking a vacation day, and went back into her bedroom where she slammed the door just because she felt like it.

At nine o'clock, Holiday tapped at her bedroom door. "Just checking on you."

"I just want to be alone," Kylie said, hearing the door open, but not moving from the facedown position she'd landed on her bed an hour ago.

"Bad mood?" There was a bunch of meaning to Holiday's question that Kylie didn't want to think about.

"Yeah, a real piss-poor bad mood." Kylie rolled over.

"Okay." Holiday bit down on her lip. "Just remember, I'm here if you need me."

"I know," Kylie said.

At ten o'clock, there was another knock. This time, the knock sounded at her cabin front door.

"Go away," she yelled out.

A minute later, Derek walked into her bedroom without being invited. That pissed her off even more. Then, she remembered something else that had pissed her off that she hadn't spoken with him about yet.

"Why didn't you tell me about the whole erasing thing?" she blurted out.

He dropped down on her bed. "Burnett kind of said I shouldn't tell everyone."

"Am I everyone?" she asked, and sat up, pulling her knees to her chest.

Whether it was her tone, her question, or if her mood was contagious, she didn't know, but she recognized pissed off when she saw it. And Derek was pissed off. "Maybe if you'd been more accessible to me, instead of worrying that someone might figure out you liked me, we could have spent more time talking."

"I think I've apologized for that." She hugged her shins. "Not that it means you've forgiven me," she said with a touch of sarcasm.

He shook his head. "Okay fine, so maybe I don't have a right to be mad about *that*."

His inflection on the word *that* led to her next question. "But you're mad about something, right?"

He frowned. "I shouldn't be." He ran a hand through his hair and looked at her. The deep emotional hurt that Kylie saw in his eyes chased away her own bad mood and she started to worry about him.

"What is it that you shouldn't be mad about?"

He stood up from the bed and paced across the room. "You never lied to me. Not really. And I could see you still had feelings for him. You'd feel guilty and I knew you were probably thinking about him. I knew it, because I felt it. Yet like an idiot, I kept on pursuing you, even when you refused to go out with me."

She shook her head. "You're not making sense."

He stopped walking and let go of a deep breath. Then his beautiful, warm, and still-hurting eyes met her gaze again. "I can only be mad at myself."

"For what?" she asked again, her bad mood trying to move back in.

"But what I can't get over is that you didn't tell me."

"What didn't I tell you?" She felt confused and yet . . . not really. She sensed he was talking about Lucas. Not that it really mattered, because she and Lucas were history. She'd made up her mind.

Yeah, there were the dreams. And she felt the guilt creep around her again.

He waved a hand in the air. "You see, this is how you feel half the time I'm with you. Guilty." He shook his head. "Tell me it's not true. Tell me that you haven't been getting letters from him this whole time."

His question bounced around her head. "I . . . I never wrote him back." She wanted to assure Derek that she hadn't done anything wrong. But the truth hit and it hung on like a big mean dog to a bone he considered his own. If he'd been getting letters from some girl who'd kissed him, she would have been jealous. She wouldn't have liked it. Certainly not if he'd been having sexy dreams about her, too.

"Derek," she said softly, "I swear to God, I didn't mean—"

"To hurt me," he finished her sentence. "I believe you. I know you didn't do this to hurt me. You aren't cruel or mean. You don't have a devious bone in your body. You're just . . . confused."

She stood and walked over to him and tried to take his hand in hers, but he pulled away. His withdrawal hurt. Meeting his eyes, she tried to find a way to explain it. "You're right. I'm confused about a lot of stuff. But I'm not confused about what I feel about you. I care about you. A lot. When I'm with you, I feel safe and when you kiss me I feel everything. Everything looks so beautiful and . . . and I don't even care if you're doing it anymore. I just want that feeling, okay? I want to go out with you."

"If you'd really wanted that, you'd have said something earlier."

"I did want to, I was . . . just confused. Like you said."

"Because of Lucas?"

"No." She offered him the answer she'd offered herself. "Because I'm still trying to figure out what I am."

"But I told you that what you are isn't important."

"It is to me," she said. But deep down, deeper than she wanted to look, she knew what he said was true. Not knowing what she was, was only part of the reason she hadn't agreed to go out with him earlier. The other part was Lucas.

But that didn't change how she felt about Derek, she insisted to herself. It was just like Holiday's aunt Stella. She might feel an attraction for Lucas, but she wouldn't act on it. She tried again to take his hand, but he wouldn't let her.

"You have to decide, Kylie, because I can't stand living in this limbo. I have too much limbo in my life with my father and I just can't deal with it anymore."

"I've already decided," she said. "It's you. I was going to tell you yesterday and then . . . everything happened."

He stepped closer and her heart sighed with relief. She leaned in for a kiss. She wanted him to kiss her so badly; she wanted to make him see how much she cared about him.

He touched her cheek. "Until you're sure about what you feel about him, then you can't trust how you feel about me."

"That's not true." She tried to kiss him, but he put a finger over her lips, stopping her.

"No. No more. Until you've made up your mind, we're just friends. Just friends." Pain and hurt echoed in his voice and took a flying leap, landing right in her heart.

She didn't want to just be his friend. She wanted more. "Please don't do this, Derek. I never meant—"

He put his finger over her lips again. "I know you didn't mean to hurt me, Kylie. But it does hurt. I feel . . . everything. That's what makes this so hard." He took a step back. "I'd better go."

Pain welled up inside her. Tears filled her eyes. She was going to lose him. She knew it as well as she knew her own name.

He got to her bedroom door and turned back. "As your friend, I'm telling you this. Fredericka is back. She wants to hurt you. And

I don't think she'll stop with just telling me about the letters. Be careful. Especially until after tonight. Weres are hyper-aggressive before they turn."

Kylie felt her own aggression boil up inside her and she swiped at the tears sliding down her face. Until he mentioned it, she hadn't stopped to guess how he knew about the letters Lucas had sent her. And now that she knew, she didn't like it one iota. Fredericka had told Derek about the letters.

And in doing so, she hadn't just hurt Kylie, she'd also hurt Derek.

Kylie closed her hand into a fist. "Don't worry," she said. "I'm not as helpless as I used to be."

"Helpless, no," he said. "But she's got meanness on you hands down. You don't want to tangle with her."

An hour later, heart still breaking, Kylie checked her e-mail and found her mother had finally sent her the scan of Daniel's obituary. Maybe her emotions were already primed and ready to go because of her already sucky day, but when she read about her father's death, Kylie dropped her head on the desk and wept. She wept for Derek and she wept for Daniel.

She recalled the dream/vision she'd had about his death. He'd been leaving a war-torn village and had returned to save a woman from some insurgents. He had not only given his life for his country, he had given it to save a stranger.

"I love you, Daniel." She wished he would drop in for a visit.

She noted his parents' names and that they lived in some place called Gladlock, Texas. A search on the Internet showed it was a small city about seventy-five miles outside of Dallas. With her heart still hurting, she did a search for a phone number for

Kent B. Brighten. The computer hadn't completed the search when the door to the cabin swung open.

Kylie glanced up, expecting to see Miranda or Della. But nope. Fredericka had come a'calling. And she'd bypassed the proper etiquette of knocking before entering, too.

Chapter Twenty-five

"Well, if it isn't the ghost girl." Fredericka's smartass tone hit Kylie the wrong way.

"She's got meanness on you hands down. You don't want to tangle with her." Derek's words rang in Kylie's head.

Okay, so Derek was right. She didn't want to tangle with Fredericka, but Kylie wasn't sure she had an option now considering the werewolf stood less than six feet away. Kylie had no way out. Too late to run and hide under the bed.

Kylie stood, staring at the girl's dark eyes and hoping the she-wolf wouldn't see Kylie's streak of insecurity.

Yesterday with Selynn, Kylie hadn't felt fear. Nope. She'd been acting on instinct to protect her mother. Now the only one needing protection was Kylie herself; the kick-ass instinct had a taken mini-vacation.

"Gosh, I didn't hear you knock." Kylie tried to imitate Fredericka's curt tone and defensive posture, hoping to bluff her way through this.

The glimmer of a smile danced over Fredericka's lips as if Kylie's bluff had fallen short.

"I thought it best if we got this little talk over with." Fredericka glanced around the cabin as if taking in the furnishings. Not that it was much to look at or different from the other cabins. The over-stuffed brown sofa was paired with an overstuffed gold chair that almost matched. Kylie's mom had brought her a few throw pillows that added splashes of color to the room. The end tables had utili-tarian lamps with plain white shades, and Miranda had added a few crystals around the room.

Behind Fredericka, Kylie saw Socks freeze in a panic at seeing a stranger in the cabin, and the skunk unfroze long enough to bury himself under a red and gold sofa pillow.

Kylie didn't blame him, either.

"What talk is that?" she asked. "The one where I explain it's rude to walk into someone's home without knocking?" Her snarky comment might set Fredericka off, but Kylie sensed this was a test, and to show fear felt more dangerous than provoking the she-wolf.

Fredericka released a low growl, and her eyes brightened. When her uninvited guest's gaze shifted up and down Kylie's stance, it took everything Kylie had not to crawl under the pillow with Socks.

Fredericka's brows twitched. Kylie, never prouder of her new talent, twitched back. The she-wolf's pattern looked much like those of the other weres she'd noted at the river yesterday, but the dark-ened edges appeared ominous. Did that mean anything? Kylie re-ally needed to sign up for Brain Pattern Reading 101.

"I hear you might be one of my own kind." Fredericka's eyes tightened.

The idea of sharing a bloodline with this bully made Kylie feel sick. Her gaze went back to the trembling pillow on the sofa. She recalled what Holiday had said about her not being were because felines had an abhorrence of werewolves. Kylie hoped Holiday was right about that. Even drinking blood for the rest of her life felt like a better option than bring a were.

Kylie held her defensive stance. "I wouldn't believe everything you hear."

"And if I were you, I wouldn't forget that if you do turn, we'll likely meet. And on full moons the emotions are always generally out of control, resulting in high casualty rates."

"Then I'm sure you will be watching your back," Kylie said, really bluffing now.

Fredericka's brows pinched. "Especially when a female feels another is making advances toward her mate."

"So, you still having a hard time holding on to your man?" Kylie fought back her fear.

The gold in Fredericka's eyes grew brighter. "What's that smell?" Fredericka held her nose up in the air.

Kylie didn't dare glance at the pillow hiding Socks. "Wouldn't know, but if it's offensive, the door is right behind you."

"It smells sort of like . . . I don't know, lion, maybe?" Fredericka's left eyebrow arched.

Kylie didn't blink. "I knew you did it."

"Did what?" Fredericka's smile turned into more of a smirk. Then she shifted back a couple of steps and dropped down on the sofa with an exaggerated plop, as if she planned on hanging around a while.

The sound of the sofa giving up air was quickly followed by a half-hiss and half-meow. The pillow fell away and a black and white tail sprang up into the air. Fredericka turned just in time to take the full spray directly in the face.

Twenty feet away, the stench had Kylie covering her nose, but she couldn't stop smiling.

The she-wolf screamed and dove at the animal. While Socks had gotten in touch with his skunk side, he obviously hadn't forgotten his feline roots. He flew off the sofa in full frightened-cat

mode. His ascent into midair sent the lamp on the end table crashing to the floor.

Wiping her eyes with her palms and howling, Fredericka shot
off the sofa after Socks. Socks, now perched on top of the over-
stuffed chair, reacted accordingly and flew in midair, bouncing off
the walls as he ran for his life.

The thought of what the she-wolf would do to her kitten had
Kylie giving chase. Wooden chairs cracked against the floor, the
microwave flew across the room, the computer desk nearly fell over,
and a few dishes left on the counter shattered beside the chairs.
Everything spun in circles with one kitten-turned-skunk, one she-
wolf, and one unidentifiable supernatural chasing each other around
the living room/kitchen, each with their own agenda.

Socks to live.

Fredericka to kill.

Kylie to protect.

Unfortunately, Socks was no match for the angry she-wolf, and
in seconds Fredericka had Socks cornered by the refrigerator. A
loud roar filled the cabin. A wash of adrenaline shot through Kylie
as Fredericka dove for the poor animal.

Just before Fredericka latched her paws on to Socks, Kylie latched
on to the girl's forearms. Picking her up in the air, she hauled the
struggling Fredericka over to the front door and tossed her out.

She landed about eight feet from the porch with a loud thud.
Her eyes, now a bright gold, stared up in horror at Kylie. The she-
wolf rose off the ground on all fours, her knees bent, shifting back
and forth, as if revving up to pounce again.

Kylie didn't flinch.

She breathed in.

She breathed out.

She welcomed another round.

"You bitch!" Fredericka growled, and tossed her head back.

"You hurt my cat and you'll see how big of a bitch I can be!" Kylie voice sounded as animal-like as the she-wolf's. Then, suddenly frightened, not of Fredericka, but at what Kylie would do if the girl came at her again, she stepped back and slammed the front door. The whole cabin shook from the impact. And right then a cold presence filled the room.

Company.

Great. The cabin smelled of skunk, she had a majorly pissed-off she-wolf outside, and *now* the spirit wanted to drop by.

Five minutes later, Kylie still stood with her back to the refrigerator, breathing through her mouth so she wouldn't gag at the pungent odor, and trying to calm herself and a very scared skunk-kitten. Socks, seconds after Kylie had come inside, had climbed up her leg, cuddled into her arms, and buried its little pointed nose in her armpit. Kylie wondered if the nose in the armpit wasn't so much his need to escape the smell as it was to hide.

The ghost paced the tiny living room as though she was trying to think. Kylie watched the spirit walk in circles before realizing the ghost's wardrobe.

"Why are you wearing a hospital gown?" Kylie asked, but the spirit didn't answer. And when the ghost faded, relief flowed over Kylie. She closed her eyes and tried to recall the calm she'd gathered at the falls about the whole "Someone you love is dying" situation.

Then the door to the cabin swung open. Thinking it could be Fredericka again, Kylie tensed and then un-tensed when she saw Holiday and Miranda.

"Are you okay?" Holiday asked.

Kylie nodded and Socks, hearing more commotion, snuggled

tighter into Kylie's armpit. Miranda and Holiday both covered their noses and their wide-eyed gazes moved around the ransacked cabin.

"What happened?" Holiday asked.

Fredericka happened, Kylie almost answered, but then bit back the words. She'd never been much of a tattler and didn't want to start now. "Socks got startled." It wasn't altogether a lie.

Holiday, her hand still plastered over her nose, squinted at Kylie. "I know Fredericka was here." Her voice came out muffled behind her palm.

"She told you?" Kylie asked.

"Didn't have to," Miranda piped in. "We smelled her when she walked past the office."

"What happened?" Holiday repeated her question from behind her fingers.

Miranda took a step closer. "She was spitting mad," Miranda broke in again, humor in her voice. "Seriously spitting. Did Socks get her in the face?" The witch laughed and wrinkled her nose at the smell again and waved her hands around the air as if to perform a bit of magic.

Kylie's next intake of air didn't include the skunk stench. "Thanks," she said to Miranda, surprised that her roommate had removed the smell without any goofs.

"Welcome," Miranda said with a sense of pride. "Odor removal is a piece of cake. Learned in the potty-training stage."

Holiday dropped her hand. "Miranda, can I have a minute alone with Kylie?"

Miranda rolled her eyes. "Why is it that everyone is always sending me away?" She stomped off into her bedroom, but flashed Kylie a smile before shutting the door.

Holiday met Kylie's gaze. "Now, what happened?"

Fredericka just stopped by to remind me that she tried to kill me once by putting a lion in my room and once might not be enough for her.

When Kylie didn't answer, Holiday studied Kylie suspiciously. "My job here is to show everyone that we can all get along without incident." She sighed. "I agreed to her coming back because . . . I know she doesn't have anywhere else to go. I'm afraid she'd be pulled into a gang, but if she's starting trouble, Kylie, I'll show her the gate."

Kylie knew Holiday meant what she said and she appreciated her loyalty to no end. While the temptation to tell the truth bubbled up inside Kylie, her own sense of loyalty bit down. She knew how important it was to Holiday to save every one of her campers from the dark side of the supernatural world. Even Fredericka.

Kylie wasn't sure the she-wolf was worth saving or even if she was salvageable. But Kylie didn't want to be the one to make that call. Besides, she didn't want Holiday having to solve Kylie's problems. She got a mental image of how she'd managed to toss Fredericka out the door. Maybe, just maybe she was capable of taking care of herself.

Giving the still-scared Socks a good scratch behind his ears, Kylie said, "It's not a big deal. Socks didn't like Fredericka and Fredericka didn't like Socks. No one was hurt." *Yet,* a little voice echoed inside Kylie, but she ignored it. "I'm sure we can work it out."

When Kylie looked up, she spotted Della standing behind the camp leader in the doorway mouthing the word "Liar."

Holiday looked at Della and then faced Kylie again. "You're sure?"

Kylie nodded. It felt less like a lie.

Holiday gave Kylie a hug and then took off. Miranda came out of her room, and Kylie dropped Socks to the floor and started picking up the mess. Miranda and Della did the same.

"You don't have to help," Kylie said.

"Please," Miranda said, and they continued to straighten chairs. Della lifted the microwave back on the counter. She plugged it back in and when the light came on, she said, "Good as new."

When the room was put back together, they all sat down at the kitchen table. "Okay," Miranda said. "Give us the details and don't leave out the good parts. And by good parts, I mean when little Miss She-wolf got sprayed in the face. Something tells me that that is going to be my favorite part. Heck, I'll bet you're even glad I turned Socks into a skunk now, right?"

Kylie leaned back in her chair and told them the whole story, including the part about Fredericka telling Derek about Lucas's letters and even the part about Fredericka halfway admitting she'd been the one to put the lion in Kylie's bedroom.

"Why the crap didn't you tell Holiday?" Miranda asked.

When Kylie didn't answer right away, Della piped up. "Because she's too damn nice."

"It's not that," Kylie said. She bit down on her lip. "Okay, maybe that's part of it, but it's Holiday I'm worried about—not Fredericka. Plus, I want to deal with this myself."

"Now, that part of it I can respect." Della crossed her arms over her chest. "Then there's the saying about how you should keep your friends close, and your enemies closer."

Miranda frowned. "Fredericka's meaner than a rattlesnake. Are you sure you can handle her?"

"If she can't, I'm always up for kicking a little werewolf ass," Della said.

Emotion swelled in Kylie's throat and she barely managed to

swallow it. "Is Lucas here, too?" Kylie recalled the hurt in Derek's eyes. The emotion in her throat doubled.

"Not yet," Della said. "I heard Fredericka say he was showing up tomorrow."

Kylie blinked, hoping to contain her tears. Then she recalled the dreams and how hard facing Lucas would be.

Miranda leaned in. "Do you think Derek's serious about breaking up?"

"He didn't break up with her," Della corrected in a harsh tone. "They weren't going out."

But he might as well have, Kylie thought, and that's when a couple of tears slipped out. Standing up, she said. "Thanks guys, but I'm . . . I just want to—"

"You still feeling pissy?" Della asked.

"Yeah," Kylie answered. Her gaze shifted to the computer showing her grandparents' phone number. She was even too distraught to deal with that right now. Tomorrow. Kylie got to her bedroom, shut the door, and dropped facedown on the blue-and-white bedspread. She had just closed her eyes when she heard Miranda sigh. A sigh Kylie shouldn't have been able to hear through her closed bedroom door.

"Do you think she's werewolf?" Miranda asked.

Kylie grabbed a pillow and covered her head, but it didn't stop Della's answer from filtering through the foam to reach Kylie's supercharged hearing.

"Probably," Della answered. *"But I'm not going to hold it against her. She'll be the nicest werewolf that ever existed."*

"Me, either," Miranda said. *"Not all weres are bad. Not that I've ever been close to any of them."*

Great, Kylie thought. Her friends seemed certain she was doomed to a life of nasty moods and howling at the moon. Kylie tried to imagine what it would be like to morph into a wolf. Then she remembered that Fredericka was going to be waiting with bated wolf breath for a chance to get even with her when—okay, if—she did turn.

And then she recalled Derek saying that he didn't want her to be a werewolf because she'd have that in common with Lucas. Was that why he'd pulled away? Gawd, why did life have to be so damn hard?

Kylie stayed in her room the next few hours. Feeling an emotional storm rage inside her, she tried to think of anything that could take the edge off. She'd napped, actually fallen asleep, but had awoken when the temperature dropped in the room. She looked around for the ghost, but the spirit didn't materialize. Remembering the ghost's appearance after Fredericka left, Kylie asked, "Do you have something to say?"

Her question vibrated in the still coldness of the room. Kylie hadn't expected an answer, but asking was her job, right? Staring at the ceiling, she jumped when something crashed to the floor. Turning around, she saw her phone had fallen from the nightstand. When she picked it up, she heard someone on the line.

"Hello?" Kylie recognized Sara's voice.

"Hey," Kylie said.

"What's up?" Sara asked.

Kylie huddled under the covers to ward off the cold. "Nothing. Did you call me?"

"No. You called me," Sara answered.

"Oh." Kylie glanced at her cell. "My phone fell off the nightstand. It must have dialed you accidentally."

"Oh." The awkwardness rang louder than Sara's voice.

"Where are you?" Kylie asked, just to chase away the uncomfortable silence because just hanging up felt too rude. It wasn't as if Kylie could say what's on her mind like, *Hey guess what? I just tossed a werewolf out of my cabin for trying to kill my kitten that's now a skunk, and tonight, I might turn into a wolf myself.* Right then Kylie realized she'd been blaming Sara for the distance in their relationship, claiming Sara had changed. Well, hell, now look who had undergone the most change.

"At the mall with Tina," Sara answered, her voice sounding strangely tight.

"Tina?" Kylie asked, hoping to show interest in Sara's life.

"Tina Dalton. She just moved here."

"Is she nice?" Was Tina Sara's new best friend?

Sarah chuckled. "Not really, but her brother is hot."

"Hmm," Kylie teased. "Good thing I didn't have a brother or I'd think you were just interested in him all these years."

Sara laughed and Kylie joined in. A little of the awkwardness faded.

"It was strange that you called," Sara said. "I was just thinking about you. Do you remember when we were thirteen and you did that backward flip and knocked both of us off the trampoline? Our moms took us to the emergency clinic by our neighborhood because they thought you had broken an arm and I had a goose egg on my head."

"Yeah," Kylie said. "What made you think about that?"

"Who knows," Sara answered with the same tight voice.

Kylie leaned back on her pillow. "You thought the doctor was cute."

"He was cute." Sara sounded normal again. "Any hot guys at the camp?"

"Yeah." Kylie took in a deep breath and when she released it, it came out as a fog. Strange. She'd thought the spirit had left but she was moving closer.

"You hooked up with any of them?" Sara asked.

Kylie's heart tugged. "Kind of, but . . . we sort of . . . called it quits." *Or he called it quits.* A shiver ran down Kylie's back and she looked around again for the ghost. She still hadn't materialized, but her chill filled the room.

"That sucks," Sara said, and in the background Kylie heard someone call out Sara's name. "Hold on a sec."

The line went silent as if Sara had covered the receiver. But Kylie's ears picked up Sara's intake of air. Whether Sara had moved her hand, or if it was Kylie's hearing abilities, she wasn't sure. She still didn't grasp how this whole gifted hearing thing worked. It came and went. Just like her strength.

"No, I'm not using my insurance." Sara's voice filled the line. "I'm paying cash. Of course my mom knows. Look, is the doctor going to see me or not?"

Kylie frowned when she realized that Sara had lied about being at the mall. The reasons for the lie filled Kylie's head. Had she run out of birth control pills? Or did she think she was pregnant again? Tightening her grip on the phone, Kylie was reminded of how different they were. How sad was it that they couldn't share things— neither werewolves or sex?

"Kylie," Sara said. "I need to go."

"Okay. Bye." Kylie put her phone back on the nightstand. When she looked up, the ghost sat at the foot of her bed, appearing incredibly sad. Kylie started to speak but the spirit faded.

"Great," Kylie muttered. "Communicating with spirits is almost as bad as communicating with old friends."

• • •

At eleven thirty that night, Kylie walked with Della and Miranda to the campfire. Her heart swelled with the fear of what would or wouldn't happen to her tonight, but she refused to show it. Of course, Della pretty much knew what she was feeling because she kept studying Kylie with an enormous amount of sympathy.

The moment the three of them cut through the clearing, Kylie spotted Derek standing in a group of four other fairies. He glanced at her. The full moon offered enough light for her to see the soft concern in his eyes.

No doubt he could read her fear. Stopping, she muttered to Della and Miranda to go ahead and let her talk to Derek. Her two roommates walked off.

Kylie waited for Derek to come and offer her his comforting touch—just a touch to ebb the fear from her heart. She could really use a little of his calm right now, not to mention his touch. His gaze met hers, but instead of moving over, he glanced back at his circle of friends. That's when Kylie got the first hint of how things would be between them from now on.

Obviously, being *just* friends meant no more kisses and touches.

Kylie's first impulse was to beg him to stop this nonsense. Her second impulse didn't involve begging. Anger crowded out some of her fear. Even though she knew Derek was partially right—in the beginning, there was some truth to her confusion with Lucas stopping her from going out with him—didn't Derek trust her enough to know she wouldn't cheat on him? His lack of faith in her just plain ol' made her mad. Really, really mad.

Sure, it might be her uncontrollable werewolf-related aggression bringing on the fury, but she felt it all the same. And once again, being mad felt better than being hurt, even better than being frightened, so she clung to the anger and hoped Derek would read it. She even stepped closer, giving him ample opportunity.

She knew it worked when he turned back around and his green eyes met hers. She didn't blink, didn't attempt to look away, wanting to make sure he read every bit of her anger. A frown tightened his brows and he walked away, probably wanting to get out of emotion-reading range. While tempted to follow him and cloak him in her emotional state, she didn't.

Just go. Her chest tightened as the hurt crowded out the anger. *Just remember, I wasn't the one who called it quits.*

Taking a deep breath, she looked around until she spotted another lone soul who looked almost as miserable as she felt. Perry stood by himself, leaning against a tree and watching Miranda chatting cheerfully with a group of guys—one of whom was Kevin. Knowing misery loved company, Kylie went to join Perry.

Perry snarled at her when she walked up. "What? Are you going to tell me how much she likes me again?"

"Nope," Kylie said. "I've come to the conclusion that anything to do with the opposite sex should be banned and considered illegal."

Perry studied her through his brown eyes. "Trouble in paradise?"

"Yup."

He sighed. "Maybe we should hook up and teach a few people some lessons."

"In your dreams," Kylie said.

"Not even there." He frowned. "The only girl appearing in my dreams lately is the girl who is too busy flirting with everyone to even say hello to me."

Kylie gaped at Perry. "I can't believe you." Where did he get off thinking Miranda should talk to him when he'd been the one to call it quits? Like Derek.

Before she voiced her opinion, Luis, the were in charge, called for everyone's attention. Kylie's anger with Perry and over Derek dissolved and she fell right into the lap of fear again.

Her heart thudded. She felt the moon's rays on her as if it were the sun. Her skin actually stung and it took everything she had not to stop and stare up at the huge orb in the sky and scream for it to stop.

"It's not as scary as you think," Perry said.

Kylie met his gaze. "Does everyone know what's going on with me?"

"Pretty much." His eyes, now a bright blue, studied her. "It's not bad."

They moved closer to where the ceremony was taking place and she looked up at Perry and gave him credit for his sincere concern for her "I didn't think shape-shifters and werewolves were the same thing."

"We're not," he said. "But we both shift and I've spent a lot of time talking about it with others. They all say the same thing, 'It's not a big deal. Like a muscle cramp.'"

She bit the inside of her cheek and recalled Lucas describing it the same way. Unfortunately, she'd never been fond of muscle cramps. A thousand questions started stirring in her head. Why hadn't she found more answers? She felt her heart stop, start, then flutter like a trapped butterfly.

Swallowing fear, she searched the crowd for Fredericka. "Will I know who I am?" she asked Perry. Her lungs felt too tight to breathe even though she didn't spot the she-wolf.

"Sure you will." His gaze shot over Kylie's shoulder. Kylie feared he saw Fredericka behind her.

"You okay?" Holiday's comforting voice came to her ear.

Kylie turned just as Holiday motioned for Perry to move on.

Kylie leaned in and her voice caught as she confessed the truth. "I'm scared out of my gourd. I'm not ready for this." Her eyes stung with the new urge to cry.

"You're going to be fine. I don't even think . . ." Holiday didn't finish her sentence. Instead, she placed a hand on Kylie's shoulder and the majority of her panic faded. "Come on, I'll stand beside you."

They walked to the crowd and formed another circle much like they had at the vampire ceremony. Luis stood in the middle and in his hands he carried a skull. Not a human skull, it looked to be a wolf. He held up the skull. It seemed to catch the moonlight and glow. He started recounting the story of the first werewolf, and then telling about his kind's many gifts, but Kylie couldn't listen. Nothing felt right. Her gaze shot to the moon, and she could swear she saw the man in the round silver circle wink at her.

Then Kylie noticed that many of the campers were walking off. The werewolves. Kylie glanced at Holiday with questions in her eyes.

"Most prefer not to transform in front of an audience," the camp leader explained.

Kylie didn't blame them. She didn't want to do it, either. Would her clothes fall off? Would they see the hair growing on her skin?

Her only thought was to run, but Luis stopped talking and the sound that came out of his mouth was one of sheer terror. In the background, Kylie could hear what sounded like the screams of the others as they, too, turned. Air caught in her throat again. Her feet felt nailed to the ground. She didn't want to hear this, didn't want to see it, but like an accident on the side of the road, she couldn't look away.

Luis dropped to the ground, his back arched, and the sounds— half growl, half moan—continued. It was like something out of a horror movie. Kylie watched his body contort in ways no human body should ever twist. He arched his neck back so far it looked as if it would surely break. His jawbone grew, his cheeks became elongated, and where the face of a young man had once been the snout of a wolf appeared. And then came the hair.

Kylie's heart jolted. Her skin started to crawl. Her stomach knotted.

Oh, God! Something was happening to her.

Chapter Twenty-six

Kylie felt as if seltzer ran through her veins. She watched Luis, now a complete wolf, run off into the woods. Then everyone there turned and stared at her.

Watching.

Waiting.

She looked at Holiday. "I need to . . . be alone." She walked away. She didn't run—didn't want to draw any more attention to herself than she already had—but she walked fast, afraid the sounds of terror would any minute begin to flow from her own throat.

She made it to the woods before the urge to run overtook her. She moved at amazing speeds, dodging trees, jumping over stumps, and ducking under branches. How long she ran, she didn't know. But out of breath, out of energy, she finally collapsed in a heap of trembling muscles.

Stilling gasping, she stared at her hands. She touched her face to make sure she hadn't started the change.

Nothing. No change. She closed her eyes and tried to stop the feeling of her crawling skin. That's when she heard it.

A low, very ominous growl.

Opening her eyes, she saw the wolf lurching toward her. Mostly white with hints of gray and tan, its eyes glowed a bright golden. Its lips curled under and its sharp teeth were bared. This was no ordinary wolf. It was a werewolf.

Kylie tried to stand, but her muscles trembled and refused the command. The wolf seemed to notice her weakness. Its posture became more aggressive. The coarse hair on its back stood up and when Kylie looked it in the eyes, she knew. Knew with certainty the wolf was Fredericka. The she-wolf's growl deepened and then she charged.

Kylie found the strength to bounce to her feet, ready to run, when another wolf, even larger, crashed between two trees. Fredericka stopped. At first, Kylie thought she was about to be attacked by two beasts instead of one. But the second wolf, a dark gray in color with eyes that glowed a lighter gold, whipped around and growled at the oncoming wolf.

Kylie heard the competing growls and saw the two converge upon each other. She heard the sound of teeth clicking, and then, recognizing this as a chance to escape, she tore off through the woods. She ran, not as fast as before, for her energy had been spent, but she forced herself forward and didn't stop until she reached her cabin.

Collapsing on the porch steps, she forced air into her lungs. When she looked out at the woods, a pair of light golden eyes stared back Her next intake of air brought recognition. She wasn't sure how she knew, but it came with such clarity that she didn't question it.

Lucas was back.

The next morning, Kylie got her daily wake-up call with the dropping of the room's temperature. She groaned, rolled over, and glared at the clock, not wanting to believe it was dawn. But yep. It was 4:59 a.m. The spirit was right on time.

It didn't seem fair, and not just because she didn't want to face Lucas yet. Hadn't she just put her head on the pillow? She'd never had three hours pass so quickly. It had been two a.m. when she'd collapsed in her own bed.

When Kylie ran inside her cabin after seeing Lucas, Holiday had been waiting on her to make sure she was okay. Della and Miranda were waiting with the camp leader at the kitchen table, all of them looking somber. Her two cabin mates looked shocked when Kylie arrived. No doubt they seriously thought she'd made the change into werewolf. But Holiday hadn't seemed so surprised.

After thinking about it, Kylie couldn't help but be suspicious. Did Holiday know something she wasn't telling Kylie? She loved Holiday, but her belief in the self-discovery crap, the idea that a person needed to find their own answers, was chewing on Kylie's last nerve.

The cold filling the room brought her back to the present.

"You have to save her."

Speaking of last nerves . . .

Kylie groaned and sat up. The ghost stood at the foot of her bed. The sweet smell of blood assaulted Kylie before she saw the ghost had donned her bloody gown again. The spirit met Kylie's gaze and clutched her abdomen as if she was going to be sick.

"If you're going to throw up," Kylie said, "would you mind stepping away from the bed?"

The cold, uncaring sound of her own voice hit Kylie like a slap across the face. "I'm sorry," she whispered. "I'm just . . . I want to figure it out and it's frustrating not to be able to."

The ghost rested a hand on Kylie's foot. Even beneath the blanket, the icy chill took hold. *"You have the ability to stop it. Please make it stop."*

"Make what stop? Has it already started?" Kylie asked, her chest tightening. Was someone she loved already suffering? Kidnapped and being tortured by the Blood Brothers, or something even worse?

"Damn it, answer me!" Kylie yelled. "Or at least give me a vision I can understand. I don't even care how scary it is, just do it."

The one of the funeral still made no sense.

The ghost faded and so did the coldness of her touch. But then Kylie felt tingly warmth spread down the tendons to her toes and up the arches to her ankle. Kylie pressed a hand against her foot. She'd never felt that before with Daniel. Was that supposed to mean something?

Frustration welled inside Kylie, but the sound of cascading water filled her head. Was this the death angels way of saying it would be okay?

Kylie's phone beeped, announcing she had messages. There were three: one from the private investigator, one from Sara, and one from her mom.

Recalling the fear that whatever might happen could already be happening, and not caring about the hour, Kylie dialed her mom's number.

Later, at eight o'clock that morning, Kylie dropped her breakfast tray on the table and sat down beside Della and Miranda, purposely not looking around because she was afraid she might see him. Or both hims. She wasn't any more eager to see Derek right now than she was to see Lucas. Derek's avoidance of her last night still stung.

Oh, she knew she'd avoided him only a couple of weeks ago, but it had been different. She hadn't avoided him because she didn't want to be with him; she'd done it because she'd wanted to be with him too much.

Staring down at her runny eggs, which were about as appetizing as roadkill, Kylie recalled her conversation she'd had with her mom. Frankly, Kylie didn't know if her mom believed the whole "I woke from a bad dream and didn't realize the time" spiel. But when her mom confessed she'd been having some really bad dreams lately, too, Kylie couldn't help but wonder if this was because of the erasing. Were her mom's nightmares about what she'd seen at Shadow Falls?

Suddenly, Kylie felt the hair on the back of her neck start to stand up. Without even looking back, Kylie knew someone had her locked in a serious stare. Unable to resist, she glanced over her shoulder. She should have known.

Fredericka.

Turning back around, her gaze shot across the room and she found herself staring right at Derek. His eyes expressed concern, caring, but not so much that he'd come over. Could he not sense how much she needed him? She looked away, but only found herself caught in the snare of a pair of blue eyes. Beautiful blue eyes that took her back to her childhood and trying to find elephants hidden in the clouds.

Lucas glanced over at the door and nodded as if asking her to meet him outside.

Kylie had to reach deep to find the courage to do what came next.

She picked up her fork and started heaping food into her mouth as if she were too hungry to leave. Yup, she'd rather eat cold roadkill, runny scrambled eggs than talk with Lucas. Plain and simple, she wasn't ready to face him, or the dreams. Then came the fact that walking out of this dining hall to be with Lucas would no doubt hurt Derek. She didn't want to hurt Derek. It didn't even matter that he didn't seem to mind hurting her.

It was after art when Kylie arrived back to the cabin to make her two phone calls. Sitting at the computer desk, she reached for the mouse to pull up her grandparents' number again. She'd debated who to call first. The PI or her grandparents. She opted for the grandparents. Though for the life of her, she didn't have a clue what she was going to say. How did you go about telling someone you were their long-lost grandchild—but not really theirs because you happened to know their dead son had been adopted?

Oh, yeah, this was going to be easy.

When the computer woke up, the screen brought up a list of car accidents for the Springville area, Della's home. Kylie chest grew heavy when she realized Della was still suspicious of what she might have done during her changing stage.

Kylie glanced at Della's shut bedroom door. She often came back to the cabin and napped after lunch.

Opening another screen, Kylie searched for the telephone number for Kent B. Brighten in Gladlock, Texas. Unsure what she would say, she punched in the number before she lost her nerve.

The phone rang once.

Twice.

Three times.

An answering machine picked up. "Hello, you have reached Kent and Becky Brighten. We aren't home right now, but if you'll leave . . ." The voice continued.

They were still alive.

Her heart quivered. The line beeped.

Decision time. Leave a message? Not leave a message?

She hit the end button.

Ten breaths and thirty seconds later, she called the PI. Another message machine. But she left a voice message, letting him know she'd gotten a name and number of Daniel's adoptive parents.

Trying to let her mind wrap around the possibility of actually meeting the Brightens, Kylie realized she wanted to meet them for reasons other than just finding Daniel's birth parents. It would be nice to learn more about her dad. She closed the screen and another one popped up. It was a double screen of two newspaper articles about two different car accidents, each with casualties.

Kylie started to read. One was about a man in his late forties and the other was . . . Kylie's heart tugged. A woman and her six-month-old little girl.

How could Della think she could have done something like that?

A knock filled the cabin and panic filled her chest. Was it Lucas? Or Fredericka again? She cut her eyes around the room, hoping Socks was hiding. The knock came louder.

"Kylie?" Burnett's deep voice boomed through the door.

Knowing he could hear her, Kylie called, "Come in."

He opened the door and walked to the kitchen table. She grew instantly worried about the reason he was here. Surely he hadn't come back to try to pull more information out of her about Holiday. If so, he'd leave disappointed.

He nodded to a chair. "Mind if I sit down?"

"No." Then, unable to stop herself, she blurted out, "If this is about Holiday, I—"

He held up his hand. "It's not about . . . Holiday." He frowned. "Though I have to admit she still puzzles the hell out of me."

"Maybe if Selynn wasn't hanging around, then . . ." Kylie shut her mouth, realizing she was doing it again.

"Selynn's on orders of the FRU, so I couldn't send her away. But as of today, she'll be leaving."

While Kylie hadn't seen the were since the lake incident, she'd heard she was still at Shadow Falls. Someone had said she was here due to the incident with the rogue vampire. And if she was leaving, did that mean they'd caught . . .

"Has something happened? Did you catch him?" She envisioned the two girls who'd been killed, and the vision left painful footprints on her heart.

Burnett leaned back in his chair. "That's what I came to tell you. I just got word that the Vampire Council has the guy. They are going to . . . handle the situation."

"What do you mean by . . . handle?" she asked.

"Just that. They will handle it."

"Will there be a trial . . . or something like that?" Would Kylie have to testify?

Burnett looked right at her, as if remembering his promise that the guy wouldn't go unpunished. "Not really a trial. The Vampire Council basically decide his fate, but . . . they have assured me that they don't take lightly the killing of normals."

She didn't want to think too hard about what his fate would be. That might remove some of the relief of knowing that she would never have to face that rogue vampire again. But how relieved could she be? Was this incident tied to the ghost's warning? Was someone she loved still in danger?

She stared down at her hands to try and digest the information and sort out her questions. When she looked up, she saw Burnett's eyes locked on the computer screen.

"What's that?" he asked in a dark voice.

Not wanting him to suspect Della of such a horrific crime, she grabbed the mouse and hit the red X. "Nothing." Too late she remembered he could tell when she was lying. And even if he hadn't, her clumsy attempt to get the screen cleared would have told him the truth.

His gaze shot back to her eyes. "Kylie, don't do this."

"Do what?" she asked, unsure what he thought she was doing.

"Tell me you aren't investigating car accidents looking for Code-Red incidents."

Code Red. Kylie remembered that was what the FRU called a staged car accident to mask a death at the hands of a supernatural. Kylie looked back at the blank screen. "So . . . one of those accidents was a Code-Red case?" Maybe to cover up a vampire kill? Like Della had feared may have happened when she turned?

He turned his head and studied her, reading her. "If you're not investigating it, who is?"

Oh crap, Kylie thought. *What to say? What to say? It couldn't be a lie or he'd know.*

"Della?" he asked.

"No," Kylie lied again without thinking.

He closed his eyes.

"Please," Kylie said, not even sure for what she was pleading.

His dark eyes opened and he looked at her.

"She couldn't have done that," Kylie said. "She's a good person."

Burnett glanced toward Della's bedroom door. He placed a hand on Kylie's shoulder and gave it a squeeze, then he walked out without saying another word.

Two seconds after he left, Della walked out of the bedroom. Kylie had tears of guilt in her eyes.

"It's okay," Della said, but she looked scared. "I was going tell him about it anyway." She started to leave as if to find Burnett.

"You couldn't have done that," Kylie said.

Della looked back over her shoulder. Tears brightened her eyes. "I hope you're right."

Kylie sat there for about thirty minutes, numb with guilt. If she hadn't been reading the screen when Burnett came in, this would not have happened. That's when she realized she couldn't just sit here. She had to do something. She tore out of the cabin, running with everything she had to the office where she expected Burnett would have Della.

Because everyone was either in a class or a meeting, the trail was empty. Kylie hadn't gone too far when she felt it—that feeling of being watched—but her heart and mind weighed too heavy on Della to care.

Kylie made it to the opening of the trail when she saw Burnett's car, with Della in it, pull out of the front parking lot. "No."

"It's okay," Holiday said from behind her.

Kylie looked back, and because the same worry she felt was etched on Holiday's face, she knew that Holiday had been informed about what happened. "It's my fault." Guilt filled her lungs, making it hard to breathe.

Holiday guided her to the office where she gave Kylie a hug. "It's okay," she repeated, sending a surge of calm into Kylie.

"Where's he taking her?" Kylie swallowed a lump of emotion.

"To the FRU office to do some tests. DNA and bite-mark imprints."

"So one of the accidents was a Code Red?" Kylie asked.

"Both," Holiday confessed.

Kylie's heart felt like it folded over onto itself.

"Is everything okay?" a male voice spoke from the doorway.

Lucas leaned on the door frame. Worry filled his eyes.

"It's fine." Holiday waved him out.

He didn't move. "You okay?" he asked Kylie as if he needed to hear it from her.

She had yet to speak to Lucas since he'd been back and for some reason, her voice box refused to work now. All she could manage was a nod. He walked away, leaving a wake of genuine concern.

Holiday pulled Kylie over to the sofa and they sat down. "It's really going to be okay." She pressed a hand on Kylie's back and sent comforting warmth washing through her.

But the image of Della with fear in her eyes filled Kylie's mind. Della and fear didn't mix. Della was strong, and bold, and way too kind to hurt someone. "She didn't do this," Kylie told Holiday. "It's stupid to put her through the tests."

"Della wanted to do this. She needs to know."

"But she didn't do it," Kylie said again, realizing Holiday hadn't agreed with her.

"That's what we're hoping, Kylie. But if she did, there are extenuating circumstances. She was undergoing the change. The FRU will overlook it, I'm sure."

Kylie inwardly flinched at Holiday's words. She didn't know what bothered her more—that Holiday could believe Della could do this, or that new vampires could kill innocent humans and not be held accountable.

Holiday called three hours later and told Kylie that Della would be returning. She gave permission for Kylie and Miranda to take the rest of the afternoon off and wait for her. And that's just what Kylie and Miranda did. They sat at the kitchen table waiting. Kylie turned a Diet Coke around in her hands. Miranda didn't even move.

"She didn't do this," Kylie kept saying. "How can they think it's possible?"

Miranda groaned as if tired of Kylie's litany. "This isn't the same world you used to live in. Shit happens here. Bad shit. Teenage girls die. Cats get turned into skunks. Werewolves come into your cabin and try to kill you. And when a vampire turns for the first time, they can . . . do things that they wouldn't do in their right minds."

"You think she did it!" Kylie accused.

"I don't know," Miranda said. "But if she did, it wasn't her fault and I won't stop loving her. And damn it, Kylie, you shouldn't, either. She thinks you walk on water. If you turn your back on her, it'll kill her."

Tears filled Kylie eyes at even the suggestion that Della could've done something so terrible. But deep down she knew, even if it was true, she wouldn't turn her back on her friend.

Ten minutes later Della, eyes red, walked into the cabin and dropped into a chair. "The bite marks weren't mine. None of the fingerprints, either."

A smile spread across Kylie's face and her heart. "I told you."

Tears slipped from Della's dark eyes and rolled down her pale cheeks. "They think Chan did it."

Miranda looked from Della to Kylie. "Who's Chan?"

"My cousin," Della told her, no longer caring about keeping the secret. "He helped me through my change. He didn't have to do it. But he did."

"Oh," Miranda said.

"Now they want to me to find out if he did it," Della went on. "To go undercover and get the proof of his guilt." She hiccupped. "But he was there for me when no one else was, and now I have to—"

"Just tell them no," Kylie said.

"You don't tell the FRU no." Della took in a deep breath. "Besides . . . they showed me the pictures." Sorrow filled Della's dark's eyes. "There was a baby. It was awful. If he did do this, he has to be stopped before he does it to someone else. I don't think I could live with myself if I let that happen."

That night Kylie attended a mandatory camp meeting because somebody had tampered with the security alarm again. According to Burnett, the alarm was being shut off—what he didn't know was if it was by someone on the inside or outside, but he was determined to find out.

Kylie wondered if her feeling of being watched coincided with the security alarm being turned off. Because now that the alarm was guarded, she didn't feel a thing, except safer.

After the meeting, she had headed back to the cabin alone and had taken the first step up onto her porch when a noise startled her.

So much for feeling safe. Her heart pounded and she turned. Her thoughts shot to Fredericka.

"How long do you think you can avoid talking to me?" Lucas leapt up on her porch.

Kylie shifted a bit closer to the light fixture above the front door, where insects buzzed, and looked at her watch.

"Obviously only about twelve hours," she said, noting it was nine o'clock on the dot. Today when she'd seen him in the office, she'd been too concerned about Della to worry about her Lucas issues with the dreams. But not tonight. She stepped out of the light, hoping he wouldn't see embarrassment color her cheeks.

"So you admit you've been avoiding me?" Humor laced his deep voice.

Humor she didn't appreciate. She met his eyes before looking away. "I'd deny it, but you wouldn't believe me." *Besides, avoiding things that make me uncomfortable is my specialty.*

Instantly, she recalled confessing to Holiday about how confronting her dad had made her feel better. Was it too much to hope that confronting Lucas would have the same effect?

One more peek at her cabin door and she knew she had to do this. Face him and get it over with.

"So, if you're not going to deny it, dare I hope you'll explain the reason you're doing it?"

She raised her gaze again and while she wanted more than anything to believe he didn't know about the dreams, she couldn't believe it. Obviously, she was much better at avoidance than denial.

"Reasons," she said.

"What?" He stepped closer and his scent, woodsy and rich, invaded her air.

"I have more than one reason."

"Okay." He caught the end of a strand of her blond hair and rubbed it between his fingertips. "Tell me the reasons."

She pulled her hair from his hand and took a step back. "Tell you? And take all the fun out of your trying to figure it out yourself?" She had meant for the words to sound curt, but she must have missed her mark because he chuckled.

She frowned.

His humor faded. "Okay, my first guess is that you're beginning to realize at least some of your gifts. Dreamscaping, for example?"

She flushed but didn't look away this time. "Now that I understand it, it won't be a problem." She prayed she was right. Holiday had said Kylie would get more control over it, hadn't she? Surely that meant she could shut it down. God, she hoped it was true.

He studied her. "That's a shame." His tone came out flirty again.

She glanced back at the door. She'd said what she needed to, hadn't she?

When she reached for the doorknob, he caught her arm. His touch wasn't rough, not even a little bit. It was tender and that gave her more pause. She'd had a hell of a day and could still recall how he'd seemed genuinely concerned for her in the office.

"Give me a few more minutes. Please."

She continued to stare at the door, so aware that he didn't drop his hand from her arm. So aware that his touch sent feel-good tingles down her arm.

"So what are the other reasons?" he asked. When she didn't answer, he continued. "Why are you so angry with me, Kylie? And don't deny it. I might not be able to feel your emotions like . . . some people . . . but I see it in your eyes."

Kylie didn't question who he meant by "some people." He must have heard about her and Derek. Good, she thought. But then, whatever he'd heard was history. Derek had ended it.

His hold on her arm tightened slightly. "Tell me what you're upset about so we can get past it."

One word sat on the tip of her tongue. *Fredericka.* But admitting she was upset about his being with Fredericka meant she cared about him in a boy-girl kind of way. She didn't want to admit that to Lucas. She hadn't liked admitting it to herself. And it wasn't even really true. She was just confused.

"I'm tired." She risked looking at him.

His blue eyes looked brighter in the golden hue of the porch light. He still had his hand around her arm and his thumb started brushing against her skin. "You got my letters, right?"

"Yeah."

"Is it the dreams that have got you upset, because I didn't—"

"I know—it was me, not you." She pulled her arm away.

He raised his eyebrows as if contemplating. "It wasn't all you," he said as if it cost him a lot to confess it. "Not the first dream. I mean . . ."

When he hesitated, her mind took over. "So you were doing it? You came into my dream?"

"No, I don't have that ability. But when you came into my dream the first time, I was already dreaming about you." He shrugged as if to knock some of the guilt off his shoulders. "At first, I didn't realize you were really there. Not until it became so vivid and real. And I didn't say anything later because I could tell you didn't understand what had happened. If that's what you're upset about. I probably should have stopped it but . . . It was a dream. And oh, hell, I didn't want it to stop."

Even if she had to give him credit for being honest, she was still upset. He should have stopped it. Or at least told her so she wouldn't have gone back the second time. Then again, she didn't know how she'd have reacted if he'd told her this then. A lot had happened in these past weeks. She'd accepted things now that she probably wouldn't have been able to accept then.

"The second dream, however, that was all you." His eyebrows rose as if the thought made him happy.

Caught off guard by the blue twinkle in his eyes, she said the first thing that came to her mind. "I bet Aunt Stella dreamed about Tom Selleck, too."

Chapter Twenty-seven

Confusion filled his expression. "What? Tom Selleck?"

Embarrassment filled her chest. Had she really said that? "What I'm trying to say is I don't think it will happen again. So let's forget it, okay?"

"Why won't it happen again?" His gaze became heavy, and he lowered his face an inch closer from hers. "It's obvious that you feel the same about me as—"

"As you do for Fredericka?" She wished she could snatch the question from the air before it reached his ears.

His brow creased and he leaned back on his heels. "So that's what you're angry about."

She didn't deny it. Not because she didn't want to, but because she didn't think she could pull it off.

"Look, Fredericka and I—"

"It's not important."

"It is to me. I never touched her while we were away. Not once."

"It doesn't matter because . . . what you two are, or what you do, is your business. Because you and I . . . we're just friends."

"We could be more," he countered. "It feels like more already."

"No." She looked him directly in the eyes, hoping he'd understand she meant it.

He pushed a strand of her hair behind her ear, and his thumb brushed over her cheek. "The last time we stood on the porch, you invited me inside and I think that invitation included more than just . . . being friends."

She remembered standing here, almost begging him to come inside, wanting . . . so much more than his company. But that was then—before her feelings deepened for Derek.

She caught Lucas's hand and moved it from her face. "But you said no. And you were right."

"You really believe that?" He tenderly folded his fingers around her hand.

Yeah, she did, because he'd run off with Fredericka.

"She followed me, Kylie. I didn't ask her to come. I would have sent her home, but it turned out I needed her."

Kylie tried to pull her hand from his, but his hold tightened.

"I didn't mean need her like . . . like that. I left to help someone." He paused. "I didn't tell you in the letters because if Holiday found out she'd have had a fit. I have a half sister. She'd been pulled into one of the gangs. I had to get her out, Kylie. She didn't deserve to . . . I should have been there for her earlier. She called and asked for help a few months before, but I didn't do it because I would have had to face my father. It was my fault it happened and I had to help. Then Fredericka helped me."

Kylie tilted her head back. "She helped you. She tried to kill me."

He shook his head. "She wouldn't have killed you last night."

It *had* been him. She'd known, but hearing him say it made it more real.

"She just wanted to scare you," he continued. "She doesn't like you because she knows how I feel about you."

"You had to fight her to stop her from charging me."

"That doesn't mean anything. That's the way we deal with things when we're changed. We don't stand around and use psychology when we're in our natural state."

"But last night wasn't the first time she tried to put me six feet under. She put a lion in my room before you left."

His expression darkened. "She did what?"

"She put a lion in my room. One from the wildlife preserve. If it hadn't been for Derek I could have died."

Disbelief filled his expression. "She wouldn't have done that."

Kylie yanked her hand from his. She couldn't believe he was defending Fredericka. But why was that unbelievable? He'd admitted to having sex with her. Then he ran off with her.

He raked a hand through his hair. "She's not like that, Kylie. I know she's harsh but . . . you don't know her like I do."

"You're right," Kylie said. "I don't know her like you do. And since you two have so much in common, why don't you go find her right now and . . . and be with her? That's where you belong."

"She's not the one I want." His words came out terse. "It's you. It's been you since . . . since the minute I first saw you."

Kylie closed her eyes and shook her head. This was all happening so fast. She'd finally gotten used to him being gone, and now here he was shaking up her life all over again.

"Tell me you didn't feel it," he whispered. "Tell me that you didn't feel the bond we had when we first met."

She had felt it, but she'd been five years old. She met his gaze again. "I don't know what to think, Lucas. You're telling me that there's nothing between you and Fredericka, but she obviously has other ideas. Maybe you should sort things out with her before you start something up with me." Her heart clutched when she realized this was basically the same thing Derek had told her.

"You make it sound as if I haven't already tried to do that."

She shrugged. "My life's really complicated right now. If you'd been around these past weeks, you'd know that. So for now, we can be friends. That's all."

Kylie heard voices on the trail. When she looked up, Derek and a few of his friends walked past. Derek didn't even look her way. She suspected it was because he'd already seen them. Seen them and assumed the worst.

Guilt filled her, but she pushed the emotion back, hoping Derek hadn't been close enough to sense it. She hadn't been doing anything wrong. Breath held, she watched the group of guys walk out of eyeshot.

When she looked back, Lucas studied her. "Is he why? Are you two serious?"

"That's not even important. You and I are just friends, Lucas. Just friends."

She turned and opened her door. Right after she shut it in his face, she heard him say, "Not if I can change your mind, Kylie Galen."

The next morning, Della had an early morning ritual and would be a no-show for breakfast. Miranda announced she'd be skipping as well. Kylie got a feeling the witch was up to something. Probably trying to reverse the spell on Socks. Kylie had almost asked but she'd fought sleep most of the night for fear she'd lapse into a dream with Lucas, and she didn't have the stamina for a long conversation about possible curse reversals.

Walking into the dining hall alone, Kylie felt everyone's stares and knew they were all twitching like crazy checking out her brain pattern. After she grabbed her tray of a Danish and fruit, she hesitated in the back of the room, searching for a seat. Today everyone had chosen to sit with their own kind. Since Kylie didn't have a kind, or at least know what kind she belonged to, she marched over to an empty table.

For the life of her, she didn't know why it was so hard to sit alone. She should have more self-esteem than to let something so silly make her feel uncomfortable. But calling it silly didn't change how she felt. She stared at her Danish and tried not to look as pathetic as she felt.

Hearing familiar laughter, Kylie glanced up and saw the fairy table all in chuckles. Everyone there looked content in their cozy circle of friends. Everyone but Derek. Hurt filled his eyes, but what was she supposed to do? She hadn't done this. He had. And she had a distinct feeling if she went to him, he'd walk away from her. That would hurt too much.

Picking up her pastry, she took a bite. It was her favorite kind with raspberry and cream cheese, but she barely tasted it. She swallowed another flavorless bite and felt as if everyone in the room stared at her. Her new shifting brain pattern hadn't stopped being the topic of conversation from what she'd heard.

Suddenly, a tray dropped down on the table beside her. Thinking it was Della back early from her morning event, Kylie sighed the words, "Thank you," and turned with a smile.

Not Della.

Lucas smiled. "Thanks for what?"

"Nothing," she said, and almost asked him to leave. But damn it, hadn't she told him they were friends? And as friends, there was no good reason why he couldn't sit at a table with her. Well, aside from a certain she-wolf who would want to kill her because of it.

His blue eyes twinkled with humor. "You've got jelly." He brushed his finger across her lip. Then he popped the digit into his mouth.

"That's what napkins are for," she said, reaching for one and giving her tingling lips a good swipe.

He chuckled.

Realizing Derek might be watching, Kylie cut her eyes to his table. He was gone. Which meant he'd seen them and taken off. Great. She let herself feel guilty for a second and then she got mad. She wouldn't be in this situation if he would have come over and sat with her. Nope.

Taking a deep breath, she reached for her milk and took a long sip. Then she looked at Lucas who was watching her.

"You are so damn beautiful," he said.

She rolled her eyes and put down her milk. "Just friends," she insisted.

"Okay. But you're still beautiful." His grin widened. "Even with a milk mustache." He handed her a napkin and chuckled. Then he grew serious. "Burnett told me about what happened with Della. Is she going to be okay?"

"I think so." She didn't go into any detail, or mention Chan. She didn't know how much Burnett had said, or how much even Della was supposed to be telling anyone about the Code-Red incidents.

"I heard about what happened in town and then with your mom," he added. "It sounds like you've had a crappy time since I've been away."

"Yeah, pretty crappy."

He picked up his pastry and took a bite without getting anything on himself, of course. "I also heard . . ." His eyes brightened in humor. "About what your skunk did to Fredericka. I'm sure she deserved it."

"She did." Was this his way of showing loyalty to Kylie over Fredericka? Not that he had to choose between them. Kylie and Lucas were just friends. And if she could just stop remembering how good it had felt to kiss him, she really thought they could be friends, too. "Your last few weeks didn't sound too great, either. Is your sister going to be okay?"

He nodded. "I think so. I've got her staying with some friends. I'm going to talk to Holiday about her enrolling here for school. You are signing up, right?"

Kylie pinched off a piece of pastry. "I'm hoping so. My mom said she's thinking about it."

The thought of what Kylie would do if her mom really said no caused her stomach to knot. She belonged here, with the others. Her gaze shifted around the different tables hosting what looked like families of supernaturals. Hopefully, soon she'd even discover what table she belonged to.

This isn't the same world you used to live in. Kylie heard Miranda's words from last night echo in her head. No, it wasn't the same world. It was dark and sometimes very dangerous, but it was her world now.

Chapter Twenty-eight

"How do I make it stop?" Kylie, exhausted from lack of sleep, asked the question as she dropped into a chair across from Holiday's desk at the start of their two o'clock appointment. "I don't want to do this whole dream crap anymore."

Holiday sat back and pursed her lips. "This gift is too special to call crap. And you can't stop it, but you can control it with practice."

"Okay, how do I control this shit then?"

Holiday chuckled. "Haven't you sensed yourself moving in the dream world?"

"You mean, like flying?"

"Yeah, like flying."

"Sure, but sometimes I don't wake up until I'm already in the dream."

"Okay, here's what you do. Before you go to bed . . ." Holiday rattled off a series of techniques to train herself to wake up from a dream. It wasn't a guarantee Kylie could control it but Holiday thought it was a first step.

They had moved on to the subject of the ghost when Holiday's cell rang. She picked it up from the desk and glanced at the caller's number. Her eyes lit up. "I . . . need to take this call. Can you give me a few minutes?"

Kylie started to get up, but Holiday sprang from her chair first and started toward the door. "Hello, Mr. Eastman."

Holiday shut the door behind her with a firm *click* and Kylie settled back and closed her eyes.

"Yes, I'm so excited that you're considering my offer." Holiday's words filled Kylie's ear.

Kylie snapped her eyes open. Not again with the sensitive hearing!

"I can't tell you how much Shadow Falls needs someone like your-self on our board."

Kylie put her hands over her ears, not wanting to eavesdrop.

"Yes, a hundred thousand should cover it."

Kylie frowned when the voice continued to sneak through her palms. Then she realized what this meant. Holiday had found an-other investor for Shadow Falls, which meant Burnett would be leaving.

Kylie's chest filled with a strange kind of achiness, a sense that this was all wrong. Not that there was a damn thing she could do about it.

After a few minutes, she heard Holiday tell Mr. Eastman that she'd be in touch soon and send him the papers to sign. She heard Holiday hang up and Kylie quickly started debating whether she should tell Holiday that she'd heard her phone conversation.

Several long minutes passed and Kylie came to the conclusion that she didn't need to tell. When Holiday didn't come back into the office, Kylie went to find her.

Holiday stood in the back room staring out the window at the basketball court. When Kylie joined her, she noticed that Bur-nett was shooting hoops with a group of boys. Kylie's gaze shot to

Derek, but she suspected it wasn't Derek who intrigued Holiday. No doubt the camp leader was having second thoughts. Hopefully even some third ones about turning down Burnett's offer.

Right then, Derek turned. His gaze found the window and she knew he'd sensed her. He didn't smile or wave. He turned back to the game and ignored her. Just like that, Kylie made up her mind. Enough was enough. She and Derek needed to talk.

The next morning, Kylie woke up refreshed. When the cold at dawn hit, Kylie had slept for about five straight hours. Holiday's tips on how to wake up before the dreams started had worked. She'd woken up twice to the sensation of flying. Once, she'd even seen Lucas, but she'd been able to pull back before he'd noticed her. She felt certain he hadn't even known she'd been there. Or at least she hoped that was the case.

Pulling the covers up to her chin, she looked around. No ghost appeared, but the cold hung on so Kylie knew the ghost hung with it. When Kylie's phone fell off the nightstand—again—she remembered how it had done the same thing the other day.

"Are you doing that?" she asked the spirit. "Wanna tell me something?"

No answer came back. Reaching for her phone, wondering if she'd find someone on the line again, she was relieved when there wasn't. Then seeing her blinking message light, she remembered she hadn't deleted her old messages.

She'd spoken to the PI and given him the new information she'd discovered about her grandparents. He said he would try to contact the Brightens. Not that it stopped Kylie from also calling them. She'd made a dozen calls to the number yesterday afternoon, but each time she'd only gotten the message machine.

Kylie went to delete the messages and realized she had one from Sara that she hadn't played. Remembering the mixed emotions she'd felt the last time they'd spoken, she put the phone down and gave herself permission to avoid it until later. Besides, she needed to get her speech straight to get Derek to come to his senses. She hoped her plan worked.

Kylie waited out in the dining hall before breakfast, looking for Chris. Don't let him walk up with Derek, she prayed.

When she spotted Chris walking up with Jonathon, she relaxed. When he got closer, she motioned him over. He said something to Jonathon and then started walking her way. Kylie could see curiosity spark in his eyes about why she wanted to speak to him.

It wasn't a secret that Chris, one of the head vampires, thought he was a total stud muffin. And Kylie would admit, with his blond hair and light eyes, he had sort of a California-beach-cute-guy look going for him. His body wasn't all that bad, either. But if he was thinking Kylie had a thing for him, he was about to be disappointed.

"What's up?" He smiled.

Kylie hadn't given much thought about how to approach this, so she just blurted it out. "I need a favor." Chris was in charge of Campmates Hour, where names were put in a pot and drawn and you would spend an hour getting to know this person better.

"What kind of favor?" His gaze shot to her breasts.

She almost called him on it, but considering she needed him, she let it pass. "I heard that if someone wanted to make sure they drew a certain name, you could arrange it."

"Oh." He looked disappointed, which told her he'd thought

she'd called him over for different reasons. He recovered quickly, though. "Did you also hear there's a price for doing it?"

"A pint, right?"

"Yep."

"Fine. I'll tell Holiday I'm donating." She started to walk away, but he caught her arm.

"You forgot to tell me who it is." He wrinkled his brow. "Let me guess. Lucas?"

Kylie frowned. "Derek."

Derek wasn't around when the names were called, so she went in search of him. He stood in the dining hall talking with Steve and Luis. Derek frowned when he saw her step beside him. That hurt. Forcing a smile, she leaned over and whispered, "Guess what?" She waved the slip of paper with his name in the air.

He said good-bye to the guys and motioned for her to follow. They walked outside past the crowd. She wondered if he just planned to go to their spot at the rock, but he stopped.

His green eyes studied her. "Did you rig this?"

"Rig what?" She feigned innocence.

He caught her arm and turned it over. She knew he looked for a bandage, or a needle mark, but his touch sent tiny pain-like currents running through her. "Did you buy my name with blood?" He dropped her arm.

She squared her shoulders. "So? You did it for me. Twice."

So much emotion filled his eyes that her breath caught.

"We have to talk, Derek. This . . ." She moved a hand between them. "It isn't right."

He raked a hand through his brown hair. "What isn't right is that I care about you while you care about someone else."

"Fine!" Kylie felt herself growing angry and losing hope. "Do I care about Lucas? Yes. But I don't care about him the way I care about you."

He shook his head. "You can't lie to me, Kylie. I can read your emotions and when you're around him you're . . . attracted to him."

"Okay, I'll even admit I'm attracted to him. But that doesn't mean anything."

"The hell it doesn't!" He started to walk away.

Kylie grabbed his arm. "You're no different."

"What?" His eyes brightened with anger and hurt.

"I saw you looking at Miranda when we were swimming."

"I didn't—"

"Yes, you did!"

"This is stupid." He started walking away again.

Kylie almost let him go, but she remembered that she was going to have to pay a pint for this. Damn it. She wanted her blood's worth.

She caught up with him. "Perry even noticed because he started giving you the evil eye."

He continued walking and so did she.

"Did I get bent out of shape about it? No, I didn't because I know that while you might have thought she was pretty in her bathing suit, it didn't mean you didn't like me."

He stopped and turned to face her. "That is different."

"How is it different? If I could read your emotions, like you can read mine, I would have read lust loud and clear."

"Yeah, but . . . but I'm a guy."

Her mouth dropped open. "So only guys can be attracted to someone? Please! What century are you living in?"

His eyes tightened. "I didn't mean it like that."

"Then what did you mean?"

"I meant . . ." He clenched his jaw. "Christ. I don't know, but it's still different."

"It's not, Derek! Don't you see? You're getting all bent out of shape because you're jealous and you have no reason to be."

"It's more than that," he said. "You just said you care about him. This isn't just—"

"Yeah, I care about him. We met a long time ago. And maybe that bonds us somehow. And yes, he's nice looking. But . . . I want to be with you."

She thought she was getting through to him, but he looked away. "I can't do it, Kylie. Until you can prove to me that he doesn't mean anything to you, I can't do this." He walked away again.

"Derek?" she called.

He turned around. "What?"

Her chest grew heavy. "You lied to me."

"About what?" Frustration colored his voice.

"You said we'd be friends. This isn't how you treat a friend."

He looked up at the sky before he met her eyes. "You're right. I'm sorry. I guess I can't be your friend." He walked off.

This time she let him go.

It was hard to get through the day. Kylie wanted to ask Holiday to let her skip the scheduled events, but she'd begged off too much. So she went to art, took a hike, and lost herself in cake decorating.

Every time she started to think about Derek, she'd mentally snap a rubber band around her heart. She was so focused on decorating her cupcakes that half the class was over before she realized Miranda wasn't there.

As soon as it was over, she ditched music class and found Della walking to the lake for kayak lessons. Della had been pretty low-key lately, still recovering from the whole FRU visit and testing. And she dreaded having to go undercover to try to help catch her cousin for murder. Of course, worrying about that meant she wasn't worrying about parents weekend. Hey, you had to find the silver linings where you could.

"Have you seen Miranda?" Kylie asked.

"No. Is something wrong?"

"She just wasn't in cake decorating. I was going to see if she was at the cabin."

"You want me to come with you?"

"No," Kylie said, remembering that Della had been looking forward to kayaking. "If I can't find her, I'll find you. I'm sure it's nothing."

Unfortunately, right before Kylie reached her cabin, she was certain she'd been wrong in her assessment. Her first clue? The high-pitched scream coming from inside.

Taking off at a dead run, Kylie reached the front door before she realized that the screams weren't Miranda's. Not that this realization slowed her down. Someone was in her cabin and screaming bloody murder. And Miranda was missing.

Jerking the door open, Kylie ran inside. "Miranda?"

"In here," Miranda called from her bedroom, her words barely heard over the shrieking.

Pushing open the bedroom door, Kylie thought she was prepared to face anything. She couldn't have been more wrong.

Chapter Twenty-nine

Kylie gaped at the screaming redheaded girl locked in the big purple cage in the middle of Miranda's room. Then her gaze shot to Miranda, reclining in the middle of her bed, painting her toenails as if it were a lazy Sunday morning.

"Let me out of here, you bitch!" The girl shook the cage.

Miranda finished spreading fuchsia pink on her pinky toenail before she glanced up. "What's up?" She smiled extra wide at Kylie.

"Bitch!" the girl screamed at Miranda then glared at Kylie. "Make her let me go!"

"I think I should be asking you what's up," Kylie said to Miranda, and then she looked back at the girl. A quick sniff of the air said there hadn't been any blood lost.

Yet, anyway.

"Release me!" the prisoner snarled.

Kylie glanced back at Miranda and raised an eyebrow.

"See what I caught." Miranda giggled. "Remember I've been telling you that someone was lurking around our cabin? I set a trap. And damn if I didn't catch Tabitha Evans."

"Do you know her?" Kylie asked.

"Yup, she's one of the witches I'm competing against in two weeks."

Tabitha shook the bars so hard that the cage rocked. "I'm the witch that is going to put a hex on you if you don't let me out!"

"Don't worry," Miranda said. "Her powers don't work as long as she's kept in my special cage. And I put a silencer about a hundred feet away, so no one can hear her yell."

"What's she doing here?" Kylie asked, concerned for the prisoner.

"Trying to undermine my confidence so I'd drop out of the competition."

"And if I'd known you were such a screw-up I wouldn't have wasted my time," the girl screamed.

Okay, so Tabitha deserved to be caged. "Do you think she's the one who's been cutting off the security alarm?" Kylie asked.

"No, this was done with magic. Pathetic, barely excusable magic, of course." Miranda glanced at the caged girl.

Tabitha hissed. "You're the one who's pathetic."

Miranda raised an eyebrow at her prisoner. "And you're the one in the cage."

The girl returned to shrieking. Miranda beamed with pride.

No doubt, catching Tabitha was good for Miranda's ego. Kylie hated to pop Miranda's bubble, but . . . "As cute as she looks in the cage, you do know you can't keep her."

"I don't plan on it," Miranda said. "I told her that as soon as she turns Socks back into a kitten, she can leave."

"And I've told you that I didn't do that! That was your screw-up! All you!"

"Please," Miranda said. "For weeks almost everything I tried to do came out wrong."

Miranda swung her feet off the bed and leaned close to the cage. "Change the skunk back into a kitten and you can go."

"And for the millionth time, I didn't do that!"

Miranda glanced back to Kylie. "Do you want me to paint your toenails?" Doubt filled Miranda's eyes.

"Look," Tabitha snapped. "If it wasn't you who did it, then maybe it was that old guy."

"I've got some nice reds," Miranda told Kylie, ignoring Tabitha.

Kylie wasn't so good at ignoring. "What old guy?"

"Don't believe anything she says," Miranda said.

"I don't know who he is, but he's vampire. But he has some other powers, too, because he was here using a similar spell as I was. Scary old guy."

"Please," Miranda said. "Tell me something I can believe."

"I'm telling the truth," Tabitha snapped.

Miranda rolled her eyes. Then she wiggled her pinky.

"Wait," Kylie said, but too late, the cage and Tabitha disappeared.

"Wait for what?" Miranda asked.

"Where did she go?"

"You said I couldn't keep her."

Kylie frowned. "What if she was telling the truth about the weird old guy?"

"Please, she's making up crap. Della would have smelled a vampire. Tabitha's crazy."

Kylie had to admit Miranda had a point. Della could sniff out vampires a mile away.

Miranda dropped back on the bed. "Can you believe I caught Tabitha Evans. I'm good."

Socks came slinking into the room cautiously. His puffy black and white tail pointed in the air as if ready to blow and go if needed. Kylie looked back at Miranda. She might be good at setting traps, but she hadn't quite gotten the spell down to turn Socks back into a kitten.

Then Kylie remembered her conversation with Derek. She mentally reached for the rubber band to snap herself out of thinking about him, but the dang rubber band wasn't there. All she could feel was a big empty hole in her chest where her heart used to be.

"I'm gonna lay down." Before she went into her bedroom, she stopped at the fridge. Yanking opening the freezer, she grabbed one of the many quarts of ice cream Miranda had bought to nurse her broken heart.

Snatching a spoon out of the drawer, Kylie wondered if there was enough ice cream in the universe to make her feel better.

She really didn't believe so.

The next week passed in a haze of heartbreak. Kylie gave her pint of blood and ate at least ten pints of ice cream. Derek continued to avoid her; Lucas continued to show up. Not that she could even get mad at him. He never made any passes. He was just being a friend. With her heart on the mend, she could use another friend.

Of course, they never discussed Fredericka or the dreams— and thankfully she'd managed to keep the dreams at bay. He had asked about Derek, though, and Kylie told him it was a sore subject. The only thing Lucas said was that Derek was an idiot. For some reason, Kylie appreciated Lucas saying it.

She also appreciated the fact that Fredericka had stayed out of her way. Kylie wasn't sure, but she suspected Lucas had something to do with that, too.

The ghost showed up every morning. Sometimes she'd speak, but she never offered anything that helped Kylie figure out who was in danger. Whenever Kylie would start to worry about the ghost's warning, Holiday would take her to the falls. They'd gone three times. Kylie kept leaving with the same message: stay focused and keep the faith.

Holiday hadn't mentioned anything about Burnett in all this time. Kylie wondered if she'd told him she'd found another investor, or if she was reconsidering his offer. Kylie caught Holiday spying out the window and watching Burnett and the others play ball at least six times. Two or three of those times Kylie had even stood with her, just so she could watch Derek. Not that he didn't know she looked on. He would always glance at the window.

Their eyes would meet. Kylie would remember how much she missed him while he appeared annoyed.

"You want to talk about it?" Holiday had asked the last time it happened.

Kylie had agreed to spill her guts, but only over ice cream. She'd eaten all of Miranda's stash and needed more. So Kylie and Holiday took the afternoon off and went back to the ice cream parlor where they ate their weight in cold creamy scoops of bliss.

"Why does ice cream go with a broken heart?" Kylie asked.

"Because if you eat enough of it, it freezes the heart and numbs the pain for a bit," Holiday answered, and they both laughed.

Daniel hadn't visited since the day her mom had broken into the camp and had to be erased, but her stepdad had called twice. Kylie had taken his second call. They talked about his job, about the weather, and then he mentioned the possibility of Kylie attending the Shadow Falls boarding school. He hadn't been positive or negative and said it was up to her mom.

When she hung up, she realized that her mom and dad must be talking for him to know about the boarding school. Kylie wasn't sure how she felt about that. Was her mom ready to forgive him? Kylie almost called her mom and asked, but with parents weekend less than one week away, Kylie figured she should wait and do it in person.

Miranda seldom mentioned Perry anymore. Not that it stopped Perry from watching Miranda. Anytime he was within a hundred feet of her, he had his gaze locked on her. Kylie knew that Miranda noticed it. She chose to ignore it. Not too hard considering her stress about the upcoming competition that her mother had entered her in during parents weekend. If she wasn't practicing for the event, she was attempting to solve the puzzle of what happened to Socks.

After two weeks, Socks didn't seem to mind being a skunk. He seemed to understand the power of his tail, and he'd raise it up in a threat at the least provocation. He even had Della walking a line. Thankfully, he hadn't sprayed again.

Della dreaded going home. And now she dreaded coming back to the FRU job waiting on her. Going undercover to find out if her cousin was responsible for the murders wasn't going to be easy for Della. A grumpy Della and a stressed-out Miranda meant the two were at each other's throats. Kylie often wondered if she didn't intervene if the two would really kill each other. But she loved the two of them too much to chance it.

The PI had finally discovered that Kent and Betty Brighten had taken a long vacation in Ireland. So Kylie's quest to discover what she was had been temporarily put on hold. Wasn't that just lovely?

The one good thing that happened lately was Kylie no longer felt that strange sense of being watched. She wondered if Tabitha had been the cause of it. But when she'd recall Tabitha, Kylie would remember what the girl said about an old vampire hanging around.

For some reason, that bothered Kylie. Not enough to mention it to Holiday, because in doing so she might get Miranda in trouble. And after the Burnett incident with Della, getting friends in trouble was the last thing Kylie wanted to do.

On Tuesday morning, Kylie woke up with what felt like an extra chill in the air. Either the ghost was trying to send a message or Kylie had more than one spirit hanging around. Great. That's all she needed, another ghost.

"What do you want?" Kylie trembled beneath the covers.

Her phone started croaking. Either her phone's ringtone had gotten changed or Miranda had managed to turn it into a frog. Kylie grabbed her phone. It stopped making the hideous sound and went directly to her voicemail messages.

First it played the one her dad had left, then one the PI left a few days ago. Next it played one that Kylie hadn't heard. From Trey, her boyfriend from the past. How had she missed this call? He asked her to return his call, saying it was important.

"Yeah, right," she muttered. "What, did you find out my breasts got bigger and you want to see them?" She shut the phone off, but not before deleting his message.

She had no sooner laid it back on the nightstand when the cell commenced croaking.

Grabbing it, she looked at the dang thing to make sure it was off. It was. So how did it make noise? She hit the off button again. The croaking continued.

"Are you doing this?" she asked the spirit. "If so, stop. Because it's not funny. And it's not telling me crap about what I need to know."

The phone went silent. The ghost appeared at the foot of her bed. *"You have to do something soon. She's dying."*

Just like before, the spirit didn't offer a freaking clue as to who the mysterious "she" was.

Kylie got dressed and decided to visit Holiday. She doubted if hearing Holiday say she thought everything was going to be okay would take the edge off the fear, but she had to try.

She hadn't even gotten to the office porch when she heard the voices ringing in her ears.

"Tell me it isn't dangerous?" Holiday insisted, sounding furious.

"I can't tell you that," Burnett said. *"This work is always dangerous."*

"Then no. He can't go."

"I didn't come to ask you," Burnett said, sounding equally annoyed. *"He's gotten permission from his mother. He'll be leaving today around noon."*

Kylie turned and started walking in the opposite direction. She would have covered her ears, but that had never worked before, so she just kept walking, hoping the voices would fade.

"It's wrong," Holiday said. *"First, you involve Lucas, and now Derek. I have to put my foot down."*

Kylie stopped. *First Lucas and now Derek . . . what?*

"They are both exceptional boys," Burnett said.

"And that's my point. They are boys, Burnett."

"I was sixteen when I went to work for the FRU. Lucas is eighteen. Derek is only a few months shy of that. And he's an eraser, Holiday. Do you know how few there are of those?"

"I don't care about that. I care about him."

"He'll only be gone a month or less. Back in time for the school year to begin."

"Assuming he's not killed trying to do the government's work," Holiday snapped.

"I'm sorry," Burnett said, and there was regret in his voice.

Kylie heard a door slam. Burnett had left but she didn't move. She stood there on the trail, digesting what she'd just heard. Derek was leaving. He was going to work for the FRU. He wouldn't be back for a month.

Assuming he's not killed trying to do the government's work. Holiday's words played in Kylie's mind. Her heart froze. She took off down the trail toward Derek's cabin.

Chapter Thirty

Kylie got to Derek's cabin a minute later. She spotted Chris walking out of the cabin, dressed for his morning jog, and stopped. She would have jumped into the woods and hidden, but Chris was vampire, which meant he'd probably already heard her. So she started jogging and hoped he wouldn't stop and ask any questions.

When they ran past each other, she waved. He smiled and kept going. She continued down the trail past the cabin until she felt he wouldn't be in hearing range. Then she spun around, ran into the cabin, and went straight into Derek's room.

He was in bed, still asleep. His wide chest was bare. The sheet came low around his waist and Kylie wasn't sure if he had anything on beneath the sheet. She'd heard rumors that most boys slept in the buff. But she'd seen him naked and that didn't scare her away.

"Derek?"

He dropped his hand over his face.

She moved over to the bed and touched his shoulder. "Derek?"

His eyes popped open and he shot up. He stared at her but didn't look awake. "You've got your clothes on, so this isn't a dream." He flinched as if he realized he'd said that aloud and then he dropped back on the bed and stared up at the ceiling.

"It's not a dream." She sat beside him. "I heard what you're planning to do and I don't want you to go. Please, don't go."

He looked over at her with heavy-lidded eyes, but she could tell he was awake. "How did you find out?"

He hadn't answered her question, so she didn't answer his. "Were you not even going to say good-bye?" Tears filled her eyes.

He sat up and pulled the sheet around his waist. "I was going to say good-bye."

She blinked away the emotion. "You're doing this because of me, aren't you?"

"No. Not completely." He touched her arm and the floodgates of emotion really started pouring.

"Please, don't go," she said in tears.

"I have to. I need to get my head on straight." He blinked. "You were right. Well, partially right. I still think you have issues you need to resolve about Lucas. But . . . you were right about me being jealous. My ability to read emotions is getting stronger. And I don't know why, but with you, it's as if I feel everything you feel but . . . more. I don't know if it's because I care about you so much or what. But when you feel something I don't like, an attraction for another guy, anger, or even disappointment at someone, I . . . I go crazy inside. It's like someone is shooting me up with emotional adrenaline." He raked a hand over his face. "I've either got to learn to deal with this or . . ."

"Or what?" she asked. He didn't answer, but Kylie knew what he meant. He either had to learn to deal with the emotions she unleashed inside him, or walk away from her. But wasn't that what he was doing? Walking away?

"And you've got to deal with Lucas and . . ." He paused. "I'm also going to confront my dad. And when I come back in a month, we'll see how things stand. You may have fallen in love with Lucas by then. And if that happens, I'll have to accept it."

"Would it be that easy to accept?"

"No. But I don't see what other choice I have."

"But you do have a choice. Stay. Give us a chance. We'll work through this."

He shook his head. "I can't, Kylie. I just can't."

She looked at him and as hard as it was to accept, she finally did. Derek was leaving. He had made his choice, and it wasn't her.

Chin high, vowing that she'd done everything she could, she turned and walked out. He might have broken her heart, but he wasn't going to break her spirit. She would get over him. She would.

A week later, Kylie sat on a blanket out by the river where she and her mother had sat and talked about Daniel. Kylie just wanted to be alone to think, to try and wrap her head around how she was going to get her mom to sign her up for Shadow Falls' boarding school. And maybe, just maybe, Daniel would drop by while she was here.

She lay back on the blanket and stared up at the blue sky, and then she heard someone approach.

"See any elephants?" a familiar male voice asked.

She smiled at Lucas. "No, but I just saw a giraffe."

He looked up in the sky. "Where?"

"Over there." She pointed to the left. "Its neck is no longer connected to its body, but you can still see it if you squint."

He dropped down beside her. She thought he looked up at the clouds, but when she glanced back, she found him looking at her. He smiled. "You just get prettier every day, Kylie Galen."

She rolled her eyes. "Don't start."

"Okay, can I say I'll miss you?"

She sat up. "Are you going to your grandmother's house?"

"Yeah. We're in Houston."

She studied the tip of her tennis shoe, and decided to just ask. "Lucas, are you working with FRU?"

His eyes widened. "Who told you?"

"I overheard Burnett and Holiday talking about it."

"After I got inside the gang that had my sister, I got with Burnett to help me bring down a few really bad guys. So yeah, I sort of worked with them. And I told them if they needed me for anything else, I would be available."

"Isn't it dangerous?"

He studied her. "Are you asking out of concern for me or for Derek?"

"Both." She had accepted that Derek had left. She hadn't completely gotten over the heartbreak, but she would.

"It's not that dangerous. If you follow the game plan, things generally go okay."

He brushed a long stand of hair from her cheek. "You know I want to be more than your friend, right?"

She went to studying her tennis shoe again.

"I don't expect you to answer. I just wanted you to know before some other guy tries to move in." He leaned closer. "I'm patient, Kylie. I've waited eleven years for you. I can wait until you're ready." He pressed a kiss to her cheek. It wasn't anything like the kisses they'd shared, especially those in her dreams. But his nearness—his woodsy scent, the feel of his lips against her skin—sent a hundred butterflies into full flutter mode.

When she looked over at him, he was gone.

And obviously so were Kylie's wits. Because for the life of her, she didn't know what she'd planned to do, reprimand him for kissing her . . . or kiss him back.

And maybe it was better if she didn't answer her own question, too.

Friday morning, Kylie, Miranda, and Della, each carting suitcases, walked the trail to meet up with their parents. They walked slowly, like condemned prisoners moving to their executions.

"I'm going to be peeing on a drug test stick every hour," Della muttered.

Miranda sighed. "I'm going to screw up at my competition and my mom is going to give me up for adoption."

"I'm going to a ghost hunt," Kylie added. Both girls looked at her. "Don't ask."

Holiday met them at the end of the trail, channeling her normal, peppy self. "Smile, guys. It's only for a few days."

They all turned and looked at each other again. Kylie dropped her suitcase and hugged them both. "I expect a phone call from each of you twice a day."

"Twice a day," Della said. "I hope you don't mind if I call when I'm peeing on a drug test stick, because that's what I'm gonna be doing the whole time."

"Just don't flush," Miranda said. "I hate it when people flush when they're talking to me."

Five minutes later, over in the dining hall, Kylie gave Holiday a big hug. "Take care of Socks," she told her.

"I'm planning on bringing him over to my place," Holiday said.

When Kylie and her mom started out of the dining hall, Perry came over and gave her a nudge with his elbow. For Perry, that was equivalent to a hug. Kylie gave him a warm smile.

"It seems like you've made good friends here," her mom said.

"Yeah, I have, Mom. They're special."

Kylie almost ran out the door when Lucas stepped in front of her. "Hello, Mrs. Galen," he said. "My name is Lucas. I just wanted to say good-bye to your daughter."

Kylie's heart raced as she worried her mom might recognize him.

"Nice to meet you, Lucas," her mom said, and stepped away to give them some privacy.

He smiled. "Take care."

"I will."

He leaned in. "Dream of me," he whispered.

She rolled her eyes, but he just grinned and walked off. Kylie headed over to her mom.

"He's kind of cute," her mom said, but she had that tone—the tone she got before she started handing out the sex pamphlets. They walked out of the dining hall and headed for the car.

"Yeah," Kylie agreed, and for the umpteenth time, she hoped that the weekend went okay. No unexpected surprises, no long, uncomfortable silences with her and her mom.

When her mom started the car, the cold that filled the interior was more powerful than any car air-conditioning.

"Wow. I've never had this car get cool so fast." When her mom pulled out, Kylie glanced in the backseat to stare at the ghost in her bloody nightgown. Suddenly the ghost lurched forward and threw up all over Kylie's shoulder. The stench was awful.

Kylie fought to keep her gag reflex from bouncing up and down her throat.

"So," her mom said, oblivious to it all. "Where would you like to go for an early lunch? I'm starving."

Chapter Thirty-one

Kylie wasn't sure who it was who said you couldn't go home again. But he had it partly right. Oh, you could go home. It was just going to be awkward as hell. Amazingly, it didn't stem from her mom. They'd actually had a good three-hour drive home, phantom puke aside. The problem was the house. It felt cold, not just because the ghost had decided to tag along, but because of her dad. Or lack of dad. There was nothing, not one thing here that reminded Kylie that he'd ever lived here. Even the pictures of their father-daughter trips were gone, replaced now with pictures of just Kylie.

She couldn't blame her mom, but damn. For the first time since it all happened, Kylie worried about how her mom might really feel with her going away to boarding school. And maybe she even understood her mom wanting to sell the house.

"Doesn't it feel so good to be back?" Her mom hugged her.

Being back? Not so good. The hug felt nice, though. So nice it even made the house feel less awkward.

When Kylie went into her room, she couldn't help but laugh. On her nightstand was a whole set of pamphlets on all the sex-related topics Kylie had missed while away. The one on top, obviously the one Kylie's mom thought most important, covered info on safe oral sex. Oh yeah, crucial need-to-know information. Kylie was planning on running out tonight and having oral sex.

Her mom had the entire weekend scheduled with items from her We Gotta List. We gotta bake your favorite cookies. We gotta go eat at a new pizza place. We gotta be at the haunted house at six.

When, Kylie wondered, was she going to have time to run out and have "safe" oral sex?

Kylie added a big Gotta to the list. *Gotta convince Mom to sign me up for boarding school.* Even with her reservations about leaving her mom, Kylie was a supernatural and felt like a fish out of water back at home.

At six that evening, after baking cookies and enjoying some together time with her mom, Kylie crawled her fish-out-of-water butt into the car to go to the ghost hunt. And she seriously hoped that the B&B owner didn't mind if she brought a visitor along because sitting in the backseat—still bloody, still puking—was Kylie's ghost, who wasn't any more communicative here than she'd been back at Shadow Falls.

And to prove the point, the ghost disappeared before they arrived at the B&B.

Once they'd all gathered in the lobby of the B&B, the owner, a tall, heavyset woman in her late fifties, with dyed red hair, waved them into a semicircle. "Welcome. Welcome to Anderson's B&B. My name is Celeste Bell. Some of you may remember me from my many television appearances."

Kylie didn't but several of the other guests nodded their heads. Celeste was a professed ghost whisperer who had appeared on some cable show as an expert on haunting. She wore a long white gown, as if dressing spooky would help intensify the experience.

"The house was built in the late eighteen hundreds by Joshua Anderson, but tragedy struck before he ever moved in when his young bride was killed on their wedding day in a carriage accident. Joshua took his own life in the master bedroom. The place was subsequently sold and reopened as a saloon. More tragedy soon followed. Now, before we get started, let's talk about the rules."

The rules were simple. Stay together. No unnecessary chitchat. Celeste also insisted they turn off their cell phones because that kind of energy could chase away ghosts.

Funny, Kylie thought, her experience said ghosts really liked tinkering with her cell.

Kylie actually checked Celeste's brain pattern to see if maybe she was supernatural, but nope. The ten attendees, with the exception of Kylie and her mom, were all card-carrying senior citizens who no longer had to show their IDs to get their free coffees at their neighborhood Chick-fil-A. Moving slowly as a group, half of them using walkers, they followed the woman through the first floor of the house. In each room, Celeste stopped to tell another haunting tale, most from the house's days as a saloon.

Thus far, the place looked ghost-free.

While Celeste may have sucked as a ghost whisper, she was a good storyteller and she had everyone on pins and needles listening to the spooky tales.

"Now, we're going to have dinner. And I'll tell you about what happened in the early nineteen hundreds. Go ahead and sit down." Celeste motioned to the dining room table, with plates already filled with spaghetti. "For some reason," she whispered, "this room is always a bit colder than the rest of the house."

As if on cue, the temperature in the old parlor dropped a good forty degrees. Kylie's ghost materialized next to her. The patrons all huddled together, hugging themselves, as steam rose from their lips. The look on Celeste's face would have made attending the ghost hunt worth it if Kylie hadn't seen the look of sheer terror on her mom's face.

"It's okay, Mom," Kylie whispered.

"It's so friggin' damn spooky." Her mom never said *friggin'* or *damn*.

"Probably just a trick," Kylie lied.

"It's time. Time for you to do something!" the ghost screamed.

Show me what I have to do, Kylie said in her mind.

Right then, every cell phone in the room started ringing. Well, all of them except Kylie's. Her phone croaked like some demented frog. And since they had all been turned off, that brought some serious gasps.

But not as serious as when the chandelier crashed down on top of the table, sending plates of spaghetti shooting across the room.

Celeste, the professed ghost whisperer and cable TV "celebrity," fainted. Kylie didn't know people using walkers could move so fast. But not fast enough for her mom. Kylie thought for a second that her mom was going to knock a couple of them out of the way to take the lead spot heading out of the dining room.

Kylie knelt beside Celeste. As the last of the guests fought their way out the door, Kylie heard one of them say, "Who is Trey Cannon?"

Kylie looked up at the elderly man.

"Don't know," said another lady. "But that's who called me, too."

Kylie grabbed her phone, and sure as hell, she had a voice message from Trey.

Why would the ghost send Trey's message to everyone in the room?

Kylie looked up at the ghost who stood in the middle of the room wearing spaghetti all over her blood-soaked nightgown, which definitely would be putting Kylie off pasta for a long time. "It's Trey? I'm supposed to help Trey? But you said . . . 'she' needed help."

The ghost started to fade.

"Don't you dare leave!" Kylie screeched.

"I'm so sorry, baby. I thought you were right behind me," her mom called from the other room. Seconds later, she ran back in and dropped beside Kylie. "Oh, God, is she dead?"

The woman's eyes shot open and she screamed.

Twenty minutes later, while Kylie's mom spoke to the ambulance driver who was about to cart off Celeste and one of the guests who was now complaining of chest pains, Kylie got her mom's phone and deleted Trey's message. The last thing Kylie wanted was her mom getting suspicious. She hoped her mom hadn't heard Trey's name mentioned in the mix of things.

Kylie listened to his message. All he'd said was to call him. She did. It went to his voicemail. Just freaking great!

When Kylie woke up the next morning at nine o'clock, she had two startling realizations.

First: She hadn't been woken up at dawn by the ghost. Did this mean anything? Was it a good thing? A bad thing?

Second: And this was the shocker. She wasn't alone. Nope. Completely covered under the blanket next to Kylie was a body. Dead or alive, she wasn't sure.

Biting back a scream, she touched it. More like poked it. It wasn't cold. It even made a *oomph* sound. Her mom's head popped out from under the covers. When she saw Kylie's expression, she bolted upright. "What is it?"

Kylie blinked. "What are you doing in my bed?"

"Oh." She ran a hand through her newly styled hair that really looked good on her. "I came to check in on you. I guess I . . . dropped off."

Kylie giggled. "You were scared."

Her mom did an eye roll that would put Sara to shame. "Nooo." She broke down and laughed. "Okay, yes. It was freaky. I was shocked you could sleep."

"It was just a ghost." Kylie grinned.

"You say that as if you see them all the time." Her mom touched Kylie's cheek. "I'm so happy you're home. See how much fun we can have? You don't need to go to boarding school."

Kylie's breath caught. "But I really want to go, Mom."

The spark in her mom's eyes dimmed. "Let's not talk about this now. We have a wonderful day planned."

In spite of the anti–boarding school talk, and the fact that Kylie still was unable to get in touch with Trey, her mood remained positive. The ghost had apparently decided to give Kylie a reprieve. That or she decided she'd just caused enough trouble after last night's scene. A call to the B&B informed them that both Celeste and the old man who'd complained of chest pains had been released from the hospital.

They decided to do pizza for lunch and were primed to leave when Kylie's phone rang. When she saw it was Miranda, she asked for a few minutes. Her mom took off to check her e-mail.

"Hey," Miranda said. "I got us on three-way. Say hello, Della."

"A verbal ménage à trois," Della said.

"Gross," Miranda said.

"You wanna hear gross?" Della asked. "I just peed on my hand trying to piss on this damned drug stick while talking on the phone to you."

Kylie laughed. "I miss you guys." The sound of a toilet flushing filled the line.

"Oh, double gross," Miranda snapped. "I told you not to flush while I was on the phone."

Kylie dropped on the sofa. "Miranda, have you gone to your competition yet?"

"I'm not on until four." She sounded desperate.

"You'll do fine," Kylie said.

"You will," Della added. "How was the ghost hunt, Kylie?"

Kylie checked to make sure her mom wasn't near. "You aren't freaking going to believe this." She gave them the lowdown. They all had a good laugh and then the conversation switched to how much they all wished they were back at Shadow Falls. When Kylie realized she'd been talking for almost ten minutes, she told them good-bye. They agreed to talk this afternoon.

"I'm ready, Mom." The doorbell rang. Kylie ran to the door while her mom called that she was shutting off her computer. When Kylie swung open the door all the awkwardness from the night before came hurling at her. Funny how last night's unease had stemmed from her dad not being present and now it stemmed because he was here.

"Hi, Pumpkin."

The question popping around Kylie's head was if her mom knew Dad was coming.

"Are you ready to—" Mom's tennis shoes stopped so fast at the opening to the entryway. The skid marks on the marble floor and the shock on her mom's face answered Kylie's question.

Mom didn't know. Even more apparent, Mom wasn't happy.

Her dad's gaze went to her mom. "Hi, hon." His smile wavered.

The nervousness of his grin sent a desperate flutter to Kylie's gut. Okay, her dad deserved to be nervous. But it still felt downright wrong to open the door to her dad when this had been his home. His castle. Now he was unsure if he was welcome. And if her mom's expression was any indication, he wasn't.

"I thought maybe I could take you girls to lunch," he said.

Her mom took a step back. "I . . . I should have known you'd want to see her." She waved a hand toward the door. "You two go."

"Why don't you come, too?" her dad insisted.

"I think not," her mom countered.

"Kylie wants you to come." His father's gaze shot to her. "Don't you, Pumpkin? Like ol' times, the three of us."

Her mother frowned. Kylie frowned. Her dad grew more nervous. The tension in the room grew terse.

Her mom notched up her chin. "Why not make it four? Your whore can come, too."

"Oh! This is a bad time, isn't it?" Trey's voice came right behind her dad.

Kylie's mom shot up the stairs. Her dad looked stunned. Trey looked embarrassed.

Then her dad frowned at Kylie. "Didn't you tell her it was over?"

Had she heard him right? "Huh?"

"You didn't tell her that it was over with Amy?"

"Should I leave?" Trey asked.

"Yes," her dad answered.

Kylie's head reeled. She watched Trey go. She heard her mom crying. Kylie stared at her dad—stepdad. The idea that he'd actually attempted to use her to get her mom gnawed on some very raw nerves. The fact that he'd expected her to update her mom about his relationship status pretty much nuked those nerves.

She pointed at her dad. "Don't you ever try to use me to get to my mom!"

"I thought—"

"Then stop thinking!" She slammed the door. The house shook. The small glass window in the doorframe shattered. She saw her dad's startled expression through the broken window before he took off.

She breathed in.

She breathed out.

Then she took the stairs two at a time to check on her mom.

It took Kylie an hour to convince her mom to go out for pizza again. She'd tried calling Trey hoping to see what was so important that the ghost had sent his message to everyone in the room, but she got no answer. They were in the middle of lunch at the pizza parlor, still not back to their prior jovial mood, when her phone started croaking.

"Oh, honey," her mom said. "Change that ringtone." She hugged herself and called out to the waiter, "Can you turn down the air?"

Kylie grabbed her cell. There was no call, but an old voice message played.

"Hi, Kylie. It's Sara. I'm sorry I had to hang up like that. I . . . had something I had to take care of. Listen, I really want to see you when you're home. Please make sure to call me?"

"Who was it?" her mom asked, then lowered her voice. "Your dad?"

"No. A message from Sara."

Kylie stared at her pizza and got the strangest feeling. "Mom, would you mind if I went to see Sara after lunch?"

"Hi, Kylie," Mrs. Jetton said an hour later. "Sara will be thrilled to see you."

Kylie studied Sara's mom's expression. Her eyes looked red and her face pale. The somber mood filling the air ratcheted up Kylie's concern for her former best friend.

"She's in her room," Mrs. Jetton said.

Kylie almost asked what was wrong, but the chill running down her spine prevented her from talking. That short walk from the living room to Sara's door filled Kylie's head with dozens of memories. And for some odd reason, those memories brought tears to her eyes.

"*You have to save her. You have to save her.*" The ghost's words vibrated in Kylie's head. She swallowed and told herself she was overreacting, that everything was fine.

Sara's door stood ajar and when Kylie saw Sara, Kylie gasped.

Sara looked . . . awful. So pale that Kylie watched her chest to make sure she was breathing.

Sara opened her eyes. "She told you, didn't she?"

Kylie used both hands to wipe the tears from her cheeks. "Told me what?"

"What the doctor . . . If she didn't . . . why are you crying?"

"Happy to see you." She tried to smile.

"You always were a lousy liar." Sara pulled the covers up. "Mom, can you please turn down the air? I'm freezing in here."

"Honey, I already did," her mom called from the living room. "I phoned the electrician. Something's wrong with the AC again."

A photo album on Sara's bedside table plopped to the floor.

Kylie picked it up. She wasn't surprised when she saw the face staring up from the album. Then she looked at the foot of Sara's bed at the same spirit of the woman. She'd lost the spaghetti and the bloodstained gown, but her expression was just as dire as before.

"Who is this?" Kylie passed her finger over the face. Sara leaned over to see. It appeared to hurt her to move. "My grandma. She died when I was four. Of the same kind of cancer. Isn't that freaky?"

Cancer. The word brought another gasp to Kylie's lungs and she had to work to keep her lips from trembling. She looked at the spirit. "I can't fix this."

"Yes, you can!"

"Can't fix what?" Sara looked at the album as if Kylie had broken something.

"Nothing." Kylie sat down beside Sara. The memories of them on this bed, sharing secrets, laughing at the stupidest things, filled Kylie's head.

She swallowed emotions that threatened to overpower her. "Do you remember when we laid here and practiced kissing mirrors before the sixth-grade dance?"

Sara smiled. "Yeah." She leaned on the pillow and closed her eyes. Her long brown hair looked thinner and it lacked its normal luster. The silence grew longer. Sadder.

Kylie stroked Sara's arm. "What did the doctor say?"

Chapter Thirty-two

Sara opened her eyes. "The oncologist said he'd try to get me into experimental trials, but . . . he thinks it's too late." A sheen of tears filled Sara's eyes. "Mom says I'm doing it, but . . ." Sara swallowed. "I don't want to die." Her lips trembled. "But I can still hear my mom saying dozens of times that if *she* ever got cancer, she'd rather die than go through what they put her mama through. She said they butchered her mom. I don't want to deal with that. The one surgery was bad enough."

Kylie recalled the dreams of knives coming at her. She looked at Sara's abdomen. "When did you have surgery?"

"Last week," Sara answered. "I'd missed so many periods. The clinic doctor felt a mass when she was checking me. Two days later, I was in the hospital."

"Why didn't you call me?"

Sara bit down on her lip. "I did. I didn't tell you that I thought I had cancer, but . . ."

Guilt filled Kylie's chest. The ghost, Sara's grandmother, had been trying to get her to listen to the message. The same message she had played earlier.

"Couldn't they take it out?"

Sara shook her head. "There's too much. It's everywhere."

The ache in Kylie's heart doubled. She recalled Trey's message that had been sent to everyone at the B&B. Why had the ghost sent Trey's message? "Trey?"

Sara looked down at her hands. "I'm sorry. I swear I didn't mean it to happen. I'd drunk too much. He'd drunk too much."

"What?" Kylie asked.

Sara looked up. "Shit. He hasn't told you, has he?"

It took only a second to digest what Sara said—it took less time for Kylie to know it wasn't important.

"I asked him to tell you because I couldn't stand it. He promised he would."

"He tried. I didn't take his calls. But I don't care, Sara." She took Sara's hand in hers and squeezed. "Trey and I are . . . so over. You're what's important."

Another tear crawled down Sara's pale cheek. "You're not just saying that because I'm dying, are you?" Sara tried to make it a joke.

Kylie didn't laugh. "No."

Sara pulled her hand out of Kylie's. "You're hot."

"You can do it." The ghost's voice came right behind Kylie's ear. *"It's your touch."*

Kylie looked back at the spirit. "Do you mean . . . like Helen?"

"What?" Sara asked.

Kylie continued to stare at the ghost.

"Do it," the ghost said. *"Please. Heal her. Before it's too late."*

"I don't know how," Kylie muttered.

"Am I hallucinating or are you talking to yourself?" Sara asked. "I mean, I am on some pretty good drugs right now."

Kylie looked back at Sara. "No." She felt the cold of the ghost inch closer.

"No, I'm not hallucinating or no, you're not talking to your-self?"

"No to both." Kylie tried to think. Could she really do this?

She looked down at Sara's grandmother's picture. "What's her name?"

"Fanny Mildred Bogart." Sara laughed. "I'm glad Mama didn't name me after her." It obviously hurt Sara to laugh because she moaned and dropped back on the pillow. When she opened her eyes, she stared at the photograph. "Do you want to hear something crazy?"

"What?" Kylie asked, but she thought she already knew what Sara was going to say.

"Sometimes I think she's here."

"She *is* here." Kylie took Sara's hand again and struggled to know how much to tell Sara.

Sara chuckled. "Now you believe in ghosts, huh?"

"Yup." Kylie inhaled. "You'd be surprised what I believe in now."

"Like what?" Sara asked.

"Like miracles." Kylie looked at Fanny.

"I could use a miracle." Sara smiled and tried to pull her hand away. "Why is your hand so hot?"

"How do I do this?" Kylie asked the spirit, holding on to Sara's hand.

"Do what?" Sara asked, her voice sounding as tired as her eyes looked.

"I don't know how, I just know that you have the power."

"That's not helpful," Kylie responded.

"You're talking to yourself again," Sara said, but she'd stopped trying to pull her hand away.

"I know," Kylie told Sara. Then Kylie remembered how Helen, the fairy who had the ability to heal, had touched Kylie's head when she'd checked her for tumors. And Helen had said that's what she'd done when she had healed her sister's cancer.

Dropping Sara's hand, Kylie scooted up to the head of Sara's bed. She brushed Sara's bangs from her brow. Then she reached over with her other hand and touched both of Sara's temples.

"What are you doing?" Sara asked, looking at Kylie and making a funny face.

"Trying to help you relax," Kylie said, knowing it sounded lame.

"Okay, this camp has turned you weird," Sara said, and started to reach up to move Kylie's hands.

"Tell her that your mom did this for you when you weren't feeling good," Fanny said.

Good idea. "My mom used to do this to me, and it really made me feel good."

Sara dropped her hands down. "Okay, but if you try to kiss me, I'm screaming for my mom." Sara giggled.

"What? I'm not your type?" Kylie asked, and giggled, and then she tried to concentrate on positive healing thoughts.

It was after nine that night when Kylie left Sara's house. When she'd been there for about an hour, Kylie had slipped into the bathroom and called her mom. She cried when she told her mom about Sara's cancer. Her mom said she'd call Mrs. Jetton tomorrow and that Kylie should stay with Sara as long as she wanted but to call before she started home.

Kylie didn't leave until Sara went to sleep. She had forgotten to call her mom, but since she lived close, she didn't worry.

Her neighborhood was dark, no streetlights—no lights on in

the houses, either. A power outage, Kylie told herself as she fought an urgent sense of unease.

And that's when it happened.

Something large hit the windshield of her car.

Chapter Thirty-three

Kylie's heart stopped when she saw the body against her windshield. She slammed her foot on the brakes. Oh, my God. She must have hit someone.

Then she saw the face staring through the windshield at her. The rogue, the vampire who'd killed those girls in Fallen. But how? Hadn't he been "dealt" with?

She accelerated and swerved, hoping to throw him off the car. It didn't work. Clinging to the car like a spider, he inched over, smiled, and punched his fist through her car window. Glass shards went everywhere. She screamed and pushed the accelerator harder. He reached for her. His fist wrapped around her neck and squeezed. She couldn't breathe. Couldn't move. Fireworks exploded before her eyes. Her last thought was of Sara. She hoped she'd healed her. One of them should live.

When Kylie woke up, she sat up on a cold, heavy wooden chair. Her head and throat throbbed. She went to rub her temple, but her hands wouldn't move. She heard a clinking noise, metal against metal. Chains?

She pried open her eyes but saw nothing. Pitch-blackness surrounded her.

Shuffling her feet, she heard chains rattling again. Aware of
cold metal bracelets against her ankles and wrists, her mind started
rationalizing. Her arms and legs were bound with some kind of
metal chain. She attempted to shift her limbs to test her theory.

Yup. Chains.

She hated being right, too. The memory of the rogue filled her
head. A scream lodged in her throat.

She blinked and hoped to see something but only blackness invaded her senses. She inhaled. The scent of dirt and concrete filled
her nose.

The lightest intake of air reached her ears. "Is someone here?"

No answer came. "I know someone's here," she said. Trying to
test her strength, she pulled at the chains.

She was barely able to move.

"So the rumors of your strength were just rumors." A raspy
male voice echoed in the darkness.

"Release me!" Panicked even more, she fought against the chains
that bound her, but she couldn't free herself.

"You shouldn't struggle, Kylie. You'll spend your energy use-
lessly. Save your strength to think. To make wise choices."

Forcing herself to calm down, she listened. The voice echoed in
the room. She didn't recognize it. She remembered the rogue vampire who had crashed through her windshield. Panic clawed at her
raw, dry throat. She tried to remember what his voice had sounded
like. She could hear him in her head, but it hadn't been the same.
Had it?

"What kind of choices?" she asked.

"We have much to talk about." Definitely not the rogue and not
a voice she'd heard before. It sounded . . . rusty, almost . . . old.

From the way the voice bounced around the room, Kylie sensed she was in a tunnel.

"Where am I? Who are you?" She would have asked what he wanted, but she was too scared to know. Face it, when you find yourself in chains in a pitch-black room, tea and scones weren't usually going to be offered.

The only noise she heard was the sound of her own breathing and the lighter short breaths from the man with the rusty voice. Her mind shot to the visions with the ghosts and she wondered if she had misread them. Was Kylie the person who would be tortured?

Taking a deep breath, she pulled against the chains. She couldn't free herself. Where was her strength? "What do we have to talk about?" she asked.

The light flickered on with blinding brightness. She blinked and on the second rise of her eyelids she saw him. He wore a strange robe, like a monk. His skin was wrinkled, leathered. She tightened her eyebrows and saw his brain pattern. As she suspected, vampire.

An old, weird vampire like Miranda's enemy Tabitha had described. Kylie's gut had tried to tell her not to ignore it. She hoped this didn't turn out to be her fatal and final flaw.

"You were watching me."

"You have keen instincts." He stepped closer, frighteningly closer. His eyes were cold and gray. Dead gray. "Do you purposely keep your mind closed?" he asked.

She wondered how much she should tell him, or if she should tell him anything at all. Then again, if he thought she was blocking him on purpose, he might get angry. And she had to remember not to lie.

"I don't know how to open up."

The sound of metal scraping concrete rang out. Kylie looked behind the old man to a door being pushed open. Her heart stopped and her throat ached as she remembered the newcomer's hand cutting off her airway.

"I told you to wait," the old man scolded.

"But, Gramps, I'm just eager to see my new bride." The rogue moved closer.

Bride? Kylie yanked at the chains, repulsed by the idea of being his bride.

"Leave now!" the old man roared. His voice might be rusty and worn, but his tone demanded obedience. Frightening obedience.

The rogue stopped two feet from her. His auburn hair wasn't soaked in blood this time, but she could still see it in her mind. She knew the minute she looked into his cold, gray eyes, he was the same vampire who'd slipped into her dressing room—and the one who'd crashed through her windshield. "She's so pretty. Don't keep her from me too long."

He shot off. The sound of the iron door slamming shut echoed throughout the room.

Kylie glared at the old man. "He murdered two young girls."

"Yes." He hung his head as if ashamed. "My grandson made many mistakes. But he will grow wiser."

"The Vampire Council was supposed to . . ." Kylie remembered something Della had said about the Council, namely that they were all old, and just like that, she knew. "You are part of the Council. You lied to them."

He looked up. "I did not lie. I said I would deal with this. You are part of my plan."

"He kidnapped me." Could she shame the old man into letting her go?

"On my orders."

So much for that hope.

He moved closer. A sense of power moved with him. "In my

day, when our young men acted out, only one thing could tame them. A woman strong enough, pretty enough, to give them a reason to settle down."

"He can't be saved." Her pulse raced as the old man inched closer.

"He's wild now, but you fascinate him. Do you have any idea how many hours he spent in those woods by your camp, risking being caught, and for nothing more than a chance to see you?"

She shivered with disgust, knowing it had been him all those times.

"I was curious about who had stolen my grandson's heart and I followed him. Once I saw you, I could understand what drove him. You are very fascinating." He leaned down, his face inches from hers. His breath came against her cheek and she felt sick that they shared the same airspace. "What are you, Kylie Galen? Do you even know? Is there vampire in your blood?"

"He's a murderer. I would rather die than let him lay a finger on me."

His right eyebrow arched. "Death is always an option. Not one I recommend, though."

The panic started to claw anew in her chest.

"I saw you drink the blood." His cold touch on her arm made her skin crawl. "But you are still warm. I saw the strange wolf befriend you, but you did not turn on the day of the moon. Normally, I would seek a vampire as his mate, but you . . . my grandson is right. You are special."

She pulled again at her chains. "Let me go."

"You seek a family, Kylie Galen. We shall be that to you. You will bear me great-grandchildren, and with my genes and yours, they will be even more powerful. And you will teach my grandson to be a man."

"Not happening," Kylie sneered.

"We will convince you."

"I'm not easily convinced. And if your grandson isn't a man, maybe it's because he's lacked a role model."

The old man's eyes tightened. "I will tolerate much, but I demand your respect."

"You have to earn respect." It was her mom's favorite saying, and it never rang so true as it did now.

He shook his head. "In our world, respect is won by the person who has more power. Right now, my dear child, I hold all the power."

He disappeared. Vanished. Kylie didn't even see him turn into a blur. What was he? She remembered Tabitha, the witch who Miranda caught snooping around the cabin, saying he was more than vampire, and Kylie feared the girl was right.

He might have power, Kylie thought, but she still didn't respect him. And by God, she wouldn't bear his great-grandchildren either.

She yanked at her chains again, sought the strength within herself to get free. The strength didn't come. She considered screaming but something inside her said it would be a waste of energy. She needed to think. She needed to use her brain to get out of this.

She called out for Daniel. He was a no-show. Would the death angels or whatever it was at the falls come to her aid?

She closed her eyes and asked for help. Begged, actually. The thought of being touched by the rogue meant she wasn't above begging.

In the deep corners of her mind, a voice whispered, "You have the power within you."

"Please, that sounds like an old *Star Wars* movie!" When only silence answered, she continued, "This isn't any time for self-discovery." She yanked again at the chains, thinking the power she had was to break loose. She struggled until she felt her wrists and ankles bruise.

"He wants me to bear his great-grandchildren. I could use some help here!"

Trying to remember to breathe, she considered what power the death angels meant. She was a ghost whisperer, she could run fast, and occasionally found unknown strength to toss werewolves long distances. And she had special hearing that came and went. There was also a possibility that she could heal—she hoped so for Sara's sake—and she could dreamscape.

I can dreamscape! Wasn't that as good as a cell phone? If she could get Lucas, Lucas could get Burnett. Burnett would get her out of this. He would. He'd bring the whole FRU down on this old dude's ass.

She counted sheep. One hundred, then two. Every noise and some-times the lack of noise kept her awake. Her eyes grew tired. She eventually grew tired. Finally, the floating sensation pulled at her subconscious. Then she flew, whooshed through the clouds. She saw him.

"You came." Lucas sat up on a king-size bed. He wore a sexy smile and no shirt. Not that now was the time to notice such things.

"The rogue has me. Get Burnett." She spoke quickly, afraid she'd wake up.

"What?"

"You heard me."

"Where are you?"

"Don't know. A tunnel. There's a lot of concrete. Iron doors, too."

He looked at her in panic. "I have to know where you are."

"I was unconscious when they brought me here."

"They?"

"The rogue's grandfather. He's one of the Vampire Council."

Lucas pushed both hands through his dark hair. "Listen, Kylie. The way dreamscaping works, you can fly. You're going to have to fly back to your body, but slowly. Look down and see landmarks. Then come back and tell me where you are. I have to know where you are or I can't help you."

"What if I can't come back? What if I wake up and can't tell you?" The panic made her feel heavy and it sounded in her voice. She didn't want to leave Lucas. Although she knew it was a dream, she felt safer here.

"You can do this, Kylie. Go!" He waved her away. "Hurry."

Kylie did what Lucas told her to do. She started flying back. Too fast. She concentrated until she found how to reduce her speed. Then she looked down. She saw a skyline. Houston skyline. She dropped lower until she saw a large building, the Toyota Center, she recognized it. Then she remembered her father had taken her downtown into the Houston tunnels.

Flying through the tunnel, unstopped by the walls, Kylie didn't slow down until she saw herself. Her heart hammered against her ribs. Seeing oneself slumped over in a chair, chained like a scene in a horror movie, freaked her out. She heard a noise. The iron door began to open. She felt herself falling into her body.

"No!" She had to get back to Lucas. She had to give him directions on how to find her.

Chapter Thirty-four

Fighting the pull to move back into her body, Kylie swung around and flew back the way she'd come. The speed prevented her from breathing.

Someone called her name. Not Lucas. It was the old vampire.

The clouds were thick. Wasn't Lucas just through the layer of fog? She felt herself being yanked back. She was about to wake up. "Lucas, I'm in the Houston Tunnel System. Under the Toyota building. Can you hear me?"

"What are you doing?" the dark, rusty voice growled.

Kylie jerked her eyes open. The old vampire stared at her. She remembered she couldn't lie. "Dreaming."

"What kind of dream? I felt the energy."

"A disturbing one. I . . . used to have night terrors when I was younger." No lie there.

He appeared resigned to believe her, but remained suspicious. Was there something for him to be suspicious about? Had Lucas heard her?

"I have some old friends interested in meeting you. For your own well-being, I hope you will be on your best behavior."

"Who are they? And why do they want to meet me?"

"I think, Kylie Galen, that you are even more special than you know."

"How am I special?"

He didn't answer. "If you can tell me that you will not try to escape, I will release the chains."

The thought of having the heavy metal bracelets removed sounded like heaven. The words were on the tip of her tongue, but they would have been a lie.

"We both know that if there is a way to escape I will take it. Your job is to make sure there isn't a way."

He laughed. "I appreciate your honesty."

"Enough to unchain me?"

"Not that much," he said.

She met his aged gray eyes. "I see no way to escape the room. Unless you believe I have the power to overtake you when the door is open. And since I can't break these chains, are you saying that your powers are weaker than this metal?"

He studied her. "You are very intelligent, my child. Dare I worry that you are as cunning as you are smart?"

"If I was that smart and cunning, would I be here?"

"Let's compromise." He closed his eyes and the metal bracelets around her arms and one from one ankle disappeared. Her right ankle was now attached to a long heavy chain.

Shocked at his ability, she stared at him. "What are you?"

He smiled. "See, I am already winning your respect."

"You misread curiosity for respect," she countered.

His eyes tightened, but a slight smile crept from behind his anger.

"What are you?" she asked again.

He folded his aged arms over his chest. "What's wrong, dear? Are the similarities frightening?" With that, he disappeared into the thin, cold air.

"What's that supposed to mean?" she yelled, and stood to see how far she could get with the chain attached to her ankle.

No nearly far enough.

Kylie tried to fall back asleep, to get back to Lucas, but she couldn't. She could only hope her message had gotten through and that he'd already phoned Burnett and they were on the way here now. How long would it take?

What if they didn't come? What if her message never got through? She attempted to pull the chain free, but her strength wasn't there. What was it with her strength? Why did it come and go?

Kylie started pacing, dragging the chain as she went. She couldn't reach the thick door, though it wouldn't have mattered if she had. When the vampire had disappeared, so had the door-knob. Opening it would have been impossible. Still she paced and tried to come up with a way out, with or without any help from Burnett. She glanced back at the door with its missing knob. What the hell was he? And what had he meant by that whole similarity crap?

The chain clattered against the concrete floor. She remembered she hadn't phoned her mom before she left Sara's house and she hoped like heck that she wasn't worried. Turning again, pacing toward the right wall this time, Kylie was surprised to hear voices. Was the old man back with his friends? She stopped moving and listened.

It wasn't the old dude's voice, but that of the rogue. Oh, great, was he planning on visiting again? Her body tensed and she looked around for anything that could be used as a weapon. Before her gaze swept the room, she heard the rogue's voice clearer.

"Who are you and what are doing snooping around here?"

Where were the voices coming from? She hesitated and moved closer to the wall. Suddenly, a loud thump sounded as if something heavy had been tossed across the room.

Or someone?

Her heart stopped. She moved even closer to the wall trying to see if the voices were coming from behind the wall. Another clatter echoed and she felt almost certain that it was.

"You will tell me!" the rogue hissed.

Fear filled her gut. Who was the rogue talking to? Was it . . . was it someone who'd come looking for her? Her thoughts and heart shot to Lucas.

"Unchain me and fight like a man!" Lucas's voice roared.

Her chest swelled with regret. She'd gone to him for help and . . .

"Why? You would only fight like the dog you are." A loud thud followed, and Kylie knew Lucas had taken a blow.

Her muscles tightened. A surge of energy shot through her. She grabbed the chain with one hand and yanked it out of the concrete. Then, turning to the wall, she charged at it with her shoulder. Only a flicker of a second before she hit did she consider how it might hurt.

Oddly, she felt nothing. Chucks of concrete fell around her. She knocked the big pieces from her face and then, realizing she stood on the other side of the room, she stared through the cloud of dust. Lucas lay on his side, still chained to a chair, much like the one she'd been in moments earlier. She saw his face, a bloody mess, and his eyes were closed as if he was unconscious.

Or dead.

She breathed in raw fury and looked around for the rogue. When she saw him, the shock on his face didn't surprise her. She charged him, but right before she had her hands on him, he disappeared.

"So you are not so powerless." The old vampire's voice boomed around her although she could not see him. The concrete wall behind her reformed and she sensed it grew thicker this time.

"What are you?" she hissed, knowing no ordinary vampire could build a wall back up.

"Did I not ask you the same thing?" he answered.

She ran to Lucas. A hand to his chest told her he was still alive. She yanked his chains off and dropped beside him on her knees. The gravel on the concrete floor bit into her skin.

Remembering she possibly had the power to heal, she moved her hands over him, then remembering what she'd done for Sara, Kylie pressed her palms around his head.

"Talk to me, Lucas. Please." The memory of him saving her from the bullies and of him looking up at the sky for elephants filled her mind and tears filled her eyes. "Please be okay."

She tried to think positively, tried to think about her hands sending warmth into his body. She didn't know if this was how it worked, but for Lucas's and Sara's sake, she prayed it was. Her heart filled with hope when the swelling on his face disappeared.

"Now talk to me," she whispered, and she began to lean down.

His eyes shot open, panic marred his expression, and he swung his fist.

She tried to catch it but whatever power she'd had was gone.

She did manage to avoid the punch to the face. Instead, his fist slammed against her shoulder. Pain exploded. The blow knocked her clear across the room.

"Christ!" He lunged to his feet. "I'm sorry." He picked her up and cradled her tenderly against his chest. "Are you okay?"

She nodded. Thankful he wasn't vampire and wouldn't know she lied. Her shoulder throbbed like a bad toothache. "Down," she managed to say.

He complied but her knees buckled and he had to catch her. "I'm sorry."

She looked into his blue eyes. "It's okay." He hadn't meant to hit her. "I don't think it's broken."

"Did you get . . ." She stopped talking, remembering the old vampire was probably listening.

"Burnett?" she mouthed the name, and looked up at him with a question in her eyes.

He nodded and she prayed he'd read her lips correctly and this meant Burnett and the FRU were coming.

Her shoulder pounded. Her legs shook. She leaned against the wall and slid down to sit on the cold concrete floor. Lucas sat down beside her. She shivered and he must have felt it because he put his arm around her. His body oozed heat. She leaned into him to soak up his warmth.

"You are so hot," she said.

"It's about time you noticed," he teased.

She would have smiled if her energy hadn't felt spent. In spite of the pain, she felt safe.

"It's a werewolf thing," he said. "Our body temperatures run hotter."

"What time is it?"

"After midnight," he answered.

She remembered her mom who must be panicking by now. Then feeling too exhausted to think, Kylie closed her eyes and leaned closer into his chest, careful not to move her shoulder.

He shifted her into his lap. His warmth surrounded her. She felt him moving a hand through her hair. "You've got something in your hair," he said.

"Probably concrete, from when I . . . came through the wall," she said.

"What wall?" he asked.

She recalled he'd been unconscious then. Did he even know she'd healed him?

"That one." She nodded. "He put it back together, though."

"I think I hit you harder than I thought."

She didn't have the strength to argue. "So tired."

"Rest." He pulled her closer. "Soon," he whispered.

Was he saying that it would be over soon? God, she hoped so.

"Kylie. It's time."

Lucas's words stirred her awake some time later.

She felt Lucas jump up with her in his arms and she became instantly alert. Loud noises came from behind the wall and, in one easy leap, he had them against the back of the room, away from the noise. Before she could insist Lucas put her down, the front wall collapsed and Burnett and several other FRU personnel hurtled though the cascading concrete.

Burnett rushed forward. "Is she okay?"

"Fine," she said, embarrassed that Lucas held her like a child. "Put me down."

"Her shoulder," Lucas said. "I think it's broken. My fault. I did it . . . accidentally."

"I'm fine." She went to move her shoulder to prove her point, and winced.

"They're here!" someone screamed from down the hall. Lucas, Burnett, and the other men ran through the rubble that had once been a wall. She stood alone in the cloud of dust their hasty departure had created. The sound of men fighting in the distance reached her ears. Feeling useless, she started to follow, hoping her strength would return, but she hadn't taken one step when she felt the rush of air move past her.

The young, evil-eyed rogue stopped beside her and before Kylie could do more than scream, he had her in his arms. Forgetting about her shoulder, she struggled. Pain exploded in her arm, but she continued to fight. But his hold was strong, and her own strength spent.

"No!" the deep rumble of Lucas's voice filled her ears.

"Put her down," Lucas demanded.

"She's mine," the rogue hissed.

"Over my dead body," Lucas roared, and his eyes deepened to a burnt orange.

"That will be my pleasure," the vampire roared back, his gray eyes now glowing red.

Realizing her opportunity, Kylie jabbed the palm of her hand into the rogue's throat. He dropped her, and she had no more than hit the ground when she saw Lucas attack. The sound of fist pounding into bone filled the room. In horror, she watched as Lucas was thrown across the room. She felt her own strength returning, but before she got to her feet, Lucas was back, holding the vampire by the throat. The sound coming from the vampire's throat left Kylie with no doubt that Lucas's hold was crushing his airway.

"Drop him!" The voice of the old vampire filled the room and made the air heavy. "Drop him or she dies."

While Kylie could see no one, she felt a hand close around her throat. She clawed at the invisible force that choked her and tried to pull air into her lungs. None came.

She saw Lucas's gaze shoot to her. Dark sparkles started filling her vision, and right before everything went black, she saw Lucas drop the rogue, who then disappeared. No wind, no air. Obviously the old man's magic had taken him away.

Still attempting to gasp air into her lungs, she collapsed to her knees. Lucas pulled her up.

Burnett suddenly appeared at their side.

"He came back for her," Lucas said.

"We need to get her away," Burnett said, and reached out and took her in his arms. "The FRU are following them."

"I'm going with them," Lucas said.

"No," Kylie said, forcing the words out of her bruised throat. But she wasn't in the room anymore. The wind hit her face so fast she couldn't breathe. Burnett readjusted her, and buried her face against his chest, a chest that wasn't near as warm or comforting as the one she'd just been sleeping against.

When he came to a stop outside a single-story building, Kylie raised her head. "Where are we?" She touched her neck.

"A clinic," he said, and moved her hand to check her neck.

"I'm fine. Put me down."

"Not yet. You might be fine, but Holiday would have my ass if I didn't have a doctor check you out."

She remembered Lucas. "You should have stopped Lucas from going after the rogues . . ."

"Couldn't have stopped him," he said. "Werewolves are too damn stubborn. But Lucas can take care of himself."

"He got captured," she said.

"Only to get inside to you," he said.

The realization made her gut clench. "He could have been killed."

"He wasn't." The lights came on in the building and Burnett moved in.

Kylie read the sign on the door as he carried her inside: PRO-TECT YOUR PETS AGAINST HEARTWORMS. "Wait. You're taking me to a vet?" Kylie looked around the small office with pet pictures posted on the walls and noticed the smell of animals.

"A vet and supernatural doctor," he said.

A man walked out of the door from the back. "In here," he said.

Burnett introduced her to Dr. Whitman as he carried her though the door. A big orange cat followed them into the back. When Burnett placed her on an examining table, the cat jumped up beside her. "I'm fine," she told Burnett and Dr. Whitman.

"Her shoulder," Burnett said. "And her neck."

When the doctor reached for Kylie's shoulder, she flinched. "I'm just bruised." She looked back at Burnett. "I've got to get back to my mom's. She's probably already at the police station."

Burnett picked up the phone and walked to the other side of the room.

Dr. Whitman moved Kylie's shoulder and studied her. Kylie flinched a bit, but she knew it wasn't broken. His eyebrows twitched as he looked at her forehead. "What are you?"

"Beats me," she said, and looked at his brain pattern. He was part fairy. The cat walked across Kylie to rub against the doc's side. She suspected he could communicate with animals the way Derek did, too. The thought of Derek had her heart remembering how much she missed him, but she pushed it away.

"Well, the girl's right. Her shoulder isn't broken," Dr. Whitman said as Burnett moved back over.

"Told you so," Kylie couldn't resist saying. "Now, would you please drop me off at my mom's house?"

"Thank you," Burnett said to Dr. Whitman, and motioned for him to leave the room. Once they were alone, Burnett turned back to Kylie. "I'm going to get you home. But first I need to know what happened tonight."

Kylie told him everything she remembered from the time the rogue had landed on her car, to right before Burnett burst through the concrete walls. She informed him that the rogue who'd killed the girls in Fallen was the grandson of one of the Vampire Council members. As well as the fact that it had been the vamps who'd been watching the campgrounds off and on all summer. Most of what Kylie had to say turned the vampire's eyes bright with fury.

"So, what's the deal with him wanting me to marry his grandson?" she asked when she was done.

Burnett shrugged. "In the past, our grandparents chose our mates."

"Even if the mate wasn't willing?"

"Afraid so." Burnett's expression filled with remorse. "You were right, Kylie. This was about you. I should have listened. I won't make that mistake again."

She nodded, sensing how hard it was for him to admit he'd made a mistake. "The old man, he's weird. His brain pattern says he's a vampire, but he's more than that."

"I know the man you are talking about. I've met him during my visits with the Council. He's vampire, but you're right, he's strange."

"He's more than vampire," Kylie said. "He put the wall back together after I broke it down."

"Maybe he had help from someone with other powers."

"I think it's more," she said.

"Maybe," he said, but Kylie could tell he didn't agree. "Okay, I'll get you home. And I'll have someone watching your house so you'll be safe."

He picked Kylie back up. "Hold on." She knew this time to bury her head against his chest.

In seconds, Burnett set her down in front of her house. "What do I tell her?" she asked.

"Don't know. I've never been good dealing with parents," he said. "But be creative."

"You're not a lot of help." She bit down on her lip. "Oh, crap, my car."

"We found it when we were looking for you. Someone will get the window replaced and have it back here before daybreak."

"Thanks."

He nodded. "I'm glad you're okay, Kylie. We'll go over everything again tomorrow evening when you come back to the camp. And call Holiday the first chance you get. She won't sleep until she talks to you."

Kylie reached up and hugged him. He looked unprepared for the show of affection. "Thank you," she said.

"You're welcome," he answered, obviously uncomfortable with the conversation as much as the hug.

She looked around at the darkness. The silence didn't even scare her because she knew Burnett was the one who caused it.

"I've got two men watching the house," he said as if he'd misread her expression.

"I believe you." She watched him leave. Then she went to the door. When she realized she didn't have her keys, she found the spare her mom kept inside the fake dog poop behind the azalea bushes.

She barely got the door open when her mom flew at her and wrapped her arms around her.

"Oh, God. I was just about to call the police. Where have you been, young lady?"

Her mom's hug squeezed her shoulder and made it hard to breathe. Pulling back and trying to mask the pain in her voice, Kylie said, "I forgot to call. And then . . . I was so upset over Sara that I just needed to think."

Tears filled her mom's eyes. "Oh, baby, I'm so sorry. The power went out. I fell asleep on the sofa waiting on you to get home. I woke up fifteen minutes ago and when I realized you weren't here, I called Sara's house. Her mom said you'd left, but she didn't know when."

Luckily Sara's mom had already gone to bed when Kylie left so she couldn't have known what time Kylie really left. "Well, I'm fine."

"I didn't hear the car pull in," her mom said.

Think quick. "I parked it on the street." She hoped Burnett was right and the car would be returned by daybreak.

Kylie faked a yawn. "You know, Mom, sleep sounds really good right now," she said, wanting to get to her room and call Holiday. But she'd have to use the home phone because her cell was back in the car.

"Okay, but we'll talk about Sara tomorrow."

Yeah, Kylie thought. They also needed to talk about her going to Shadow Falls for the next school year. But she decided to worry about that later, too. She hurried to her room and dialed Holiday's number.

"Have you heard from Lucas?" she asked when the camp leader answered the phone.

"Yes," Holiday said. "He's fine. But . . . last I heard, the people responsible for taking you weren't captured. Burnett is watching you, though. Don't worry."

"I know," Kylie said.

"Are you okay? I wish I could I touch you and calm you down."

"I'm fine," she lied.

"If you close your eyes and imagine the falls, it will help push away the panic."

"I will," Kylie said, and this time she wasn't lying.

Sunday morning, the ringing telephone woke Kylie at almost ten. She sat up, reached for the phone, and actually looked around, hoping she'd see the ghost. Hey . . . after over a month of seeing her first thing in the morning, she sort of missed her.

Pushing the talk button, she recalled her conversation with Holiday from last night. It had worked; imagining the falls had taken the edge off her panic.

"Hello," Kylie answered.

"Are you okay?" Della and Miranda's voices exploded at the same time over the line.

"I'm fine." Kylie leaned back on the pillow. "How did you find out?"

"When you didn't answer the damn phone all night, I called Holiday," Della said.

"Spill it," Miranda said.

Kylie gave them the short version and promised she'd tell them all the gory details later. Then she asked about their weekend. Miranda moaned and groaned about the event, but ended by telling them that she'd taken second in the competition.

"And the bitch Tabitha took fourth," Miranda said with pride.

"How are you, Della?" Kylie asked.

"What does this tell you?" The sound of a toilet flushing filled the line.

"Gross," Miranda said.

"I think my parents are shocked that I haven't shown positive yet."

After a few more minutes of chatting, they said good-bye. Remembering the car, Kylie scrambled out of bed and looked out the window. Burnett had been true to his word. The car sat on the street outside the house, looking as good as new.

If only everything else in her life could be fixed as easily.

"You're up," her mom said as Kylie walked out of her bedroom a few minutes later. Her mom had a towel wrapped around her head and wore her bathrobe as through she'd just gotten out of the shower. "Give me a minute and I'll fix us breakfast."

Thirty minutes later, Kylie was having pancakes and eggs with her mom. They talked about a lot of things but mostly about Sara. Kylie's mom told her that Sara's mom had called to make sure Kylie had gotten home okay.

Her mom picked up her plate and carried it to the sink. "Sara's mom said that Sara's was feeling good today, too. She's supposed to go to the doctor tomorrow to talk about her options. I sure hope it works out."

Kylie stood and helped clear the table.

"*She doesn't need options,*" a voice whispered behind Kylie. "*You did it.*" The temperature in the room dropped a good twenty degrees.

"I swear that air-conditioner has been acting up for a month now." Her mom shivered and went to check the thermostat. Kylie wondered if her mom's AC was really out, or if it had been Daniel causing the cold.

Kylie turned and saw the ghost. She looked healthy and young.

Beautiful. Kylie suspected that Sara would look just like her when she hit her thirties.

"Thank you. I knew you could do it."

"You don't have to thank me. She's my friend."

"Did you say something?" Her mom stood in the kitchen doorway.

The ghost smiled and faded.

"Yeah," Kylie said. "I said we need to talk about school." Kylie went and gave her mom a big hug. Her shoulder hardly hurt now. When she pulled back she just spouted out the words before she lost her nerve. "I know it's hard for you. I know you love me. But I need this right now. I really need this."

He mom touched Kylie's face. Then tears filled her mom's eyes.

She breathed in.

Then out.

"Baby, I'm sorry. But I just can't let you go."

Chapter Thirty-five

Kylie's heart squeezed. The room went cold again. Daniel appeared. He smiled. "Remind her . . ." he said, but before he could finish, he disappeared. Somehow Kylie knew what he'd meant.

"Mom," she said. "Remember how you told me that when you met Daniel, you just knew he was right for you?"

Her mom looked shocked that Kylie had brought up Daniel. "Yes, but—"

"This school is my Daniel, Mom. I know it's right for me. I know it in my heart. Please, don't take that away from me. Don't take this away from me, like Daniel was taken away from you."

"Don't I even get to walk you inside?" her mom asked, after she pulled to a stop in the parking lot outside the gates at Shadow Falls later that afternoon.

"It's not visitation day," Kylie said, and barely glanced back at the new spirit who'd hitched a ride with them as they passed the cemetery in Fallen. The dark-haired woman, wearing a pink fuzzy housecoat, appeared to be in her late twenties. She also looked completely confused and kept staring at Kylie and asking where she was. Kylie had tried talking to her in her mind, but the woman didn't hear. Plus, Kylie's mom had bitched the entire way about how the car's air-conditioner must be broken, too.

Scooting over, Kylie gave her mom a big hug. "Thank you," she said. Her mom had reluctantly agreed to sign the papers for Kylie to go to school that fall at Shadow Falls.

Sighing, her mom pulled back and rested her hand against Kylie's cheek. "I still don't like it."

"I know."

"Remember the condition," her mom said.

Kylie hadn't meant to argue, but the words slipped out. "I don't get it. You won't forgive him. You don't even want to see him, but you expect me to call him twice a week."

"He's your father," her mom said.

"Daniel's my father."

Her mom winced. "Yes, but Tom loved you like his own."

"I know. And I plan on forgiving him, but . . . it still hurts. And when he tried to use me to get to you, well . . ."

"I know," her mom said. "He was wrong. He's not perfect. Neither am I. I'm sorry I caused a scene when he showed up."

Kylie looked into her eyes. "Do you still love him?"

"I don't know. When it stops hurting so bad, I might figure it out."

They hugged again and a few minutes later Kylie watched her mom pull away. The ghost had decided to stick with Kylie and now stood beside her. She opened her housecoat and looked down at a big gaping hole in her abdomen. Why the heck couldn't Kylie get haunted by a ghost who died peacefully in her sleep?

"What happened to me?" the ghost asked.

"I don't know." Kylie watched the spirit fade. But Kylie had a feeling she'd be back. And she'd expect Kylie to help her figure everything out, too. That in itself frustrated Kylie to no end. How could she figure out the ghost's problems when she couldn't figure out her own? She checked her phone to see if the PI had returned her call she'd made to him right after she'd collected her phone from her car this morning. He'd left a text and said he had news, but didn't even hint at what the news might be.

When Kylie got to the gate, the feeling of being home made her heart race. This really was where she belonged. Holiday and Burnett were waiting for her as soon as she walked inside.

Holiday gave her a big, soulful hug. Burnett took her bag and motioned for her to follow him.

As they passed the dining hall, Kylie saw that several campers had also arrived early. Holiday had called Kylie and asked her to come back an hour early to talk. They walked into the office cabin and Kylie was stunned when Lucas stood right on the other side of the door.

His blue eyes met hers. "The shoulder okay?"

Kylie got a feeling he wanted to touch her, but he waited for her to make the first move. As tempting as it was to wrap her arms around him, it didn't feel a hundred percent right. Last night it had felt as natural as breathing, but now she wasn't so sure. "Only a little sore. Thanks."

"If you ever hit her again, accident or not, I'm going to come after you with a pitchfork," Holiday said. From the tightness in her eyes, Kylie knew the camp leader meant it, too.

"It wasn't his fault." Kylie stepped closer to Lucas and obviously he took that as the sign he'd wanted earlier. He moved his hand ever so slightly and touched her wrist. A simple touch, but it sent sweet warmth through her.

"Yes, it was." Lucas met her eyes. Guilt rang in his voice. "I have to learn to think before I swing." He looked at Burnett and

Kylie got a feeling Holiday wasn't the only one who'd given Lucas a talking-to.

Slowly, Lucas's hand slipped into hers and gave her palm a light squeeze. Ambivalence bounced around Kylie's stomach. She wasn't sure she was ready to give herself to the possibilities of where that touch could lead them, but neither was she willing to pull away. He'd risked his own life to save her. Remembering she should focus on something other than Lucas, she looked at Burnett. "Any luck on finding them?"

"No." His eyes brightened with anger.

"But we will," Burnett and Lucas said at the same time.

"The others in the Vampire Council have been told about what happened. I imagine there will be consequences."

In a few minutes, Lucas was asked to leave and then Burnett and Holiday took Kylie into Holiday's office. Burnett made Kylie go over everything three or four times. While it felt about as easy as eating rocks, she didn't complain about his drilling. Holiday's eyes filled with pride when Kylie told them about healing Lucas and possibly also Sara.

Finally, the question that had been brewing in her mind came out. "The thing I don't understand is why I couldn't use the strength to save myself."

Holiday gasped as if she'd come to a sudden realization. "You're a protector. I should have guessed after the incident with Selynn. When we were at the lake, you only gained strength when you thought your mother was in danger. It also explains why your real father, Daniel, wasn't able to save himself the day he died."

"Does that . . . tell you what I am? What he was?"

"I'm afraid not, but . . ." Holiday's gaze went to Burnett who looked equally surprised and amazed. "Being a protector is very rare and only is bestowed on the extremely gifted."

"Really gifted," Burnett said, and he sounded a little awed. "I've only met one other protector in my life."

A protector? Kylie didn't know what all it meant. "So, I have other gifts beside the ones I have now?"

"Probably." Holiday smiled. "I knew you were special, Kylie. I knew it from the moment I saw you."

"Could one of these gifts perhaps be the gift of figuring out what the hell I am!" Frustration colored her voice.

After a minute of being told the same thing: *It would eventually happen. She needed to be patient, make it her quest . . . bla . . . bla . . . bla . . .* Burnett went back to asking questions. "Did Mario say who these friends were that he wanted you to meet?"

"Mario?" Kylie asked.

"Mario Esparza is the old vampire's name."

She closed her eyes, not sure if she liked knowing his name. "No." Kylie shivered, imagining the kind of friends he probably kept. "What do you think he meant about the similarities he said we had? Do you think he believes I'm somehow like him? Could he be a protector or . . ."

"I don't know what he meant," Burnett said. "But I don't think he's a protector."

"You're not like him, Kylie," Holiday insisted. "He wasn't born at midnight."

"So he's evil?" Kylie asked.

Burnett looked at Holiday as if he wasn't sure what he should say. Holiday nodded as if giving the okay.

"Yes, he's evil. He's been a thorn in the FRU's side for years. We tried to get him thrown out of the Council, but we never had enough proof."

Kylie took a deep breath. "Do you think he'll come for me again?"

Again, Burnett glanced at Holiday before continuing. "I wish I could tell you that I thought it was over. He doesn't like to lose, but you have my personal guarantee he won't win this one. I will stop him, no matter what it takes."

Holiday reached for Kylie's hand and squeezed. "We need to wrap this up," she told Burnett. "I think most of the campers are in the dining room."

He didn't look happy. "Okay, but I may want to ask you some questions later."

Kylie nodded. They all stood. Burnett started out.

"Burnett?" Holiday said, her tone filled with uncertainty.

He turned around and for a second his expression was one of a puppy who sought affection and acceptance.

Kylie watched Holiday pull a piece of paper from her desk drawer. "You might want to take this. Read it over carefully before you sign."

"What is it?" he asked.

Holiday hesitated. "It's the paperwork. I thought you wanted to be an investor in Shadow Falls."

He glanced down at the paper and then back at Holiday. "So, you couldn't find any other investors?"

Her right eyebrow arched. "I suppose the school isn't considered the best of investments."

Kylie had to bite back a smile when she recognized Holiday's method of avoiding a lie for the purpose of hiding a different truth. She didn't want Burnett to know she'd had other offers, and Kylie knew why, too. To admit that she chose him over the others was admitting she didn't want to lose him.

"I will insist on having more of a say in how things are run around here," Burnett warned.

"And I'm sure I'll fight you on most of it," Holiday countered.

A slight smile whispered across his lips. "Fair enough."

Holiday nodded. "Most of my conditions are listed."

Burnett went to Holiday's desk and signed the paper.

"Don't you think you should have read it first?" Holiday asked.

"Let's just say that I look forward to fighting with you." He handed her the paper and walked out, leaving a sweet kind of tension in his place.

Kylie waited until she was sure Burnett was out of super-hearing earshot. "I know you had another investor lined up."

Holiday rolled her eyes. "And you know not to say anything about it, too, right?"

Kylie grinned. "You didn't want to lose him, Holiday."

"He's growing on me," she said. "But that doesn't mean—"

"Right." Kylie laughed.

Holiday frowned. "I'll bet Della and Miranda are waiting for you."

Kylie hugged Holiday before leaving. When she walked out of the office, Kylie looked toward the dining room and suddenly she wasn't so sure she was ready to face everyone. So much had happened and she hadn't even had time to adjust. Right then, she felt a hand slip inside hers.

She jumped and started to pull away, but stopped when she recognized the warmth of the palm in hers.

"Hey," Lucas said, and gave her a tug. "Let's take a walk."

She let him lead her behind the cabin that housed the office. The moment they stepped in the secluded spot beneath the trees, he stopped and turned and faced her.

"I'm really sorry I hit you." His hold on her hand tightened.

She shook her head. "You didn't mean to do it."

"But I still did it." He gave her hand another light tug and drew her closer. "Burnett said you . . . you healed me."

"Yeah," she said, feeling the warmth of his chest even though she wasn't pressed against him. She inhaled and realized that Lucas smelled like the woods. The scent of the trees and the moist earth clung to him.

"You might have even saved my life," he said.

"Yeah, but I was the reason you got hurt in the first place."

"Doesn't matter." He shot her a sly smile. "You know there's an old vampire legend that says if someone saves your life, you must stay with them forever."

She cut her gaze up at him. "You're not vampire."

He leaned down. His lips were so close to hers that she could taste them. "And for the first time in my life, I wish I were." He inhaled. "But since I'm not vampire, I think the least I can do is give you a thank-you kiss."

"The least you can do," she said, and then his lips touched hers. It wasn't overtly sexy like the kiss they'd shared at the falls, or the ones they shared in the dreams, but it didn't make it any less special. Or any less harder for her to pull away from. But she did pull away. It was just . . . too soon. But later, maybe . . . yes, maybe.

"We . . . we should probably go join the others."

"Yeah." And they walked in silence and he didn't let her hand go until they walked into the dining hall.

Kylie was nearly overwhelmed by everyone wanting to make sure she was okay. She wasn't sure who had spilled the beans about what had happened but it was clear they all knew.

Della, Miranda, Perry, Helen, and Jonathon all gathered around her. Lucas stood back as if giving her space. But he'd meet her eyes every few minutes. Once she even waved him over, but he shook his head, as if somehow he knew she'd been unsure about offering him the invitation. Or maybe it was because he was werewolf and his kind just always seemed to stay together. Nevertheless, she got an odd kind of feeling as if he was guarding her. She remembered how he'd protected her from the bullies when she'd been six and again she felt the bond that connected them. Now what Kylie needed to figure out was just exactly what that bond meant.

An hour later, Kylie's closest friends were all still eating pizza and chatting about how their home visits went. "Oh," Miranda said in her usual peppy voice. "I think I figured out what I did wrong with Socks. I'll have the little stinker back to his old self in no time."

"So, Miranda, your competition went okay?" Perry blurted the question out, sounding nervous. It was the first time he'd spoken to Miranda. Kylie knew this was his way of saying he wanted to start over with her, and Kylie would have hugged him if she hadn't been afraid Miranda might zap her with her award-winning pinky.

"It went fine," she said, but Kylie couldn't read Miranda's expression.

"Why don't you two just kiss and make up already?" Della said. "And then you can go somewhere alone and really suck face."

Miranda shot Della a huge frown that for sure meant an argument would follow later. Perry's eyes went black as he stared at Della, and then he walked off, looking a little rejected. Kylie just leaned back in her chair and wondered if things would ever change.

But then . . . some things had already changed, hadn't they? She found herself looking around for another face. While she tried really hard not to admit it, she missed Derek. More than that, she worried if he was okay. She decided to go find Burnett and ask, but her phone beeped with an incoming text.

She glanced at the caller ID. It was from the PI. Then Kylie saw she had a text from Sara. It read, "What did you do? Don't lie. I know you did it."

Kylie's heart lurched. Great. What was she going to tell Sara?

Her phone beeped again. When Kylie read the message from the PI, she gasped. "Grandparents back. Spoke yesterday. They want to see you ASAP."

Hope stirred inside her heart. Would this lead to the answer about who she was?

"Kylie?" Mandy called her name from the door.

Kylie turned around. "Yeah?"

"Holiday said for you to come to the office. Someone is here to see you."

"Who is it?" Kylie asked, feeling panicked at the thought of it actually being them. Was she really ready to do this? Was she ready to meet Daniel's adoptive parents? Her grandparents?

"I don't know, but there was an old couple knocking on the gate a few minutes ago."

And just like that Kylie heard the sound of cascading water. Something caught her attention out of the corner of her eye, and she looked toward the log wall where a mixture of light and shadows swirled in soft, almost hypnotic patterns. Dancing death angels.

She glanced at Della and Miranda. Neither reacted. Apparently, Kylie was the only one to see the show playing on the other side of the room. And then,

"Go and uncover your past so you may discover your destiny."

"Is everything okay?" Della asked, looking concerned.

Kylie took a deep breath. "Yeah. Fine."

And she hoped she was right about that, too.

You won't believe what happens next!

Read on for a preview of the third book
in C. C. Hunter's Shadow Falls series

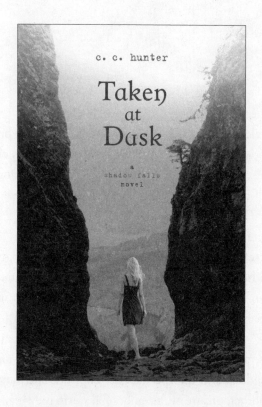

c. c. hunter

Taken
at
Dusk

a
shadow falls
novel

Available from St. Martin's Griffin in April 2012

They were here. Really here.

Kylie Galen stepped out of the dining hall into the bright sunlight and looked over at the Shadow Falls office. Birds chirped in the distance, a rush of wind rustled the trees, but she mostly heard the sound of her own heart thudding in her chest.

Thump. Thump. Thump.

They were here.

Her pulse raced at the thought of meeting the Brightens, the couple who had adopted and raised her real father. A father she'd never known in life, but had grown to love in his short visits from the afterlife.

"Daniel?" she whispered her father's name, almost as if requesting his presence. The one word seemed to be snatched and carried away by a sudden and unexpected gust of wind. She took one step and then another, unsure of the emotional storm brewing inside her.

Fear.

Excitement.

Curiosity.

Fear. Yes, a lot of fear.

But of what?

A drip of sweat, more from nerves than Texas's mid-August heat index, rolled down her brow.

"Go and uncover your past so you may discover your destiny." The death angels' mystical words replayed in her head. She took a step forward, then stopped. Even as her heart ached to solve the mystery of who her father was, of who she was and, hopefully, what she was, her instincts screamed for her to turn and hide.

Was this what she feared? Learning the truth?

Until only a few months ago, before coming to Shadow Falls, she'd been certain she was just a confused teen, that her feelings of being different were normal. Now she knew better.

She wasn't normal.

She wasn't even human. At least not all human.

And figuring out her nonhuman side was a puzzle.

A puzzle the Brightens could help her solve.

She took another step. The wind, as if it was as eager to escape as she was, whisked past and picked up a few wayward strands of her blond hair, scattering them across her face.

She blinked and when she opened her eyes, the brightness of the sun had evaporated. Glancing up, she saw a huge angry-looking cloud hanging in the sky, directly overhead. It cast a shadow around her and the woodsy terrain. Unsure if this was an omen or just a summer storm, her heart danced faster.

Taking a deep breath that smelled of rain, she took one step when a hand clasped around her elbow.

What now?

Panic shot through her veins.

She swung around.

"Whoa. You okay?" Lucas asked, and his clasp around her arm lightened.

Kylie caught her breath, and stared up at his amazing blue eyes.

"Yeah. You just . . . surprised me. You always surprise me. You need to hum or whistle when you come up on me."

"Hum or whistle," he repeated, and almost smiled. Of course, he would see it as humorous. Werewolves were famous for being sleek, soundless, and intense. And Lucas was one hundred percent werewolf and, at least where she was concerned, completely, overwhelming intense.

"Sorry." His thumb moved in soft little circles over the crease in her elbow. She could feel her pulse rushing and fluttering against his touch. And somehow that light brush of his finger felt . . . intimate. How did he make a simple touch feel like a sweet sin?

A gust of wind, now smelling like a storm, stirred his black hair and tossed it over his brow.

He continued to stare at her; the hint of humor in his gaze vanished. "You don't look okay. What's wrong?" He reached up and tucked a wayward strand of her hair behind her right ear.

She looked away from him to the cabin that housed the office. "My grandparents . . . the adopted parents of my real dad are here."

"I thought you were looking for them? Wanted to meet them?"

"I do. I'm just . . ."

"Scared?" he finished for her.

She didn't like admitting it, but since werewolves could smell fear, lying wouldn't help. "Yeah." She looked back at Lucas and again saw humor in his eyes.

The thought that he was laughing at her caused a frown to pull at her lips. "What's so funny?"

"You," he said, as if she amused him. "I'm still trying to figure you out. When you were kidnapped by a rogue vampire with ties to an underground supernatural world, you weren't this scared. And now you reek of fear."

"I reek?"

He appeared to purposely bite back his grin. "Not reek . . . just . . ." He paused, and then leaned in and lowered his voice. "Seriously, if this is the same couple I saw walking in here a few minutes ago, then they're old and just humans. I think you can take them both, with both hands tied behind your back."

Just humans. If she didn't know and like Lucas so much, his choice of words might have annoyed her.

"I'm not scared like that. I just . . ." She closed her eyes for a second, unsure how to explain something she wasn't clear on herself, but then the words spilled out as if they'd been sitting on her tongue waiting for their chance to be acknowledged. "What am I going to say to them? 'Oh, I know you never told my father he was adopted, but he figured it out after he died. And he came to see me. Oh, yeah, he wasn't human. So could you please tell me who his real parents are? So I can figure out what I am?' "

He must have heard the angst in her voice because his expression went from amused to concerned almost instantly. "You'll find a way."

"Yeah." She wished she shared his confidence. Knowing she had to hurry, she started walking. His warm presence took the edge off her fear as they moved up the steps.

He stopped beside her at the door and brushed a hand down her arm. "You want me to come inside with you?"

She almost told him yes, but stopped herself. He'd rescued her from that rogue vampire, but she knew this was one thing she needed to do alone. She thought she heard voices from inside and glanced back at the door.

She wouldn't exactly be alone.

No doubt Holiday, the camp leader, waited for her inside,

prepared to offer moral support and even a calming touch. Normally, Kylie objected to her emotions being manipulated, but right now might be an exception.

"Thanks, but I'm sure Holiday is in there."

He nodded, his gaze moved to her mouth. His head dipped down ever so slightly and his lips came dangerously close to hers.